"ARE THEY EVER GONNA STOP COMING?"

Viet Cong streamed from the barracks buildings beyond the villa compound. *The entire command must have been assembled for some reason or other*, reflected Peterson as he aimed at the first of four VC who rushed his position.

So intense had the firing become that, at first, no one heard the rhythmic *whap-whap* of rotor blades. Not until the radio crackled in the ear of the RTO did anyone become aware that help had arrived.

"Blunderbuss, this is Mongoose One. What we see is a hell of a fire in the middle of a sort of parklike area. Is that the bad guys? Over."

"Roger that, Mongoose One. We'll mark targets for you. Over." Over the din of battle, Wally Ott shouted to the SEALs. "Grenade Launchers, give 'em some Willie-Peter!"

White phosphorous rounds sped toward the enemy, bursting in white pyrotechnic displays, fragments streaming through the air. A second later the roar of chain guns drowned out the *whap-whap* of the rotary wings of the AH-1G Cobra gunships. The roar of ripple-fired 2.75-inch missiles filled the air, followed seconds later by a staggered series of loud blasts as the warheads detonated among the charging enemy.

Another thunderous symphony of death was unleashed on the Viet Cong, who now sought nothing more than to escape with their lives. Most ran heedlessly toward anything that offered a promise of safety. Few of them made it.

SEALS
TOP SECRET #4
Operation: Shell Game

CHIEF JAMES "PATCHES" WATSON
and MARK ROBERTS

AVON BOOKS ◆ NEW YORK

This is a work of fiction. Names, characters, places, and incidents either are products of the author's imagination or are used fictitiously. Any resemblance to actual events, locales, organizations, or persons, living or dead, is entirely coincidental and beyond the intent of either the authors or the publisher.

AVON BOOKS, INC.
1350 Avenue of the Americas
New York, New York 10019

Copyright © 1999 by Bill Fawcett & Associates
Cover art © Brian R. Wolff/IIPI, All Rights Reserved
Published by arrangement with Bill Fawcett & Associates
Library of Congress Catalog Card Number: 98-94821
ISBN: 0-380-80575-8
www.avonbooks.com

First Avon Books Printing: July 1999

Printed in the U.S.A.

WCD   10   9   8   7   6   5   4   3   2   1

CHAPTER 1 _____

THREE VARIETIES of pigeons cooed softly in the trees of the park opposite the old Metropole Hotel, converted in 1959 to the Ministry of Defense of the People's Socialist Republic of Vietnam, yet their soothing ululations went unheard by the large, stony-faced man who emerged from the rear of an aging Citroën. Likewise the antics of a pair of red and gray rollers went unnoticed. The loud, raucous voices of a treeful of barbets failed to penetrate the red haze of anger that boiled beneath the placid surface of General Trang Van Key, Chief of Operations (G-3) for the General Staff of the People's Liberation Army (NVA). They were late for the most monumental meeting as yet to be held in Hanoi. And Key blamed his driver.

Not that the driver, Senior Sergeant Dien Minh of the NVA, was entirely an innocent victim of his passenger's wrath. Sergeant Minh was in love. And being a man in love, he tended to dawdle. She was a beauty, the only daughter of a minor Party functionary, an aspiring actress in the State Cinema Arts school who had already received small parts in four critically acclaimed short films (read propaganda movies) on such diverse subjects as "Your Tractor—Replacement for the Water Buffalo," "The Enemy to the South," and "Sunrise over a Reunited Vietnam." Beyond that, two of the Citroën's tires had been flat when he reached the motor pool that morning. The man who repaired them, a political

1

prisoner, was not inclined to work at a rapid pace. Which made Minh even later. But a sergeant, even a senior sergeant, did not make such excuses to a general of the stature of Key. So Senior Sergeant Minh bore General Key's silent wrath without visible sign of discomfort.

"Wait for me at the west portico," General Key snapped as he crossed to the front entrance to the Metropole.

Right then the pair of rollers, which had been in straight and level flight, suddenly broke into their tumbling act. Red and brown feathers puffed into balls as they performed half a dozen somersaults, then resumed normal flight. *Like puffs of AAA fire*, General Key mused, roused for the first time from his black mood.

Key was a big man for a Vietnamese. In his late forties, he towered over most of his contemporaries, evidencing at least some Chinese in his ancestry. A barrel chest, bedecked with medals commemorating his service with the Viet Minh, and later the Pacification of the North, swelled with confidence and pride. His gray-green woolen uniform with the red pips on his collar and shoulder boards was pressed to razor sharpness. He wore a wide black patent leather belt, complete with magazine pouch and pistol holster of the same material. The firearm case rode high on his hip and the cross-strap of the Sam Browne–style harness slanted below the collection of awards for heroism. A huge Soviet-style "flying saucer" hat bedecked his large head, a wide red band with gold star at the front under the mushrooming crown. High black boots encased his surprisingly small feet and muscular calves. His shirt was tan, his tie black. His mood matched his tie and leather accessories. With considerable effort he adjusted his attitude when his superior, General Gao Dien Ghe, Commander in Chief of the People's Liberation Army of Vietnam, stepped out through the huge, tall multi-doors of the main entrance of the old hotel and greeted Key with open arms.

"Comrade General, we had begun to worry that something unfortunate had delayed you," General Ghe declared, as his old friend and colleague approached. After exchanging salutes the two men embraced.

"Nothing unfortunate, Gao. Merely a lovesick puppy for a driver and some idiot worker throwing nails in the street where my car could drive over them," said Key, revealing that he knew at least as much as the Senior Sergeant. He chuckled to show that he himself was not making excuses and patted the side of his attaché case. "I have everything here as you commanded."

Ghe beamed. "Good. Good, then. Shall we go inside? There are only three others yet to arrive."

Despite the presence of the supreme commander, it proved necessary for General Key to present his identification card to a battery of sentries and clerks as the pair penetrated deeply into the aged hotel. Gilt-trimmed white pedestals lined the splendid main hallway, each topped by a draped scarlet gold-trimmed cloth upon which sat a character, either real or mythical, from the past of Vietnam. Key stifled a shaft of uneasiness. No matter how many times he entered this facility, the inspection of those many unseeing eyes unnerved him.

A wide, gracefully curving staircase interrupted the parade of busts. It gave way to the mezzanine and second floor. The leather heels of the boots of Ghe and Key clicked loudly, setting off echoes in the spacious former lobby of one of the most famous hotels in Southeast Asia. The pair swept past the base of the stairway and Ghe led the way to a pair of tall teak doors that gave access to what had once been the grand ballroom.

Antique gaslight sconces remained along the bare white-plastered walls, the heavy burgundy velvet drapes had long since been removed by the prudish communist functionaries who had redesigned the hotel as a military facility. Always champions of the status quo, the military brass had been overwhelmingly exceeded by the inflexibility of the party's enforcers of political correctness. The only specimen of past aristocratic decadence was the huge crystal chandelier.

Perhaps it was its size and weight that had saved the

1920s Art Deco object from the zeal of the revisionists. Fully
15 feet in diameter, the massive light fixture was suspended
from the third floor ceiling of the ballroom by a gilded log-
ging chain. Crystal fobs, obelisks, and orbs dangled in profusion and emitted spectacular bands of colored light, divided
as sharply as though projected by a spectrograph, the source
being the bright, stark floor lamps that ringed the gigantic
oval teak table in the center of the parquet dance floor.

Seated around the enormous slab joined in only one place
at the center, Key recognized the general staff of the armed
forces of the People's Socialist Republic of Vietnam: General
Hu Lian of the Air Force, General Dong Vu of the Anti-
Aircraft Service, General Li Dao of the People's Militia,
General Kao Tri of the State Security Service, and Admiral
Phon of the Navy. As the senior service, the Army was represented by the entire staff—the G-1, G-2, and G-4, as well
as himself. There were civilians present also. Key knew them
by sight: the Foreign Minister, with three lesser bureaucrats
in fawning attendance upon his wishes; the Minister of the
Interior, with only two minor functionaries; and, of course,
the General Secretary of the Communist Party. He had seven
suits flanking him. Key wanted to laugh out loud, or at least
smile in a condescending manner at this display of conspicuous excess but forcefully restrained himself. He headed instead toward the empty chair immediately to the left of the
one to be occupied by General Ghe. There was a stir behind
him as two of the tardy attendees made their presence known.

One of them was Colonel Fong Xiguyen, Commandant of
the POW camp in Hanoi known by the American enemy as
the Hanoi Hilton. Key had invited him, following the development of intelligence from agents in the south who swore
to the veracity of their discoveries, as the G-2 had related to
him. For a moment, the scabrous, mustard-yellow walls of
the infamous Long Don political prison flashed behind his
eyes. The recollection caused him to grimace. Worse still
was the interior. A stench hung over the place, a blend of
vomit and despair and human excrement that rose from the
odious holes in the floors of the cells that served as sanitary

facilities. *Sanitary!* The slightest scratch or abrasion festered in there and swiftly turned into a mass of yellow infection and eventually vile putrefaction that could easily become gangrenous. Good enough for political dissidents, Key reasoned. But the majority of prisoners were now foreign enemies of his country. As such, they were also soldiers, like him, and deserving of better treatment. Key quickly bit off that thought. To give voice to such sentiments, he knew, would be to invite a closer scrutiny by the agents of General Tri and the State Security Service. He briskly strode the last few paces to his chair and lay his briefcase on the polished teak surface. Opening it, he glanced around the table as the third and final latecomer entered the room.

"Comrades, before we address the issue which has brought us here, I must regretfully call your attention to other matters. We have unanticipated problems," he informed those gathered at the table, dismissing any preamble. "Following the recent face-destroying incursion into Long Don prison by enemy forces—forces we believe to be the notorious U.S. Navy SEALs—it is now the estimate of the G-2 for the People's Liberation Army that a raid in force is being prepared to free our prisoners of war confined here in Hanoi."

"Impossible!" General Kao Tri exploded. "My Security Service has an iron ring around the entire country. The only access the enemy has is by air. And if they come that way, we will ferret them out, isolate them, and eliminate them. Not one will cause the least problem."

Such arrogance, Key thought to himself. *He actually believes that his twenty-one week basic officers course at the Frunze Institute and a six-week matriculation with Faculty Number Two in basic Counterintelligence at the Andropov Institute, the FDC training school, makes him a competent spy master. Truth is, the youngest, most inexperienced KGB agent could run rings around him.*

"I am sure you have the situation well in hand, Comrade Tri." Key's tone was condescending and patronizing. "However, it is the recommendation of the G-2 that the prisoners be moved. Covertly and at the earliest opportunity.''

Tri looked to Xiguyen for support, found none, and rounded on Key with a sputtering protest. ''But why such unseemly haste? Such an operation would require weeks—months to organize, plan, rehearse, and prepare for.''

Key shook his head and shot a glance at the Chief of Staff. ''All the same, speed is of the essence. Particularly in light of the upcoming tri-powers meeting in less than two weeks' time.''

Another hand raised. General Nhung, the G-4. ''Where would the war criminals be housed?''

General Key appeared to consider that for a moment, as though he did not have the issue fully summarized on the pages fanned out before him. ''There are several small camps scattered in the hills of Northeastern Bac Phan province. In particular I am thinking of the confinement complex on the western slope of Fan Si Pan.''

He referred to the 3,143-foot peak of a long ridge that formed the steep sides of narrow valleys through which the Na and Black Da rivers flowed. It was a good 180 kilometers from Hanoi, and there were no roads, only narrow trails, between isolated villages. In fact, the only access over the last 95 kilometers was by water. As Chief of Operations, it was his number one choice. He passed around copies of the movement scenario he had produced, complete with section maps—due to the inherent paranoia of a totalitarian regime, and a communist one in particular, maps of the entire country were never provided to anyone, except a limited few on the general staff—showing the five internment camps designated to receive prisoners. Most of those present studied the documents with care—all, Key noted, except General Tri.

When the other generals and Admiral Phon had returned their attention to General Key, General Tri waved a hand dismissively over the map. ''I am familiar with the location and conditions of all of these camps. I find them totally unsuited to accommodate the increase in prisoners you propose. This is entirely unsatisfactory. Besides, there is no possible threat the enemy can offer to necessitate such an action being undertaken.''

At that point General Ghe entered the fray, his words coated with sugared venom. ''Fortunately, the final decision is mine, not yours, Comrade Tri.'' He cast his gaze around the assembled officers. ''Is there any other reactionary thinking in this room?'' Negative shakes of several heads replied to him. ''Well, then, the matter is settled. Comrade General Key, you will please prepare for us an operations order covering the relocation of the prisoners in Long Don prison. Now, next on the agenda is the intelligence report of Comrade General Bac.''

Short and birdlike, General Bac rose in place and passed out copies of his report to all present, except Colonel Xiguyen. He made his comments brief. He thanked Ghe for the opportunity to enlighten the staff and resumed his seat.

''Very well. It was indeed enlightening. So much so that when I first received it, I turned it over to Comrade General Key for the preparation of an operations order. That he assures me had been completed and he is prepared to hand it over to me at this time.'' Key gave the Chief of Staff a copy of the order, and one to each G-section leader. Ghe read it rapidly. Privately he considered it to be a bit over-ambitious, but it would suit the purpose for which it was intended.

''Excellent. I am prepared to activate this operation immediately.'' He raised the ops order and gestured to his staff. ''I am hereby ordering a major offensive south of the Demilitarized Zone. Inablement will commence at once. Finally, the main topic of our meeting is the last item for consideration. You are all aware of the impending high-level meeting of our political and military leaders with their counterparts among our comrades of the People's Republic of China and the Union of Soviet Socialist Republics. It is scheduled to begin thirteen days from now.

''There will be representatives from the Soviet Foreign Ministry, the Politburo, the Communist Party, and the KGB,'' Ghe continued. ''Also, at least two general officers from the Red Army and two colonels from GRU. The People's Republic will send three members of the Great Assembly of the People, two from the Foreign Office, and three generals of the People's Liberation Army, and no doubt someone from Black House. Our nation will be represented by the First Secretary of the Party, the Minister of Defense, myself, and three members of the general staff of my choosing.''

Always the complainer, General Tri raised a finger to interrupt Ghe. ''Why is this meeting being held?''

Ghe fought back a scowl. Key did likewise, although he failed. ''Are you not aware of the honor it does our country? When the meeting is over and everyone has returned to his home, releases will be made to the world press, complete with film footage made by our Ministry of Information of the meeting and signing of certain accords. It will mark the entry of the People's Socialist Republic of Vietnam into the league of world leaders.''

Tri snorted contemptuously. ''Preposterous. We are a small country, a Third World country, I might point out. Granted, we have heavy industry here in the North and a university second to none in Asia. But until we are reunited with the South, we have no agricultural base to make us independent, let alone a world leader.''

Ghe gave Tri a gimlet eye. ''Be careful you do not misspeak yourself, Comrade General Tri. That sounds like reactionary, negativist thinking. This meeting can do nothing but redound to our greater glory. Coupled with a successful campaign into the South at the same time, it will only add stature to that glory.''

Key stepped in to fill the gap of silence that followed. ''Might I enlarge on the anticipated results of this meeting?'' At Ghe's nod, he went on. ''We will be negotiating increased aid from both China and the Soviet Union. Much of it in the form of military hardware, granted, but also in the tools and machinery necessary to expand our own industrial base. And, Comrade Admiral Phong, you will be happy to hear this. We are to receive three Dugalev-class submarines from the Soviets. Also a small pocket aircraft carrier. But there is a catch to this generosity. Training of pilots to make carrier landings and takeoffs, and training of submariners, will take time and be costly. We must gird the people to accept even more stringent limitations of material goods, foodstuffs, and, of course, another increase in taxes.''

General Tri looked at Key with mixed doubt and wonder. "We get all of that, and all we are required to do is compel the people to suffer a bit more privation. Incredible.''

General Ghe took up the thread. "That is not all, Comrade General. The Chinese will provide us with fifty thousand of the newest Type 53 assault rifles, their copy of the Soviet AK-47, lightweight mortars and what amounts to an unlimited supply of ammunition. All at prices far below market value. Planning for this meeting will commence tomorrow morning. That is all.'' The others began to depart, and Ghe gestured to Colonel Xiguyen.

"Remain, please, Comrade Colonel. There is something I wish to discuss with you.''

"As you wish, Comrade.'' Small in stature, slim, with elegant gestures and a pencil line of mustache on a thin upper lip, Fong Xiguyen actually gave an appearance of class to the utilitarian service uniform of the People's Liberation Army. In the electric blue tunic, scarlet trousers with blue stripes along the outer leg seams, knee-high boots, and reverse colors on his flaring flying saucer hat of the dress uniform, he was a fashion plate.

Colonel Xiguyen was a recent replacement for the former warden of Long Don prison. His predecessor had born the burden of his laxness and abject failure in the matter of the penetration of the prison by an enemy force and the subsequent recapture of the bomb by the Americans. Blame for the breaches of security, first at the coast, then later in Hanoi and in Vinh province, had to be assigned to someone. Colonel Dao Nguyen Dao had been subordinate to all the generals who should have shared the fault, Fong Xiguyen mused, as he awaited General Ghe's revelation. It was his earnest intent not to repeat the errors of his forerunner.

"Yes, Comrade General," Xiguyen prompted. He noted that General Key had remained also.

"Comrade Colonel, I wish you to prepare a detailed plan for the movement of the enemy prisoners under your control. Include a logistics report on means of transportation and duration of the transfer for the G-4. Coordinate your efforts with G-3 Key, if you please. I will expect a preliminary draft this Monday. That is all, Comrade Colonel." General Key turned away and made a gesture to his aide that indicated he was ready for his breakfast.

Thus dismissed, Colonel Fong Xiguyen saluted crisply, did a sharp about-face, and left the former ballroom. Behind him, Key commented to the Chief of Staff, "Now, that's a soldier. He has a superb military bearing."

"Better still," Ghe replied, "he takes his orders without argument or question. And based on his record, he carries them out to the letter."

CHAPTER 2

"PARTY TIME!" Machinist Mate 1C Charlie Sturgis brayed, as Chief Tom Waters ushered Kent Welby and Francie Song into Phon Bai, the best, and only, full-service restaurant in Tre Noc. "Ain't ever' day a guy turns twenty-five, Doc. 'Specially out here. C'mon, we got the Flower Water Room all to ourselves."

Doc Welby grinned boyishly and ran his large spatulate fingers through sandy yellow hair. His cobalt eyes flashed with enthusiasm, especially when they gazed upon Francie Song. The young couple allowed the leader of Bravo Squad to direct them into the private dining room on the main floor of Phon Bei. Chief Tom Waters, Platoon Chief of First Platoon, Team 2 SEALs turned from the bamboo-fronted wet bar and raised a glass in salute.

"Hiya, Doc. B'God, you're gettin' to be over the hill. Twenty-five years. You gonna put in for your Social Security?" His gibe brought a chorus of guffaws from the other SEALs in the room.

Boatswain Mate First Class Rodriguez grinned broadly. "Remember when I had to haul your sorry butt over the gunwale of my PBR? I didn't think you'd see another birthday that time." Rodriguez was a member of PBR River Section 534, and coxswain of one of the Patrol Boat River craft that ran interdiction patrols along the Mekong and Bassiac rivers.

11

They also transported the "Men with Green Faces," as the SEALs had been labeled by their enemy, to and from operations in the Delta. He and several of the other River Rats (Riverine Force sailors of RS 534) had been invited to Kent's birthday party by Tonto Waters. More than once Rodriguez and his PBR sailors had bailed First Platoon out of some extremely deep pucky. For their part, the SEALs considered Rodriguez and the 534th to be right up there with the guardian angels. Apparently the attractive young Vietnamese woman who nestled in the crook of the muscular arm of Rodriguez felt the same.

She smiled winningly. "So you are the one he told me he 'hauled you in by the'—how you say?—'seat of your pants'?"

Kent shot Rodriguez a dark look, not without a large dose of gratitude. Tonto Waters' bright blue eyes twinkled under a thick shock of dark brown hair as he gestured to Francie. "Don't just stand there, get the lovely lady a drink."

Grinning, Kent Welby crossed to the bar and ordered a Mai Tai for Francie and asked for a beer. Idly he wondered how long Happy Hour would last. Knowing the SEALs, he concluded that it could be interminable. As a college student and a pledge to *Lambda Chi Alpha* national collegiate fraternity, Kent thought he knew quite a lot about drinking. That was before he'd joined the Navy and later become a SEAL.

Never in his life, before or since, had he seen men with the ability to consume the hopsy suds like a gathering of SEALs. The night after they completed "Hell Week," Kent recalled, his teammates consumed an average of a case of beer each. Yet they had not violated the 2200 hours curfew. Every one of them had been standing at the foot of his bunk, some of them albeit a bit unsteadily, including Kent Welby, when the Duty Petty Officer had checked their barrack. Never a heavy drinker, Kent had limited his consumption to eight cans of beer. That had proved to be about four too many, which he discovered the next morning. He quickly offered up a silent prayer that tonight's birthday bash would not bring about a repetition of that binge.

Sighing, he turned away from the bar and handed Francie her drink. Then he took a long pull directly from the bottle of Tiger brought in from Singapore by the owner of Phon Bai. Richard Golden approached, his walk a blend of swagger and sea legs roll. He grinned broadly, a thick-fingered paw extended to congratulate Kent. Large orangy freckles writhed on his face below a thatch of carroty hair. Those features had early in life earned him his nickname, Archie, after the comic book character Archie Andrews.

"Yer lookin' good for an old man," Archie gibed.

Doc Welby made a face. "I'll give you *old*, grandpa. Don't you have a kid that's a little more than half my age?"

"Right you are. Matter of fact, I've got one who is 19 and another seventeen. David is thirteen. And . . . by the way, he had his Bar Mitzvah Saturday two weeks ago, my wife wrote me. Tonto was right, too. My younger brother stood up with him and everything went great. He read off all that Hebrew without a slip. Hell, it took me four weeks' extra hours with Rabbi Liebman to get just a three-verse passage from Exodus down so I didn't make it sound like Russian. Man, am I hungry," Archie changed the subject. "Don't they have any munchies around this joint?"

His words might have been the cue for which a quartet of waiters had been listening. They appeared now from the double swinging doors that connected to the kitchen. One held aloft a large platter covered with crushed ice and a huge mound of steamed and shelled giant prawns. Another bore a silver salver with canapes made of tea-smoked duck medallions, a soft cheese, and red caviar, all resting on thin slices of minute French bread. The third carried a gigantic bowl filled with wooden skewers of Vietnamese barbecue; ground pork meatballs, tiny bulb onions, wedges of green pepper, and pieces of lotus root and bamboo shoot. The fourth had a tray of mini-Imperial rolls. At the sight of the appetizers, Francie Song's eyes brightened and she clapped her hands enthusiastically.

"Oh, it is all so wonderful," she declared, like a small

girl at the circus. Then her practical side took over. "But Kentwelby, it costs so much money."

"Not mine," Kent reminded her with a grin. "C'mon, let's dig in."

Over the preprandial repast, conversation avoided the one obvious topic. No one mentioned the war, the VC, or anything else unpleasant. Finally, at least among the healthy young Americans present, talk turned to life in the World. Their words, Kent Welby thought, had a faintly nostalgic flavor to them.

"I wonder what's big on TV this season?" asked Chad "Repeat" Ditto, one of Kent Welby's Alpha Squad mates.

"Same thing we're gettin' here, Repeat. Only two years newer," came a laconic retort from Andy Holt.

"What do you know about it, Randy Andy?" Porfirio Agilar riposted. "The only television broadcasts in-country come from Saigon, an' they have French dubbed over the dialogue." He gave his listeners a "so-there" smug smirk.

"There is AFTV, Zorro," Andy Holt came back defensively. "At least they get it at the hospital in Bihn Thuy."

"Armed Forces Television! Talk about golden oldies, Randy," Zorro sneered.

"I'd still like to know what's big back in the World," Repeat Ditto stated again.

Andy took pity on Chad. "I'll bet that really cool one that came on just before we shipped out of Little Creek last year is still doin' fine. You know, *Star Trek*?"

"Awh, who watches sci-fi?" one of the River Rats depreciated the space opera.

"Infidel!" Chad rounded on him with a laugh.

A moment later the door to the Flower Water Room opened to admit Lieutenant Carl Marino, CO of Team 2. No one called the room to attention; SEALs were not that big on formality. Rather the conversation died as they watched the olive-complexioned Marino stride across the room to the bar.

"First a drink, then congratulations are in order, I understand."

Kent Welby came the closest to the position of attention of anyone. "Thank you, sir—uh—thanks, Pope."

A leonine mane of hair rose from a pronounced widow's peak to cover Pope Marino's head with an ebony mantle. He shot black brows and softened his voice when he addressed Francie Song. "Ah, the lovely Francie. How's our soon-to-be SEAL?"

Shocked surprise numbed the tip of Kent Welby's tongue. *Their secret* was out and Pope Marino, his by-God commanding officer, knew. Who else, he wondered, knew all about the baby on the way? With another shaft of cold, Kent realized that Marino could not know anything "officially" about the pending blessed event. If the lieutenant took any official notice, Kent would have a negative entry in his 201 jacket. Worse still, Betty might find out about it.

Thought of his estranged wife cast a blanket of gloom over the festivities. Kent and Elizabeth Welby had been married three years now. Betty had wanted a divorce when Kent had refused to leave the SEALs rather than go to Vietnam, in order that she might tailor his life to how she thought he should live it. And then she didn't want a divorce. In the meantime, Kent had met and fallen in love with Francie Song.

He had hardly reconciled himself to giving up Francie and remaining married to Betty when Betty had changed her mind again. She wrote to tell him that she agreed with the sentiments in his last letter; she accepted divorce as inevitable. All that during the first two months the SEALs were in-country. Tet, the Vietnamese New Year, had come and gone and Kent had found out Francie was pregnant. No problem. When their tour was over, he would arrange to get her out of Tre Noc, and out of Vietnam entirely, through the kind offices of Eloise Deladier, the Saigon correspondent for the popular French magazine *Le Monde*, who happened also to be the girlfriend of Chief Tom Waters.

His first tentative approach to the subject had been well received by Tonto Waters, who encouraged Kent to go for what would make him happy. The Chief promised to discuss the possibility of getting Francie and her seven-year-old son out of Vietnam. To Kent everything was going along swimmingly. At least until Betty's next letter had arrived. She had had a long discussion with her mother and their parish priest, she informed him. She had come to the conclusion that divorce was not the way to go. If he could find it in his heart to make room for her love, she would make room in hers for his being a SEAL. And there the matter stuck. Kent Welby made a considerable effort to banish such dark and brooding thoughts and return to the festivities of the hour. He flashed a big smile.

"I'm gonna have another beer, hon," he confided to Francie. "Why don't you find our place at table and I'll bring you another Mai Tai?"

Francie flashed a brief frown. "It is not good for the baby. Too much alcohol. Wang Sheng, the herbalist, tells me this is so. I want to have wine with our dinner, so no more drinks now, is that—uh—okay-dokay?"

Kent beamed at her. "It's okie-dokie by me. But . . . you don't mind if I have a bit more?"

"It is your birthday, you can do what you want. I love you, my big American Kentwelby."

"I love you, too. Later, I have every intention of proving that to you."

Her eyes sparkled mischievously as she contemplated their immediate future. She looked forward eagerly to the time between the end of the party and when the curfew would demand that her Kentwelby return to the Navy base.

Four NVA soldiers preceded the small, dapper man dressed in civilian clothes. Night animals made grunting and snorting sounds in the near distance, kindling some primitive aversion in the silent man and his escort. The trooper at point halted abruptly, his head and upper torso invisible in a pool of blackness. Only from the waist down did the wan light of a quarter moon illuminate his uniform and boots. A challenge came from the dark and he whispered a reply.

"Advance, Comrades," the unseen sentry commanded in

a louder tone. They complied, and when the civilian came into view, the speaker barked abruptly in the accent of the South, "Halt! Who is this man?"

For the first time the man in a Western-style business suit spoke. "I am Colonel Kahm-thi-Hue of the People's Liberation Army of Vietnam."

"Do you have identification? Travel documents?"

"Of course. I will show them to you if you will relax your finger on the trigger of your weapon."

The young VC challenger felt a sensation of wonder and awe. How had this stranger known how tense he had become in challenging five men, four of them obviously armed? Did he know about the tunnel complex? The entrance lay not five *li* away. Forcefully he commanded his body to relax from the strain. He took a deep breath, licked dry lips, and extended his hand for the papers.

When he received them, he read carefully, developing a new fear now. This was indeed a colonel in the army of the Socialist Republic of Vietnam. And here he was, Fanh Cau, son of a peasant farmer, speaking rudely to such an exalted personage. His punishment, he firmly believed, would be swift and severe. Hand atremble, he returned the documents.

"I had no way of knowing, Comrade Colonel. Welcome to Cap Lahn," Cau declared using the name of the nearest village. He gestured over his shoulder. "If you will come this way, I will take you to my captain."

"Excellent. I have orders for your commander," Hue stated matter-of-factly.

Once in the maze of tunnels, Hue was conducted past several cubicles in which earnest young men were being indoctrinated in the principals of the Socialist Revolution. In others, more seasoned fighters were cleaning and oiling their weapons. Among them was one no longer a youth, a combat team leader named Vinh Nhon. He looked up and gave long study to Colonel Hue. The NVA officer was led to the largest bunker in the tunnel complex. There, three Viet Cong officers sat at a low table drinking tea.

"Captain Hien, I am Colonel Kahm-thi-Hue of the People's Liberation Army," Hue introduced himself. "I have brought you new orders and some maps which you will need to show your team leaders."

"I will summon them at once," Hien declared as he rose.

"That will not be necessary. At least for the present, Comrade Captain. First I wish to brief you on a major operation that will unfold over the next two weeks. I shall take as little time as possible."

"D'ya hear anything?" Repeat Ditto asked, as he ambled out of Phon Bei.

Beside him, Archie Golden paused, straining to make out some specific sound. "No, as a matter of fact. Nothin' but the critters in the bush."

Chad Ditto, Boatswain's Mate 1C, waggled a hand and pulled a droll expression. He was more than a bit tipsy. He was, in fact, shit-faced. "Tha's what I mean. No friggin' mortar attack. Ya think they laid off in honor of Doc's birthday?"

Archie steadied his own somewhat rocky condition. "No, I don't, and you're drunk an' we've gotta get back to the compound. Let's make tracks, kid, what say?"

"Yeah—yeah." Repeat looked longingly along the narrow, twisting street taken by Rodriguez and his girl. "Man, I sure wish I had me one of those little Oriental dollies to play with. I bet they've got lots softer mattresses than my bunk."

"No, they don't," Archie corrected him. "They sleep on pallets on the floor. Just a thin pad with little rice straw stuffing."

Repeat gave him an owlish look. "How d'you know? I thought you were the original faithful-to-his-wife dude."

"I was and I am. Momma Rose at Mi Flower told me about how the Vietnamese sleep for the most part. I saw a whole lot of these striped cotton bags hangin' in the laundry one day not long after we got here. I asked her about them. She said they were mattress tickings. From the way they were sewn, you could tell they wouldn't hold a hell of a lot.

Even if they got stuffed with clouds they'd be mighty uncomfortable to sleep on."

"Uh-huh. So says you. I'll bet you slipped off some night an' dipped yer wick in some of the local talent—right, Archie? Right?"

Archie bit off the sudden flare of anger. "Don't make shrewd with me, Ditto. Like that clever you ain't already." Ordinarily, Richard Golden spoke with the refinement of a college graduate, which he nearly was. Only the greatest of stress brought out traces of his origins. The more the pressure, the thicker his Jewish accent, until when in an extreme situation, he would curse colorfully in Yiddish.

Chad Ditto raised both hands in a defensive gesture. "Okay, okay, I'm sorry. Didn't mean anything by it. Let's go, shall we? We can enjoy the lack of shrapnel on the way to the base."

Kent Welby checked the diver's watch on his right wrist as he and Francie turned toward the covered stairwell leading to her apartment above the apothecary's shop. "We have only an hour."

"We can hurry," Francie Song assured him.

Kent rested one hand on her pert, taut little buttock. "I don't want to hurry. I want to make long, long, slow love with you."

Kent felt her shiver with delight as she spoke. "Oh, yes— yesss. Someday we can do that all night, every night. For now, we must follow the regulations of your Navy."

"You work for the Navy, too."

"Yes, I know. But for me it's different. I'm a civilian." Her long exposure to Americans had begun to register on Francie's speech patterns. She had recently started to use contractions in their correct context.

Kent quickly caught up a step and nuzzled Francie at the juncture of neck and shoulder. "Ummmm. We'll do our best."

Francie unlocked her door and they entered. "I want to check on Thran," she whispered.

In the darkened alcove that served as the eight-year-old's bedroom, Francie let her eyes become adjusted and peered at her sleeping child. Thran lay atop his futon, clad only in a white diaper-like garment that covered his loins. To her he was the picture of innocence and so very beautiful. What, she wondered for the thousandth time, would her new child look like? Would he be big and strapping, like his father, or slender and delicate, like Thran? She blew her boy a kiss and turned back to Kent.

Her eyes widened when she saw he had already speedily removed his clothes. His wide white grin added to the insistence of the large erection that swayed at his groin. With a small mew, Francie went into his arms. Through her thin silk gown she felt the hot tumescence of his manhood. Hungrily she thrust herself against it, willing it to be deep inside her, surging and plunging. Their embrace lasted long minutes.

"Do you—do you want something to drink?" she asked hesitantly, when Kent released her.

"I just want to drink in your beauty."

"Ah! And a poet, too. Well then, maybe I should reveal a little more of it so you can drink deeper."

"Oh, yes. Do, please do." Wildly aroused now, Kent helped her to undress.

Smoothly he lowered her to the large futon and knelt between her open, inviting legs. Slowly he decreased the distance between them until his maleness touched her heated passage. With a deftness born of much practice he slowly, gently penetrated her. Her moan of immense satisfaction was genuine. Her hands sought his firm, small buttocks and pulled him deeper into her welcoming body.

After a long, slow, delightful coupling, the breathless couple lay side by side, idly touching one another in sensitive spots, working toward new titillation. Francie's eyes roamed her small apartment.

"When the baby comes, I am going to need a larger place to live. Thran should have a room of his own."

Tenderly, Kent kneaded an erect nipple. "I'll get you a

small house. Hell, I'll get you a mansion, if that's what you want."

"No—no, I just want you. Now, then, forever and forever, my dear Kentwelby."

Midnight had come and gone before Colonel Hue had completed his briefing of the combat team leaders and the staff of the area VC commander, Captain Hian. Those not immediately affected by the orders and their men were then dismissed to their homes. Among them went Vihn Nhon. The three-quarter kilometer walk along a narrow jungle path to his home village went by in silence. When he reached home, all lay in quiet, the villagers asleep. Soundlessly Nhon went into his hooch. There he knelt beside his sleeping mat and turned the rice straw–stuffed pad back.

Nhon cast a nervous although totally unnecessary glance over his shoulder before he brushed aside a rectangle of dirt to expose a wooden lid. This he opened to reveal a hidden compartment. From that he extracted a compact, powerful VHF radio set and an encryption machine, an aged M-209 converter, obsolete for U.S. forces since not long after the Korean War, but as yet beyond any technology possessed by the Viet Cong.

Next he lighted a candle and settled it in the secret compartment to partly shield its glow. Lower lip clamped between his teeth, he checked the SOI for the code sequence key for that day. He double-checked the setting and closed the machine. Then he methodically set about translating his message into five-letter code groups. Slowly the message spilled out onto a thin paper tape as he set the correct letter and turned the handle of the M-209:

LDXRV
QMPTA
FCBUJ

On it went until the whole of his information had been reduced to neat blocks of letters. Random cams on the print wheels inside the encryption device prevented any duplication of a printed letter. Thus, *PAPER* would come out:

CJRWY

one time and perhaps the next:

MXPZK

The trick was to make sure both encoders were set on the same key.

"Now comes the hard part," Nhon whispered to himself, as he blew out the candle and left his hooch.

Half a klick into the jungle a small clearing existed far enough off the trail to avoid easy detection. In the dim light of a lowering quarter moon, it would be impossible to learn of its presence if one did not already know of it. It was here that Nhon came with his radio.

He first checked to determine that no other human being could be in the immediate vicinity. Then he skillfully scaled a tree and secured one end of his fine copper wire antenna. Back on the ground he went to another tree twenty meters distant and climbed it. There he affixed the other end of the antenna's arms. He lowered himself with caution and went to where he had secreted his radio. He attached the antenna lead and powered up the set. Using a key plugged into the proper receptacle, he sent his message in Morse code. He would receive no acknowledgment; he could only wait for a later contact.

Daa-dit-daa-dit came through the speaker above the radio set of the River Section 534 monitoring station at Tre Noc. The night duty operator standing watch took down the string of Morse letters, then noted the "hit" in the watch-keeper's log. He then gestured to a young seaman nodding off in a fan-backed rattan chair liberated a long time ago from the house of a VC village chieftain.

"Hey, Jimmy, go over to the SEAL barracks, to the

Chief's quarters, and awaken Chief Waters. Tell him Mouth has sent an urgent.''

"Aye-aye." The kid yawned expansively. "Damn, I wish I had that crow sittin' on my sleeve. Then I could send some-one else.''

"Just do it, all right?"

Ten minutes later, Tonto Waters appeared in the doorway, hair tousled, eyes somewhat glazed by the residual of sleep, his body encased in rumpled BDU trousers and a green skivvy shirt. "Whatcha got?" he demanded of the watch stander.

"Like usual, a whole string of letters. Is this guy on the level?" the Second Class Petty Officer inquired.

"Sorry, no need to know. Thanks, I'll take it along and see what Mouth has to say.''

With that, Tonto departed for some much needed sleep. The decryption could wait until after morning mess.

CHAPTER 3 _____

FORTUNATELY, NIGHT had always been the friend of the SEALs. Tonto Waters spent an hour the next morning decrypting the message from Nhon, known to Tonto by his cover name of Mouth. Nhon was a former Viet Cong and graduate of the *Chieu Hoi* program. He had become a member of a company of Kit Carson Scouts and reinserted into his former VC territory to act as a deep-cover intelligence agent for the Americans. Because the Chief was closer than any CIA field officer, Jason Slater, CIA Station Chief in Binh Thuy, had given Mouth to Tonto Waters to operate. What Waters made of the report gave him an unpleasant surprise.

What came with Mail Call gave him a surprise of a far different sort. A most pleasant surprise, he would call it. Eloise Deladier would be in Saigon briefly, starting four days from then, as Tonto figured it. Great news. Since he was slated to meet with Pope Marino after noon chow to discuss the report on the arrival in the area of an NVA colonel, he'd take the opportunity to ask Pope for special liberty, in order to take some time with Eloise in Saigon. Nothing could be easier, right?

Wrong, as he would soon find out.

Pope Marino made a face. "The best I can do is twenty-four hours. One time. If what your source said is correct, everyone from the DMZ to Ba Dong here in the Delta is gonna be as busy as the towel boy in a whorehouse when the fleet's in. When do you contact him again? . . . No, I don't want to know that. Never mind. Try for some more solid proof of this invasion. You ask me, I'd say the NVA brass has gone around the bend. It's absolutely nuts for them to try something like this.''

''I'll get on it, Pope. And—ah—thanks.''

Colonel Kahm-thi-Hue paced agitatedly before the assembled cadres of the Sunrise Liberation Company of the Viet Cong. In strident tones he exhorted them to maintain duty, loyalty, and valor. ''For the first time, Comrades, you will be fighting as equals alongside your heroic Comrades from the North. Shoulder to shoulder, you will provide the anvil against which the enemy will be smashed by the hammer of the People's Liberation Army. Total victory is close, Comrades. I see a united, liberated Socialist Vietnam within the next three months. This is but the first chapter in a glorious book to be written on the solidarity between the workers and peasants of the South and the industrial and military might of the North. Be prepared to lay down your lives, if necessary, to advance the rising tide of Marxist Socialism in Southeast Asia.'' A cacophony of cheers rose spontaneously. ''You will receive your orders and where to go when the time is right. Until then, keep the faith and stand ready to raise your weapons in defense of our cause at a moment's notice. I will leave special orders with your Captain detailing exactly where you will engage the enemy and to which unit of the People's Liberation Army you will be attached. There is nothing ahead for us but victory and glory. Long live Ho Chi Minh!''

After the cheering had ended, Colonel Hue retired to a private cubicle to rest and prepare for the final meeting with the combat team leaders. Vinh Nhon left the tunnel complex and took a direct route back to his village. He knew he was taking a tremendous risk by contacting his control during daytime. But if the Americans wanted to know what had been revealed to his VC company by Colonel Hue, they would do best by capturing the NVA officer, he was con-

vinced, and so informed Tonto in code. And it would be wise
if they moved swiftly, he added.

Late in the afternoon, Lieutenant Carl Marino stood before
the SEALs of First Platoon, seated on the ground under the
shade of a huge, ancient teak tree. Its leafy branches screened
out even the slightest sunlight. On a corkboard in front of
the gathered men were a map and blown-up aerial photos of
an area of jungle. At first glance, and even after careful study
by one uninitiated in the science of photo interpretation, it
appeared as though nothing out of the ordinary existed in
this stretch of jungle.

The truth was strongly to the contrary. The first of the
over-flights during which these photographs had been taken
occurred six months ago, shortly after the insertion of the
agent known as Mouth, with monthly updates since. The subject of those pictures was the area near Cap Lahn, in which
was located the tunnel complex where the company to which
Vinh Nhon belonged underwent training and stood duty
watches to defend the area from the Foreign Aggressors and
Running Dogs of Capitalism (read the Americans and their
South Vietnamese ARVN allies). Marino indicated the sali-
ent features on a composite photo-mosaic with a pointer
made of a length of teak dowelling, tipped with the slug from
a .50 caliber machine gun round. The shell casing formed
the base.

"This is the village of Cap Lahn. There are some thirty
families living there, mostly farmers. Some are VC. The others are harmless. Now, look closely at this portion of the
middle and lower left photo overlaps. You can see there are
ventilation pipes here, here, and here. There are plenty more,
but they are under the tree cover and could not be photo-
graphed. Memorize their position in relation to the entrance,
which is here." Pope Marino tapped the largest, separate
photo again.

"Both squads will be employed. Alpha will sweep the
surface area around the tunnels. Bravo will make the first
assault on the complex. With Alpha in reserve, all exits will

be covered. No one, I repeat, no one is to escape." After a careful check of the area around their briefing spot, Marino removed an eight-by-ten glossy print from a manila envelope. "Study this face. Learn it well. He is a deep cover agent known to us as Mouth. He is a Kit Carson Scout who returned to the Viet Cong as an asset for Christians in Action."

"He some kinda missionary, sir?" cracked the new man, Signalman Second Class Bobby Santoro.

Marino sighed. "No, Wise Guy, he's not. For your benefit, let me explain. Over here, we've taken to calling the spook class 'Christians in Action,' for CIA. Got that?"

"Yeah, sure, Pope. Considerin' some of 'em it fits."

Bobby understood well enough, though he did not like his nickname. Yet, he reasoned philosophically, what could a guy expect when his folks were second-generation Americans from Sicily and there was this big-time Mafioso walking around Jersey with the same name? No relation, his indignant and outraged mother had drummed into him since he was old enough to comprehend what she was talking about. Which put it from about the age of three, Bobby reckoned.

At least Chief Waters understood. He was from New Jersey also and knew all about the way the Cosa Nostra guys just about ran the whole state. Especially Newark. Hell, that old Don, Gianini, had actually organized the Columbus Day parades for about ten years in a row. And even in his own parish, Bobby knew, if someone was down on their luck even if they went to the Knights of Columbus, the Altar Society or the St. Vincent DePaul Society for help, they wound up at Abruzzi's Athletic Club if the kind of help they needed wasn't just money. Worse still, since the age of ten, Bobby Santoro had worked for four years as a lookout for the numbers dealer who operated out of the candy store on a corner two blocks from their house. His sainted mother would die of shame should she ever find *that* out. And it had been a kindly precinct sergeant named Graviato who had aimed Bobby in the direction of the Navy, which took him off the road to first prison and then becoming just what his nickname implied: *un buono uomo*, a good fellah, a wise guy . . . a Mafia hood.

Bobby Santoro could have easily navigated that other path. Although he had the face of an angel, with black curls, shoe-button eyes that shined with intelligence and mischief, a pug nose, and a sweet, winning smile, he also had a three-alarm temper and the strength in work-hardened arms to enforce his frequent rages. PAL had channeled that rage and saved him from a life of crime that would be far from a trite phrase.

Carlo Graviato had introduced young Bobby to the Police Athletic League and to the manly sport of boxing at the age of fourteen. Learning and perfecting the science of fisticuffs had taken a long time. The knowledge had come fast that rage robbed him of smarts and had cost him more than one hell of a beating in the ring before he'd learned it. And always there were the rules.

If one chose not to follow them to the letter, the rules got you in the end and you were out on your ass. Carlo Graviato and Mike Doolin, a detective sergeant on the organized crime squad, drummed that into Bobby often enough. At last it took root. He shaped up, finished high school early at the age of sixteen, and at age 17, visited the Navy recruiter to join up. It was the best decision he had ever made, Bobby admitted to himself, as he forced his attention back to Pope Marino, who was going on with the briefing.

"The purpose of this operation, called 'Timelapse,' is to capture an NVA colonel—alive, if possible—along with any documents, maps, and charts he may have in his keeping. We will be going in by slicks, with backup available from Cobras if needed. The idea is to be stealthy. Cap Lahn is only three-quarters of a klick away, so we will approach from the south. The LZ will be located two klicks away from the tunnel complex. That is right here, at Charlie-Quebec three-two-five-zero. Route march approach to the objective, with two flankers out. The next two men behind the point man will carry hushpuppies. Use them to take out any sentries.

"Everyone else will carry personal arms; Bravo's will be

suppressed. We will take six claymores for perimeter security during the operation. After all external security has been taken out, we drop CNDM grenades (vomiting and tear gas) down the ventilator pipes. That's why you are to memorize their location. Hard Case,'' he addressed Brandon Mitchell, Bravo Squad's demo man, ''You will take one satchel charge, a twenty pounder, for opening the front door. Bravo enters and makes a quick sweep action, and hear this: absolutely no frag grenades underground, *none*. Mop up by Alpha, leaving three personnel topside for security. When we've got what we came for, we leave; ignore any VC that are left alive. Extraction will be from a different LZ, here a hundred meters from the objective. Finally, and I saved the best for last, our rules of engagement. And believe me, it makes me question what political asshole thought this up,'' he remarked rhetorically. ''The idiots want us not to shoot unless shot at.'' He paused a pregnant second. ''But I think we can arrange to have that happen easy enough. At least, that's the way it will read in the After Action Report. We jump off an hour after full darkness. Go draw your equipment, chow down, and grab some Zees. Any questions?''

There were none. ''Dismissed.'' Marino gathered the briefing materials and headed for his office. Behind him, Chief Tom Waters addressed the SEALs.

''All right, troops, let's get ready to go kick ass and take names.''

Recently promoted *Polkovnik* (Colonel) Pyotr Maximovich Rudinov, KGB *Rezidentura* for Cambodia and South Vietnam, sat at his desk in his comfortable lair in the provincial capital of Kampong Cham, Cambodia. Only recently had he cast off his guise and the uniform of a *Spetznaz* lieutenant and donned the required austere, poorly tailored business suit of a KGB agent in the Foreign Directorate. Seated across from him, in a natty Saville Row suit that must have cost around 50,000 rubles, was General Major Vladislav Nikoliavich Ludvinov, his superior in the First Directorate, KGB. Both men drank from glasses of tea poured by Rudinov himself from his ancient family heirloom samovar.

Ludvinov smacked his lips in appreciation of the sweet-ened brew and spoke first. "You are aware, of course, that your presence will be required in Hanoi during this confer-ence."

Rudinov frowned. "Why is that? My area of responsibil-ity is the South."

"You are also the senior KGB officer in Southeast Asia, as of your recent promotion, for which let me congratulate you, Colonel. Your major concern will be with developing credible deniability for Soviet participation in the conference. Also to supervise a high-visibility security force for the screening of the meetings and protection of the participants."

"One crisis at a time if you please, Comrade General," Rudinov interrupted with a smile, to show he was not criti-cizing. "Our deniability must be predicated in not being there at all. So what do I do? Go around in my full-dress uniform? I think not."

"No. You will wear mufti unless otherwise ordered by some superior."

"Such as, Comrade General?"

Vladislav Ludvinov produced a bleak smile. "General Colonel Yevgeni Deguriev will be representing the Red Army. He is, as you know, next in line for a baton as a Marshal of the Soviet Union. He might opt for formality no matter what we know to be for the best. Whatever the case, it can be dealt with when and if it arises. Be assured you will have an ally in the person of Boris Konstantinovich No-vorat, who will represent the politburo. He is most concerned our presence is not verified. Likewise Feodor Litvanoff, Sec-retary General of the Party, will be cautious. You should be able to remain out of uniform."

"So then, all our people will be arriving by separate air-craft and route, the usual for covert meetings?"

"Yes, Pyotr. And no media fawning over them, make that clear to our comrades in the North."

"Well, that said, and the manual on Disinformation seems

to have covered the subject adequately. The next issue you brought up is security, am I right?''

''Correct.'' A smile raised the corners of his thick-lipped mouth. ''Of course, you have the manual on Meeting Security which you can consult. But this assignment requires considerably more inventiveness and originality than described in that respected tome. I trust you are up to that aspect, because it is anticipated that an endless string of imagined scenarios will be presented to you.

''The NVA,'' Ludvinov continued in a complaining tone, ''suffers from acute paranoia. Generals Kao Tri of the State Security Service and Gao Dien Ghe in particular, though both for different reasons.''

Rudinov pulled a long face. ''May I ask what those reasons are?''

Ludvinov laughed, a short, barking sound. ''I would be disappointed if you did not. It seems that they see U.S. Navy SEALs in their closets and under their beds. Tri has bought into the idea of General Bac, the G-2, of a massive raid into the north to free prisoners of war. He has geared his available personnel to withstand such an incursion. Ridiculous, of course.''

''Certainly,'' agreed Rudinov.

''Ghe is somewhat less hysterical in his dark suspicions. He reasons that since some SEALs managed to get into the country once before, they might do it again. This time their logical target would be to disrupt the tri-powers meeting. Accordingly, his G-3 has devised an operations plan for the meeting incorporating a diversion all of his security personnel into roving patrols to cover the meeting site. As unnecessary as Tri's paranoia is absurd, is it not?''

''Most surely, Comrade General,'' Rudinov allowed, although the ghost of his up-close-and-personal encounter with the last invading SEALs haunted his every word.

Tall towers of brooding clouds hovered over the triple canopy jungle of the Mekong Delta. Even before they crowded together to blot out the blue sky and brazen sun, they influenced the mood of the swarms of antlike people who toiled below the spreading arms of teak, mangrove and cypress. Palmetto fronds waved in a freshening breeze while spider and strangler vines writhed as though in agony, all of which heralded the imminent approach of a tropical storm.

Although monsoon season had long passed, the downpour would be monumental. Like bucketsful dumped on one's head, literally inches of rain would drop in half an hour or less that afternoon. The prospect did little to lighten the outlook of a redheaded U.S. Marine staff sergeant named Elmore Yates. At the best of times, it could be said that Yates lacked a sense of humor, or any trace of a positive outlook on life. If an excuse could be found, perhaps his meanness of spirit had dictated his avocation. Even now, while the temperature dropped precipitously and the wind grew in force and speed, his face was a scowling mask while he met outside the compound at Tre Noc with an Oriental whom he knew as Phon Caliphong.

Yates would have been in an even more sour mood than usual had he known that Caliphong was in fact *Starshii Serzhant* (Senior Sergeant) Feodor Dudov of the KGB. Not that Yates would betray his country to the Viet Cong and shrink from the same treason in the case of the Soviets, merely that he would have his paranoia and xenophobia fed by the knowledge of Caliphong's origins. At the bottom line, Yates was in it for the money. He was no more an ideologue than his control, Dudov. Cynical and envious, and bitter because of it, Yates sought to assuage the innumerable imagined slights directed at him by a falsely superior society with a fat numbered Swiss bank account. Even so, the redhead chafed at being given instructions like a lackey.

"Your information in the past has proven less than accurate, Comrade. My superiors are most disappointed in that. To recover face, and to ensure a continuation of your emolument, I would suggest that you be most careful in carrying out your next assignment." Dudov had no problem sounding like the inscrutable Oriental. He was a Mongol by birth, son of parents who resided in Ulan Ude, Siberia, less than 300 kilometers northwest of Ulan Bator, capital of Mongolia.

Stung by the note of supremacy in the voice of Caliphong, Yates twisted his lips into an unpleasant sneer before inquiring as to the nature of that assignment in a tone of impatience and contempt. "And what might that be?"

Dudov/Caliphong pursed his lips before responding. "We require a day-by-day, preferably an hour-by-hour, report on the activities, movement, and whereabouts of the sailors in SEAL Team 2 over a period of the next two weeks. No delays, no omissions, no excuses . . ." As though to emphasize his orders, the sky opened up at that moment and released a deluge. Although only two feet separated one man from the other, their visibility dimmed until their features blurred.

"But, that's not . . ." Yates gasped, voice weak over the roar of cascading rainfall.

Dudov raised a hand to command silence. "You did not let me complete my instructions. You will do this and you will receive the sum of fifteen thousand U. S. dollars in payment, deposited to your Swiss account. Is that satisfactory? And will it ensure your absolute compliance?"

For that much? The figure literally took the breath from Elmore Yates. In the past, sums had generally revolved around $500 to $1500 for each assignment successfully completed. Recently, in regard to the frigging SEALs, that qualifier had meant that he had received nothing for the past three assignments. He had to swallow hard before making a response. "Of—of course. More than that: I can guarantee results this time. The Song woman is entirely in my hands. Your implication that to threaten the boy's life would be a fatal mistake is obviously wrong. I am still here and still a free man. I will squeeze her and keep on squeezing for every bit of information she can extract from the Operations Section. You will not be disappointed."

"Let us hope so, Comrade. Now, good day."

CHAPTER 4 _____

LONG BEFORE the SEALs of Alpha and Bravo Squads, First Platoon, Team 2 cleared the LZ, the *whop-whop* of the rotor blades of the Huey Slicks had faded into the distance. Tonto Waters took point, as usual. The flankers went out and the small column started off through the deep jungle toward their objective. Night was their friend, darkness their ally.

Noise discipline was superlative. Not a jingle from dog tags edged with soft plastic; the SEALs had also wrapped theirs in black electrician's tape. Not a strap, nor a swivel, nor a piece of equipment had been left loose to rattle or click. Even the safety pins on their grenades had been taped lightly to the bodies of the M7 AS3 CS and M4 CD4 gas grenades.

Further, the men walked on their toes. Previous patrols had revealed that some of the more sophisticated Viet Cong tunnel complexes had been provided with motion detectors which would pick up and amplify the thud of a human heel against the ground. Only the thickest, wettest of jungle debris could cushion the careless step with heel first.

Some mighty sore calves had resulted from the first two weeks of practice back at Little Creek, Virginia, but it had paid off. It came to the SEALs naturally when they arrived in Vietnam. For their counterparts, the VC, such a manner of walking came naturally. In their earlier incarnation as the Viet Minh, the French had given them the name *Les Pieds du Chat*, the cat-footed. None of which served them well when confronted by the Men with Green Faces.

Tonto Waters came upon the first screen of sentries 800 meters from the main entrance to the tunnels. They did not have a chance to see him. He faded into the dark, halted the loose column, and silently gave hand signal instructions.

Doc Welby from Alpha Squad and Tex Goracke from Bravo slid through the dense undergrowth of ferns, strangler vines, and stunted palms. Following Tonto's directions, they skirted wide around a pair of VC watching the trail. Doc Welby moved in first. At a range of only six feet he raised the suppressed Mark 22 Model O (a modified version of the steel-framed S&W Model 39), slipped the slide lock into place, and lined up the sights on the back of a VC head. He took a final deep breath and let out half as he took up the slack in the trigger. When he reached that momentary pause in the pull-through, he increased pressure slightly.

Welby's sight picture wavered only minutely as the hush-puppy 9mm discharged with a polite chuff and soft pop as the bullet exited the Mark 3 Model O suppressor through the endwipe. A slide lock prevented even the noise of the action cycling. The targeted VC lost his gray pith helmet when his head snapped forward at impact. Already dead, he hit the ground face first a fraction of a second before his comrade went slack-kneed and pitched outward across the trail from the shadow behind a tree.

Got him! Dallas Goracke enthused silently a moment later, when the special green-tipped, 158 grain 9mm Parabellum projectile took his man down. Then the big brown eyes under a thatch of auburn hair misted over as the reality hit him. *Jesus*! He'd just killed a man.

A recent replacement, along with four other SEALs sent to First Platoon the week before, this was his first kill. His gut tightened as the VC enemy twitched violently for a couple of seconds and went still. The silence that followed alarmed Tex nearly as much as the noise made by the dying man.

He had really done it. And oh, shit, Charlie Sturgis had

made him the squad sniper. Just because he was such a damned good shot with a rifle. That was his dad's doing. From the time he was big enough to hold the small, cut-down .22 rifle to his shoulder without cocking his head off to one side and straining to keep the barrel from wobbling, Dallas had been carefully schooled in marksmanship. Now, as he lowered the Browning pistol, his mind raced backward and he could hear his father speaking.

"Good shot, son. Remember, it's not how many rounds you get off, it's bullet placement that counts." And the past suddenly tightened into sharp focus in the mind of Dallas Goracke. "It's the reason I gave you a bolt-action rifle. When I was not much older than you, my dad would give me three twenty-two shorts and I was expected to come back with three rabbits or squirrels."

"Gee, Dad," the freckle-faced eight-year-old who was that earlier Dallas Goracke replied solemnly. "What happened when you couldn't get that many?"

"Then I had better come back with the unspent ammo. Now, c'mon, son. Try the hundred yard target again. Relax and aim for the X-ring. Remember, you're shooting high and left. Adjust your aim accordingly."

Dallas had turned twelve before he'd received a rifle with a set of adjustable sights. It was a fine Huskvarna Targeteer. The freckled copper-haired boy had outgrown that weapon in two years. Equipped with an exceptionally accurate Anschuss rifle, he had taken first place in his native Kansas state NRA matches and every regional match that year, and gone on to cop second place in the Junior Rifle competition at the Camp Perry national matches. His father had been extremely proud.

Although he'd had to wear eyeglasses from his early teens, the vision impairment did not affect his expert rifleman's status. In high school, he had converted to contact lenses and his score had increased dramatically. All of that came rushing back to him in the few seconds it took the VC to twitch his last. Dallas looked up to receive a curt approv-

ing nod from Doc Welby and the two of them set off to deal
with other lookouts.

Less than 100 meters down the trail, Tonto Waters all but
stumbled on another of the VC sentries put out to screen the
tunnel complex. The small brown man was squatted down,
voiding his bowels, when Tonto nearly tripped over him and
stepped in a nasty deposit. Only superb night vision prevented the unsavory contact.

Tonto arrested his movement and caught his breath before
a gasp betrayed his presence. Lacking a pistol with conven-
ient hushpuppy, he reversed his Ithaca 12-gauge shotgun and
slammed the butt into the base of the VC's skull. A brisk,
crunching sound told Tonto that this Charlie had taken his
last crap. Crouched beside his deceased target, Waters took
a quick, careful look around, then rose and stepped back onto
the trail.

He gave the all-clear signal and continued along the wind-
ing jungle path toward their objective. A nearly inaudible
chug to his right told him that Kent or the new kid had found
another security post.

It was in fact Tex Goracke. While still swallowing hard to
keep down the gorge that rose over his first-ever taking of a
human life, he literally came face-to-face with another enemy. Charlie's eyes went wide in shock and he fumbled at
a lanyard around his neck. The VC sucked in a deep draught
of air for the purpose of blowing a shrill warning with the
whistle at the end of the braided cord.

Trained reflexes took over for Tex Goracke, whose body
and mind fell back on the patient albeit violent lessons
drummed into him and all SEAL candidates back at Little
Creek, at Roosevelt Roads and Viequez in Puerto Rico, and
later into graduate SEALs at the Jungle Warfare School—
officially the U.S. Army Jungle Operations Course 900-D-
F6, deep in the jungles of Central America, specifically the
Panama Canal Zone—and other advanced courses.

Dallas Goracke swiftly raised his Mark 22 hushpuppy and

drove the whistle through Charlie's teeth on the tip of a 9mm bullet and out the back of the head of the surprised Cong. It only made a little sound. Enough, though, to be heard and recognized by the sentry's partner. Dallas didn't gag this time. He didn't have time to.

A second Cong bounded toward him, leaping like a gazelle to avoid the fallen trunks of rotted trees. Had it been lighter, Tex could have seen the expression of confusion on the face of the VC. The young Cong had seen his comrade jerk backward and fall in a spray of dark droplets, yet had not heard more than a soft pop. Ill-trained at best, he entirely forgot about his warning signal and ignored his whistle in order to avenge his friend.

"Oh, shit," Dallas said aloud softly as the Cong crashed noisily through the bush. He quickly released the slide lock, stripped out the fired cartridge and chambered another. Then he fixed the lock, raised the Model O, and took aim.

Hastily Charlie raised his PRC Type 56 carbine, a modified version of the Soviet SKS. The "intermediate class" weapon was neither fish nor fowl. Unfortunately for the young VC, it maneuvered poorly when he tried to swing the muzzle into line with an enemy directly in front of him.

Tex Goracke calmly shot him when the Cong still had the carbine at high port. The 9mm slug from the Mark 22 in Tex's hand smashed into the wooden stock directly over the ten-round staggered-row internal box magazine. The Type 56 absorbed most of the shock, only to transmit it to the tightly gripping fingers of the youthful VC.

Those fingers flew open involuntarily and the weapon dropped into the rotting carpet of jungle floor. Dallas Goracke had so far fired only three rounds, which left him ten to expend. One more on this target wouldn't matter at all, he reasoned. He cycled the slide and tickled the trigger again. The bullet pinwheeled the VC in the center of his chest.

Shock and pain from the impact blew away the VC's intended scream in a feeble wheeze. His life quickly followed. Tonto Waters closed on Tex Goracke a moment after the body crashed to the ground.

"Damn," Waters whispered to the young SEAL. "They're comin' outta the woodwork." He did not voice his thoughts. *Must be more important doin's in those tunnels than we thought. Maybe we got here in time. The colonel Mouth reported on must still be in that place. Too much security to be otherwise.* He gestured to Goracke.

"You done good, kid. Drop back and give Zorro Agilar your hushpuppy an' send him up here."

When Zorro arrived, Tonto pointed. "Keep swingin' to the left. Tex popped a couple and there's bound to be more. I'm gonna check on Doc."

Tonto found Kent Welby bent over a dead VC. A black hole in the forehead of the enemy had a patent leather shine in the pale white of filtered moonlight. A small hand-held radio lay a few inches from the outstretched dead fingers.

Doc Welby looked wild-eyed and harried. "Th'muther damn near got out a warning. I wasted his partner and didn't even see him. Would have missed him entirely if he hadn't keyed that radio and I heard it squawk."

"All right, cool it, Doc. I'm gonna push on ahead, bring along the troops with me. Get out there an' dump me some more lookouts."

Doc Welby, Zorro Agilar, and Tonto Waters took out the last three sentries within 20 meters of the large main entrance to the tunnels. Once more, Tonto used the butt of his shotgun. But it did not prove so easy as the first.

Tonto saw a short, barrel-chested Cong rise up while two others went down for the final count. The VC's fingers reached for the clapper cord on an alarm bell as Tonto neared. No time to reverse the weapon and go in butt-first. Tonto jabbed like he had a bayonet on the shotgun. The steel rim of the muzzle cut through cloth and bit into flesh. So intense was the pain and the blow so breathtaking that no sound came from the injured Cong.

Waters jerked the Ithaca backward and across his body, quickly swiveled it as he brought it upward, and swung it over his left shoulder muzzle first. The butt streaked forward.

The steel butt plate rammed into flesh and bone, dislocating the jaw before breaking it. The heel of the butt made a deep depression in the VC's temple that slowly began to seep blood. *Kiss another one goodbye*, Tonto thought grimly, as he gave a quick examination to the wound.

Yep, another good Cong, he verified. A minute later he began a brief series of hand signals to the members of Alpha Squad. Tonto raised his right fist and extended two fingers, then closed to point with his index finger in the direction he wanted to send the men. Two more fingers paired off two more SEALs who went in yet another direction. He repeated it again and the men moved out.

They knew what to do. Quickly they spread out and found the camouflage vent pipes. One by one the SEALs pulled the safety pins on their gas grenades. Soft pops followed the release of the spoons. Each man made a three count and dropped the container down a pipe. Swiftly they capped them and moved on to other ventilators. While they worked at this, Pope Marino came forward with Bravo Squad.

His first act was to make certain the squad had their M17 gas masks firmly in place. Then Lieutenant Marino made a curt gesture to Brandon Mitchell, the demolitions man, who went forward to the brush-covered metal plate that formed the main door into the tunnels below. He bent over the hatch-like portal and worked with quick, deft movements. After attaching the satchel charge to a cleared space, he removed the safety pin and pulled the igniter cord. The pin dropped and struck a large shotgun primer, which in turn fired the frizzed open end of a short length of fuse.

"Clear!" Mitchell barked to the SEALs, as he leaped away from the depression in which the passage to underground had been created.

Five seconds later, the explosive package went off with a loud, concussive *whang*! A gout of dust and rain-damp vegetation erupted into the air and the sharp odor of burned TNT filled the nostrils of the waiting SEALs of Alpha Squad. It reminded them to don their masks also. Seconds later, with

Anchor Head Sturgis leading the way, Bravo Squad entered the tunnel complex.

Below the surface of the jungle floor, they found a scene that Dante would have loved. Hell had moved into the Delta. A section of the overhead directly behind the access hatch had collapsed to litter the floor. A tangle of tree roots hung down, writhing like snakes in the residual of the shockwave. Dim red lights glowed along the main corridor. Designed to preserve night vision, they now contributed to an impression of Hades-on-Earth. The sensation was heightened for the Bravos by the weird sound their masked breathing made. A final flavor of the Inferno likewise touched their ears with resonances that could have come from the damned souls.

Hardly human, the painful gags, moans, and retching rose throughout the complex. The audible result of unprotected exposure to CNDM gas, it registered the near-total incapacitation of the Viet Cong trapped within. Pope Marino joined the squad and motioned them forward. Anchor Head took the point and the six SEALs spread out through the warren of cross-tunnels that branched off the central corridor. Despite the calamitous properties of the tear and nausea gas, resistance came almost immediately.

With a hoarse yell of defiance, one VC unleashed a rapid string of five 7.62-by-39 rounds from his Type 56 carbine. Compressed underground as they were, the shots carried with them a physical pressure as well as ear-punishing cracks. One slug whipped past behind the head of Mickey Mouse Norton, who pivoted sharply to his left and let go a three round burst from his suppressed Swedish M45 Carl Gustaf submachine gun.

At 600 rounds per minute, the 9mm Parabellum slugs cut an upward slash diagonally across the chest of the insolent Viet Cong soldier. He spilled over backward, his Type 56 carbine flung from his grasp by the nearly instantaneous (ten per second) impact of the bullets. Movement next to the dying VC drew Norton's immediate attention.

Mickey Mouse saw what appeared to be a handgun with a pregnant barrel. The weapon made only the smallest of sounds as it fired at him. A bullet moaned past his ear an instant before he returned fire.

Not until after he had ruined the Cong's day with a three round burst did he see more clearly that the dead man held a silenced Type 67 Chi Com evolution of their rip-off of the Soviet Tokarev. The underpowered .32 caliber (7.65-by-17mm) cartridge it used gave him little consolation. It could still kill a man, and many had in Vietnam so far. He had time for only one more observation. The Type 67 had a bright, clean, shiny-new look to it. On impulse he stooped to scoop it up and take it along with him. Unwittingly his action achieved an intelligence coup.

Elsewhere in the maze of tunnels, Little Pete Peterson and Long Tom Killian had troubles of their own. In a small chamber dug off one side of the branch they had taken, they found an overturned pot of noodles, rice spilled from six bowls, and an equal number of bewildered, very sick Viet Cong.

"Move! Move! Move!" Long Tom bellowed at them, his voice muffled by the gas mask.

Not comprehending the words, nor the sudden appearance of these huge men with the hideous green faces, the VC blinked at them in growing confusion. Their secure underground world had turned topsy-turvy and their communist indoctrination had deprived them of the ability to think for themselves or evince initiative. They did know the meaning of the weapons with which the men menaced them. Meekly they surrendered. A burst of rapid gunfire jerked their gaze in the direction from which it came.

Colonel Kahm-thi-Hue had managed to get to his gas mask in time to avoid the worst of the invading irritant cloud, but not before stinging, burning fumes had caused his eyes to tear and stream like those of a frightened child. He did not believe for a moment that the incompetent Americans could have found this well-concealed tunnel warren. Which left only one possibility.

If this turned out to be an unannounced drill, laid on to impress him, then the fools who had wrongheadedly concluded that it would be the highlight of his visit would soon feel the sharp edge of his tongue, and the harsh castigation that would come from their superiors in the North. The image of a mock attack lingered until he heard the first gunfire. At once, Hue hastened to gather his profusion of maps, charts, schedules, and volumes of briefing papers.

He had only halfway completed the task when a carbine barked loudly, quickly followed by the soft discharge of two suppressed weapons outside his personal cubicle. In the next second, the teenaged Viet Cong militiaman who had been placed on guard there staggered inside. The boy spewed blood from fist-sized exit wounds in his back. Following him in came the two largest men Hue had ever seen. What he saw of their fierce expressions behind the gas masks was most unsettling. More so were the green faces that bore them.

Xachon Donasay had been a loyal supporter of the Viet Cong cause for four years. He had been a soldier for the last two of those. It gave him great pride to be fighting to rid his adopted country of the running dog lackeys of the decadent capitalist oppressors. Although his family had moved to Vietnam from their native Laos so that his father might find work, Xachon embraced the new country as his homeland. When he had been given one of the new selective-fire Type 56 assault weapons and assigned the honored responsibility of guarding the privacy of their exalted guest from North Vietnam, he had swelled with self-esteem.

When the gas had begun to spread through the complex, he did not know exactly what had happened. Yet he was young and his reflexes were fast. He reacted according to his training. Like Colonel Hue, whom he so admired, he managed to get his gas mask in place in time. It did him little good, though, when the giants stormed down on him. His Type 56 assault rifle seemed to jump into position and he fired a single shot before a terrible blow struck him in the chest. Before real pain could set in, another sledgehammer

pounded him on the opposite side of his sternum and he
dropped his assault rifle.

His legs seemed to have a mind of their own. They directed him sideways and backward through the opening to
the cubicle. Dimly he saw the green-faced men follow him.
He desperately positioned himself between them and the colonel. All to no avail. Darkness swept over him as his strength
deserted him and be began to drown in his own blood.

"Look what we've got here," Brandon Mitchell's muffled
voice came to Dallas Goracke as they looked down on the
short figure of Colonel Hue. "Unless I miss my guess, this
is the dude we're huntin' for."

"I think you're right, Bran. He fits the description we got.
Let's get him out of the mess," Tex Goracke suggested.

From the far side of the complex, they heard the distant
sounds of upheaval as Alpha Squad burst through another
entranceway and began the task of closing the trap.

It required another half hour to quell all opposition and clear
the tunnels of the occupants. The SEALs took turns breathing
fresh air by escorting groups of prisoners to the surface.
Caught among the VC militiamen was Vinh Nhon. When
Tonto Waters saw him, he stomped over purposefully and
grabbed a handful of black pajama top.

"C'mon, you. I've got some questions to ask," Tonto
growled through an interpreter, another Kit Carson Scout,
one who did not know Nhon.

Out of sight and hearing of the Viet Cong prisoners, Tonto
reached out and shook Nhon's hand. "You did a good job.
We got the colonel."

Nhon kept his grin of pride small. "He had many papers
with him. Did you get those?"

Tonto nodded in the affirmative. "Now, I think you had
better take off an' go to your village if you want to maintain
your cover. Join up with another VC cadre and keep in touch.
And . . . good luck. Oh, one last thing. We're gonna do a

little playacting here. No matter what I say or do, don't stop and don't come back.''

Nhon nodded understanding and started off into the bush. A moment after he disappeared entirely, Tonto shouted loudly, "Hey you, stop! Stop or I'll shoot." The interpreter repeated his demand in Vietnamese. Tonto let a second go by, then busted off a round from his shotgun. He nodded to the grinning Kit Carson Scout and started back to where the prisoners were being held.

His voice weighted with feigned disgust, Tonto made certain he was well within the hearing of the captive VC. "Damn him, he wouldn't answer a single question and then he made a break for it. I think I winged him. Damn well better have."

Pope Marino popped up out of the tunnel entrance like a prairie dog out of its hole. "Well, we got what we came for. Form 'em up, Chief, and let's *didi* outta here for the LZ."

Tonto Waters gave him a big grin. "Aye, sir. None too soon for me."

CHAPTER 5 _____

HUGE BLACK clouds piled up to the southeast of Binh Thuy as the lightly armed Huey swung its wasp tail around and settled on the landing pad. There would be a hell of a rain later in the day, Lieutenant Carl Marino reflected as he jumped from the bird the moment the skids touched. He bent low to clear the slowing rotor.

He swiftly moved out beyond the tips of the blades and came upright. The stiff buckram file folder he carried attracted no special attention. A jeep waited with driver lounging against the front left fender. He came to attention and saluted as Pope Marino approached.

"Good morning, sir. I was sent by Commander Lailey to meet you, sir."

Marino returned the salute. "Thank you, Yeoman. We'll go directly to the S-2 office."

Pope settled himself in the right-hand seat and adjusted the crease in his summer tan uniform trousers as the jeep engine ground to life. The yeoman who drove it must see himself as the Mario Andretti of the Seventh Fleet from the way he whipped the vehicle in and out around the other sparse traffic and the speed he maintained on the way to the headquarters building. For the bulk of the journey, Pope Marino took his mind off the Barney Oldfield of NAVSPEC-WARV and reviewed the scene that had been responsible for an important part of the After Action Report he was on the

way to file, along with the documents obtained from Colonel
Hue . . .

. . . After the SEALs had arrived at the LZ for their extraction, several men came up to Lieutenant Marino. Most wore
puzzled expressions, some appeared seriously worried as
they showed him enemy weapons they had taken in the raid.
Anchor Head Sturgis was first.

"Pardon me, sir, I picked this li'l thing up in the tunnels.
It looked like a good little side piece to keep handy. But it
got me to wonderin'."

"What's that, Chuck?" asked Marino.

"Well, it's kinda new, don't you think? Like it's not had
fifty rounds run through it. Surely not the suppressor. Absolutely silent."

"Hummm," came from Marino. "Let me see."

He took the weapon and examined it. He quickly identified it, incorrectly it turned out, as a Type 64 Chinese knock-
off of the Soviet Tokarev. It turned out to be the newer Type
67, a truly *new* development, which employed a tubular, full-
barrel, less bulky suppressor system, while retaining the original 7.65 caliber.

"This is a seven-point-six-five by seventeen mike-mike.
Uses the same cartridge as the thirty-two ACP. You're right,
though," Marino went on. "It's brand new. None of the
finish is even worn shiny."

"Yes, sir, that's what I figgered. Some of the other guys
have picked up new weapons. How you reckon on that, given
the near total shutdown of the Ho Chi Minh?"

Which had indeed been a point to ponder, Lieutenant Marino concluded, after inspecting the other examples. So had
Jason Slater when contacted about the results of the raid.
When he'd come down to escort the captive to interrogation,
he had taken along several specimens of the captured weapons. Now, Marino acknowledged reluctantly, he would have
to report on and surrender the remaining examples to Lieutenant Commander Barry Lailey. Not something he was entirely enthused about . . .

*   *   *

... The driver thundered to a stop a bare three inches from the wooden walkway that fronted the building which bore the legend "NAVSPECWARV," which stood for "Navy Special Warfare Vietnam." The white-painted structure blazed in the relentless South Asian sun. Marino stepped down, grateful to still be in one piece, thanked the young sailor again and headed for the sturdy double front doors.

He took with him an attitude born of a mixed mind. Part of him would rather not be reporting to Lieutenant Commander Barry Lailey for any reason. It was always unpleasant for both of them. Another part of him, that perverse streak of onerousness, had him always anticipating such encounters. Because, he reasoned, any personal meeting between the two men always left Lailey far more uncomfortable than himself. And that, Marino concluded, as he took the steps two at a time, was worth a two-day liberty to see.

Leaded glass panes in the upper halves of the doors reflected multiple funhouse images of Carl Marino as he approached and passed through into the headquarters of naval operations in this part of Vietnam. The chief yeoman at a high, police precinct–style desk in the lobby recognized him and waved him on down a hallway to Marino's left.

Offices gave off the hall: S-1 Personnel, S-2 Intelligence, S-3 Operations, S-4 Logistics and Supply. Lieutenant Marino turned into the reception area. A YO/2C looked up from a mass of paperwork on his desk and, copping an attitude from his boss, asked snottily, "Yes . . . *sir*?

Marino bit back an angry retort, well aware the yeoman knew him on sight and knew the reason for his being there. "Lieutenant Marino, SEAL Team 2 to see the S-2."

With a curl to his upper lip that came close to a sneer, the yeoman took his sweet time examining an appointment calendar. At last he looked up at Pope Marino. "You're not on the list . . . *sir*."

"I am expected. I called ahead."

"We'll—ah—see . . . *sir*."

Patience deserted Marino. "Tell me, do you like being a second class petty officer?"

When the subject of conversation turned to himself, the sailor brightened. "Oh, yes, sir. I'm strikin' for First next month."

"Humm. I'm thinking that if you don't watch that attitude and mouth of yours, it could be arranged for you to become an SA two-striper damned fast."

Seaman apprentice? The thought chilled him. He quickly rearranged his outlook. "Commander Lailey is expecting you, sir. Go right in."

"Thank you, Yeoman—ah—Parker," Marino replied, after a quick glance at the nameplate on the desk.

It let Parker know that Marino had made note of his name. It even suggested that perhaps he had chosen the wrong role model. After all, rumor had it that Lieutenant Carl Marino had a lot more influence and respect around NAVSPEC-WARV than Lieutenant Commander Barry Lailey. While Parker ruminated on this, Marino strode past his desk and paused outside the closed door to Lailey's office.

He raised one fist and rapped with hard knuckles. "Come," came a brusque reply. The tone implied that the occupant of the room knew exactly who had knocked.

Pope Marino removed his cover, tucked it under his left arm and turned the knob. Without hesitation, he crossed the room in almost a march step, halted in front of Barry Lailey's desk, and executed a sharp salute.

"Lieutenant Marino, First Platoon, Team 2, sir."

Lailey spoke in a tired voice, as though bored with all the mundane information that passed over his desk. "I know who you are, Marino. What's this shit you brought me?"

Accustomed to this hostile environment, Marino did not hesitate. He sat his file folder on the edge of a conference table behind him in the middle of the room. Without a comment he undid the straps, turned back the stiff buckram lid, and removed a sheaf of documents.

"Quite a few papers in Vietnamese, which will require translation." He began listing the contents. "There's a manual here that covers a new sight for their antiquated Soviet M43 eighty-two millimeter mortars. It's my impression that this sight will bring the accuracy up to a par with our eighty-ones.''

Lailey could not hide the condescension in his voice. "What do you base that on?"

Marino opened the book and flipped to a series of photographs. "The illustrations, sir. Also the ranging charts." He turned to a series of firing tables.

Without examining the evidence, Lailey scoffed openly. "You're an artilleryman now? And you read Vietnamese?"

"I am checked out on our sixties and eighty-ones as you well know, sir. The Vietnamese use Arabic numerals and basic math is still basic math. The firing tables speak for themselves."

"Very well, I'll accept that, pending a translation of the text. What else?"

"Maps, sir. Some of the best I've ever seen. I don't think they are Viet Cong standard issue. The most important thing is that they show troop disposals by unit size and numerical designation. Also routes of march and what appear to be proposed engagements, with assault positions and Order of Battle drawn in."

To Marino's surprise and consternation, Lailey came alive at mention of these. He reached for them eagerly and pored over several examples. "Now, *that* is interesting. I've been hearing . . . rumors lately. About something these maps just might verify. It looks to me that you've made quite a find, Marino."

That was as close to a compliment as Carl Marino could expect from Barry Lailey. It appealed to his mischievous streak and gave him wicked satisfaction to have wrung at least this small praise from the man who hated him. Lailey continued, once more in his acid mode.

"This prisoner of yours . . . when can I arrange for his interrogation?"

"Right now, MI Team Six has him," he evaded. "After that, Jason Slater wants to have a chat. I'd say you can see him about the middle of next week, sir.'' Marino portrayed an air of indifference.

Lailey's face suffused scarlet. "What the hell? He's our capture. We should have him here."

Marino responded calmly. "The Military Intelligence teams are experts, sir. And they have excellent interpreters. Well, at least some of them are numba one. Besides, it will take you about that long to get those documents translated. What an asset that will be to your interrogation. It will make you look like you know a great deal more about him and his business than you actually do."

That idea appealed to Lailey. "All right. All right. I'll get someone on these maps and papers right away. Thank you, Marino. You're dismissed."

"One more thing, sir. We encountered an unusual and unexplained situation. The VC seem to have been able to be supplied with the newest equipment, regardless of the near total interdiction of the Ho Chi. We have weapons as examples, all Chinese and nearly unused."

Lailey scowled. "I'll want them, of course. See that they are sent here at once. Now, you are dismissed."

"Zah vashe' nastrovia, tovarish gayneyral."

Colonel Peyotr Maximovich Rudinov raised the tall, slender glass, threw back his head, and tossed off half of the three ounces of freezer-thickened Moskva Petrovka, pepper-flavored vodka.

" '*Nastrovia*,'' responded General Major Vladislav Nikoliavich Ludvinov in a tone of bored indifference. Form and tradition meant little or nothing to him, except for the ritualistic traditions of the KGB, of course. Eyes closed, he took time to savor the icy bomb that slid into his stomach.

Doubt coloring his voice, Ludvinov asked, "You still favor Moskva over Stolichnaya?"

Rudinov smiled, wondering how a thick brush of Stalin-style mustache would look on his upper lip. "Naturally. Stoli is horse piss, made for export to dolts who do not appreciate the true nectar of Mother Russia."

Ludvinov laughed heartily. He gestured with his empty glass and Rudinov reached into the freezer compartment of his tiny apartment-sized refrigerator. "You are prepared for your journey to Hanoi?"

"Certainly, Vladi Nikoli'ch. Am I a child who must have his coat buttoned and his fly zipped? Certainly not. I have been ready since you informed me of my new, hopefully temporary, assignment. I cannot stand close association with these slope-headed, saffron-skinned midgets."

Ludvinov uttered a snort of laughter while Rudinov poured more vodka. He nodded to the bottle. "How much of this have you packed to take?"

"Enough," Rudinov answered aloofly, then relented. "A case. I figured three bottles as gifts for our hosts, the rest to take the bad taste out of my mouth from their food, but mostly from having to deal with them."

Ludvinov drank, smacked his lips. "Those are hardly the charitable thoughts of a compassionate Communist, Pyotr Maxim'ich."

"*Bloodyeet Kommunesm!*"

" 'Fuck Communism,' Comrade?" Ludvinov asked coldly.

"No—no, I misspoke myself, of course." Then he warmed to his subject. "But you and I, we're soldiers, Vladi Nikolai'ch. We both served in *Spetznaz* and on the border with China. We are also intelligence operatives. We have seen a lot of the world, have we not? Where was the poverty, the suffering, the tyranny we were told as children we would find? Be truthful with yourself. We saw tyranny, poverty, starvation, primitive living conditions, and backward, out-moded technology only in Africa and in other communist nations, right?"

Ludin's expression of perturbation changed rapidly to one of cautious fear. "Be careful where you say such things, Peyotr. That what you point out is also true makes it even more dangerous. Now, the subject is closed. We will speak of it no more. And . . . Comrade Colonel, you will specifi-cally forget that I agreed with you."

"Of course, Vladi Nikolai'ch," Rudinov agreed with amusement. "I never said anything critical of our beloved Communist State, and you never agreed with me. How's that?"

Ludvinov made a face. "*Esprjaneyee*," he muttered under his breath, then repeated, "Shit. I would never have favorably endorsed your promotion papers if I did not trust you, Peyotr. You are indeed your father's son."

"Thank you," Rudinov responded, with a humility he sincerely felt. In his childhood, Maxim Rudinov had been like a god to the small boy. A general colonel of the Red Army, the senior Rudinov had been a role model like no other could possibly be.

Maxim Rudinov also had a soft side. He loved to take his son fishing in summer. To this day, Peyotr remembered that magnificent day when he had hooked a sturgeon. It was a small one, barely five years of age and perhaps fifteen kilos in weight, but to little Peyotr it had seemed a whale. Although he ached to ensure the lad's success, Maxim had held back and let Peyotr fight the fish, work it in, let it run, haul back on the rod, and reel in again.

At last, sweat dampening his long, curly blond locks, black eyes dancing with excitement, Peyotr had landed the fish. Maxim praised him fulsomely. The ten-year-old had literally vibrated in the warmth of his father's accolades. He had ridden home on the broad shoulders of the man he loved more dearly than life itself. Although his arm ached after the first fifty meters homeward, Peyotr held the sturgeon high, its tail flipping against his father's shoulder. The next year, Peyotr had entered the preparatory school for the Freunze Institute and his fate as a soldier of the Soviet Union had been sealed. Colonel Pyotr Rudinov fought off the bitter memories of his father, General Colonel Maxim Rudinov, discredited by a malignant and vengeful Lavrenti Pavlovich Beria, humiliated and stripped of his medals, including three citations as Hero of the Soviet Union, and dead these ten years in some obscure *gulag*. Suddenly the victim of the "Russian Curse," he surreptitiously wiped at the sentimental moisture that filled his eyes and misted his vision.

He produced a broad, albeit weak, smile. He put a comradely arm on the shoulder of his guest. *"Poshal! Zahlnom!"* He urged himself, more than Ludvinov, repeating as he steered them both toward the vodka bottle, "Come on! Drink up!"

Birds chattered in the three-layer canopy of the jungle. Typical of the time of year, the day was hot, dank, and humid. A sewage plant appeared to have mated with a garbage pit to produce the rank odor of the jungle rot that permeated the area around the small villa. Located 15 kilometers northwest of Tre Noc, its sole purpose for existence was to provide shelter and a place to raise the younger children of the rice farmers and teak loggers who resided there. There were two businesses of sorts: a mercantile that sold blackmarket American cigarettes, cooking utensils, rice, herbs and spices, charcoal, and, of course, beer. The other was a noodle shop. It sold all sorts of noodle dishes: plain noodles in rich chicken stock, pork noodles, prawn noodles, duck noodles, and the local delicacy, dog noodles.

Tonto Waters sat opposite Vinh Nhon over bowls of thin rice-thread noodles and evaporation cooler chilled quarts of *bahmibah*. Nhon had ordered and out of respect for his control, did not tell Tonto which type dish he had acquired for them. It looked good: huge bowls with a layer of Chinese parsley (cilantro) topped with sliced brown-edged light gray meat, then noodles, followed by a layer of bok choy and tissue-thin meat, more noodles, then matchstick partially cooked julienned carrot and meat, noodles, more Chinese parsley and another layer of meat and noodles. Grated ginger and toasted sesame seed covered that, all of it floating in a rich, clear broth. Better yet, it tasted great, Tonto concluded, although he winced when Nhon added to his own generous shakes of *nuac mam* and red pepper sauce. They ate with chopsticks, holding the bowls close to their faces and using a pinch-and-scoop action to move food from container to mouth. Between assaults on the noodle dish, they paid attention to mounds of steamy shrimp fried rice and prodigious gulps of beer. They said little until the food had been reduced to stray scraps.

"Now, why is it you had to see me in person?" Tonto asked after a pause to cover his mouth with the back of one hand and issue a soft belch.

Nhon leaned forward and spoke softly. "It is not safe to send more than a contact call from where I am now. Since your successful capture of the NVA colonel, I have learned something very important. Too much detail to transmit in code from my new base. I am no longer allowed to live in my own village. It is too far away, for one thing; also, those of us who escaped the raid on the tunnels are suspect. So I come to talk to you."

Tonto shot a quick, penetrating look at the distant edge of the jungle. "Are you sure you were not followed?"

"Yes. It is a holiday, one instituted for the Viet Minh by Ho Chi Minh himself. Everyone is off getting drunk on beer and making love to their women." He lowered his eyes and blushed. "Some of them are buying the services of little girls to satisfy their needs. Including the cadre officer assigned to watch me."

Another slow, careful sweep of the fringe of dense bush satisfied Tonto for the moment. "Okay, so tell me?"

"The offensive below the DMZ that Comrade Hue brought us information on is only a ruse, a massive diversion. There is something big about to happen up north," he continued and went on to tell Tonto about it.

When Nhon had given over everything he knew and answered as many of Waters' questions he could, Tonto called for the check, paid, and they rose to leave. Still impressed with the excellent food, he asked Nhon what was the meat in their noodles.

Nhon cocked his head to one side and looked at Tonto with a bright light of humor in his eyes. "Haow-haow," he said slowly, using the Vietnamese phonic for a dog's bark. "Haow-haow."

*   *   *

A curtain of white filled the air as a freshening breeze blew in across the Potomac River. Flurries of pink-edged snowy cherry blossoms swirled in the brisk eddies and danced along the Mall, lending a deceptive, sweet fragrance to the air. With a soft sigh, the President of the United States reluctantly turned away from the two-inch-thick Lexan windows of the Oval Office. It was morning briefing time again. He gave his attention to his chief of staff. Lyman Clark, the COS, indicated Preston Adams, the CIA deputy director for Operations.

He was charged with delivering the intelligence brief for the President on this particular day. A deep, vertical furrow between bushy eyebrows gave the only indication of the strain felt by Adams as he cleared his throat and tried to keep a casual tone in his voice.

"Our first item, Mr. President, is what information we have so far developed on a supposed upcoming meeting of high-level Soviet, Chinese, and North Vietnamese officials in Hanoi. ELINT—electronic intelligence—intercepts have been descrambled in the case of telephone and voice transmissions and decoded in the case of code. They all appear to verify what our assets in both the Soviet Union and Laos have developed. Also, intercepts of Chinese transmissions indicate that some sort of uneasy truce has been achieved between the People's Republic of China and the Soviet Union."

"For the purpose of attending this meeting?"

Adams sighed and deflated slightly. "We are not positive of that. There has been no direct reference to such an arrangement. What we do have is some unusual movement on the part of high Soviet officials, likewise for the Chinese."

"Any direction on this movement?" the President pressed.

"The Soviet ministers and Red Army ranking officers are moving east, the Chinese to the southwest." Adams shrugged. "Best scenario is that they are all headed to Hanoi."

"I want you to keep a close eye on these jolly travelers. And watch what is going on in Hanoi."

"Not so easy. We do not have any triple-A qualified assets in place there. And certainly none of our own."

"Why not?" demanded the President.

Uneasy, Adams cleared his throat. "We—ah—we have had singularly poor success at recruiting Orientals to serve as field officers. Translators, photo interpreters, cultural analysts, yes. But not field officers."

The President scowled, his lower lip protruding in a familiar sign of anger. "You are trying to say you don't have any Oriental agents operating in Southeast Asia?"

"We—ah—don't have any operating *anywhere*, sir."

"Then get some, by damn, and meanwhile keep me posted on everything . . . every cotton pickin' thing that relates to this supposed meeting in Hanoi. Lyman, what's next?"

"Joint Chiefs' report, sir."

"All right. Adams, get your butt outta here and bring me some answers."

CHAPTER 6

THREE BOYS, naked except for diaper-like loincloths, played in the dirt at the edge of the village. They laughed and giggled at the antics of a small, fat, wriggly puppy that they baited by dangling a chunk of meat from a length of string. It was surprising that their parents had not called them in already.

Darkness had fallen an hour earlier and only a silvery net of moonlight lay upon their bare backs and heads of dark black hair, bowl-cut to a rigid uniformity. The reason for their unsupervised nighttime adventure was that their father, the local Viet Cong chieftain, was holding a lavish party and did not want the children, each a son by a different one of his four wives, in the way. So absorbed were the lads in their cruel play that they failed to notice the furtive movement of eight men among the trees.

Their faces done in green and black, the shape of their heads broken by slouch boonie hats, tiger-striped camouflage blending into the night, the SEALs of Bravo Squad, accompanied by platoon medic Filmore Nicholson, advanced on their objective. Anchor Head Sturgis gave curt hand signals clearly seen by squad sniper Dallas Goracke though barely perceived by the rest of the squad. Soundlessly they closed on the brightly lighted outer walls of a colonial era villa.

Lilting dinner conversation, spiked occasionally with barbs of laughter, drifted from the open French doors of the white-stuccoed manse in the center of the village. It had been the country house of a French planter back before Ho Chi Minh. It now belonged to Bao Dak Thom, commander of the Red Harmony Battalion of the Viet Cong infrastructure. Austerity and sacrifice are supposed to describe the ethos of the ''good'' Communist. In fact, ideal and reality are rarely the same.

Thom lived in the opulent splendor of an old-time warlord. His wives wore silk, gold, and pearls. He favored an ice cream suit and white Panama over the black pajamas and conical straw hat of the typical VC. For holidays and civic occasions, he actually wore a pair of white bucks, the shoes meticulously powdered to perfection with ground chalk from a bunny bag. Unfortunately, all of his artifice failed to achieve his desired goal.

Bao Dak Thom had a moon face and a lumpy build that defied his best efforts to cut a sharp figure. For all that, he could move with deceptive speed when required to do so—especially if his life was in danger. Unlike many of his fellow commanders, Bao led from the rear. Not that he was a coward. He simply wanted to enjoy his vast fortune, acquired by judicious application of the Viet Cong agenda.

Only those area residents and businesses of middle class wealth were targeted for ''liberation'' by the Red Harmony Battalion. For the wealthiest, Bao conducted a stealthy program of extortion. He made it known to the rich that for certain considerations, usually in the form of U. S. dollars or Swiss francs, he could see that Red Harmony left them alone. Payment could also be made in the form of the best vintage wines, choice champagnes, gold, and jewels. So it stood to reason that he would do everything to prolong his life in order to savor his affluence. The mission of the SEALs who would soon descend upon him was not only to capture Bao Dak Thom, but to do this entrepreneurial Viet Cong leader as much financial harm as possible.

They had all that it would take. In addition to their personal arms, each SEAL carried four M26 fragmentation grenades, two smoke grenades—one white, one green—a fifty-foot coil of det cord (primacord), an HDP primer, a fuse cap, and half a pound of C-4 in quarter-pound blocks. Pope Marino figured when he planned the mission that with the haughty villa reduced to rubble, the loss of face alone would diminish Thom's influence. Add to that his seizure by the Americans, which would utterly destroy him in the eyes of his superiors. Reason enough to make this foray, Bravo Squad had been told.

Each squad member had been given a specific task and a portion of the villa to mine with his explosives. This would be done even if Thom managed to escape. Every man knew his part and looked forward to the fireworks that would result. "Nothing like a big bang to raise a feller's spirits," as Archie Golden, demo man of Alpha Squad, always put it. Provided, of course, that nothing got in the way.

Garbed in a white jacket, Lien Xeang, one of Bao Dak Thom's VC cadre sergeants, poured wine for the guests assembled in the Music Room, where string quartets and smaller ensembles used to give concerts. The district commander, Militia Colonel Cuong Thien Minh, was drunk . . . had been, Xeang noted, when he arrived. The rank and file had no idea that the man responsible for their operations over a fifty-square-kilometer area was a hopeless alcoholic. Minh raised his champagne flute and inclined the outer edge of the rim toward the host.

"Bao, my friend, you never fail to amaze me. Each dinner party you give is better and more opulent than all previous ones. I should make you chief of commissary for our entire militia."

Not loath to boast, Bao Dak Thom accepted the toast with a wry remark. "You haven't the treasury to support my tastes, Comrade Cuong. Seriously, I have been fortunate." His moon face glowed with hidden avarice as he launched into an explanation. "Several of the more reactionary businessmen whose assets I have liberated proved to have far more put away than I had anticipated. Have I not always met my quota for the financial support of our People's Liberation Front?''

Minh considered. "Yes. And with more than required on many occasions. You have been successful beyond the dreams of most area commanders." A frown momentarily creased his inebriate's usually placid visage. He waved an unsteady hand around to encompass the opulence of Thom's lifestyle. "Although I look at all this and sometimes wonder if perhaps your acquisitive zeal has not compromised your dedication to our Socialist principals."

Thom blanched. His shock at this accusation quickly stifled, he hastened to reassure his superior. "Not in the least, Comrade. I am as I have always been, a loyal, faithful servant of the People's Liberation Front and a good, true Communist." He closed the short distance between the heavily laden white-draped cocktail buffet table and the drunken district commander. He spoke softly, confidentially. "I—ah—have arranged to have delivered to your guestroom tonight a substantial contribution to the fund for your campaign for the National Assembly. I agree that from inside this corrupt government you can work so much more effectively to bring it down. I will gladly support your efforts to the utmost.''

At fifty meters from the villa, Long Tom Killian encountered the first sentry. Bao's lifestyle bred laxity among his subordinates. This soldier guarding the commander's home had leaned his Type 56 carbine against the low plaster wall that defined the park area which surrounded the villa. His silhouette indicated that he wore a pith helmet and puttees, obviously contributed by the NVA. His features could be seen intermittently in rose and brown as he took deep drags on a cigarette. In fact, he did everything wrong.

Rather than facing outward, toward any potential threat, he had turned to gaze toward the sounds of revelry inside the brightly lighted villa—his mistake, he'd found out an instant before his death. Tom Killian came up behind him in a silent, swift move, K-Bar knife at the ready.

With a big hand over the VC's mouth, Killian plunged

the blade into first one kidney, then the other, completely destroying both of the man's organs. Intense pain robbed the sentry of the ability to make a sound and locked him in momentary paralysis. Killian's knife moved again, this time upward to make a long swipe across the guard's throat, slicing through the larynx and severing the carotid artery and jugular vein on the right side. Mobility returned to the hapless VC, who quivered violently for several seconds, then went slack. Tom Killian lowered him to the ground. With utter confidence, the SEAL continued toward the villa. To his left, QM/2C Pete Peterson aimed a Smith and Wesson Mark 22 at the side of another sentry's head. The Model 0 chuffed softly and the guard went down in a spray of his blood, bone, and brains. Pete, too, moved on, a satisfied smile on his face.

Around the perimeter of the park, similar scenes were enacted as each of the eight SEALs took out a sentry. So far the mission had gone so flawlessly that they arrived at the building at almost the same time. Mr. Ott, who led them, signaled to spread out and place their charges. No alarm had been given and no other VC troops could be seen around the building. With two men to a side, the charges went into place quickly. Inside, dinner was announced. Mr. Ott had taken a quickie course in Vietnamese and understood it well enough to recognize that phrase. The guests streamed from the spacious ballroom into an ornate dining room lined with watered-silk wall hangings which framed plaster medallions that held beveled-edge mirrors which reflected the light of a crystal chandelier hanging over the large oval table in the center of the room. The time had come for the SEALs to act.

Thom's chef, a renegade Frenchman, looked up in stunned disbelief as two outlandishly dressed persons entered the kitchen. They had to be human, although to the eyes of François Guillom it appeared they could be from Mars. Their faces were a hideous green, distorted by swaths of black, heads distorted by soft denim cloche hats, bodies made lumpy by loose-fitting clothing in an outlandish pattern of stripes and blotches. François simply did not have the vocabulary to correctly describe boonie hats and tiger-striped cammies. The weapons they carried were frightening.

"*Sacré nom!*" François gasped under his breath. One of the weird apparitions winked at him, made a limp-wristed gesture, indicating he should remain silent and passed close enough to the frightened chef that François could smell the odor of gun lubricating oil and cold metal.

Rather than react in fear, François sniffed and made a little moue of pique. *The crude villain,* he thought to himself, *to imply that I am a pouf. What could that brute possibly understand about the finer qualities in life?* Before the last of these offended thoughts had been formed in François's head, the evil-looking men had moved on past him and the three Vietnamese cooks, who stood gaping with terror. Unlike François, they had a good idea who these terrifying men might be.

In the reception hall, the major domo of the villa gaped, open-mouthed, when two heavily armed men burst through the double doors and menaced him with silent fury. The weapons they carried brought authority with them. One approached in swift silence and shoved him against the wall. Unseen by the butler and general factotum, the tense but efficient intruder raised his weapon and struck downward against the older man's head.

Brightness exploded in the majordomo's head, along with a brief burst of intense pain, then he knew nothing more.

On the balls of their feet, the four squad members made not a sound as they invaded the house. Startled servants gasped at the sight of them but made no sound, intimidated by the array of weapons. One knocked out an older man and the pair moved on toward the double doors to the dining room. There they kicked open the tall wooden panels and leaped inside, dividing to put their backs to the wall. The other two filled the opposite doorway that opened on the kitchen. A young woman let out a shriek, echoed by a gray-haired dowager across the table from her.

"*Chow ong.*" Wally Ott used the manner of address as a superior to a little child when he said his sarcastic hello in Vietnamese to Colonel Cuong Thien Minh a moment before he put a bullet between the district commander's eyes. Bao Dak Thom read the situation in a flash and reacted with remarkable alacrity.

He thrust violently with powerful legs. His force sent the chair over backward with him still in it. He hit the floor and continued in a backward roll to clear the encumbering furniture, drawing his Chi Com Type 51 service pistol from under his dinner jacket. The plan was to take Thom alive, so when the area commander opened fire, Tex Goracke aimed at the VC leader's legs. His M21 sniper's rifle, equipped with a Sionics noise suppressor, spat quietly twice. But Bao was moving too fast. Both rounds missed. Before any of the SEALs could react, Bao bolted through a concealed exit behind a set of heavy drapes. Bullets chased him, only to whack loudly into thick cloth without touching flesh.

"He got out," Lieutenant (j.g.) Ott informed Anchor Head Sturgis over a handheld radio.

"Copy that," Sturgis clipped sharply.

The other four SEALs had remained outside the villa to cover the area. They had been ideally placed, they suddenly learned. Viet Cong soldiers appeared abruptly in the entranceway to a small outbuilding on the grounds. Apparently the disturbance inside the villa had aroused them. Mickey Mouse Norton dropped one of them with a suppressed M10 Ingram. The big .45 slugs of a three round burst literally ripped open the chest of his target.

Three more interior guards appeared in second floor windows. They shouted to their dying comrades, demanding to know what was going on, and pointing at the SEALs. Anchor Head shot one of them, but the roar of his 12 gauge shotgun only served to announce the presence of trouble to more VC lodged in a barracks building 100 meters from the villa. Even as Dallas Goracke and the other three SEALs exited the building, resistance began to thicken.

A squad-sized unit of VC charged toward the besieged villa, weapons held at high port. Anchor Head pulled the pin from an M26 fragger, counted a quick two, and hurled it at them. His point of aim put it slightly in front of where they would be in another two seconds and at waist height. It went off with a loud crack and cut down four of the seven men. Another took several bits of shrapnel in his right arm and side, but kept coming.

He made another five steps before Brandon Mitchell dropped him with a three round burst from his CAR-15. More Viet Cong poured from the building in the distance and wasted no time forming up, but simply spread out and rushed toward the villa. Before they could reach the point of conflict, an automobile engine roared to life and a large, boxy 1958 Mercedes-Benz town car backed out of a garage. Dust billowed as its rear wheels spun in loose gravel.

Wally Ott quickly grasped the situation. "The generalissimo is in that vehicle," he barked into the hand radio.

"I'm on him," Tex Goracke replied calmly from beside the young officer.

Goracke took careful aim and squeezed off three rounds from the M21 (a modified M14). Both tires on the left side went flat with bullet holes through them, but Bao Dak Thom's driver gave no indication of the damage done. He geared down and goosed the powerful Mercedes engine. Goracke fired twice more. The slugs stuck the high, squarish trunk lid and bored through to the passenger compartment. He sent another round chasing after the departing vehicle, although he could not detect any positive results through his light-gathering telescope.

Mr. Ott watched the Mercedes speed toward the jungle and thought he saw it slew sharply to the left after the last shot fired by Dallas. Then he looked in another direction and saw that they now faced almost the entire VC battalion. Too much firepower for them to survive.

"Pull back," he commanded aloud. "Blow the villa, then head for the LZ. I'll call for a hot pickup."

His RTO (radio telephone operator) joined him and Wally Ott got on the AN/PRC-25 VHF radio and called the Aviation Support Squadron at Binh Tuhy. "Blue Sky, this is Blunderbuss. We've got a bad situation here. Over."

Painfully long seconds of static followed. Then a faint voice crackled through the air. "Blue Sky here, Blunderbuss. State the nature of your situation, over."

What? "Shit, can't you hear?" Wally Ott barked, as the volume of fire increased and bullets cracked past his crouched figure. "We've got about a battalion of VC out to kick our asses. We're pulling out for our LZ. It will be a hot pickup."

"Do you have your cargo with you? Over."

"Negative, Blue Sky. But he's headed the same way we are. We'll make another try for him. By the way, we could use a little help getting out of here. Any Cobras in service tonight?"

"Roger that. We can send a pair."

Wally Ott grinned. "That'll do just fine. We'll illuminate the target when they get here. What's your ETA?"

Silence followed while the Marine operations sergeant consulted the map that displayed all missions laid on for the twenty-four-hour period. "Twenty minutes, Blunderbuss."

"Make it ten or there won't be anyone to pick up. Blunderbuss out."

"Faster! Drive faster, you son of a clubfooted whore," Bao Dak Thom shrieked at his driver, as the Mercedes slewed wildly around a poorly banked curve in the narrow path that served as the only road in this portion of the province.

Intimidated as much by the terror of his superior as by the frightening sight of monstrous men with green faces and horrid weapons, the driver ducked his head in a nod of acquiescence and jammed the accelerator to the floor. He scrupulously avoided looking at the rapidly dropping fuel indicator. He did not want to know how little they had left. One of the bullets fired at them must have punctured the petrol tank, he reasoned. Before long they would be standing still.

It happened long before he had mentally prepared himself for it. "What now?" demanded Thom. "Did you not fuel the vehicle, you dolt?"

"No, Comrade Commander. I topped it off when I brought François back from the fish market."

"Then what is it? Why aren't we moving?"

"I—I fear that a bullet has pierced the tank, sir. The petrol has poured out."

A loud crack jerked the driver erect as Thom drove his fist into the back of the front seat. "Americans! It is the damned Americans! We have to keep going," he uttered his impromptu plans aloud. "You didn't see what he did to Minh."

"No, sir. What, sir?" Sergeant Pham Nguyen bit his lip, conscious that his commanding officer was losing it.

"Shot him right between the eyes. One of the Green Faces, it was. Killed him right at my table." Suddenly aware he was babbling like a frightened child, Thom pressed his lips tightly closed, regrouped, and then spoke calmly.

"We must leave the car, keep on the move. We can contact another cadre, lead them back to my villa, reinforce my battalion, and exact vengeance on these Americans."

"D'you hear the latest?" Randal Preager, CBS's chief correspondent in Vietnam asked Don Colbert of NBC over martinis in the Carousel Lounge.

"No, what's that, Ran?" Don drawled lazily. It had been a four-martini dinner.

"I got this from some of my contacts in Studies and Observations. There's supposed to be a super-secret operation laid on to raid a veri—veritable Viet Cong fortress and capture the VC area commander. He's supposed to be some guy who fancies himself an old-style warlord. Lives it up in an old French Colonial villa called "Le Fleur Rouge." All the best food and booze, you know?"

"Ummm," Colbert digested this information. "So what?"

"So it's time to crank out another of those 'Tragic Defeat for U.S. Forces in Vietnam' pieces, right? Got to let the folks back home know how things are falling apart out here, huge casualty lists an' all that, right?"

Suddenly Colbert regretted the last three martinis and the two bottles of wine with dinner. "I'm becoming persuaded that doing that sort of story is not in the best interest of our viewers, nor the American effort in Vietnam, for that matter."

Preager gave Colbert a look that declared his belief that his colleague had lost his mind. "Whaddya mean? That's hot news back home. The more stories we send in showing lots of GIs in body bags, the better our editors like it, am I right?"

Colbert's mouth turned down. He tried to derail the course of their conversation. "If this is so super-secret, how are we supposed to get shots of our troops in body bags?"

Preager shrugged and signaled the waiter for another round of the Benedictine liqueur they had been consuming after dinner. "We've got file footage for that, right? All jungle looks alike, all body bags look alike, and sure's hell all scared, green kids look alike after a firefight. So what's the problem? I'm gonna have one more, then head for my room. I have a big tragedy to write about."

CHAPTER 7 ————————————————

BLOOP! BRANDON Mitchell fired the 40mm grenade tube under the 5.56mm CAR-15 barrel of his XM-148. The small bomblet went off with a bright white flash and a loud *krang*. Three VC screamed in agony, one cut off quickly when he bled out from a shredded throat.

He died without avenging the spectacular destruction of the magnificent villa where his commanding officer lived in the opulence of the Kahns. The C-4 charges had erupted with characteristic soft *whumps* as the detonators had discharged, followed almost in the same instant by a sharp crack and bright flash. The walls bulged inward, only to be caught in more hellfire as the explosives planted inside went off in their turn. A mighty gout of plaster dust, churned earth, and smoke formed a huge billow which rose above the age-dried timbers of the villa and burst into flame, lighting the underbelly of the slowly forming mushroom. Gentle rumbles continued for three minutes while the once impressive structure imploded on itself.

Although they had blown the building, the SEALs had been unable to break clear of the surrounding Viet Cong troops. They had taken positions behind the low stone wall at the perimeter of the property and fought a desperate holding action.

"Shit, are they ever gonna stop coming?" Little Pete Peterson asked rhetorically, while more of the Viet Cong streamed from the barracks buildings beyond the villa compound. The entire command must have been assembled for some reason or other, reflected Peterson, as he aimed at the first of four VC who rushed at his position behind the low wall that surrounded the once less-than-modest country home.

"That's what we should have blown up," he grumbled under his breath.

So intense had the firing become that at first no one heard the rhythmic *whap-whap* of rotor blades. Not until the radio crackled in the ear of the RTO did anyone become aware that help had arrived.

"Blunderbuss, this is Mongoose One, do you copy?"

"You gotta be kiddin'," Wally Ott began, the moment he had been handed the hand mike and told the call sign. "Cobras and mongooses don't mix. But we're glad you're here."

"Cross a cobra with a mongoose and you get a mean muthafucker, Blunderbuss. What we see is a hell of a fire in the middle of a sort of parklike area, more fires in some barracks beyond. Is that the bad guys, over?"

"Roger that, Mongoose One. We'll mark targets for you, over." Over the din of battle, Wally Ott shouted to the SEALs. "Grenade launchers, give 'em some Willie-Peter."

White phosphorous rounds sped toward the enemy. They burst in bright white pyrotechnic displays, fragments streamed through the air in front of the advancing VC enemy, and snowy smoke billowed in long streamers.

"I've got you now, Blunderbuss. Making a pass from right to left, at three hundred."

"We'll keep our heads down."

Within a minute, the rotor flutter grew extremely loud. A second later, the roar of chain guns drowned out the *whap-whap* of the rotary wings of the AH-1G Cobra gunships. The roar of ripple-fired 2.75-inch missiles filled the air, to be followed seconds later by a staggered series of loud blasts as the warheads detonated among the charging enemy.

"Beautiful, Mongoose. Lay it on again. We're gonna boogie. Suppress fire to your right and we'll *didi* outta here. On the next pass, open a path through your bearing two-seven-zero. Do you copy that? Over.''

''Mongoose One copy that. What's your plan?''

''We have to find someone, Mongoose.''

''Yeah, heard about that. Good hunting. We're making that pass now. Mongoose out.''

Another thunderous symphony of death unleashed on the Viet Cong, who now sought nothing more than to escape with their lives. Most ran heedlessly toward anything that offered a promise of safety. Few of them made it.

Which was quite all right with Lieutenant (j.g.) Wally Ott and the SEALs. The moment the two Cobras opened up, they vaulted the low wall and ran forward, firing as they went. Two VC fell to their fusillade.

''Keep moving,'' Anchor Head Sturgis encouraged his squad mates. ''We got a train to catch.''

Behind them, the Cobras continued to mop up. The fury of their action faded as the SEALs pressed deeper into the jungle.

Nighttime quiet surrounded them the further they progressed along the narrow pathway taken by the fleeing Mercedes-Benz. ''This is a sorry excuse for a road,'' grumbled YO/2C Dallas Goracke, the newcomer.

''More than better for us, Tex,'' Anchor Head Sturgis told him. ''Chances are that Kraut Can won't get far. Them high-priced buggies are all sorta delicate.'' He stopped abruptly, turned slowly in a full circle, and sniffed loudly. ''You smell something?''

''Yeah,'' Mickey Mouse Norton piped up, wonder in his voice. ''Gasoline. Hey, kid, you done good. Nailed him in the gas tank, I'd say.''

Dallas Goracke grinned broadly, relishing the first sincere praise he had received since joining the squad, although he could not be seen under the dense canopy of jungle foliage. ''Yep,'' he said softly. ''I thought that last round connected with something important.''

''Keep movin', guys,'' Ott urged.

"Can't be far now," Little Pete Peterson speculated happily.

They found the abandoned Mercedes 300 meters farther down the trail. Even in the subdued light of a waxing quarter moon, filtered through the jungle canopy, the signs of flight could clearly be seen. Anchor Head pointed the way, thick finger extended at the end of a raised arm.

"We're in luck, buds. The head VC honcho is makin' for our LZ. Won't that just make his friggin' day?"

Major Thom—for all his pretensions, that was all the rank Bao Dak held—was completely lost. Raised in the city, educated in Hanoi and later at the Military Institute of the People's Liberation Army of China, he had never truly developed the woodsman's skills needed to keep track of oneself in vegetation as dense as this cursed jungle. Now he found himself dependent upon the abilities of Pham Nguyen, the sergeant who had so stupidly allowed the auto to be shot in its petrol tank. Did the dolt know where he was going? Biting back a sense of life's betrayal, Bao Dak Thom trudged on in the wake of Nguyen.

Sergeant Pham Nguyen had grown up in this country. He knew it well. His mind clear of doubts, he trudged through the underbrush with a definite goal in mind. A large clearing lay in this direction, and beyond it the village of Ham Cao. Actually not more than a cluster of primitive brush hooches, made of windfall branches and tar paper—the latter undependably provided by the government in Saigon when they were in the mood—Ham Cao belonged to the Viet Cong. There were armed freedom fighters there, and messengers who could be sped off to rally more troops. If only Major Thom got hold of himself and quit thinking just of his personal loss, Pham might even expect to be rewarded for his initiative.

"My villa! My beautiful, beautiful villa!" wailed Major Thom, oblivious to the need of silence to foil any pursuit.

*   *   *

"Hey, we're bein' followed," Brandon Mitchell, who had the drag position, announced. "They're comin' fast. A whole hell of a lot of 'em."

Wally Ott frowned. "Not good. I suspect we oughtta call for our pickup now, so they'll be there for us when we reach the LZ. Might not hurt to bring in another Cobra for cover, huh?" Why he asked when he was the officer in charge was a testament to his intensive training in Navy OCS. *Juniors* never made decisions. They only took orders. He reached for the hand mike and called Binh Thuy.

"This is Blunderbuss, Blue Sky. We're about ten minutes from the LZ. We need an immediate pickup. Oh, yes, we're being pursued. A large force of VC, from the sound of it. Can you arrange to have a Cobra come along? Over."

"Roger that, Blunderbuss. We're on the way."

Chief Tom Waters looked down at the radio operator in the Aviation Section at Bihn Thuy. Some premonition had brought him here. Not that he doubted Anchor Head's ability to lead the men, or Mr. Ott's to officer the operation satisfactorily . . . rather that something in the briefing had alerted him to a potential danger not taken seriously by the men going or those who had planned the operation.

"Sounds like they're in some deep stuff. You got room on that Cobra for a passenger?"

The signalman third shrugged. "Not really. How are you as a weapons officer? Or maybe crew chief?"

Tonto shrugged. "Not my bag. I like my shotgun because usually I can't hit crap with a rifle or pistol. And machines and I are total strangers. I even have the service station change my oil."

With a nod in Tonto's direction, the radioman explained further, "With about a hundred and eighty pounds of you on board, the bird would be short that much ordnance. And you do want your guys outta there, right?"

"Okay, okay, so how do I get there?"

"Ride one of the slicks. Replace a door gunner."

Tonto beamed. "Now, that I can handle. I love an M60. They're real cool."

"We have to stop," Thom panted, his shirt soaked at the underarms and a swath down his spine.

"I will go on," Pham Nguyen offered. "We must alert the men of Bright Victory company. Do you have a weapon, Comrade Major?"

"Yes—yes, I have my pistol."

"That is not enough if the Americans come. Here, Comrade Major, take my submachine gun." Sergeant Nguyen held out his Czech-made Model 25 SMG. "Unfold the tubular metal stock if you need to fire at any range. And remember, the magazine well is in the pistol grip."

"You are a good man, Sergeant," Thom responded, his reason returning for the moment. "Get Bright Victory headed this way quickly."

Sergeant Pham Nguyen turned to depart when a bullet cracked past his head close enough he felt its wind in his ear.

"We're about there, Mr. Ott," Anchor Head advised the young J.G.

Suddenly, Long Tom Killian, who had the point, halted abruptly and made a signal. Someone had been sighted in the clearing that would be their LZ for a quick extraction. He pointed a thick index finger to his eye: "*I see.*" Then he extended his arm, raised his wrist, and raised two fingers in a "V": "*Two people.*" Next Killian raised his weapon high and clear of his body: "*Armed.*" He then released his M16 with his right hand, raised that arm, and made a wide circle in the air, ending with his trigger finger poking through the middle: "*In the center of the clearing.*"

Mr. Ott observed this silent conversation and nodded his understanding. He used the same method of communication to divide his command—placed half of the squad on the right, the rest on the left side of the trail. When they had spread out in a line-of-skirmishers formation, he signaled the advance.

Silently, with grim concentration, the SEALs moved out. Fifty careful, measured, silent paces brought them to the edge of the clearing. Barely discernible in the sparse light, two figures could be made out approximately halfway between the center of the opening and the far edge of dense vegetation. Immediately the SEALs halted. Mr. Ott edged over to Dallas Goracke, who was hunkered down in the rifleman's sitting position, his rifle to his shoulder, sighting on the close-in targets through his scope.

"Tex, can you drop our target with a leg shot without bleeding him out?"

Dallas grinned. "Sure. I can kneecap him if you want. He won't go anywhere."

"Are you really that good?"

"I don't mean to brag, but yes, sir, I am. I took First in Junior Rifle competition twice in a row at the Camp Perry matches. I took Second twice in adult civilian competition at Camp Perry and once in military."

"*God*," Ott breathed softly, a prayer rather than blasphemy. "I should have read your record much more carefully. Well, then, do it, okay?"

"You say when, sir."

"Wait one." He slid away and had the word passed that when Goracke shot, the SEALs moved. He came back to where Tex sat, legs crossed, knees up like two church steeples. After a long count, during which the targets came within 50 meters of safety in the dense brush, he touched Goracke lightly on one shoulder. "Go."

The modified M14 made only enough noise to alert the rest of the SEALs. They were up and charging before Bao Dak Thom jerked violently and collapsed to one side, his support shot out from under him. At his side, Sergeant Pham Nguyen turned in astonishment. *How can this be?* he asked himself a second before he saw the dark forms rush out of the jungle screen and streak toward him. Acting on training and instinct, he bent to retrieve his commanding officer.

"No, go on. Leave me. Go and alert the command," ordered Thom.

Bullets from a suppressed submachine gun snapped past Nguyen as he turned to obey. A 5.56mm slug made a loud crack near his right ear and added greater speed to his headlong dash for concealment in the bush.

"Damn! One of them got away," complained Anchor Head.

"Never mind," snapped Mr. Ott. "Secure the prisoner."

Sturgis quickly accomplished that task, then turned to the squad. "Take positions inside the screen of brush ahead of us. We want those gooks who are coming after us to have to cross all that open ground, if they get here before the Slick."

Quickly the SEALs set up in ambush position well inside the thick undergrowth, yet they left clear fire lanes to the killing field that the LZ had suddenly become. All they could do now was wait. For all the danger it entailed, the "hurry up" part of combat they didn't mind so much as the "wait" part that gave them time to think. It proved all too easy to visualize that one special bullet with one's name engraved on it.

Tonto Waters peered out the open door of the UH-1H Huey chopper that vibrated violently enough that he had multiple impressions of the trees which flashed past beneath them. He held the aircraft type dual grip of the M60 machine gun. During takeoff, the weapon had been stored in the secured and locked position. It now swung free on its pintle, the chamber charged and ready for action.

Privately, Tonto hoped it would not be needed, but he had little doubt that reality would catch up to him and they would be for sure going into a hot LZ. "How long?" he asked into the boom mike that hung before his lips.

Static crackled, blended with the jet engine hiss and rotor thump in the big padded headphones Tonto had clamped on over his boonie hat. "Six minutes at best, Chief," came the reply.

Tonto wanted to ask them to crank on more speed, but refrained. He knew they were doing their best. His most persistent thought returned to nag him. What was going on down there on the ground?

Bao Dak Thom groaned and tried to move. He had a metallic taste in his mouth, coppery and sour. He opened one eye and saw that it was still night. He also saw the hard face of an American with a huge head, hawk nose, and cold eyes. The apparition spoke and his words sounded like thunder in the aching head of the former area commander of Viet Cong Liberation Forces.

"He's awake," Anchor Head declared.

So fiercely had Thom resisted capture that the SEALs had been compelled to club him into unconsciousness with a rifle butt. The pain in his leg became meaningless when the ugly Americans surrounded him and peered down at his helpless form. The first one to bend and touch him received a vicious kick from his good leg for his efforts.

He managed to hit another a solid blow in the chest and bite the web of a third SEAL's hand before bright flashes of prismatic light exploded in his head and he lost consciousness. Now the one he had kicked in the crotch leaned over him and spoke quietly.

"I know you can understand English, so listen up. Where did that Cong with you go? What's he up to?"

"Go fu—" Thom did not get the expletive out before a hard backhand blow from the big SEAL loosened several teeth.

Anchor Head Sturgis cautioned him before repeating the question. "Mind your manners. Now, where'd he go and what's he supposed to do when he gets there?"

"I am a legitimate prisoner of war, and as such I demand proper treatment under the Geneva Convention."

In a swift move, Anchor Head grabbed the front of Thom's shirt, balled it in his huge fist, and half-raised the man off the ground. "You're a fuckin' terrorist and I'll do whatever I damn well please to you."

Stall for time. That's all he had to do. Sergeant Nguyen had only five hundred meters to go to the village. Bao Dak steeled himself and worked his dry mouth in an effort to produce a thick wad of saliva. His reward was scant indeed. Enough, though, that when he spat in the face of the menacing SEAL, a fat gob clung to one cheek. Totally unexpected, the big man jerked Thom off the ground and used the front of the VC major's shirt to wipe his face.

Sturgis had cocked a fist for a hard rap to the mouth when Little Pete tapped him on the shoulder. "We got company, Anchor Head. There, on the other side of the clearing."

Anchor Head clamped a big hand over the mouth of their captive and turned to stare in the indicated direction a second before three black pajama-clad figures stepped out into the clearing, some 120 meters away. Widely separated, they came on, followed on the trail itself by a column of silent men dressed in khaki uniforms and gray pith helmets. A quick check told Anchor Head that the rest of the SEALs had seen them. Now all they could do was wait in silence.

Then, to the amazement of the Americans, the troop commander ordered a halt in the center of the clearing. The VC militiamen broke out cigarettes and lighted up, most refreshing themselves from their canteens. It was the haughtiness of their commander that had equipped them with uniforms very like those of the North Vietnamese Army, but all that arrogance could not drum into them the necessary discipline to survive in the jungle against professionals. Anchor Head looked on in disbelief.

At first he felt, rather than heard, a rhythmic *thump-thump*. Faintly then, far in the distance, Anchor Head could make out the fluttery *whop-whop* of rotor blades. Time to stir up the sleeping fools. He signaled the squad and then took careful aim.

One tallish, slope-shouldered VC jerked and went rigid for a second before he fell in a boneless heap. At once the other SEALs opened fire. At least their training on ambushes had been more than adequate, Sturgis noted, as the VC charged forward into the ambush rather than attempt to with-draw to the concealment of the bush. Which suited him quite well.

Running legs came into contact with trip wires, which in turn pulled the pins on detonators affixed to three claymore mines. The deadly above-surface devices went off with ear-splitting roars and sent showers of thousands of .18 caliber BB shot flying in an arc from each curved backplate.

Eleven men died, several of them shrieking out their last seconds on earth from savage multiple wounds. That had the effect of halting the others in place, nicely positioned for a clean-up. Another eight went down to the guns of the SEALs. The remaining dozen or so made hasty retreat to the protection of the trees and thick underbrush on the far side of the clearing.

"That's that for now," Anchor Head observed.

Tex Goracke pointed over his shoulder. "Before the fire-fight started, I thought I heard a chopper."

"Two choppers, to be precise," Anchor Head affirmed.

"We're out of here, then?" Dallas sounded relieved.

"If our friends over there don't get in the way."

Confirmation of that possibility came from the VC as several opened fire on the unseen positions of the SEALs. Wisely the battle-hardened sailors did not return fire. Tempt-ingly, little yellow fireflies danced among the trees and called to be answered. Resisting the urge, the SEALs waited while the chopper noise grew louder. The radio crackled to life and the RTO handed the mike to Mr. Ott.

"Blunderbuss, this is Bowser. Light up your LZ. Do you have a hot situation? I say again, do you have a hot situa-tion?"

"Couldn't be any hotter, Bowser. We got Charlie on our doorstep. D'you bring along anything bigger than a door gun? Over."

"Roger that, Blunderbuss. City Boy is sitting on my six. He's fat with two-seven-fives an' a lot of twenty mil he can unload. Where do you want it?"

"We'll illuminate, Bowser. Over."

"Roger," the Slick pilot advised Anchor Head. "He's on our net, and is coming up into place now. Fire your light rounds now."

"Let 'er go," Anchor Head told Brandon Mitchell, and the demo man fired a WP round from the XM148. Mickey Mouse Norton did likewise from his M79 grenade launcher. Seconds later, the two white phosphorus rounds went off against tree trunks at the opposing flanks of the enemy.

"Now give 'em flares," Anchor Head ordered his grenadiers, and pulled a 30mm flare pistol from his belt. He aimed it high over the center of the VC line and let go.

Seemingly at once the air hissed and seethed with a prolonged salvo of 2.75-inch rockets fired from the pod attached to the starboard hard point of the AH-1J Cobra gunship. In the nose, the 20mm chain gun roared to life and spit sudden, explosive death in a long, narrow stream along the entire illuminated front. The big chopper swung around and lined up for another pass, and the whine of the big 1,625 shaft horsepower–rated General Electric CT7-2 jet engine grew to an ear-shredding volume.

All fire from the enemy suitably suppressed, the chopper pilots held a brief conversation and the Huey waddled in to lower itself onto its skids and take on passengers. Mr. Ott stood beside Anchor Head to watch the descent. Even before the skids touched down, he waved the SEALs forward.

"C'mon, guys. It's *didi maou* time."

They ran for the chopper, while Tonto Waters stood in the edge of the door manning the M60. Only when flashes of yellow began from the near-side brush did the pilot discover his mistake in landing the way he had. Several slugs smacked into the tail boom and fuselage of the Huey while he grabbed frantically for the collective and the cyclic to make a quick liftoff.

"On our six!" Wally Ott yelled into the mike. "On our six. The fuckers got behind us." Unaware of the belated arrival of help from the distant village, he got that one wrong.

At once, the ugly snout of the AH-1J turned and the nose dipped slightly as the boom rose and their forward momentum increased. The gunner began firing a full complement of their onboard ordnance even before the craft had reached the grounded Huey. Already the SEALs scrambled aboard their extraction vehicle. Anchor Head had to physically manhandle Mr. Ott aboard, throwing the officer through the door a moment before he, too, dived onto the inner deck and the crew chief yelled to lift out of there.

Once airborne, Tonto Waters got in his licks. Half a dozen VC ran into the open to fire at the helicopters and he hosed them down with the M60. The last to fall uttered a futile curse, spat blood, and keeled over into a bowing position on his knees, his forehead touching the ground. Sergeant Nguyen had accomplished his mission, only to die for his efforts.

"Here it is again, sir," Anchor Head Sturgis told Lieutenant Carl Marino upon the safe return of the squad to Tre Noc. "It don't add up, Pope," he went on, as he handed his platoon leader a shiny new Type 56 assault rifle. "Just like that other place more'n forty klicks away. Hell, some of this stuff ain't just new, it ain't got all the Cosmoline cleaned off yet."

"You've got a point," Pope Marino agreed. "The Air Force has been interdicting the Ho Chi Minh day and night for over two weeks. I don't know how many thousands of tons of explosives have dropped. The raids with Puff at night have been the most effective. Yet even this far south we're finding brand new weapons and equipment. It's getting here somehow and I'd say for some special reason. They have something brewing. What we need to find out is what and where."

"And when we do, Pope?"

Marino produced a wicked grin. "We go take it away from them and spoil their fun."

CHAPTER 8 _____

EARLY THE morning following the return of Bravo Squad to Tre Noc, a mass movement of NVA troops, trucks, and even a brigade of armor along the front between the nations of North and South Vietnam came to the attention of reconnaissance overflights of the DMZ and North Vietnam. So vast was the southward migration that Major Herman Dorfman, photographic surveillance officer in one aircraft, could make out the movement with his naked eye even from 35,000 feet. He remarked on it over the intercom to the pilot.

"D'you see what we've got down there?"

"Yeah. Looks like a friggin' invasion. They wouldn't be that crazy, surely. That would sure as hell take the wraps off no bombing of Hai Phong."

"Don't we wish," Dorfman remarked with a chuckle. "Wait until we get the prints developed. I'll bet the photo interp weenies will tell us it's some sort of joint training operation."

The pilot rubbed his thin line of mustache in a thoughtful gesture. "Just so no one on either side gets trigger happy."

A second large column on foot and by bicycle and moped began a swift march along the Ho Chi Minh Trail. It was this second thrust that drew the immediate attention of U.S. Army Special Forces troops.

Captain Kevin Morgan stood in the forward OP (observation post) of his large mountaintop firebase at the southern knob end of a ridge overlooking the Ba Lu River, north of Dac To. He ran short, stout fingers through his close-cropped light brown hair and lifted a pair of powerful 750-by-90 binoculars to his pale hazel eyes. *Friggin' place could be beautiful*, Morgan thought to himself, as he scanned the river valley. *A cabin and a fishing dock along that river would be cool. Guy should be able to take some real lunkers outta there*. He lowered the glasses to turn and gaze back at the raw red and ocher scars made by carving out ammo and personnel bunkers, mortar emplacements for the big four-inch tubes, and artillery pads. It was his job, and that of both of his twelve-man Special Forces A Teams, to provide security for the firebase and act in concert with their Montagnard mercenaries in preserving the peace of the surrounding countryside.

"Win their hearts and minds," the slogan ran. *Yeah*, Kevin Morgan thought bitterly. *The truth was that only if you grabbed 'em by the balls would their hearts and minds be sure to follow*. Kevin felt they were spinning their wheels, wasting time. They were supposed to fight the silent war far behind enemy lines, recruit assets for intelligence gathering, and serve as leaders for resistance fighters when and if the enemy faced an invasion. Here he was playing nursemaid to a lot of artillery weenies in a not-so-friendly "friendly" country. There were exceptions, of course. The "Yards," as the mountain folk were known colloquially, were fiercely loyal to the Americans, if for the most part they hated and reviled the central South Vietnamese government. They were great warriors, too. They fought like hell in any scrap. Essentially members of two separate tribes, the Hre and the Bru, the young men—they were very young, some no more than 16—had grown up in mountain villages where everyone was family. Wives were found from outside the community. The Hre tribesmen lived by the old ways—they had their own laws, an elected headman, and their own doctors. They hunted, fished, and raised rice for their sustenance. Life was peaceful, Kevin Morgan recalled being told by Vihn Dei, the leader of the CIDG (Civilian Irregular Defense Group) strikers assigned to Phon Xueh firebase, more often called by its English name, "Loadstone."

Vihn told Kevin that he and his fellow Hre tribesmen had every intention of continuing their pacific, uncomplicated way of life until the Viet Cong came one day. The headman was severely beaten and his life threatened. The Viet Cong demanded the people provide them with food and conscripts for replacements among their ranks.

"We did what they told us. We were afraid they would kill us all." Vihn Dei hung his head and flushed with shame as he recounted this to Kevin Morgan. Then the young Montagnard raised his head and a fierce light of loyalty flared in his ebony eyes. "Then they went away and you Americans came. We were given medicines and food and offered money if we would leave our villages and go to a place to be trained how to fight the Communist enemy. We agreed and made the long journey. There in a camp near Lang Vie we were given weapons, marvelous guns with which to defend ourselves against the Viet Cong." He grinned a broad, white slash in his dark face. "And with which we could kill a lot of them."

Now Captain Kevin Morgan trusted Vihn and his Yards as much as he did his own men. They had proved themselves two score times over since coming to Firebase Loadstone. In the near distance he recognized Vihn returning with a patrol. Kevin left his vantage point and strode to the fire control bunker where Vihn was headed.

"What did you find?" Kevin Morgan asked, after greetings had been exchanged.

Vihn had lost his grim expression only during his exchange of welcomes with his friend. "It is not good, *dahwi*. Many soldiers are coming along the Ho Chi Minh Trail. One large column has broken off and is headed directly here. We kept ahead of them and left no sign."

Captain Morgan nodded approvingly of this application of skill. It came naturally to the Hre and the Bru. Tribal history spoke of past warfare between them and the Laotians and Cambodians. Even a time in the far past when the tribes had warred among themselves. Their great warrior traditions and skills had been handed down in their hunting practices. Morgan needed to extract the finest detail.

"How many of them?" he probed.

Vihn's high, smooth brow furrowed in concentration. "You would call it reg-i-men-tal in strength, I think it is the word."

Cold formed along the spine of Kevin Morgan. "A regiment? You're sure?"

"Oh, yes. Maybe more. What is bigger than regiment?"

For a moment, Morgan wondered if Vihn had any concept of the numbers involved. "A brigade? Eleven thousand men?" he added rhetorically.

Vihn shook his head emphatically. "Not that many. Maybe two regi-ments." Vihn squatted and drew a line in the dirt floor with his knife. "The main force is spreading out along the trail. They will turn east, I think. We listened to their talk. Then they will follow those who come our way." Vihn nodded vehement assurance.

"These are VC?" he asked Vihn.

"No—no. They are regular soldiers, in green uniforms. Real helmets hanging from backpacks. Funny gray hats on their heads, not peasant straw."

NVA, sure's hell. He's talking a fuckin' invasion. Kevin Morgan thought through the cold revelation. He had to get men in close, some of his own, check this out, make certain of the route of advance for these troops. Once that had been verified, he would have to get some serious map work done, establish some firing tables for the mortars and field pieces. That was, provided they were not ordered to pull out.

It wouldn't be the first time in this upside down war. Pull out the people, leave the heavy stuff behind. No thermite down the barrels, no taking the breech blocks, just leave it all behind for the enemy. Yeah, a great way to fight a war. Hell, he was almost ready to buy into the theory that flew around among some combat commanders that the official Washington position was a no-win policy. Truth was, they sure as hell seemed reluctant to do what needed doing to ensure a clear-cut victory. "Never mind *their* hearts and minds," Kevin had heard a battalion commander declare, referring to the secretary of defense, the secretary of state, and the Pentagon crowd, "first they each gotta *grow* a set of balls." Whatever, if this currently developing situation resulted in an ignominious retreat, it would for sure fuck up morale.

Not all of them, he acknowledged, might recover from a blow like that. More than one trooper, more than one outfit, for that matter, had turned *dinki dow* . . . gone nuts. With a turn he realized that his long silence had been watched with growing anxiety by his XO and the yard CO.

"Uh—just trying to digest what all you told me, Vihn." To his executive officer he reeled off the plan that formed complete in his mind. "Get Sergeant Curtis. Have him form up a patrol and take them out to the west. They're looking for a large concentration of NVA troops headed our way. There is to be no contact. Observe, take numbers, and withdraw without a trace."

Half an hour later, Captain Morgan met with Sergeant Curtis. "Jimmy, there's more riding on this than I like to think about. Get everything you can, but first and foremost, do not allow contact, and don't let the enemy see you."

"I gotcha, sir. No sweat on that. We'll bring you the next best thing to a close-up picture."

"Don't wait to bring it—report on numbers, weapons, and support elements by radio immediately after you exfiltrate from their area."

Jim Curtis raised an eyebrow. That important, eh? Didn't sound like a repeat of Tet. Those are supposed to be regulars out there, and in big numbers. He'd do what it took to get a fix on them.

"You're leaving early," Amanda Blakely, a civilian employee of the Navy at Tre Noc, remarked to Francie Song.

Petite, her slender figure not yet betraying the signs of her pregnancy, Francie smiled easily at the American woman she judged to be in her mid-thirties. "Yes. I have a doctor's appointment."

Amanda closely examined the rose-frosted, golden hue of Francie's complexion, not without a tiny hint of jealousy. "You are seeing a doctor? You have the glow of absolute health. As a matter of fact, I don't think you could convince me you've ever had a sick day in your life."

If you only knew what gave this glow, Francie thought secretly. "Nothing serious, of course. Just a regular check-up."

"Don't worry, I'll cover for you. Nevertheless, that healthy bloom makes me green with envy."

Green? Francie thought. She didn't understand. Her only experience with green people had been when Kentwelby had shown her how he and the other SEALs looked when they went on patrol. Scary, and Amanda did not look the least like that.

Outside the Navy compound, Francie waved off a hopeful cyclo driver and chose to walk. An early shower had washed clean the air and lowered the temperature by 15 degrees. The respite would be all too short and she wanted to take advantage of it. Unlike the sprawling base that housed the SEALs and the 534th River Section, PBR, the village of Tre Noc was compact and small. With the exception of the old Imperial Gardens, with its neat, trim pagoda and carp pond, one could walk across the bustling community in under fifteen minutes. Francie enjoyed the clean, sweet scent of the light breeze while she strolled toward her doctor's office. Once there, her apprehension returned.

"Doctor Chu has an unexpected emergency to handle. It will be a few minutes," the receptionist informed Francie, when she entered the waiting room.

Dr. Chu, a Vietnamese citizen of Chinese extraction, did not have the usual array of magazines so common in American medical offices. Rather, there were racks containing government pamphlets written in a stern, judgmental style. These preachments covered a variety of conditions, ranging from proper tooth care to bone loss and memory failure

among the aged. Cardiovascular ailments were lumped together under the less than accurate term ''Heart Attacks,''
while all respiratory diseases were summed up as ''Consumption.'' It would have come as a surprise to Kent Welby
and other Americans to learn that nearly none of this litera-
ture dealt with oncology. There was little incidence of cancer
among the Vietnamese. Francie ignored the governmental
exhortations and sat primly on the edge of a hard, straight-
backed wooden chair. When she was summoned by the office
nurse, she hurried inside.

''We must weigh first,'' the nurse told her in a prim tone.
''Here we are.'' She set the balance arm and made a fine
adjustment. ''Ummm. Up only a half pound. That is very
good, Miss Song.'' She gave Francie the accustomed condescending and disapproving expression of the properly married woman to a soon-to-be unwed mother.

''In here, please. Doctor Chu will be with you in a moment. Please disrobe and put on the examination gown.''

Dr. Chu came bustling in ten minutes later, squinting at
a chart, eyeglasses perched above a high, widely spreading
forehead. He laid the folder aside and paused, facing Francie,
his hands folded together in front of him.

''I have received the results of the tests we took last
month. I am afraid the news is not good. Coupled with my
external physical examination of the fetus, I am afraid that
the child will be born horribly malformed.''

He might as well have stabbed her through the heart with
an icicle. Enveloped in the frigid grip, Francie Song spoke
with measured precision. ''I do not understand, Doctor.
Everything has been so—so ordinary. My pregnancy has
gone so easy. Easier even than with Thran. And there have
been no cramps, nothing to indicate injury to the baby.''

Dr. Chu pursed thin lips. ''Even so, it is my conviction
that the child will be—grotesque, to be the most charitable
I can be. I know it is contrary to our religious beliefs, but in
this case, I feel it is merited. Let me suggest that you see the
Chinese herbalist for a potion to terminate this pregnancy.''

No! Francie wanted to shout, yet she cut off the explosive sound in time. From a calm corner of her mind came the clear thought that Dr. Chu was actually prejudiced against the child because the father was white. He had, she knew, a reputation as a xenophobe. Mastering her boiling emotions, she turned in a most credible performance. Lowering her eyes, she gasped and affected a sob.

"That is most hard to take. I do not—I cannot make that decision now. I must examine it, and examine my conscience as well. And I must pray for guidance."

A dark frown creased the brow of Dr. Chu. "I am giving you all the necessary guidance you require. Purge this disfigured creature at once and get beyond the incident."

If she had not known better, Francie would have believed she was in North Vietnam. Her doctor *ordering* her to abort the child of Kentwelby? *Not this day or any other,* she vowed silently. Once more she caught herself before her rebellion flared openly. Drawing a deep breath, she made a demure response.

"If you say it is the only course open to me, I will see the apothecary tomorrow."

Dr. Chu smiled and laid a gentle hand on Francie's shoulder. "That is a wise decision. There is truly nothing that can be done to save the child. Please return after the herbs have done their job."

Dr. Chu watched her depart in aloof silence, all the while thinking, *What a beautiful young woman. How I would like to make the clouds and the rain with her. But she has defiled herself with that* quai fan lo. Dr. Chu's fondness for things Chinese was evident even in his thoughts.

Outside the office, Francie's resolve expressed itself in a favorite stubborn declaration of Kentwelby's. "I will like hell," she murmured aloud.

Elizabeth Welby, Betty to her husband, family, and friends, found the small apartment she had retained in Norfolk, Virginia, to be cramped and stifling. As a result, she welcomed any opportunity to absent herself from the little nest she had prepared in order to be close when Kent and the rest of the

SEALs returned to Little Creek. The small size of their quarters would please Kent, who resented her family's wealth and had determined from the outset to provide for his wife, and presumably family, on his own.

How foolish, Betty mused, as she tripped lightly down the single flight of stairs to where Megan and Sue waited. First off, she did not want children. She was horrified at the thought of ruining her figure with ugly pregnancies and the inevitable stretch marks. Besides, children were demanding and dirty and noisy. She was all Kent needed, she constantly maintained. Her self-absorption had been the subject of several arguments. At least it was one of only two topics that had created dissension between them. The other, naturally, was Kent's remaining in the SEALs and going to Vietnam.

Both girls were wives of young SEALs. Betty had made this concession to her attempt to try life as a Navy wife. Meg Killian and Sue Peterson were what she considered dirt poor, their husbands grossly underpaid, as was Kent, she reminded herself in a momentary pique. But they were sweet, and amusing company, if a bit undereducated and vacuous.

"Hi," she greeted them brightly, and then herded Meg and Sue toward her Olds convertible.

The trip to the Winn-Dixie took little time—long enough, though, that the conversation took an unfortunate turn. Sue was first to express her concern.

"Isn't it just awful?"

Meg quickly agreed. "Yes, it is. I'm worried sick it's worse than we've heard."

"Heard what?" Betty asked, her own suppressed anxiety surfacing.

"Didn't you see the morning news?" Sue prompted.

Betty shook her head, long blond hair aswirl around her nicely shaped head. "No. I never watch the news anymore. Why? What did you learn?"

"They said that our boy—er—husbands in First Platoon went on some sort of secret operation yesterday. That it went bad and they took huge losses. They even showed the—the body bags. Lots of them,'' blurted Megan, who ended with a sob.

''They said it was so bad that the Navy was not telling anyone about it. Covering up the whole thing, you know?'' Sue contributed.

Panic nearly choked Betty Welby, yet she managed to complete the drive, walk woodenly along the aisles of the large supermarket, and numbly select items from her shopping list. Sue and Meg continued manufacturing fears for the rumor mill on the way to the enlisted family housing area, where the Killians and Petersons lived. Then Betty drove to her apartment in a blind rush, heart pounding.

What could she do? How could she learn the truth? Oblivious to what she did, she carried her grocery bags into the apartment, put everything away, then surrendered to her horror. Sprawling across her bed, she gave rein to her imagination, visualizing Kent in a body bag and again cursing him and the fates for his stubbornness to remain in the SEAL team and go to Vietnam in the first place. When and how would she learn what had really happened?

Daddy! Yes, that was it. Daddy had defense contracts and high-up contacts in the Defense Department. He could know who and how to call someone who knew the truth.

Thin shafts of pale yellow light shone from the slitted headlight masks on the Porsche 600. It marginally illuminated the roadway that led to the military airport outside Kampong Chong, Cambodia. Behind the wheel, Colonel Pyotr Rudinov drove with single-handed impetuosity, his usual doctrinaire 10-and-2 o'clock grip abandoned for the time being. His cavalier attitude toward road safety had been dictated by his anger toward the news he had only that afternoon received, along with instructions to take the night flight to Vihn in North Vietnam. And why?

Vihn happened to be the headquarters of the NVA Second Army. Commanded now by Colonel General Wahn Sahn Chee, replacement for General Hoi Pak, the new CO eschewed a fancy colonial baronial mansion for the politically correct communist austerity of a drab gray office building on the edge of town. Colonel Rudinov had previously visited General Pak on several occasions.

Frankly, although he found Pak's sexual preferences disgusting, he preferred the opulence of the then headquarters to what he expected to find as the lair of the zealot Wahn Sahn Chee. He glanced ahead to see the sleek, whitepainted side of the Tupilov 124K2, twenty-two-passenger jet glistening in the bright lights of the private side terminal. Idiots! Didn't the Cambodians know they were making an easy target of their airfield? The American Air Force could pop across the border, below radar coverage, and crater every runway, wipe out every aircraft on the ramp and be gone before these dolts knew it. A barbed wire–topped gate separated him from his goal. Immediately Rudinov began to downshift. At the last moment he braked.

Already the gate was swinging open. The guard in the sentry box saluted him as Rudinov slid through in the metallic gray Porsche. It came as a shock when he realized that although he was only in his late thirties, advancing age already worked depredation on his eyesight. The letters of the Soviet government-owned airline—which performed certain covert duties for the military—blurred at this distance and did not come clear until he halted the hot German sports car at the base of the boarding ramp. There, he could see them clearly now; ДероФлоТ, *Aeroflot*. He loosed his rein on his temper as he climbed from behind the wheel.

"Turn off those goddamned lights, you idiots!" he bellowed, as he placed his foot on the first tread. "This is not Sheramantyevo, and we're not headed for a dacha on the Black Sea."

As if obedient to his barked demands, the floodlights dimmed and died. Only soft yellow glows came from the pilot lights placed every third step on the boarding ramp. Satisfied, Rudinov mounted, the pair of leather attaché cases tightly gripped in his left hand. Cambodian customs and immigration officials were conspicuous by their absence.

An hour-and-twenty-minute flight to Vihn did little to improve Rudinov's humor. The entire idea of a massive invasion across the DMZ into South Vietnam was idiotic, to his way of seeing things. "It invites certain massive retaliation by the Americans. Can't our Comrades in the North see that?" he dictated into a portable tape recorder that rested on the foldout desk along one wall of the twenty-two-passenger, all-VIP seating Tu-124K2.

Outside the well-insulated cabin, the twin D-30 Srs II Soloviev turbofan engines whispered with the soft, steady undercurrent rumble typical of the world's first turbofan airliner. The maiden flight of a Tu-124K had been in 1960, when the rest of the world relied on the ancient Boeing 707 for passenger jet service. Most airlines still depended on the Douglas DC-7, with its four internal combustion engines, as the mainstay of their air fleets. For once, at least, Rudinov mused in retrospect, the constant assertion of the Soviet propaganda organ was correct. The Russians had done it first. It did his mood little good, though, when his flight landed at Vihn.

There was no sign of a military greeting committee, let alone a vehicle to transport Colonel Rudinov to General Chee's headquarters. At this late hour, 2340, there was in fact not even a commercial taxi available. An old man in a peasant's conical straw hat and single diaper-like garment sat drowsing on the front seat of a battered cyclo. His anger gathered tightly to him, Colonel Rudinov stomped over and engaged the primitive vehicle for the ride across town to the military headquarters.

When he reached his objective, he allowed his mound of fury to explode over into shouting demands of the sleepy duty sergeant, who hastily sent word of the esteemed comrade colonel's arrival. The duty officer would be there at once, Rudinov was assured.

An office door opened halfway down the hall and a young captain hastily approached, buttoning his tunic as he came to where Rudinov paced the reception area. "Yes, Comrade?"

"*Polkovnic Rudinov* of the *Komitet Gosudarstvannoy Bezopesnosti* of the Soviet Union."

That got an eye-widening response from the captain. "Yes, Comrade Colonel," he gulped, as he snapped to attention. "Were we expecting you?" he asked lamely.

Rudinov let his anger flow. "That is a stupid question. If you were not, I would not be here. Why was there no one there to meet me at the airport?"

"Simple, Comrade Colonel. It is all part of our massive deception. If no show of importance is made, the enemy will not understand what is actually going on."

Unsatisfied with that response, Rudinov let it hang for the moment. "I will require quarters for the night and for so long as I shall be here."

"At once."

A corporal appeared and conducted the way to a small suite on the third floor of the headquarters building. An elevator had never been installed, so Rudinov was obliged to climb three flights of steep stairs. Inside his room, Colonel Rudinov opened the small wooden ammunition case that a pair of NVA privates had struggled to bring upstairs. The small ice chest contained two bottles of his precious vodka. He quickly poured a glass and drank deeply.

A sigh announced the first relaxation since he had received his orders to come here that afternoon. Perhaps tomorrow would prove more informative and far less nerve-racking. Perhaps, he reminded himself as he poured a second shot of vodka.

Kent Welby leaned down and kissed Francie Song lightly on the lips. "Ummm. That was good. Really, really good. You're the best, my little Lotus Blossom."

They had just finished a long, slow, delicious bout of intense lovemaking that had left them both wrung out and sweaty. Kent longed for a cold beer, or anything to slake the thirst their amorous endeavors had generated. He settled for a sip of tepid fruit juice.

Francie Song giggled. "Don't call me that, Kentwelby. It

makes me sound like one of the bam-bam girls in Saigon bars.''

"How would you know about them?" Kent asked as he reached for his green slingshot skivvy shirt. "Well, wasn't it wonderful?"

"Yes. For me . . . very special. It should be maybe our last before the baby comes. Father Jacques gave me a pamphlet. The church says that last three months we should abstain. That it is not good for the baby. Not a sin, exactly, but dangerous."

Kent frowned. "That's old-fashioned. It don't count any more. All that went out back twenty-five years ago in the States. American Catholics don't have to do that anymore."

"But aren't American Catholics supposed to be married to the women who will have their babies?"

A low groan escaped Kent. Francie was not giving him a hard time, or badgering him over something he didn't want. It was only that . . . that Betty had set her stubborn head to "making the best" of their marriage no matter what.

"Please, Francie, don't go into that. You know we cannot be married while I am in the Navy. At least while I'm in-country. We've gone over that often enough. You know the plan. Eloise gets you to France first. Then, when I'm rotated back to Little Creek, I send for you. You come to the States and we get married."

"Me and Thran?"

"You and Thran and the baby."

Francie produced a pout. "We must wait that long?"

"I'm afraid so."

"What about . . . your wife of now?"

Kent shrugged. "She's bound to change her mind again. And when she does, I'll sign the papers and zip them off Emergency Mail through the Red Cross."

Francie fixed him with a deep, emotion-laden stare. "And if she does not?"

"If . . . she doesn't," Kent wavered, "then I'll have to do something about it myself."

Fear replaced the intensity on her face. "The Church . . ."

she gulped. "If we cannot be married in the Church, we would be living in sin."

Kent Welby looked around the room and at Francie, then himself, as though revealing their circumstances to her for the first time. "That bothers you?"

Before their exchange could develop into a full-blown emotional stew, the feathery burble of incoming mortar rounds announced the nightly visit by the local Viet Cong company. The projectiles detonated at a distance, inside the Navy compound, yet close enough to cause Kent to grit his teeth.

"Right on time," he grunted.

Francie twined her arms around him and drew him close. "Come, my love, there are better ways to get through this awful bombing."

"I have to go. There'll be a roll call after the mortaring lifts."

"No," Francie countered. "Stay here with me, protect me and Thran. And we can make delicious love again and again until the Viet Cong quit."

"Ummmm. That sounds like a good idea," murmured Kent Welby, as he bent toward Francie Song and nuzzled his nose in her small but prominent cleavage.

An hour and twenty minutes later, after the last mortar round had blasted into the empty space of the parade ground at Tre Noc River Patrol Base, Kent and Francie exchanged languid, passionate goodbyes. He hurried off to rejoin the SEALs on base, his mind divided between sweet memories of Francie's incredibly sexy body and how he would connive to get back on base without getting on report and being counted as present during the mortar attack.

Both minor infractions—being out after curfew and being absent at roll call—Kent handled with unexpected ease. The Marine guard at the main gate gratefully accepted the bottle of high-proof Chinese liquor, contraband provided by Francie, with an eagerness that astounded the young SEAL. A promise to stand the next night's duty watch for Anchor

Head Sturgis, who was CQ (charge of quarters) that night, got Kent Welby ticked off as present at the roll call. Ten minutes later, he slid off into the deep slumber of the well and thoroughly loved.

CHAPTER 9 ⸻

COFFEE AND croissants on the verandah, accompanied by a mound of uncolored sweet butter, thick Scottish orange marmalade, and gossamer-thin slices of smoked salmon, put Pyotr Rudinov in a better mood. All the breakfast lacked, he mused, was a few tablespoons of good Russian caviar. He was to be in the office of General Chee at 0830 hours according to a note delivered by an aide to his quarters while he slept. He had retrieved it from a small silver salver in the phonebooth-sized foyer when he arose at 0630.

He ordered more coffee. He smoked his way through two strong black Russian cigarettes, which had long coarse paper tubes instead of filters, before enough time had passed for him to make his way to the third floor office.

His surprise showed on his face when he entered and found General Major Ludvinov there ahead of him—there at all, for that matter. "Comrade General," said Rudinov formally in the presence of onlooking strangers. "How good to see you here."

"*Spàsibo, tovàrish Polkovnik*," responded Ludvinov in Russian. "You had a comfortable journey?"

"Yes—yes, physically, at least. I cannot understand what has possessed these people to attempt an invasion of the South. I have said it before and I say it again, it's madness."

Ludvinov smiled benignly, confident that none of the Vietnamese could understand their exchange in rapid-fire

Russian. "I'll let General Chee explain that to you." He glanced up at the aide standing in the doorway to Chee's inner office. "Shall we go in? Comrade General Chee is expecting us," Ludvinov went on, switching to Vietnamese.

Once in the inner sanctum, General Chee greeted them effusively. He produced a broad smile, shook hands energetically, and made repeated bows. At last he gestured expansively to a pair of chairs drawn up in front of his desk. To Rudinov's relief, Chee got right to the point.

"Comrades, it has been given to me the pleasure of a major announcement," he declared in ungrammatical, terribly accented Russian. "Effective this morning, as of seven hours, a major offensive has been launched against the outlaw, upstart government of the South. This invasion in force has been authorized by General Diren Gien Ghe, commander of the Chiefs of Staff."

Rudinov could not contain himself, his pleasant morning banished in a few words. "But why? We, the Soviet Union, consider any large-scale invasion of the Republic of South Vietnam to be hazardous at the least, possibly disastrous."

Chee raised a hand to stem the flow of protest. "*If* it were to be prosecuted to the fullest extent, we would agree. However, and this is the genius of the situation, the invasion is nothing more than a diversion, to direct the attention of the world's media away from the monumental policy meeting in Hanoi at the end of next week. It is, to be more explicit, a mere ploy."

Astounded by this, Rudinov worked to form some forceful retort when to his utter amazement, General Ludvinov spoke up, his voice rich with tones of approval. "You have greatly relieved my mind. We, the Soviet Army, have been wondering about your military buildup along the DMZ. I am confident that the reason you give will be officially considered, as I already do, as a brilliant strategy. Does your General Ghe play chess?"

Ludvinov went on to explain, "This greatly reminds me of our international chess champion Karpov. He constantly

uses the tactic of getting his opponent to look the other way.
And it always works.''

Colonel Rudinov could not believe it. *Who had whose
nose more deeply buried in the other's buttocks*? He could
not believe Ludvinov was serious. Then again, he had never
known his superior to be deliberately obtuse. Nor to be deceptive in so ingenuous a manner. He could do nothing but
sit there and endure it. He silently ground his teeth and made
curt one-word answers when necessary until the meeting had
concluded.

Then he stomped out of the office in search of vodka and
the solace it could bring.

Early morning brought Captain Kevin Morgan an entirely
different sort of worry from that of Colonel Pyotr Rudinov,
albeit one from a common cause. The recon patrol from
Team 1 had returned at 0241 hours. They had not needed to
go far to verify the report from the Montagnard strikers.

Five klicks to the west of Loadstone, they had encountered three columns moving rapidly toward the ridge that
contained the firebase. The six Special Forces troopers had
taken a careful count and later compared notes. They determined the enemy strength at near three regiments. Two of
them had even encountered some light armor rumbling along
the highway that connected Da Nang to Kon Tum. Captain
Morgan had slept on their report, although not well.

When he took his pre-breakfast stroll around the perimeter
of Firebase Loadstone, Captain Morgan found the valleys
below filled with a swarm of North Vietnam Army units.
They streamed around the finger of high land on which the
firebase stood, and Captain Morgan surmised that they either
did not know of the existence of the American base or were
totally indifferent to any supposed threat.

A closer examination of the southernmost unit indicated
that they had halted and begun to inspect the slope above
them. Any second now, Captain Morgan allowed, Loadstone
would be discovered. Better, he decided, to bring the fight

to the enemy. A nice little Time On Target barrage would do fine.

"Sundance, this is Loadstone. We have a fire mission for you. Over."

At Firebase Sundance, the RTO keyed the mike while he waved at a Pfc seated near the folding table that held the field radio. "This is Sundance. We copy, and wait one, over."

"Roger, Sundance. We're holding."

Three minutes went by before the private returned with Lieutenant Dornan, the OD. The RTO keyed his mike. "Okay, Loadstone, what do you have for us? Over."

"I have about half of the North Vietnamese Army, Sundance. They're all around the base of our hill. I need your three batteries to lay it on at Charlie-Sierra two-zero-six-niner."

"Copy Charlie-Sierra two-zero-six-niner. You want us to range it?"

"Negative, Sundance. Fire one round for effect, we'll adjust from that, then use that as your center for a TOT. Over." Static crackled over the net for a few seconds.

"Copy that, Loadstone. Wait one while we verify and get authorization."

Captain Morgan's voice took on an edge. "What do you want to do, Sundance? Come up here and take a look. Screw that. By the time you can verify and authorize they'll be down there visiting you. Get off the stick, man. Any second they're gonna start up after us. Over."

Lieutenant Dornan and the radio operator exchanged looks. "At least I had better clear it with Captain Parsons."

The RTO nodded encouragement at that, then keyed the mike. "Okay, Loadstone. Stand by. One hot one on the way." Then, off the air, "That'll keep him zipped until you get a chance to talk to the old man."

"Thanks, Sullivan," offered Dornan on his way out of the bunker. "I'll remember you for that."

"Yeah. Like how about at beer ration time, sir?"

*   *   *

Captain Kevin Morgan divided an anxious twenty minutes between the commo bunker and the perimeter fence, eyes fixed on the enemy below. He watched in fascination as what appeared to be a platoon strength unit formed up and started to climb toward the encampment when a shout came from the RTO.

"One round on the way, sir."

It seemed only a second went by before Captain Morgan heard the thin shriek of the descending projectile. Rapidly it grew to a freight train rush as its arc ended deep in the valley. The blast came as a surprise to everyone except Morgan and the radio operator. The Special Forces captain ran to the commo bunker.

"Left two, down one, and fire," shouted an inordinately pleased Kevin Morgan. The shot had been far closer than he had expected.

A Time On Target barrage is an awesome thing. The four-inch mortar battery fired at a different time than the 105mm howitzers and the 155mm self-propelled guns. Yet all three had been calculated to arrive at the coordinates given at the same instant.

Only fractions of a second lapsed between detonations as the first rounds plunged into the V-shape of the valleys around Firebase Loadstone. Intense actinic flashes were followed by huge gouts of dirt that erupted, mingled with balls of orange and exclamation points of black and white smoke. Even 1,127 feet above, the noise was tremendous. At the point of impact it was literally deafening.

Even among those who escaped being torn apart by the explosions or shredded by the slew of shrapnel, a number of NVA soldiers went about dazed as blood streamed from their ears. Those who had been closest would never hear again. The so-called lucky ones would recover, though the slightest sound would keep them in constant pain. With hardly a breeze blowing, a pall settled over the impact area. The screams of the wounded went unheard by those nearby.

Their howls ended sixty-five seconds later when a second

salvo landed. The bodies of the living and dead were torn apart and the power of the explosions forced blood to infuse many an eyeball and partially blot out the white. By then, Captain Kevin Morgan was all but jumping up and down in his excitement. He loved it! Kicking NVA Regular tail. What a high! What a fan-fucking-tastic high.

The sudden sight of limbless, shattered torsos cartwheeling through the lacerated air sobered him. God, war was more gruesome than even he had imagined. All at once he felt sorry for those poor bastards. But at least his precautionary move had succeeded in keeping them safe. The barrage had blown the entire platoon off the hillside. He would soon discover how big a mistake it had really been.

Elizabeth Welby climbed from behind the Mercedes-Benz 310S that her daddy had bought for her as a congratulatory gift when she had departed the family home and headed for the apartment she had retained in the Norfolk area. The Virginia weather was ideal for a convertible. Betty wore a yellow cotton dress with white polka dots and lace trim and quite incongruously, a large, matching Southern belle–style sunbonnet. To her immense satisfaction, she succeeded in turning male heads in the parking lot of the shopping center where she had come to buy groceries at the Winn-Dixie. One of those who cast an admiring gaze was a young, handsome visiting yachtsman, who in a different era would have been called a playboy. Anyone could tell by the expensive mid-thigh white linen shorts and torso-hugging light blue Lacoste polo shirt that he absolutely dripped money.

Betty startled herself to discover she was observing him appreciatively when she made note of his long, sun-browned, nearly hairless legs that stretched between the shorts and his trim ankles, encased in handmade white Ferragamo loafers. He had a nice smile, too, which he dazzled about a thousand watts of on her as she approached where he stood near the door to the Chesapeake Oyster Bar.

''Hello,'' said the vision of masculine pulchritude in tones so melodic that it made Betty go suddenly weak inside.

Her joints turning to water, Betty could only stammer a response. "Hu-hu-hello yourself. Ummmm."

"I'm Bill," he said, by way of introduction. "Are you trying this place for the first time, too?" he inquired with a nod toward the well-known watering hole and seafood deli.

Betty made an instant decision based on her absolute conviction that Kent didn't love her—could not, or rather than being in Vietnam he'd be there with her to be a foil to such an obvious pickup line. "Why—ah—yes, yes I am. And I'm Betty." She smiled warmly and offered her arm.

He took it, twined it around his own, and turned away from the Winn-Dixie to sweep her into the cool, darkened interior of the Chesapeake Oyster Bar. Guiltily, Betty acknowledged how glad she was that her fingers had been slightly swollen of late and she could not wear her wedding ring.

"I've heard that they serve a marvelous chardonnay here that goes even better with oysters on the half-shell than sherry. Shall we try a bottle?"

"Let's," Betty agreed. "Maybe even two."

"Ummmm. And you know what they say about oysters. The effect they have?"

Prodigally, Betty cast aside most of her inhibitions. "I hope so. Oh, how I hope so."

And an hour and a half later, in the large bed of the upscale hotel room they had rented, she cried out, "Oh! Oooh, yess—yess. God . . . it . . . feels . . . soooo . . . goood!"

She would hate herself tomorrow, be absolutely consumed with guilt. Yet for now, that didn't matter, she thought breathlessly. She needed a man so bad. Had needed one for seven long, aching months. Especially one like Bill, who turned out to be silken angles and muscles and brown all over and long and hard, and filled her with so much joy.

His calling down artillery had only attracted attention from the NVA troops surrounding Firebase Loadstone. Captain Kevin Morgan reluctantly admitted that to himself as the ten-minute pounding lifted and the survivors rallied themselves.

Driven by anger, an assault in earnest began on the ridge.

Although they had the disadvantage of coming from the low ground, the NVA soldiers clambered up the slope with fiery determination. The first barrier of razor wire lay concealed in tall grass. It slowed their charge for the moment. Then three of the four .50 caliber machine guns inside the compound opened up. Firing downslope, the gunners walked their half-inch-diameter bullets into the massed men who attempted to cross the wire. M60s took up the rat-a-tat chorus. That broke the NVA force utterly.

The unity of their assault shattered into a chaos of frightened individuals who fled for their lives. Officers and NCOs bellowed in Vietnamese in an effort to stem the onrush of demoralized troops. Captain Morgan watched from above, suddenly aware that these were green troops who had never before been exposed to combat. Slowly the rout ended. Whistles shrilled and the troops formed up. Shouted orders passed down the ranks.

In better formation now, some seven hundred NVA troops started back up the slope. Disciplined troops are hard to stop in a determined charge. The first barrier of concertina wire failed to stop them. They slowed only to allow the lead men to throw themselves on the wire at close enough intervals to create passages for those who followed.

Past the wire, they surged forward until the second defensive line, a triangular stack of razor wire strung entirely around the outermost perimeter. What the NVA soldiers did not know was that trip wires had been threaded through the concertinas so that when the lead element threw themselves on it, they detonated a series of Claymore mines.

A platoon of Regulars died in the resulting blasts, flayed by 18mm steel balls. The bulk of the NVA force recoiled momentarily, then pressed on. Above them, Captain Morgan called for more artillery. He received a quick response this time.

"Fire mission!" shouted the soldier monitoring the radio in each battery at Firebase Sundance. "Range adjustment, up two, left one. Firing TOT.'' Within seconds the rounds were on the way.

Three more companies joined the assault as a second wave before the first rounds dropped on the new target. Forced by converging parallel lines of concertina into funnel-like corridors, fully a third of their number fell instantly when the incoming shells detonated above them. Captain Morgan stayed on the radio, constantly sending adjustments so that the artillery walked up the hill with the advancing enemy.

For all the murderous fire, the soldiers of North Vietnam continued to struggle up the hill. A third wave was thrown into the mix, bringing the total to near 1800. It rapidly developed into a human wave that the badly outnumbered Special Forces troopers and Army artillerymen could never hope to prevail against.

This, too, Captain Kevin Morgan recognized, and he altered his plans accordingly. "Get me the air base at Loc Ninh," he commanded his RTO.

When he got the Air Force operations officer on the line, Morgan quickly outlined his need for air support. "You'll have to talk to Flight Operations. And you'll need a priority number in order to get a mission laid on," he was told.

"Look, I'm up to my ass in alligators out here and you want to play bureaucrat. My priority number is that if you don't get some A6s up here ASAP, you people are going to lose three batteries of artillery and about a hundred men."

"You are absolutely certain of the identity of the assaulting force?" asked the S-3 at Loc Nihn with maddening blandness.

"Hell yes, I am. There's more than three thousand of them around the hill we're perched on, and more coming. Now, get me the man who can send us aircraft, and make it fast."

Undaunted by the outrage in Morgan's voice, the by-the-book staffer asked primly, "You're Army, right?"

"Damn right. Now, transfer this call."

"What you need to do is get ahold of the Army Aviation

Service detachment here at the field. They can send Chinooks to extract your personnel.''

''Our orders do not include the possibility of extraction and the abandonment of our equipment. What the fuck happened to inter-service cooperation? Goddamnit, get me the man who can get air support up here.''

Somewhat chastened, the Air Force S-3 relented. ''It'll only take a couple of seconds.''

''Flight Operations, this is Sergeant Lowery, sir,'' crackled in Morgan's ear.

''Sergeant, this is Firebase Loadstone. We need immediate close air support. We have a FAC (forward air controller) and a FAG (forward air guide) on base. They will talk your people in.''

''Yes, sir, very well, sir. What is your priority number, sir?''

''Five-thousand-fucking NVA surrounding the ridge we're perched on. How's that for starters, Sergeant Lowery?''

''Ummmm. I think it will do, sir. I'll tell our captain an' he'll tell our colonel. You should have some relief within half an hour. Any special ordnance, sir?''

''Yeah. They keep hittin' us with assaults. So far our defenses have held them, but that ain't gonna last forever. Send up some napalm. Lots and lots of napalm. And make it fast.''

Lieutenant Dave Colton loved his L-19. The little four-passenger high-wing aircraft handled like a dream. Outfitted with wing slats that allowed it to fly far below normal stall speed, it made an ideal reconnaissance plane. Without weapons or armor, the L-19 could cruise around even longer than its Cessna 170 civilian counterpart.

So far, Dave had made three passes over Firebase Loadstone. He could see the attacking force and estimated its strength at slightly higher than had the base defense commander. He had reported back accordingly to the approaching flight of five A-6s. Then he had contacted the Special Forces detachment commander on the ground below.

"Yeah, this is Morgan. Even though we're under attack, we want to make it hot for these slope bastards. Can you fly to the west of here and report back on the range to the nearest column of NVA approaching our area?"

"Roger that, Loadstone. Will do."

Dave Colton banked left, flew over the ridge, and plowed into the cumulus-dotted distance. It did not take him long to find more NVA troops on the move. Quickly he reported back to Morgan.

"I've got 'em, Loadstone. About two thousand yards out, a large column, including several vehicles and some sort of Russian scout car, light armor, all that. Over."

"That's good news, Hawkeye. What are the coordinates? Over."

Colton gave them and wished the unseen artillerymen luck. Then he cut south out of the immediate area. Artillery shells cannot distinguish by nationality. Within thirty-three seconds he made out the blurred images of 155mm rounds slowing to naked eye visibility at the peak of their arcs. A fraction of a second later, they nosed over and plunged toward the earth.

In ripple effect, the proximity fuses of the big shells set them off twenty feet above the ground. Blast and heat put fifty NVA down for the final count. Shrapnel slashed into seven dozen more. Consternation ripped through the peaceful ranks.

Another salvo landed seventy-one seconds later. Satisfied with his handiwork, Dave Colton turned east and started back to Loadstar. He reached a point ten miles beyond the firebase in time to welcome the A-6s. "Good hunting," he offered the flight leader, as the pilots digested his briefing of the situation.

"Loadstone, this is Blue Dog One. We have you in sight. Where are the bad guys? Over."

Morgan's forward air guide gave precise locations of the enemy forces deployed around the firebase. He concluded with the observation that they would mark the target area with red smoke.

"This is the FAG at Loadstone," came a deep bass when the flight of A-6s came well into view. "I have multiple targets halfway up the ridge on both sides and the face. Co-ordinates are . . ." He quickly read them off. "Use Anti-Pam to toast 'em, Blue Dog. Over."

"Roger that. Hold onto your brassieres, kids, here we come."

The big engines of the A-6s rose in pitch and volume as the aircraft dived toward attack altitude of 850 feet. From the base at Loadstone, the Special Forces troopers looked on in fascination while the long, silvery aerodynamic canisters of napalm dropped from the port wing pylons and did lazy somersaults as they descended. When they hit, long streams of jellied gasoline spewed out to cover nearly every NVA soldier on the slope. Instantly the deadly fuel mixture ignited. The screams of those afflicted with the deadly jelly were horrible.

"Loadstone, we're gonna make another pass, we'll be shootin' 'em this time."

Salvos of 3.5 inch rockets erupted from the pods on the belly hardstands of the A6s. Twenty millimeter gatling guns in the nose blisters slashed deadly swaths through the ranks of NVA troops. Thoroughly demoralized, the attackers broke and ran, some of them living torches that screamed horribly. The American aircraft flashed silver in the sunlight as they completed their climb-out and made ready for a third pass, lower this time.

From under the starboard wings fell canisters of Anti-Pam to douse and cook the members of the stalled columns halted by the necessity of neutralizing the American firebase. The slaughter reduced their numbers by a third. Again the A-6s pulled up from attack attitude and circled in the air before descending again to deal out mortality.

In all they made three more passes, which expended all their stores. "Okay, we ran dry, Loadstone. We're outta here."

"I think we almost have 'em licked, Blue Dog. Can you

load up and come back? One more work-over should do it.''

"We'll try. Y'all hang in there.''

General Major Sun Voy sat in his Soviet-made ACRV-2 (command and reconnaissance vehicle) and watched three Zil trucks burn. His fury mounted when his radio operator told him that the advance elements of the invasion force had met with disaster at an unexpected American firebase at the junction of two valley systems above Doc To.

They had been subjected to an artillery barrage, then air attack. More than a thousand dead and no known harm done to the Americans. Silently, Voy fumed. He would not, he vowed to himself, tolerate such a loss of face. He rose from his bucket seat in the lightly armored vehicle and grabbed the mike from the hand of his radio operator.

"I want that firebase destroyed. Reduce it utterly. Close off all access. No one in and no one out until they are crushed. Do you understand?''

Face white with outrage and with some little fear of his superior, Xeang To, commander of the afflicted regiment, he responded in a flat tone. "Yes, sir. It shall be done as you say.''

CHAPTER 10

FOR ONCE, Tom Waters appreciated the Vietnamese practice of dining late. Way back in colonial times, the French had introduced that to their culture and it had not been rejected so far. At five in the afternoon, when business was light, he met with Mouth at the nearly empty *phon bai*. They both knew it was risky to get together at such an open place, yet the situation dictated the necessity. The one most vulnerable, Vihn Nhon, had asked for the meeting, so Tonto knew it to be important. They sat at an obscure corner table behind one of the many privacy screens used in the place, mostly by individuals and families of Chinese origin. So urgent was his information, Nhon abstained from the usual ritual greetings and polite talk and got right to the meat of his imperative request for a meeting.

Chief Waters lifted an Imperial roll wrapped in a lettuce leaf and bit off a sizable portion. He chewed thoughtfully while he considered what Nhon had just told him. One thing for certain, he did not like the sound of it. Not one damned bit.

"You say that this offensive that's kicked off in the North is only a diversion. And the reason for it is some ultra important, high-level meeting in Hanoi?"

"That is correct, *dawi*."

"Chief. I'm just a Chief, Vihn, not a Captain."

"Yes, of course, whatever you say, *dawi*."

Tonto Waters gritted his teeth and chose to ignore it. So what if Mouth wanted to promote him to captain? "Just how high a level is this meeting supposed to be?"

"When I heard Colonel Hue and our captain talking about it, Hue said there will be ranking military men and diplomats from the People's Republic of China and the Soviet Union there." He paused to dip his Imperial roll into a tiny saucer of *nuoc mam* sauce and bit off a chunk. After reducing it sufficiently, he took a long swallow of chilled Tiger beer and continued. "I do not know the purpose of this meeting. Only that it is going to happen."

In an effort not to reveal the excitement this news had generated inside him, Tonto lifted the lid on the dark red clay pot and sniffed the savory aroma of duck and vegetables in a soy-rich sauce. He couldn't believe it, but he was getting to like this gook food. He might even learn to eat with chopsticks. Whatever happened to good old boiled beef and potatoes?

"And it's going to be at the end of next week?"

"Right. Starting on Friday. The important foreigners will begin to arrive the day before, I think. They must travel a far distance and should want to rest before the meeting begins."

A genuine smile of appreciation lighted Tonto's face. "You done good work, Nhon. And I agree. If they're really big shots, they'll be wanting all the pampering they can get. I'd say Thursday is a safe bet for them getting to Hanoi. Now, what good does it do us to know this?"

Vihn Nhon tried to be helpful. "You do not have to take so serious this invasion?"

"Ummmm. Naw, I don't think that's the way to make use of this. After all, if they don't face hard resistance, they'll just keep coming, I'm bettin'. I mean, they aren't going to say, 'This is too easy. Let's just turn around and go home.' They'll grab every bit of ground they can hold." He helped himself from a nest of crisp-fried prawns, then took some of the duck-in-a-hot-clay pot and some Chinese cabbage stir-fried with lemon grass and peanuts. Beat hell out of the noodle shop. "I have a little something for you, Nhon. Like a thousand U.S. dollars worth of piastres. I'll give it to you before I leave. I want to thank you for this information. I'll pass it along and sooner or later we might find out what's going to be done about it. Now, let's eat up and enjoy."

Lieutenant Commander Barry Lailey lifted the handset of his telephone and called the base operator. "Get me the SEAL detachment at Tre Noc," he commanded.

"Team Two, Tre Noc, Yeoman Second Goracke speaking, sir."

"Get me Lieutenant Marino, Yeoman. This is Lieutenant Commander Lailey."

"Yes, sir, right away, sir."

Dallas Goracke had the duty that evening in the platoon office. Lacking designated support troops, the SEALs took turns at the housekeeping affairs of running a military unit. That included typing, filing, answering the telephone, and running messages to anyone not readily at hand. Which meant that the young SEAL had to double-time out to the firing range to where Lieutenant Marino was leading a nighttime refresher course against the pop-up targets in their makeshift Hogan's Alley.

Marino returned with Goracke, somewhat apprehensive over what Lailey's call might portend. He knew Lailey never kept a strict nine-to-five schedule. For all his dislike of the man, Carl Marino had to admire Barry Lailey's dedication to duty. His eyebrows raised in an expression of surprise when he heard the S-2's first words. "I want you to come up here to Bihn Thuy for a briefing on the translations of the captured documents your people took off Colonel Hue."

"Yes, sir. When will that be, sir?"

"Right away, if you can manage it. And bring along your platoon chief, too. Waters, isn't it?"

"Yes, sir. Chief Tom Waters. I'll bring him along."

"Fine. Say, in an hour, then?"

"Sir, make it two. We'll have to call in a chopper if we're going to get there yet tonight."

Marino could almost hear Lailey's frown. He *never* liked to be contradicted. "Very well, Marino. Two hours."

Lailey held his briefing for far fewer people than Marino had expected. In addition to himself and Chief Waters, the CO of the 534th was there, along with Jason Slater of the CIA and the S-1, S-3, and COMNAVSPECWARV, Admiral Bates.

"Our friend Colonel Hue neglected to destroy some extremely important and enlightening documents. Our translators and those from the Agency agree for once on the interpretation. It appears that there is to be a high-level meeting scheduled for twelve days from now in Hanoi. It is purported to involve the Soviets, the Red Chinese, and of course, the North Vietnamese."

Jason Slater wore his John Wayne outfit this evening, a black Western-style suit and snowy cowboy shirt with a red velvet vest that sported a pressed floral pattern. His feet were encased in handmade M. L. Leddy boots with riding heels; and an ebony 4X Stetson rode the back of his head. The wide belt of a Bianci speed rig girded his waist. A Model '74 Colt (that's *1874*) single-action revolver filled the pocket. His issue Browning HiPower was tucked away at the small of his back. Now he stirred in his chair, a signal as clear as a schoolboy raising his hand in class. "I've heard the same thing from an unimpeachable source."

"Really?" asked Lailey, one eyebrow raised. "And who would that be?"

"His cover name is Mouth. I developed him some time ago from among some of the Kit Carson Scouts."

Lailey's quizzical expression turned to a scowl. "It's been my suspicion for some time that these 'converted' Viet Cong are no more loyal to us than are their brothers out there in black pajamas. I believe them to be agents planted among us to learn all they can. Spies, if you please," he aimed directly at Slater. Barry Lailey disliked the CIA case officer nearly as much as he did Carl Marino.

"Not this one. Not any of them, for that matter," Slater

defended. "Most recruits gained by the VC are pressed into service. They have no love for their superiors. Not when it's 'Serve or die' motivating them."

Due to the bad blood between Lailey and Marino, anything but a secret in the small world of Navy Special Operations, the S-2 had not been made aware that Marino's team chief, Waters, was the control for Mouth. Slater had more for them, a literal bombshell of intelligence.

"The Company has also developed information indicating that the prisoners in the Hanoi Hilton are to be transferred to other camps outside Hanoi."

Frowning, Lieutenant Carl Marino raised a finger to be recognized. "Where are they taking them?"

"From what we have analyzed from overflight photos and ELINT intercepts, they are headed for several internment camps scattered through the northeast provinces. Again, from ELINT, we estimate that this transfer will take place during this meeting, which is slated to last some four days. The new commandant of the Hilton, a Colonel Fong Xiguyen" (he pronounced it correctly as *Zee'win*) "is in charge of the transfer. Damnit, we don't like it any more than any of you." He changed gears and went on, anticipating the feelings of those in the room, even Lailey's. "We wanted those guys kept in one place, which we knew well, so that we might have a chance someday to go in and get them out."

"Exactly why I asked that," blurted Marino. "All of my platoon who participated in Operation Artful Dodger have all expressed how angry and frustrated—more accurately, how totally pissed off—they were at our inability to do anything for those prisoners. But the walls were high and the guards far too plentiful. And we had that bomb to babysit. Why not now," he proposed, composing his idea on the fly, "with the prisoners on the move, why don't we rescue as many as possible? Bring them out."

"Impossible!" Lieutenant Commander Lailey exploded. He looked to Admiral Bates for support, which was forthcoming.

"I tend to agree with the commander here. There's not

enough time to plan and rehearse such an operation. Then there is the logistics problem.''

Jason Slater eased himself forward in his chair, extended his big hands flat on the tabletop, and half-rose. "Well, now, I don't know about that, Admiral. As a matter of fact, I like it. We have a good thirteen days to work it out and go in there. I think I know just the ones to take this on.''

Everyone exchanged glances. "Actually, Commander Lailey," Pope Marino edged in again, "if we have a good enough diversion it could be pulled off.''

"Such as?" the admiral asked tentatively.

Always quick on his feet, Marino had a ready answer. "For starters, how about an apparent serious attack on this high-level meeting? And there could be other things. Give me a couple of days to sleep on it and I'll come up with a workable plan.''

Jason Slater gave him an approving nod. "I figured you and your SEALs would be ideal for this thing. You're the only ones who have been there, done that. First question you'll have to answer is what legend we'll develop to cover the absence of the personnel involved.''

Marino beamed a big smile. "I think I have just the one. Right before we left Tre Noc I got word by roundabout sources that there is a blankethead outfit out there in deep shit. We could be preparing to go in and open a corridor to relieve the siege.''

Jason Slater produced a beatific, sappy smile. "Brilliant. I like it.''

Barry Lailey glared. After a weighted pause, he added, "There is one more thing. A phone call came recently to NAVSPECWARV from the States. It was relayed to my office and I was obliged to handle it.'' He paused to allow his audience to digest the import of that. "Seems the wife of one of your enlisted men," Lailey nodded toward Marino, "a Kent Welby, is in a panic. She believes that all of First Platoon have been shot up or killed. She had her daddy, who is some kind of defense contractor, give us a call to get the real skinny. He all but stated flatly that he did not believe my blanket denial. Handle it, Marino. And make sure nothing like this happens again.''

Jon Quon and Harding Hastings, another CIA field officer, shifted position to ease the cramps induced by their tight quarters. Their discomfort had proved worth it, however. They found themselves in a position to observe at close quarters a planning session by the NVA generals running this new, unanticipated offensive south of the DMZ.

Headquarters for the NVA Second Army allowed for few such vantage points. The garret of a four-story colonial-style former hotel building across the small parkland that surrounded the offices occupied by the staff and command structure of General Major Chee was the only exception. Hastings grunted as he shifted the small parabolic mike he held in one big ham fist. Quon glanced at him.

"You getting anything good?" Quon asked.

"Yeah," advised Hastings. "But you'll have to translate from the recording, my Vietnamese ain't all that good. Especially this northern dialect. So much turkey gobble to me at times.''

"I'm getting some good photos. Long-range stuff, granted, but the maps they have on the wall can be blown up to legibility by photo interp's lab.''

"Don't we just hope, Jon. They're talking about them enough. If we can get good visuals, we have 'em by the ass.''

"For sure, we can't come back for a replay," Quon advised his partner. "Truth is I can't believe we've gotten away with it so long."

Harding Hastings frowned. "Why's that? Don't you think our asset is reliable?''

"We're in a totalitarian state, ol' buddy. They've got secret police to watch the secret police. Even though we came straight here in the dark of night, chances are that someone already knows about it, or they will soon find out."

"You're a pessimist, Jon. Well, sounds like the meeting is breaking up. Time to pack up our tent and silently steal away.''

"Yeah. Tonight's the night. Good idea if we clean up this mess now, pack everything away, and then take it easy until it's time to pull out."

It failed to please Jon Quon to find out that his prediction had been right on the nose. No sooner had their asset, a minor bureaucrat in the Vinh city government, arrived at their lair than agents of General Tri's State Security Service surrounded the building.

"Inside the building," blared a faceless voice from a bullhorn. "You are surrounded. Surrender. Come out with your hands in plain sight."

Harding Hastings had no more trouble understanding that than did Jon Quon. They and their guide had reached the second floor landing. Hastings and Quon exchanged glances.

"The tunnel?" Hastings asked in English.

"Yes—yes, but hurry, hurry," urged the frightened asset recruited two years earlier by CIA deep cover agent Johnny Yu, who had aided the SEALs in their previous incursion into the Hanoi Hilton and come out with them.

"You have to a count of five," came an ominous announcement from outside as the trio inside hit the first steps of the cellar stairs. "One . . . two . . . three . . ."

"Faster, please move now," the bureaucrat jumbled his scant English at the midpoint on the steps.

"Four . . ."

Thoroughly frightened now, the panicked asset wailed, "Too late now! Too late, we all die."

"Five!"

Immediately the sharp ripple of full-auto gunfire sounded. The steel jacketed 7.62-by-39mm ammunition for the Type 56 carbines easily forced through the thin walls of the old structure with loud cracks like a thousand hammer blows. At least those rounds which had received the proper amount of lead poured around their steel cores. Glass tinkled as curtains and drapes on the first floor were blown inward under the force of impact.

"Teargas," came the leader's command.

The 30mm gas guns fired with soft *plops* and the long

projectiles flashed through windows on the second, third, and fourth floors as well as the ground level.

Silence descended while the captain in charge waited for the gas to spread and do its work. When no sounds of choking and gasping came from the interior, he ordered a dozen men forward to storm all the doors simultaneously.

A few shots sounded from inside. Then quiet. After a long elapse, reports began to come in to the captain.

"No one on top floor."

"No one on second floor."

"No one on first floor."

"No one on ground floor."

"The cellar is empty."

Slowly, the captain squinted his eyes to narrow, dangerous obsidian slits. He raised the microphone of the radio set in his GAZ-58 four-by-four "Sao, they are coming to you."

Unaware of what transpired behind them, Quon, Hastings, and their guide rushed on through the short tunnel, which connected with a small stone hut at the extreme rear of the property. About the time the captain issued his alert to his second in command, Sao, the CIA asset threw back a trap-door and climbed into the confines of the former gardening shed. Hastings followed, with Quon bringing up the rear.

Bright lights flared suddenly when the bureaucrat stepped into the doorway. Immediately, a burst of gunfire cut him down. Hastings and Quon reacted immediately. Prone on the floor, behind the dying Vietnamese, Quon took careful aim and shot out one floodlight. Hastings fired from the single, small, square window, shattering the lens and extinguishing another source of illumination. Then they concentrated on the yellow-orange flickers of muzzle blast that came from the weapons in the hands of the Security Service.

Misshapen, nearly spent bullets cracked, moaned, and whizzed around the interior of the small building. Hastings dodged low and changed the magazine in his handgun. His next glance out of the window showed three dark forms rushing the wall near the square opening.

Four quick rounds brought down two of them. The third cut to his left to avoid fire from the shed, only to step inadvertently into the line of fire from one of his comrades. Two other security agents rushed one of the blind sides of the garden shed and cautiously worked their way around toward the open doorway. One of them reached it without discovery and shoved most of his weapon around into the opening. At once he triggered off a short burst.

Jon Quon returned fire and severed two fingers on the right hand of the security man. A scream came at once and the Type 56 carbine clattered to the ground. With a sudden yell the second paramilitary secret policeman rushed the doorway. Hastings fired over Quon's head and his bullet smacked into the center of the attacker's chest.

Before the dying agent could fall, a metallic sound behind him caused Hastings to whirl back to the window he defended. He fired two more rounds and blew the dark form away from the opening. But not before a small, spherical object dropped from a dead hand and made a soft thud on the wooden floor of the shed.

When the RGD-5 hand grenade detonated, Hastings' body absorbed most of the shrapnel. Only three sharp slivers of steel cut into the body of Jon Quon. Two ripped into his left thigh, the third cut a tunnel into the small of his back, fortunately missing his spine and kidneys. Before he bled too much and before the smoke could dissipate, Quon snatched up the bag containing their tapes and film and popped back through the trapdoor. Silently he closed it behind him.

He searched the passageway with the thin beam of a pencil flashlight. He could do nothing for his former partner. There was no doubt that Hastings had been blown to doll rags. Now survival was all that counted. And that looked more unlikely with each passing second. The Security Service was bound to search this tunnel. He could neither go forward nor back—at least until after the security agents left the area around the old hotel. The small circle of light slid back over a portion of the tunnel lining and a bright smile widened on his face. *How clever of them*, Quon thought. *Right in plain sight, yet all but invisible.*

Quickly Quon examined the irregular edge of the concealed swing-out panel until he located the release catch. He sprung it, swung open the low, narrow portal, and squeezed inside. Quon slid up the pants leg of his trousers and tended the wounds in his leg as best he could in the cramped quarters. He bit his lower lip to cut off sharp gasps of pain while he bandaged them with strips of cloth torn from his shirt tail, then he used other strips to deal with the laceration in his back. That accomplished, he settled in to make an estimate of his situation.

He had to get out of there, had to get to the nearest source of assistance. Unfortunately, such aid remained tantalizingly out of reach beyond the DMZ. At least, Quon assured himself, he could pass as a local. He had ID and travel documents, all expert forgeries, and enough local currency to support a legend of being a businessman on his way to Dong Hoi, the southernmost city in North Vietnam. These had been prepared in advance, in the eventuality that he'd have to travel openly through the country. Which would mean that his partner was a captive or dead. Which, of course, he was. It suddenly came to him.

Since the Security Service types knew about the tunnel and where it came out, or they would not have been staked out waiting for them, did they also know about this hidey-hole?

All he could do now, he consoled himself, was wait and find out.

CHAPTER 11

OBVIOUSLY AGITATED and clearly skirting on the edge of anger, the President of the United States paced back and forth in front of his desk in the Oval Office. The cherry blossoms were totally ignored by those in the room. The President had just received his routine morning briefing. This morning, his attitude displayed, it had been far from routine. After another progress from left to right, he rounded on his chief of staff.

"You mean to tell me that there is a major offensive going on, a fucking invasion, and we're not doing anything about it?" His angry glare challenged the Army and Air Force representatives as well as his COS.

Girding himself mentally, Army stepped into the breech. "Of course the threatened units are resisting to the fullest extent, Mr. President."

Anger clouded the bulldog face of the President. "Resisting? What the hell ever happened to carrying the fight to the enemy?" He leaned forward from his considerable height in an intimidating bit of body language.

"Well—ah—there have been a couple of counterattacks," Army offered weakly.

Air Force mustered his courage. "Naturally our squadrons have been harassing their supply lines and giving close air support wherever possible."

"What about bombing Hanoi? Put pressure on their politicians. What about bombing Hai Phong?"

"Oh, but we cannot," bleated sec state. "We have agreed to . . ."

"Screw that agreement," thundered the President, his eyes flashing fury. "I want some sort of concerted action, Army, Navy, Marines, Air Force, to end this goddamned mess, and I want it now."

From there it only went downhill.

Eloise Deladier appeared to be the prototype for whom the now trite term "willowy" had been created. Tall, even for a European woman, her long blond hair hung in gently undercurled waves from a well-shaped head and framed a pleasing face. She was a lovely woman, as opposed to *beautiful*; her eyes might be a bit too far apart, her mouth a little too full and wide, her nose somewhat too Gallic, yet it all added up to a vision of loveliness that had entranced Tom Waters at first sight.

She had not lost the least portion of that enticing condition when she arrived at Tre Noc aboard the daily mail helicopter. That it was 0445 hours made not the least difference. She was as flawlessly turned out as though she had only moments ago stepped from a Paris beauty salon on the Place Saint-Michele. Had it been any other day, the duty yeoman would have met the aircraft. As it happened, Lieutenant Marino had been alerted to expect certain classified documents, including orders, and had sent Tonto Waters to meet the flight. His astonishment at seeing Eloise could be read clearly on his face.

"Ohmygod, I thought you were going to be in Saigon," Tonto blurted.

Eloise displayed a nicely turned ankle from under the hem of a baggy pair of slacks as she climbed over the threshold of the Bell UH-1 Huey. "It is better this way," declared the lovely journalist. "I am not supposed to be here, but I thought it best," she went on, as they walked away from the craft. "You know my employers have forbidden me to see you. Not here, not in Saigon, not anywhere. They would certainly take a dim view of this,'' she added, with a trill of mischievous laughter.

Tonto grunted acknowledgment of the truth behind her words. He was well aware that the employer to whom she referred was not the magazine *Le Monde*, but rather French Intelligence, the *Deuxieme* Bureau, counterpart of the CIA. He halted her safely beyond the swing of the rotor blades.

''Wait here,'' he suggested, then turned back to retrieve and sign for the classified document pouch.

Military protocol thrown aside, they walked toward the platoon headquarters hand in hand. Tonto again asked her to wait while he entered. Doc Welby sat at the desk doing yeoman duty on the dog watch. He receipted for the pouch.

''This what Pope was lookin' for?'' Kent Welby asked sleepily.

Tonto gave him a grin. ''You better hope it is, or life won't be worth living around him today. I've got somebody outside. I'll check back with you in five, okay?''

''Roger that, Tonto.''

Back outside, Tonto escorted Eloise toward the aroma of freshly brewed coffee that wafted on the early morning breeze. Her voice held expectation for all its lightness. ''I have five days—three workdays and two this weekend—in Saigon.''

''Good. I'll put in for special liberty.''

''How long can we be together?''

''Forty-eight hours at the best. More likely only twenty-four.''

Eloise took one of his big, hard hands in one of hers and patted it affectionately. ''Then we'll have to make the most of it.''

''Okay. Make a reservation for us at the Montleon.''

''I already have, Thomas.''

A soft chuckle of appreciation came from an admiring Tom Waters. ''At least we can have coffee and a good breakfast here this morning.''

''Oh, Thomas, I am sorry. I cannot. I must return to Saigon with the mail flight. It must be a cup I can carry with me or I'll even miss the coffee.''

"Who decides these things?" Tom Waters asked rhetorically. He steered her through the open doorway to the mess and called out to the River Section's mess chief. "Gimme two mugs of joe. Make 'em in takeout cups.''

"You want maybe chow to go, too? What you think this is, a White Castle?''

"Naw," bantered Tonto. "I figger it's more like a Jerkin-the-Box, ya bum. I got a lady here who has a chopper to catch. Chief Belton, Eloise Deladier, war correspondent.''

Belton mellowed at once. "Pleased to meet you, ma'am.''

"My pleasure, Chief," said Eloise sweetly. "And I really do have to be ready to leave right after your mail is unloaded.''

"Two coffees, comin' up.''

Tonto and Eloise sipped the strong, hot brew on the way back to the helipad. When they reached the edge of the large square with its three circular pads, Eloise paused and took a final swallow of coffee.

"I am really sorry to have to go, Thomas. For all its being American, that food smelled divine.''

"Belton's supposed to have studied with Escoffier.''

Eloise blinked. "He is a *French* chef?''

Laughing softly, Tonto shook a negative. "What he does isn't exactly croissants and yogurt, but bacon and eggs have a certain universality, don't they?''

"Yes. Now, it's goodbye for today, darling. I have appointments lined up, starting at ten o'clock this morning. I will see you this weekend, *n'est-ce pas*?''

Within a minute, the jet engine of the Huey spooled up, the rotors began to turn, and Eloise Deladier lifted off from this end-of-run stop, headed back to Saigon. Tonto watched her go with a warm glow and a growing well of regret.

"Hold it right there. Put your hands behind your head.'' The commands were repeated in Vietnamese.

Without a word the challenged man complied. Two Marines in cammo BDUs stepped from a sandbag protected traffic control kiosk and approached, M16 rifles at the ready. "Who are you?" the senior of them asked the stranger who had approached this checkpoint on the road to Dong Hoy.

Greatly weakened by his ordeal and by blood loss, Jon Quon spoke softly. "I have been wounded. I want immediate transportation to Saigon."

"Do you, now? Just who the hell do you think you are that you can demand that from us?"

"I am CIA. Spec—ah—Studies and Operations Group."

The wary corporal cast a cold, distrustful glance at the obvious Oriental standing, half bent over in the roadway. "Sure you are, Chink."

"I do not like that manner of address, Corporal," Quon bit back with his last modicum of strength. "I am Jon Quon and I must have the fastest transport to Saigon."

"You have any ID?"

"Of course not. I've been deep inside the North."

"I'll bet you have. You Uncle Ho's nephew?"

"Don't be an idiot!" Quon snapped, his energy rapidly draining. "I speak better English than you do."

"No doubt," the corporal allowed. "Learned it at some Commie language school, I'll bet." His mood changed, grew even more antagonistic. "Get yer ass down. Face first on the ground, gook."

"I demand to speak to your superior. Get your sergeant here, or an officer."

"Down, or I'll knock you off yer goddamned feet."

Jon Quon went down all right, only not in compliance. He tried to summon a heated retort only to have his blood loss and exhaustion overwhelm his last reserve and send him into senseless unconsciousness.

"C'mon, Sam, let's drag him the hell out of the way. We'll chain him to the steering wheel of the jeep."

They had hardly accomplished that when a three-quarter-ton utility truck rolled to a stop at the checkpoint. The two Marine Corps officers in the rear seat, a youthful lieutenant and a seasoned lieutenant colonel, studied the prisoner with considerable interest. Before the barrier could be raised, the Lieutenant Colonel descended from the vehicle and crossed over to the jeep.

"What's this man doing here chained up like that?" he demanded of the corporal.

"NVA spy, sir," replied the corporal with confidence.

"The hell he is. I know him. His name is Quinn or Quon, or some such. He's a big-ticket spook with the Agency. You had better hope he's all right, Corporal. Now, turn him loose and get him some medical attention ASAP."

General Major Sun Voy drummed fingers against the metal surface of the field table set up beside one track of his ACRV-2. The slow play of different expressions revealed the quandary that warred within his mind. At last he gave voice to his major concern.

"Why haven't the Americans surrendered?" he asked of his executive officer. "Or at least made an effort to escape? When this situation first developed, I expected a quick, easy victory."

"Yes. And now our invasion timetable is threatened."

Voy let emotion get a momentary advantage. He balled a fist and slammed it onto the map that rested on the table. "Because they stubbornly hold on. They fight with an un-expected ferocity. They have access to air support, and that is what is holding us up. Comrade Thieu, old friend, I want you personally to take command of the Victorious Compan-ions regiment. Detail a company of suitable skill to renew the assault on this cursed hill."

"Why not the entire regiment? We could sweep the hill-top with ease."

General Voy remained impassive. He knew that face would not permit him to make a general assault, though he would not reveal it. That would be to admit that a handful of Americans were superior to the soldiers of the People's Army. "As you pointed out, we are falling behind schedule. We must maintain the majority of the brigade on the move.

See to it that this probe at least draws some blood from the enemy.''

Francie Song found herself in the frigid grip of fear as she opened the door to her apartment that afternoon after work. The first thing she saw in her living room was the imposing figure of Sergeant Elmore Yates. He was seated on the battered couch, a beer in one hand, his other on the back of Thran's neck. Her son looked petrified with fright. The red-headed sergeant gave her a lewd leer.

"How about we send the kid out to play in the street an' we can make rumpty-dumpty in that straw bed of yours?"

Francie gave Thran an imploring look. "Thran, get away from that terrible man at once."

Thran started to shift his weight to stand. Swiftly Yates changed his touch from a caress to a hard, painful grip. "Stay right where you are, boy. I have something to tell your momma." When the lad relaxed slightly, Yates returned to his gentle fondling.

To Francie the gesture looked so obscenely sensual it made her skin crawl and her stomach wrench. It made Yates' intention none the less clear, though. It was not she alone who was in considerable danger. A moment later, she realized that Yates was speaking directly to that point.

". . . So I want you to clearly understand that you will continue to cooperate with me or something really serious might happen to this cute little boy."

Francie gulped back her dread in a burst of revulsion. "Take your filthy hands off him, do you hear me?"

Yates shrugged, a sneer twisting his fleshy lips. "Whatever you say. At least for now. At least for however long you continue to collaborate." The flame-haired Marine made a show of examining the face of his wristwatch. "Oh, my, how time flies. I must be on my way. Remember, now, what I said. Keep the faith and maybe little Thran here will be around long enough to grow out of short pants."

In the second after the door had closed behind Yates, Francie spun and spat against the panel. With small, silent gulps, she fought down the urge to dissolve into tears and hurried across the room to her son. She hugged him to her, aware of his confusion and unease. Her thoughts spun rapidly until she reached a decision.

It was not one she liked, but the right one, she assured herself. She loosened Thran's grip around her shoulders and held him at arm's length. "You must," she told the boy, "go for a long visit to your Uncle Phan and Auntie Nihm. And you must do it right away."

Captain Kevin Morgan watched grim-faced as the NVA soldiers in company strength labored up the steep slope toward the firebase. Not for the first time did he wonder why the hell he ever volunteered for Special Forces training after graduation from West Point. His reasoning always returned to the same thing.

He had inherited his spirit of adventure from his dad. More than that, he had also been endowed with his father's stubborn determination that what was right was right, no matter how many heads nodded in silent surrender to some off-the-wall concept or idea that flew in the face of his good old-fashioned Catholic upbringing. Kevin remembered from his childhood the whole family gathered around the radio to listen to Bishop Fulton Sheen's regular Sunday broadcast. The cleric often spoke praises of the Breen Office, that organ of censorship in Hollywood that kept those notoriously licentious actor and entertainer types in line.

"He's right, too," the senior Morgan frequently said of the good bishop.

And Sheen found time and glowing accolades for the efforts of the Knights of Columbus also. "American Catholic gentlemen," Sheen called them. Bishop Sheen was as big on America and loyalty as was his father, Kevin recalled. "Be the best you can be," he always urged the young people in his nationwide audience.

Although not yet in first grade when World War II ended, Kevin vividly remembered Sheen with a clarity that amazed him in later years. Perhaps the impression made by the bishop during the Korean War accounted for that. His father had been recalled to active duty during Korea. Yet the family continued to listen to Bishop Sheen on the radio. So maybe the bishop had to share blame with his father for his decision to "be the best." Whatever the case, it had gotten him here, in the middle of Vietnam, in the middle of an invasion.

Small consolation. The NVA troops had passed through the ruined initial lines of defense and swept rapidly up close to the inner perimeter. With a heavy sigh, he gave the signal to open fire. Kevin Morgan reached up under his left arm and drew the 1911 A-1 Colt from its shoulder holster. Quite against regulation for other than special warfare troops, he had paid to have the weapon altered to incorporate a beavertail hammer and an extended magazine that held twelve rounds. The former prevented the pinching of the web between thumb and forefinger and the latter allowed for the greater firepower of thirteen rounds when the .45 was carried in Condition One (cocked and locked). At the same time he reached for the mike to call for air support.

"They're down, Loadstone. We've got fog you can cut with a knife. At least three hours according to Met."

All of which made Captain Morgan wish that he was 9 years old again and the only prospect that scared him was the impending occasion of his first time serving as an altar boy.

"Fog don't hamper artillery, Cap," Sergeant Clark reminded his CO.

"Damn! You're right, Clark." Captain Kevin Morgan set about rectifying his lapse.

A lusty cheer rose from the charging NVA troops as they neared the inner wire. So far, opposition had been light. It encouraged them to hope for a quick, easy victory. Their shouts drowned out the first flutter of mortar fins. But not the shriek of 105mm and 155mm shells as they rained out of the sky onto the ground between the charging enemy and the thin line of wire that kept them from the base.

*   *   *

General Major Voy slammed the handset of the field telephone into its cradle with enough force to knock the instru-
ment over. Fury suffused the planes of his high-cheekboned
face a dark magenta under its usual olive-brown hue. His
picked company had failed again.

"Unacceptable!" he shouted to the four winds.

"Yes, Comrade General?" his sergeant-driver responded,
unaware for the first moment of his commander's rage.

"We have run out of time and we have yet to capture this
impudent American base," Voy continued talking aloud to
himself more than the sympathetic noncom at the wheel of
his ACRV-2. Voy lifted the handset again and reached out
to set the compact unit upright and turn the ringer crank three
times.

"Victorious Companions Regiment, Sergeant Prang, sir."

"This is General Voy. Summon Colonel Thieu."

"Yes, Comrade General. At once, sir."

It took three minutes for Colonel Thieu to come on the
line, during which General Voy only fed his wrath. When
Thieu identified himself, Voy spoke sharply, his rancor clear
in the tone of his voice.

"Our schedule will not permit me to continue to commit
an entire regiment to punishing those impudent Americans
who continue to defy us. We must move on and ignore this
small outpost."

"By your orders, Comrade General," Thieu snapped
crisply, fully aware of the extent of his commander's ire.

"No," Voy amended. "I want you to hand-pick a company strength unit of the very best among the Victorious
Companions. Charge them with the responsibility of bringing
down these running dog lackeys of the Capitalist enemy.
They are to reduce this installation utterly. They are to remain here, investing that hill, until the task is accomplished.
See that they have all necessary supplies and support."

"As you wish, Comrade General," Thieu replied with
correctness. "Will I be rejoining the brigade command?"
Voy thought a moment until a small smile, the first since

their initial encounter with the Americans, spread on his face. "No. I want you to command this elite unit. The presence of so senior an officer should inspire them to excel. That is all, old friend. Good fortune."

CHAPTER 12 _____

A SPRAY of bullets cracked and rang through the cab of the six-by-six truck. A second later, thick green smoke engulfed the vehicle and wildly yelling men rushed it. The SEALs swarmed over the truck bed and began releasing shackled figures. These they dragged into the thick bush and disappeared from the ambush site as they reported in.

"One clear."

"Two clear."

"Three clear."

So it went through six, the tail-end Charlie, last man to withdraw from the ambush site having covered the actions of the other five. A whistle blew shrilly.

"You did that perfectly," praised Lieutenant Carl Marino. "Only thing the smoke should have gone off before you shot into the cab. The idea is to confuse the enemy. Prevent him from retaliation against the prisoners. That's it for today. Stand down, clean your gear and weapons, and hit the chow line."

Quietly, their minds replaying the training exercise just completed, the SEALs walked through the jungle undergrowth toward their barracks at Tre Noc. Each man carried the dummy he had "rescued" from the rusted hulk of the abandoned French truck. Live fire exercises such as this required the maximum in realism, but that did not extend to placing helpless living targets in the impact area. Lieutenant

Marino took a quicker way back to base. He had an appointment with the G-3 of NAVSPECWARV.

Marino had crossed the last T and dotted the final I in his scenario for the raid into Hanoi on the previous night. So confident was he that his plan, or a revised version would be implemented that he had commenced rehearsals of the critical portions of the rescue. Once back at Tre Noc, Marino showered and dressed in a crisp fresh uniform. He retrieved the file folder containing the outline and details of his strategy and walked across the compound to the motorpool.

"Your transportation is ready, sir," a young River Rat petty officer informed him. "Unfortunately, all we could get for you is a three-quarter-ton. It's sprung like a lumber wagon."

Pope Marino passed it off with good humor. "Maybe I ought to wear a kidney belt, eh?"

"It'd help, sir. No kiddin', sir. This ain't Navy issue." He referred to the comfortably riding, familiar, battleship gray painted on three-quarter-ton utility vehicles seen on Navy bases worldwide. "We got these things from the Army an' they ain't worth crap. Boxy ol' rigs they must have worn out in Korea."

"Are you going to be my driver?"

"No, sir. One of the jar-heads from the security force. There are hostile Injuns out there an' regulations say it has to be a combat-ready Marine. Shit, sir, if you'll pardon my language. We've seen more combat on the Mekong in a month than those johnnies have in a whole tour out here."

Marino laughed silently. "I hear you, sailor."

"Sir! Corporal Huntington at your service, sir!" barked a Marine in typical fashion from behind Lieutenant Marino, causing him to wince.

Pope Marino pivoted and returned Huntington's salute. "Very well, Corporal. Do you know the way to Binh Thuy?"

"No, sir. I've never made that run, sir. But the map knows how to get there."

That brought a frown to the high brow of Carl Marino.

He didn't like the idea of traveling with someone who did not know the predictable hazards of road travel in Vietnam. "Can the map show us where Charlie might have set up an ambush or two?"

"Ummm—no, sir."

"Then I'd suggest you take along something more than a map and compass and that forty-five you're wearing. Say one of those selective-fire Uzis you people have, and a couple of grenades."

For a moment, Huntington looked at Marino as though the lieutenant had lost his mind. Then he saw the cold, knowing stare of an old hand, swallowed his skepticism, and braced at attention, hand flashing upward in a Marine Corps regulation salute. "Sir, yes, sir!"

He turned with a smart about-face and all but marched off toward the security section armory. Marino turned back to the third-class machinist who spoke through a deprecating chuckle. "You see what I mean, sir?"

For the first ten miles, Huntington's opinion seemed to prevail. That all changed when a bright shower of orange sparks erupted from a flag stanchion on the left front fender.

"What th—" blurted the surprised Marine.

"Step on it. Go! Go! Go!" yelled Marino, the M16 that had rested between his legs now aimed horizontally out the right-side window.

With a lurch the truck bounded forward while Pope Marino tightened his finger on the trigger and cut off a five-round burst in the direction from which the ambush had been sprung. *Damn, it wasn't often that the VC struck in daylight, but when they did, it could raise hell*, he thought, as he fired a second burst. Loud metallic thumps announced the impact of more 7.62-by-39mm rounds. The steel-jacketed slugs penetrated sheetmetal and window glass to lodge in the inner panels of the truck body.

Faint flashes of yellow-orange came from the left side of the road and the windshield starred in four places. Greatly reduced in velocity, the misshapen rounds moaned past the ears of Huntington and Marino. At once, Pope Marino grabbed a grenade off the web gear of the Marine driver, pulled the pin, and lobbed it overhand across the top of the cab.

Four seconds later, the M26 fragger went off in the bush to their left and the firing stopped. Marino put his M16 on safe and used the butt to break out the damaged windshield. More fire from Type 56 carbines came from right and left at the same time.

"Use that fuckin' Uzi," Marino barked at Huntington.

Huntington drove one-handed, the truck still accelerating, as he swung the muzzle of the Israeli submachine gun out the left-hand window and triggered it. The 9mm sub-gun stuttered out a seven round burst, cut off and, with better control, spat another four quick rounds. Marino threw another grenade, to his right this time.

Its blast rewarded him with the sight of three small figures in the rearview mirror. They staggered onto the crudely hacked out road and one tried to fire at the truck before he toppled face first into the dirt. *Jesus*, Marino thought, *they're just kids. Can't be more than 14 or 15*. The engine screamed loudly as they bolted clear of the ambush area. Immediately Huntington put words to Marino's thoughts.

"D'you see that, sir? They were just little kids."

"Big enough to fire those Chi Com carbines. Big enough to shoot hell out of this truck, too, Marine."

Sobered by that, Huntington answered quietly, "Yeah, you got that right, sir."

Much to the obvious relief of Corporal Huntington, the rest of their journey went without incident. He pulled up in front of the headquarters building of NAVSPECWARV accompanied by the curious stares of some two dozen sailors. Marino went directly to the office of the G-3.

"Essentially, my scenario is direct and simple," Marino explained to the operations officer and the other two present. "The operation will require the entire platoon, twelve enlisted men and two officers. To ensure the maximum security, preparations will not take more than four days. We will go in by air insertion, HAELO [High Altitude Exit, Low Opening], most likely. Two waves. The distraction section and those who will be tasked with recovering as many POWs as possible.''

''What exactly will the distraction section be doing?'' asked the G-3.

''It will consist of four men, sir. The two demolitions men and both squad snipers. They are to create as much panic and draw as much attention to the site of this high-level meeting as they can. The idea is to convince the NVA defenders that the meeting is the target of all allied operations in the area.''

''Excellent. What does your plan call for to extract any recovered prisoners?''

Marino went on to tell him, outlining in detail the means whereby the freed POWs would be taken from the ground, with special attention on physical condition. ''Our team medic is assigned to Tre Noc and will be going along. So technically that makes it thirteen enlisted.''

When Marino concluded, the three senior officers conferred quietly. Marino watched anxiously as their heads nodded in obvious approval. When they reached some sort of agreement, the G-3 spoke for the trio.

''I like it. As far as it goes. The fine details can be worked out over the next few days, I assume? However,'' he qualified for Marino, ''it is an ambitious plan and will require approval from General Westmoreland, CINCPAC, and perhaps even higher up. Also, Colonel Madden here has pointed out that Jay-prick should be brought into the loop.''

''Who is that, sir?''

''The Joint Personnel Recovery Center,'' Colonel Madden enlightened Marino. ''They are a super-secret spook outfit for the most part. They are tasked with recovering captured Americans.''

Marino produced a rueful smile. ''They must be *really* secret,'' he observed. ''I've never heard of any of their successes.''

"What counts, Lieutenant, is that you've never heard of any failures," the G-3 added meaningfully.

An RPG round exploded against the rotor head of a huey which attempted to take off after delivering two forklift pads of rations to Firebase Loadstone. One whirling blade went flying end-over-end to slice into the cammo net covering one self-propelled piece in the 155mm battery. Over the chaos of combat, a man's screaming could be heard from the damaged gun. Captain Kevin Morgan gritted his teeth.

"I'll give 'em that, by God. They're getting better," he told his executive officer. "How is the wire holding?"

"Good so far, Kev. We got one breech during the night, but the gap is covered by claymores. Thank the Great Ghu or whoever that they offloaded those Cee-Rats before that RPG round hit."

Kevin Morgan shot his exec a dark look. Dan Parker's avowed agnosticism rocked Kevin's sense of the balance of things in the world. "Better reposition one of the fifties to cover the gap also. This daytime probe is light, probably only stirred up because we got a supply chopper in. They'll be back tonight in force, count on it."

"It's already do—"

Ba-whaaam! Ba-whaaam! The detonation of two claymores ended any further conversation. Small arms rounds began to kick up tiny dust devils in the ocher soil of the firebase compound. "Damn little buggers, they're gettin' through," Kevin Morgan shouted over the sudden heavy thud of the .50 caliber machine gun above them in the sandbag emplacement on the roof of the command bunker.

He grabbed for the mike. Not for the past twelve hours had he needed to call for help. It angered him that these little brown men forced him to do so now. "Blue Sky, this is Loadstone. We need air cover ASAP."

"What's the problem, Loadstone?"

"More than you can imagine, Blue Sky. I want anything I can get up here. I am," he continued to the air liaison, "surrounded by about half of the entire North Vietnam Army."

A long count of silence followed, then, "They're on their way, Loadstone. Flight of six A-6s. Full load of baggage. You like?"

"I love you, Blue Sky. Loadstone out."

Four young Vietnamese men bent over steaming cauldrons of water in the open roofed-over portion at the back of Mi Flower laundry in the village of Tre Noc. With stout wooden poles they prodded and stirred the contents while their eyes stung and teared from wisps of smoke that wafted upward from the wood fires that kept the water boiling. Elsewhere, two young women chattered pleasantly while they plied old-fashioned sad irons—those heavy, pointed oval utensils with detachable wooden and metal handles that one heated over a fire—which had been used worldwide to iron clothing for over three centuries until the invention of the electric iron, which in its turn was conspicuous by its absence.

In fact, not one modern appliance could be found in Mi Flower. Except for bare light bulbs, suspended from braided once yellow-and-green electric cords, and an ancient French-design telephone, nothing electric existed here. Beer in the tiny front room bar of the establishment was kept cold with block ice in a tin-lined wooden icebox. The phonograph was a windup Victrola of indeterminate ancient vintage. It all had the flavor of Victorian America, but it was the reality in 1960s Vietnam. Francie Song sat on a high bar stool across the counter from Momma Rose. The elderly woman's face had softened in sympathy the moment Francie had entered Mi Flower. The younger woman was clearly distraught.

Before she could draw out the reason behind Francie's drawn features, both women received a great surprise. The old French telephone began to ring. It meant that the line was working again. Momma Rose put both their thoughts in words.

"I cannot believe it is calling again. It is hard to believe with all of the activity in the area by those nasty Viet Cong."

She snatched at the handset with an almost hesitant, cautious gesture and answered in the French manner. "*Bon*?" Her eyes grew round with amazement as the person on the other end spoke, then she dumbly handed the receiver to Francie.

"Yes, who is this?" Francie demanded.

"Your Uncle Phan. I wish to report that little Thran arrived safe and sound at my farm."

Worry over the possibility that he was compromising Thran's security by this call prompted an abrupt reply. "Where are you now, Uncle?"

"At the Xeong Key store. They have one of these strange instruments. Is that really you, Frances? So far away?"

"Yes, Uncle Phan. Is Thran with you?"

"Oh, no. It is not wise that he be seen a lot of, *neh*?"

"That is correct. Thank you, Uncle, for the assurance of his safe journey. But please, for his sake and mine—do not call again unless it is an emergency."

A short pause followed. "There is something troubling you, is that not so?"

"Yes. I will tell you about it later. Now I must go. Goodbye."

Francie placed the handset in its fragile-looking cradle. Quickly she explained who had called and why. After her explanation, Momma Rose gave her a blank look and smiled sweetly.

"Now, are you going to tell me exactly why you had to send your son away? The truth, now, I mean."

Encouraged by the knowledge that her son was safe, Francie let the dike break and unburdened herself of the whole sordid story, concluding with the visit by Yates two days prior. At the end of her strength, she asked the older woman for help.

"Ummm. Yes. Why not tell your Kentwelby?"

"I cannot. It would come out that I had given this wicked person information. I would be called a spy and executed. They kill spies, do they not?"

"Not the Americans," Momma Rose assured her.

Still uncertain of her own situation, Francie made another appeal. "There has to be some other way."

Momma Rose assumed a droll, puckish expression. "You could," she suggested, "arrange for this wicked person to have a fatal accident."

Shock registered on Francie's face and she blanched in genuine horror. "Oh, no," she blurted aghast. "That would be murder."

CHAPTER 13 ─────────────

FAR FROM the jungles of Vietnam, in the climate-controlled Oval Office, the President had just received the morning briefing. Inwardly he fumed because it seemed as though everything was at a standstill. Particularly there seemed a marked lack of progress on the military front. Ordinarily, mused the big man whom the press had dubbed as having "his finger on the button," politicians longed for anything that maintained the *status quo*; in other words, nothing happening, everything stayed at a standstill.

But damnit, that wasn't his style. It hadn't been when he'd first become involved with local politics, nor when he had been in the Senate, and sure as hell not now. Thank the Lord this was not an election year. Bad enough to earn the label of a "do-nothing" president in his first year in office. At election time the ravening dogs of the media would seize on it as the ideal banner headline. Immediate events might obviate all that, though. Like his predecessor, he might find himself compelled to decline to run for a second term. His dark reflections caused him to look up expectantly when the director of operations, second in command at the CIA, cleared his throat.

"There is one more item, Mr. President."

"What is it?" Expectation brightly colored his usually somber tone of voice.

"There is a plan afoot to rescue some of our prisoners of war, sir."

"Your people?"

"No, not exactly. It will be strictly military in nature, connected to attempts to disrupt the high-level meeting in Hanoi we told you about three days ago."

"Someone's moving rather fast on this, I gather."

"Yes, Mr. President. A little background, sir?" Davis did not hesitate for an invitation, indicating the question to be rhetorical. "First off, we already have intelligence that the North Vietnamese plan to move the prisoners in the Hanoi Hilton during this alleged meeting of major players from China and the Soviet Union. In other words, our people will be out in the open at some time. The Air Force is already planning a massive air strike on Hanoi over that four-day period of the meeting. The Navy proposes introducing a rescue party and a land-based operation to attack the meeting as an additional diversion to the recovery of our POWs."

The President's dark, heavy brows closed in a thoughtful frown. "That sounds dangerous, perhaps even suicidal. Who came up with this scheme?"

"A—ah—Navy lieutenant, Mr. President."

"My God, no wonder it's so John Wayne-ish."

When he sensed himself on the defensive, Hal Davis became aggressive. "This lieutenant is a SEAL. The same officer who led the operation that penetrated the Hanoi Hilton to recover our bomb. His name is Carl Marino."

An immediate change came over the President. His scowl dissolved into a broad smile. "I want to speak to the people in charge. I want assurance this can be pulled off with minimal casualties on our side and without collateral—what is it you call it? Injuries to civilians, I mean."

"Collateral damage, sir." Davis smiled warmly, back on the winning side again.

"But, Mr. President," came the immediate protest from his chief of staff, "they are half a world away."

"Bring them here," the President commanded. "Make it

a covert visit. No one is to know. Get it in motion, Hal," he added, with a nod to Hal Davis.

Lieutenant Carl Marino pointed to a 4-by-5-foot enlargement of the bald top of a mountain. The steep-sided knob stood at the southernmost end of a long narrow ridge. Camouflage netting had been pulled aside to reveal the two artillery batteries and one of large mortars that had been dug in to the yellowish-red soil. Two helicopter pads were clearly marked with white bull's eyes and wind socks. The irregular shape of various bunkers could be readily identified.

"This is Firebase Loadstone," Marino informed the gathered SEALs of First Platoon. "There is a reinforced company of artillerymen up here. Also a blankethead outfit, to provide security. They have twenty-four Hre tribesmen with them. And they are in deep doo-doo. Part of the reported invading force of NVA troops has them under siege. From what the Special Forces commander has passed down, they are under attack day and night. Not constant, but at least one assault during the early morning and another one around midnight. Resupply became impossible yesterday when the NVA brought up RPG-7 grenade launchers and mortars and wrecked one Huey on the northern pad. Air drops are out of the question, the DZ is far too small, and there are nearly constant crosswinds. In other words, things have gotten too hot for everyone up there."

Chief Waters had a question. "I thought a relief of that firebase was to be the legend for our trip to Hanoi."

Marino shook his head. "We can no longer use it that way. This is going to be the real thing, Tonto. We have to relieve the firebase, hold off the NVA long enough to get the artillery types out by chopper, then lead the blanketheads to a secure area at Doc To."

Bobby Santoro, the new guy in Alpha Squad, had a question. "If they can't air-drop supplies, how are we going to get in there?"

"In a way, you can call this a dress rehearsal for our little jaunt to Hanoi," Lieutenant Marino replied, always ready to answer the questions of his men. "It will be a night jump, and we'll not use the standard T-10 'chutes. Instead, we'll use our Paracommanders. Steer in to a lighted DZ. Only one squad will jump in. The other will set off from Doc To northward to link up while the squad at the firebase works to open a corridor and take out the Army personnel and their Hre allies."

"Great," groused Anchor Head Sturgis, "while we take on half the North Vietnamese Army in the process?"

"No," came Marino's reply. "The estimate of enemy strength has been revised by the Blankethead captain in command up there. He thinks there's only a reinforced company involved in the siege. Mister Ott will lead this operation. He will be with Alpha Squad, which will be choppered to Doc To before Bravo Squad heads out for the jump into Loadstone. Draw equipment at nineteen-thirty, 'chute up at twenty hundred hours. Both squads will depart here by Slick to the air field at Binh Thuy. Jump aircraft will be a Boeing-Vertol CH-47 Chinook."

That drew groans from the SEALs. "Those things are way too big and easy to see," complained Anchor Head.

"You'd rather go all the way in by slick? There are regular troops down there. They have shoulder-fired surface-to-air missiles."

Anchor Head made an elaborate shrug, arms bent at his sides, palms up in a gesture of surrender. "Okay, Pope, so who's complaining?"

"Back to business. Standard ammo issue for all hands. In addition to your assigned personal weapons, Bravo squad will have issued an M55 flame projector. Alpha will take along a little gadget I had the machine shop at the five-three-four kluge together this afternoon. It's a hand-pulled two-wheel cart with a Honeywell on it." That drew expressions of awe and surprise from the SEALs. "Rules of engagement vary for each squad. Alpha will avoid contact with the enemy for as long as possible. Do not fire unless fired upon. Bravo, on the other, hand will be mixing it up with the enemy from the git-go. You are going into a free-fire zone. It moves, shoot it. If it becomes impossible to extract the artillery unit by chopper, Bravo will have to bring them out with the blanketheads. Remember, think for yourselves, innovate where necessary. Most of all, try to get everyone out alive and in one piece.''

In another ten minutes the briefing concluded.

After the orientation, Lieutenant Carl Marino returned to his office to find Jason Slater waiting there for him. With him was the head honcho for CIA in Saigon, Brian Wooster. Both Agency men arose when Marino entered the room.

''Carl, you know Brian. Hope you don't mind this unannounced call. Two things have come up that demand your immediate attention. First, a field officer has reported in with information that verifies the NVA offensive south of the DMZ is a diversion. It's designed to take attention off the meeting in Hanoi, which is definitely a reality. Which makes it even more essential to pull off an interdiction of that meeting. The Air Force is already on it. But your idea of putting people on the ground to take out some of the participants is even more attractive now. To put it as directly as I can, it is being pushed at the highest level.''

''And the second thing that caused you to pop in on me?''

''I have a feeling it pertains to the first subject. We have received a radio message. Your presence is requested in Washington, ASAP.''

Lieutenant Marino frowned menacingly. ''That's nuts. I have one operation to plan and another one running, which is far too much on my plate to go off to talk to some bureaucrats.''

''Not bureaucrats,'' Jason corrected. ''It's the President. He wants to talk to you before he authorizes this raid into the North.''

Marino thought that over for only a second. ''Then you had better make arrangements for two. I came up with the idea, but as I'm sure you know, it's the chiefs who run the Navy, so Chief Waters should come along to fill in the details.''

Slater nodded agreement. "It works for me."

Brian Wooster injected a caution. "Oh, and you're not supposed to know who it is you're going to see until you get there. So act surprised when you meet the President."

Marino cocked an eyebrow. "Politicians, or spook games?"

"It was the President's insistence that this meeting be covert," Brian explained. "It went through our deputy director, which is the only reason we know about any of this."

"All right, I'll buy that." Pope Marino stuck his head out of the office. "Santoro, get Tonto over here," he instructed Signalman Second Bobby Santoro.

"Aye-aye, sir."

In under three minutes, Chief Tom Waters knocked on the doorjamb of the doorless office. "Reporting as ordered, sir," he piped up.

"Come in and sit down, Chief."

"Aye, sir." Waters cast a suspicious glance at Slater as he took a seat.

"Tonto, we've been summoned to a meeting in Washington." Lieutenant Marino enjoyed the surprised expression that washed across the craggy face of Waters.

"Is that the state or D.C., sir?" Tonto asked with a tongue in cheek tone.

"District of Columbia, Chief. To see the President."

"Yer shittin' me, Pope."

"Straight poop, Chief. Believe it."

Jason Slater intervened. "Perhaps I should give him some of the details." When he had filled Waters in on what was proposed, he went on, "Your legend will be that the two of you are on leave. You will travel by military transport to the Philippines. From there you will be in civilian clothing and assume the cover of businessmen or tourists, whichever is most comfortable to you, and travel by commercial airline. You are to talk to no one and never show your Navy ID or reveal that you are in the military. You will enter and leave the White House covertly," Slater went on. "Only the President will be at your interview."

"Sounds spookish enough," Marino remarked. "After we leave the Philippines where do we go?"

"From Manila you'll go to Los Angeles International. You may travel together or take separate flights from LAX by round-about itinerary to San Diego, then Denver, Dallas–Fort Worth, Chicago, and New York.

"There you will be met by agents of the Secret Service who will escort you in a closed vehicle to Washington."

"How many days will this all take?" Waters asked.

"We estimate the round trip will take three days."

"All right. Sounds good. When do we leave?" asked Carl Marino.

"Tonight," Slater told him.

"Aw, hell, I just told you I have an operation laid on."

Slater's usually jovial features turned stern. "Postpone it or let it run without you. We're talking the President here, the Commander in Chief."

Marino shrugged and held his peace. Tonto Waters had looked stricken at the announcement of the timetable. Jason Slater observed this and asked him about it.

"Eloise Deladier is in Saigon for only a few days and we had a weekend planned. I even got special liberty for it. I was going to Saigon tomorrow morning to start our time together."

Slater affected a sympathetic demeanor. "You don't have much of a choice, do you?"

Tonto Waters cooled his heels while he listened to the far-off ring of the telephone in the room of Eloise Deladier in Saigon. The Montleon was not exactly a four-star lodging establishment, but it was a clean, efficiently run hotel with the faded opulence of better times in colonial days. The switchboard operator had assured him that Mademoiselle Deladier was indeed in her room. Uncomfortable with what it was he had to say, Tonto was ready to hang up when the ringing stopped abruptly.

"*Bon*?"

"Eloise?"

"Ye—yes. Is that Thomas?"

"Uh-huh."

"I was in the shower."

"Ummm. I'd like to see you right this minute."

"You're a naughty boy. But why did you call when we'll be together tomorrow before noon?"

"Uh—look, I have some bad news to tell you. I have to cancel our plans for the weekend."

"*Pourquoi*? Why?"

"Well, it's . . . something has come up out here. I mean I've had my special liberty canceled."

"But why? Carl Marino is your friend."

"He is also my commanding officer, and he says no." It wasn't exactly a lie, but it concealed the truth under a cloud thick enough for Eloise to perceive even over a phone line.

A thick stew of suspicion entered her voice. "There is something you are not telling me, Thomas."

"No—no, I've leveled with you. Pope has this op running and I'm needed. I'm sorry. I really am, but there's nothing I can do. We can—we can get together later in the week, before you have to return to Afghanistan."

"Your special liberty will not be canceled then, is that it?"

"Uh—yeah, sure. Trust me on this."

"Please, Thomas, tell me what is the real matter."

"Don't go back to that, sweetheart. I've told you all I can. Now I gotta go. Goodbye."

Tonto replaced the handset as their conversation ended in a well of heavy tension. *Oh, well,* he surrendered, *a chief proposes, the President disposes.*

CHAPTER 14

CAVITE NAVAL Air Station looked the same as it had on previous visits. As on earlier occasions, Lieutenant Marino and Chief Waters arrived at night and saw only darker black silhouettes of palm trees and low buildings. They deplaned from the Gulfstream and walked directly to a darkened hangar. There a stranger, a CIA field officer, met them and ushered them into a closed taxi.

"You can call me Chambers. Make yourselves comfortable, gentlemen. We'll be changing vehicles after we leave the base."

"Who thought all this up?" Carl Marino asked.

"I have no need to know." The CIA man let the stiffness melt a moment. "But if I had to make a guess, I'd say the Secret Service. They like to think they are as good at the spook business as some others I could mention."

"Then this is all real, like presented, Chambers?" Tom Waters remarked.

"I'm only a chauffeur. And what you could call a facilitator."

"And what would that be?" prompted Marino.

A ghost of a smile slid across the face of the Agency man. "I'm going to see you get on a commercial airliner bound for the States."

"Do you have anything for motion sickness?" Tonto asked. Chambers gaped at him as though the idea of an air-

150

sick SEAL was more than he could comprehend. "Only kidding," Waters added hastily.

They settled in the back of the taxi, Chambers facing the two SEALs on a jump seat. Curtains made of small multi-colored fuzzy cloth balls strung together obscured the windows of the rear seat and denied a view of any occupants. The driver started the engine and the vehicle rolled out of the hangar.

Although other cars were checked for liberty cards and IDs, the taxi drove through the gate without delay. Three miles down the road, they stopped at an apparently unoccupied service station. Chambers gestured to the office door.

"Go through there into the service bay. You'll find some civilian clothing there. Change into it and we'll drive to the general aviation office at the local airport. There you will take a charter flight to the international airport in Manila. From there you fly Pan Am to Guam, Honolulu, and on to Los Angeles."

"You're quite the travel agent, Chambers," Marino complimented with only a slight hint of sarcasm in his voice.

"Thank you," Chambers replied dryly. "We all serve where best suited."

When Marino and Waters came out and reentered the taxi, conversation shifted to the situation in Vietnam, and soon became a game of "Do you know so-and-so?" Eventually Jason Slater's name came up.

"Did you know that he was there back before we got involved. 'We' being the United States and 'involved' meaning officially involved. Chennault's Civilian Air Transport Service was helping fly supplies to the French until Dien Bien Phu fell and that outfit was owned by the Company. Slater was there in 'sixty and 'sixty-one—a lot of covert ops going on. You ask me, what those guys did was stir up a hornet's nest. But that's telling tales out of school."

"How are the Yankees doin'?" Marino changed the subject.

Chambers gave a small chuckle. "You've been in the jungle too long. Spring training hasn't even started yet. You ask me, though, they're gonna go in the toilet. They've lost a lot of their big guns due to retirement.''

Sports talk continued until they reached the local airport. Chambers shook hands with the SEALs and wished them well. ''From here on you are on your own. Here are your tickets.'' He handed them Pan American Airlines folders and pointed to a small, aged Beech 18 parked on the tarmac. ''There's your connecting flight. Good luck.''

In the small waiting room Marino and Waters had their first opportunity to examine their persona as civilians. Tonto wore an elaborately embroidered guiabarra in a soft green color and a pair of tan slacks. Marino was decked out in a crewneck polo shirt, sport coat, and bell-bottom faded denims.

''Wow, look at you,'' Tonto teased, ''if you had a big enough mop of hair you could pass for one of the Beatles.''

''You should talk. With that four-pocket shirt you look like a Mexican plainclothes cop . . . or a Filipino gangster. All you need is a pair of Florsheim wingtips.''

Both men lost their humor when Tonto remarked, ''I wonder how the operation is going?''

''Yeah, me, too.'' Marino checked his watch. ''They ought to be on their way about now.''

Six pair of eyes took in the spiffy new black-painted Chinook that belonged to Air America. Anchor Head Sturgis was the designated jump master and he led the squad into the helicopter by way of the aft ramp, which had been lowered.

Onboard they found a master sergeant from Fifth Special Forces. ''Andrews,'' he introduced himself to Sturgis. ''They sent me along because I know the terrain around your DZ. I won't get in your way, Chief. Just advise you guys on what to look out for.''

''I'm a petty officer first class, Sarge, an' the name's Sturgis. They call me Anchor Head. I appreciate the tour guide. The main thing is the trees.''

''There aren't any left on that hilltop. If we have to use an alternate DZ, that might pose a problem.''

"Why'd we have to change drop zones?"

"Enemy fire."

"Oh, shit. Don't even think about that."

Anyone who had been airborne-qualified knew how vulnerable to ground fire a man could be when suspended in a parachute harness. Anchor Head had practical experience in it up close and personal on two earlier occasions. He didn't appreciate the opportunity to have a third.

"Well, it is a night jump," Andrews said philosophically. "It should be a piece of cake."

The crew chief swung aboard through a side hatch and a moment later the twin jet engines began to spool up. The rotor blades started to turn as the engineer fitted his helmet and boom mike in place. To Anchor Head the kid didn't look old enough to be crew chief on this bird. The hydraulics groaned to life and the aft ramp slid upward into place. The SEALs had strapped in for the takeoff. As soon as the bird lifted off and climbed to flight level, Anchor Head released the harness and swung into place at one of the round windows that reminded him of a porthole.

Behind them he could see the dim yellow glow of lights at Binh Thuy. They faded rapidly as the Ch-47 gained speed and swung onto its heading for the distant firebase. The vibration wasn't that bad, Anchor Head mused, at least not like in a Huey. At least they got to ride all the way. Alpha squad would be choppered later to a Special Forces base nearest to invading force. From there they would go overland theoretically to link up with those his squad would be leading out. That would be quite a few, they learned shortly before departure for Binh Thuy.

Except for five helicopter loads, increasingly accurate enemy fire had prevented air evacuation for the Army personnel. Most would be walking out with his squad. That many people would make a hell of a lot of noise. He sure hoped they knew how to shoot something besides their big guns. More to the point, that they could hit what they shot at.

Outside blackness covered the jungle like a blanket. Only here and there a dim pinpoint of yellow indicated the home of some Vietnamese farmer or rice harvester. An hour into the flight, the blankethead sergeant swung inboard from the open cargo hatch he had been gazing out of. The meaning of the signals he gave were easy to understand when accompanied by the whine of the hydraulic system as the ramp lowered. Muggy air, driven by the rotors, blew away the harsh metallic odor of the interior of the chopper. At once, Anchor Head walked past the other five SEALs to a position by the opening formed by the ramp.

Facing his squad, Anchor Head used hand and arm signals to underscore his nearly inaudible words as he gave the jump commands. "*Get ready! . . .*

"*Stand up! . . .*

"*Hook up! . . .*

"*Check your equipment! . . .*"

Following his next command, the squad sounded off; "*One okay.*"

"*Two okay.*"

The countdown went on through all six men. Over the howl of the twin T-55-L-11A Lycoming turbine engines, Anchor Head uttered the fateful command "*Stand in the door!*"

At once, the RTO of Sturgis' squad, Luke Merriman, shuffled aft onto the ramp. A second later the light on the aft bulkhead flashed from red to green. Anchor Head gave Luke a swat on the rump. "*Go! Go! Go!*"

Only seconds apart, the SEALs spilled from the Chinook like a line of ducks. Above their heads, the unilluminated craft flashed by at 800 feet AGL (above ground level). A quick four-count and the first Paracommander deployed with a hissing *plop*. His fingers closed tightly around the small wooden steering knobs, Luke Merriman turned a 360-degree circle to check out the area.

For a moment he couldn't see a damned thing. Then a darker mass below him resolved itself into the ring of trees that surrounded the bare top of the hill that was their drop zone. Suddenly five bright fingers of light sprang into being, defining the four corners and center of the DZ. Luke had only a few spare seconds to wonder if the blanketheads they'd come to rescue had cleared the ground of any obstructions before he dropped below the treeline.

Feet together, toes pointed, knees slightly bent, he made ready to do a standard PLF (parachute landing fall) only to have the ground slam into him with painful abruptness. The breath jarred from him; he reacted quickly to the insistent tugging on his harness and hauled on the suspension lines.

Luke quickly grounded and surrounded his canopy. Then he hit the quick release box in the center of his chest. A second later he heard a soft *whoof* as the air was driven from the lungs of Dallas Goracke. Limping slightly, Luke and Dallas cleared the DZ. Behind them the rest of the squad grounded with slightly less distress.

From beside him Luke heard a soft whisper as Tex Goracke offered up a prayer of thanks for not being shot at by the enemy. A big man outlined by one corner light came forward and stuck out a ham-sized fist.

"Sergeant Jack Carter. Welcome to Loadstone."

"Thanks a lot," Anchor Head Sturgis said, from behind Luke and Dallas.

"I'll take you to the command bunker."

"Lead on," Sturgis replied.

Thick timbers and stacked sandbags reinforced the walls and ceiling of the deep underground bunker to which Curtis led the SEALs. He introduced Captain Morgan, who turned at once to Anchor Head.

"Where are the rest?"

"We're it, sir. We're going to lead you out of here and link up with another squad from our team."

Stunned, Captain Kevin Morgan could only stare.

"It's just my nerves," Betty Welby assured herself aloud, as she stood alone in her apartment in Norfolk, Virginia. Odd, but she could not recall his name, not even exactly what he looked like. All that remained was the tingling sensation of his turgid maleness thrusting deep within her. That, and the unspeakable shame and humiliation the recollection always engendered within her.

"I need a little tonic for it, that's all," she strived to convince herself, as she poured a generous three shots of gin into a glass, added two ice cubes, and stirred with one finger. The guilt returned with a vengeance. What could she tell Kent? Would she even try to tell him? And the prospect of going to confession terrified her. Father Flynn would know it was her. He would have not the least doubt. And he would despise her for her infidelity. It was a mortal sin. Quickly she gulped her drink in an effort to ease the pain inside her.

All of the beautiful people in New York have a martini before lunch, don't they? her thoughts nagged her as she repeated the process. *What's wrong with my having one ... well, perhaps it's two ... or is it three?*

Tonto Waters gave an angry shake to the magazine in his hand. On the cover was a photo of soldiers engaged in a firefight in a jungle. From the perspective of the lens, it made the enemy look like small children. There was an insert with a silhouette map of Vietnam. Flames leaping from a spot indicated the site of the supposed battle.

"Will you look at this? I can't believe this is *Time*. Look at the title of the feature article. 'American Imperialism.' Did we wake up in the same world?" Tonto swallowed a long pull on a plastic cup of beer. "The guy who wrote this is a liar at best, a traitor at worst. It's all lies. Every bit of it."

Disturbed by his rising tone of voice, a stewardess hurried down the aisle to where the two SEALs sat. "Please, sir, you'll upset the other passengers."

"I'll upset them, right enough," Tonto growled. A sharp look from Pope Marino silenced him.

"It's only an article," Pope reminded him, after the cabin attendant had departed.

"It's a propaganda article. Enemy propaganda."

"Not everyone feels that way."

"I'm not so sure. With this kind of crap being written, how long will it be before *we* become the bad guys?"

Marino scanned an article on draft card burners in a copy of *Newsweek* in the seat pocket in front of him. "I think we already have. And no, you don't want to read it."

CHAPTER 15 _____

ELMORE YATES prowled in front of Francie Song. Three short paces left, followed by three short paces right. "I told you to be here an hour ago."

Francie did a good job of hiding her fear. "I could not get away until the noon hour."

"Yes, you could." His cold gaze cut right through her, as though focused on the carp pool at the front of the pagoda.

"What is it you want?"

Yates stopped abruptly and shoved his face close up to hers. Francie could smell the liquor on his breath. "I need to know where Marino and Waters have gone."

"I do not know," Francie hedged, eager for some means of refusing.

"You can find out. I suggest you make it quick. Something . . . unpleasant can still happen to that little boy of yours. And oh, I hope Thran is enjoying his holiday stay with his aunt and uncle."

Stricken, Francie relented. Defeat trembled in her words. "I will check the records and see."

Two hours before dawn found the SEALs of Bravo Squad busy in the bush outside the Loadstone compound. Their faces and hands done in the notorious green and black camouflage, they ghosted from tree to tree, careful to avoid vines and clinging vegetation that would betray their presence to the enemy.

Each trio of squad members had been tasked with a 180-degree sweep of the territory occupied by the NVA troops. The night before the obligatory Texas Ranger anecdote about "One riot, one Ranger" had been related to Captain Morgan and his men. They chuckled at it, but it was obvious to Anchor Head Sturgis that they did not appreciate its application to their situation. Perhaps the blanketheads would value their recon a bit more.

Long Tom and Tex Goracke were with Sturgis, while Mickey Mouse Norton, Little Peterson, and Brandon Mitchell formed the second team. So far, only an hour into their mission, their discoveries had been astonishing.

"We've seen a lot less gooks than expected," Mickey Mouse whispered into the mike of his secure net handheld radio.

"Roger that, we got the same," growled back Anchor Head, in what for him passed as a mutter.

"There can't be more than a company over here," opined the Mouse.

"Yeah, the same on this side," the squad leader responded. *Jeez, that means more than a regiment of those buggers has pulled out here*, the thoughts of Anchor Head Sturgis ran on. "Charlie-Yankee-Alpha, ol' buddy," he advised the Mouse.

"Cover your ass, too, buddy," Michael Norton whispered without keying the mike.

He and Anchor Head had gone through BUDS (Basic Underwater Demolition School) together and into SEAL training, with Sturgis always one rank ahead of the then boatswain's mate third class. Petty Officer status was important and a requirement for entry into the SEAL program, along with a rating in one of the Navy's trades. But a crow and one chevron didn't amount to much in this man's navy, Mike Norton soon found out. In BUDS and later at the SEAL school, he and the twenty-five others of equal rank were the bottom men on the totem pole.

Later on, one of the SEAL candidates would write a song about their experience. It would become a country-and-western hit with such lyrics as *"Work your fingers to the bone, what do you get? . . . Bony fingers."* It perfectly exemplified their situation, depicting in a fanciful manner the enormous stress and incredible physical strain to which they were put daily—and nightly. Those who made it, though, were the best of the best.

No wonder, the Mouse thought, they were out here being the eyes and ears for the blanketheads. The elite Army Special Forces troopers were good at what they did. Better than that, they were *damned good*. But their mission was not the same as that of the SEALs. They held ground. They served as security for the artillery pukes, and suchlike. They went up in the mountains and organized those little short guys, the Montagnards—yeah, that's what they were called. And they were trained to recruit assets behind enemy lines and run a sort of resistance movement.

After all, Special Forces was a lot like the old OSS, determined to bring a world of hurt to the heartland of any enemy. They were an action arm of policy. And they had often been used as such by the CIA, Norton recalled. *SOG*, Special Operations Group—oops! make that Studies and Operations Group, for all it did to fool even the densest of those sorry media types—had been culled from the ranks of Special Forces and directed by the CIA. They had brought scalding pee down on the heads of many in North Vietnam, Cambodia, and Laos. They were experts in what they did, mean as hell, and damned near as good as SEALs. Which gave Norton a certain sense of superiority for being the one taking the chances in the bush instead of Captain Morgan and his boys.

Morgan had the look of one of those who had been there, done that, and lived to keep his mouth shut about what *there* and *that* were. He had the thousand-mile gunfighter's stare. Unaware that he shared that awesome look, Norton felt the reflection send a chill down his spine. Turn that Morgan guy loose and he'd kick ass and take names until the third Thursday of next week. Like a movie camera panned too swiftly, Norton's mental wanderings blurred back to sharp focus on the present by a stealthy movement to his left.

Instantly he froze and melted into the background of Vietnamese vegetation. Invisible to all but the colorblind, the Mouse eased his weapon into a ready position and touched the trigger with a fingertip. The movement came again and he saw clearly now. Two of them.

If they were Americans, Norton would judge them to be about 11 or 12 years old. But they were mature adults, one with a thick, black worm of mustache on a full upper lip. Even with their NVA pith helmets, they would not come up to Norton's armpit. The Type 56 carbines they carried made up in part for their lack of stature. If they saw him, he was dead meat. So, nothing for it but to get in the first lick. Had his Swedish Carl Gustav Model 45 SMG not been equipped with a hushpuppy, that could also prove fatal. As it happened, he not only got in the first lick, he did it *quietly*.

Norton set his Model 45 on single fire and waited until the two NVA soldiers drew to within twenty feet of him. He then popped the nearest half an inch above his left eye socket. The man jerked from the impact and its immediate effect on his nervous system. The suppressed weapon had made only a soft *phutt!* and the metallic clack of the action cycling. The dying man was folding like a limp rag when the spray of blood from the 9mm slug's exit wound struck his partner in the face. An instant later, the Mouse put another 9mm slug into the gaping mouth of the startled trooper. He gagged on his blood, clawed at his throat, and dropped to the ground, eyes rolled upward, staring at nothingness.

Mike Norton broke from his motionless concealment and swiftly dragged first one dead man then the other deep into enshrouding underbrush. That accomplished, he quickly left the immediate area and turned northward in a continuation of his sweep of enemy territory. When he had covered 100 meters, he keyed the mike again.

"Anchor Head, this is Mouse. Ran into a couple of outlaws. Had to dust them. Over."

"Anybody hear you, Mouse?"

"Nope. That Sionics suppressor works damn near as good as on a Smith. I'm following the plan. Mouse, out."

Dallas Goracke shot his squad leader a curious glance. "Mouse had to waste a couple of gooks," Anchor Head explained sotto voce, then added, "They've not run into a hell of a lot of people over there."

"And we have?" Tex Goracke asked back sarcastically.

"Naw, I'd say there's been a massive pullout of the two regiments that were supposed to be here. Another half a klick an' we'll go back up the hill."

Half a world away, Betty Welby listlessly dusted furniture in the small apartment she had obtained in the enlisted housing facility. She sighed heavily and put the furniture polish–stained rag aside.

"It would be nice," she addressed the blank gray screen of the black and white television set, "if I had a baby to care for." Abruptly she frowned. "No, it wouldn't," she continued aloud. "Not at all. It would be horrid. How could a woman alone take care of a child? I'd have to take a job to meet the added expenses of a baby. Then who would watch the kid? It's not fair. Kent should be here with me." Another soulful sigh, then Betty looked at the face of the elegant jeweled Engram wristwatch on her slender arm.

"Almost time to meet the girls," she continued her soliloquy to the TV. "I'd better get a shower and dress. And maybe there'll be a few minutes to enjoy a martini before they get here. Suzy said this place we're going is sooo swanky. Yes," she concluded decisively, "a little fortification is definitely in order."

Anchor Head Sturgis led his men back inside the Special Forces compound, inside the complex of Firebase Loadstone. He no sooner completed his report of the paucity of enemy forces than the NVA launched a sunrise attack.

*   *   *

At five-ten, Lieutenant Gao Hip was large for a Vietnamese. Only 20 years of age, he had graduated the Officer's Leadership School three months earlier and been assigned as a platoon leader in the Victorious Sunrise Regiment. Now he tightened his lips around the mouthpiece of his green plastic whistle and executed a shrill burst as the luminous second hand on his military watch crossed over the number 12. All along the line, the strident sound repeated. Close around him Hip felt the presence of his men, the soldiers of Second Platoon, Joyful Strength Company, of Fourth Battalion, Victorious Sunrise Regiment of the Army of the Socialist Republic of North Vietnam. Hip drove his right arm forward and down as he uttered a shout of encouragement to his men.

"Crush the invaders beneath our feet!"

"*Garrrow!*" came the answering agreement from thirty-six throats.

In three running paces forward the NVA troops cleared their sparse concealment and broke into the wide strip of cleared land around the mountain top American firebase. Here and there, land mines that had not been previously located and deactivated or detonated by other unfortunates went off with fierce roars. For all of how much he hated them, Hip appreciated the need for the deadly devices.

Given the "human wave" tactic most popular with his own army, any soldiers compelled to defend a given position could not hope to prevail without the use of land mines. Their fortifications would be overwhelmed in the first assault. The North Vietnamese Army and their Viet Cong allies also used mines as passive, hidden defenses. Given the tactical situation in the South, they needed them badly. The detonation of a single mine could give advance warning of an enemy approach.

The benefit of which now served the hated Americans at the firebase, Hip realized, as another loud *whang!* ripped the air close on his right and two men from his first squad began to shriek in bitter agony. A quick glance showed the lieutenant that one man clutched the stump of a severed limb, while the other struggled in vain to stuff his intestines back into his shredded abdomen. Hip swiftly stifled the terrible image and looked in the other direction.

"Keep moving," he exhorted his platoon. "This time they will all die!"

Soft pearl light lay in a widening band along the eastern horizon when the North Vietnamese whistles began to pierce the dawn. "Here they come again." Captain Kevin Morgan wore an expression of resignation rather than fear as he arose from the empty ammunition crate that served as a chair at the mess table.

He dumped the tepid contents of his canteen cup into the mess hall slop can and headed for the sandbagged entrance. One hand reached for his coal scuttle ballistic helmet while he snatched up his CAR-15 on the way. Already the heavy thump of .50 caliber machine guns sounded from the sandbag emplacements above the mess bunker. To his surprise, he found the SEALs of Bravo Squad already manning positions that provided interlacing fire on the advancing NVA troops.

"Well, I'll be damned," he muttered aloud, as his own men belatedly scrambled to their assigned battle stations. In typical Special Forces fashion, he raised a shout and jokingly chided his troops. "Hey, boys, you're gonna have to get up a hell of a lot earlier if you wanna beat these Squids."

"In your ear, Cap," replied Nick Kleiber.

So far, Kevin Morgan observed with new respect, the NVA had maintained excellent fire discipline. Not a soldier had opened up in an ineffective spray while still out of range for their Type 56 carbines. No matter, he reflected. The damn things still fired seven minutes of angle at a hundred meters. A guy had to be right on top of his target to be sure of hitting it. And that didn't take into account the frequent misfires. Morgan made a quick closeout on his line of thought and directed his attention to the immediate. To his surprise, he found himself consulting the SEAL 1C petty officer.

"What do you think, Sturgis?"

Anchor Head wrinkled his brow. "Like we told you, sir.

Not a hell of a lot of 'em out there.'' Then he added, "They're smart for holdin' their fire."

"You got that right, Sturgis. But it won't be long now."

"You gonna call for fire support, Captain?"

"I don't think so. It looks like G-2 got it right, for once. There's not enough of them out there to be a real threat."

"We saw at least two companies, sir. My best guess would be they're holdin' a third in reserve. That's a battalion at least."

"Good point. I figure that's a reinforced company out there now. If they don't commit the rest of whatever force they have, we can handle them. Keep your men's heads down."

"Hell, Captain, beggin' your pardon, sir, but if we're here, we fight."

That brought a grin to the face of Kevin Morgan. "Do your thing, then, Petty Officer. If I was in the Navy, I'd put you in for chief."

Anchor Head looked aggrieved. "Awh, heck, sir, chiefs have too much work to do." That was a lie—Sturgis thought to himself as he recalled the too-close-to-the-truth cartoon he had seen that featured a chief asleep in a swivel chair, the permanent impression of half a coffee mug in his chest—but he hoped the blankethead officer didn't know it.

This time it will work! Lieutenant Hip exalted, as the assault wave neared the outer perimeter wire. As they had been instructed it was only then that Hip and the other platoon leaders ordered their men to open fire. The Chinese firecracker patter of 7.63-by-39mm rounds masked for Hip the heavy *chunk!* of propellant detonations as four-inch mortar shells burst from their tubes.

Pointed almost vertically, the mortars of Firebase Loadstone sent the projectiles in a high, tight arc that brought them down within 100 meters of their base plates. Proximity fuses detonated the warheads 3 meters off the ground and showered the charging NVA troops with hot steel fragments. Before the first round burst, the light cough of 81mm mortars joined the fray, followed by the buoyant chatter of M60 machine guns.

Lieutenant Hip's eyes went wide, exposing circles of white, as men began to fall all around him. Shards of shrapnel whizzed past his head, two of which struck and tore chunks from his pith helmet. A swarm of 7.62mm hornets cracked past his shoulders and a sudden hot flare burned across the point of his left deltoid muscle. Hip bit off a cry of pain and fought back involuntary tears. He looked around himself frantically in an effort to locate as many of his men who had survived the mortar barrage.

To his relief, nearly the entire platoon remained intact. Conscious that he was bleeding profusely, Hip ignored his own condition to urge his men onward. Here and there, he saw, other platoons in the assault faltered. Not his platoon or any of the Joyful Strength Company, he noted with relief. Then they met a seeming wall of claymore mines at the second line of wire. The pyramid of concertina wire alone could have halted or severely slowed the attack. Combined with the 18mm steel balls of the shaped charge mines, the result was devastating.

"Pull back! Pull back!"

To his amazement and intense shame, Lieutenant Gao Hip recognized the voice as that of his company commander. Now the unrestrained tears blinded him as he and his men turned away from their objective and scurried like rats back down the mountainside to the safety of the jungle below.

"Piece of cake," Anchor Head Sturgis announced to Captain Kevin Morgan after the firefight ended. "Yep, there wasn't more than a reinforced company in that assault. More than scary if there was only us six SEALs up here, but you guys did great. I'm gonna change my guess to a positive. Yep, there's a battalion out there, three, four companies depending on their makeup, less what we wasted just now." He paused and thought a moment. "What they'll be doin' is move them around to wherever they plan to probe your defenses next.

Make it look like there's more of them. Do they ever hit you at night, sir?''

"Oh, yeah. They prefer hitting at night," Morgan answered firmly, wincing at a twinge in his shoulder wound. "Just like the Cong, whom they trained after all."

"Okay, sir. Next time we do that, here's what we do," Anchor Head Sturgis grew confidential as he lowered his voice and explained his idea to Captain Kevin Morgan.

CHAPTER 16

TIRED AND rumpled, Carl Marino and Tom Waters freed themselves from the restraint of seatbelts and stepped numbly into the aisle of the TWA 707 that had flown them from Honolulu to Lindberg Field in San Diego. Local time was 8: 35 A.M. (0835 hours). Their time sense told the SEALs that it was 2135 hours of the previous day. Tonto Waters uttered a soft sigh as he shouldered his carry-on luggage.

"I feel like someone's been pounding me with a sock full of sand," he confided to the handsome young officer in front of him.

"Know what you mean, Tom," agreed Pope Marino. "I think I've been shot at and missed and shit at and hit."

"Think we'll be met by anyone?"

Marino shook his head. "Not likely. Nobody said we'd be. You hungry?"

Waters brightened. "Yeah. What they fed us on the flight just dropped into a huge hole. I know it's sausage and hotcakes time, but I got this wild craving for a burger, onion rings, and a beer."

Marino responded in a dreamy voice. "Oh, yeah, a nice, big, fat, juicy hamburger. A half-pounder."

"Think we'll find one in the airport?"

Lip curled downward, Marino answered, "Not friggin' likely."

"Well, we've got four hours before our flight to Denver. What say we round up one somewhere?"

"I'm game," Marino readily agreed, as he took his turn exiting the aircraft and walking down the metal stairway.

This early, the terminal building on Pacific Highway at Lindberg Field was not crowded. Marino and Waters threaded their way through the sparse gaggle of early-departure passengers and the deplaning arrivals. They broke out onto the sidewalk in front of a rank of taxis. The first six were from the Yellow Cab Company, followed by two red-and-black painted, heavily built Mercurys from Veterans' Cab Company. By mutual unspoken agreement, Marino and Waters headed for the first of these.

Before they could reach their objective, the two SEALs were surrounded by a flurry of confused young men uniformly dressed in jeans, polo shirts, and penny loafers. A trio of petty officers in blue uniforms attempted to round them up. Eventually they herded them a distance away, up against the cyclone fence that separated the grassy parking strip directly in line with Runway 27R.

"Awhright, youse guys. Line up over here. Fall in two ranks facing me," bawled the familiar voice of an obviously harassed chief petty officer.

"Now hear this," continued the chief. "Youse will be in my charge until youse is processed at NTC. No smoking in ranks and no talking. Is that clear?"

There followed a few "Yeahs," "Yeps," and "Yesses," in half-hearted response. *"Is that clear?"* the chief bellowed.

Several of the young recruits blanched and tried to stiffen into some sort of position of attention. "Your response is, 'Aye-aye, sir'!"

"Aye-aye, sir," the callow youths responded.

"I can't hear you."

"AYE-AYE, SIR!"

"That's better. Maybe we'll get along all right, after all. Transportation will be here momentarily. Until then, stand at ease. You may talk, but no smoking."

A long battleship-gray bus from the Naval Training Cen-

ter slowly eased across traffic and turned into the loading
lane of the airport as they waited. Tonto Waters nudged Pope
Marino in the ribs. "Remind you of anything, Pope?"

"Umm, not really. I arrived at Anapolis in a taxi."

"It sure brings back memories for me. I'm willin' to bet
half those kids are about to wet their pants. That chief's got
them right by the short and curlies. Uh-oh, what's this?"

While he had been speaking, an unruly mob of oddly
dressed young men and women appeared around a corner of
the terminal building. They came accompanied by bright
lights, obliging TV cameramen, and eager polyester-clad reporters. As they drew nearer, their chanting became clear.

"Hell no, we won't go! Hell no, we won't go! Stop the
war. Americans stay home. Get out now!" With a sudden-
ness that was shocking, they appeared to discover the recruits
for the first time. Pointing and gesturing wildly, they changed
their chants to a beseeching mode. "You! You! Get out
while you can! Join us. Don't fight the fascist's war."

"Git outta here," brayed the chief.

"Yeah. To hell with you. We're joinin' the Navy," one
of the bolder recruits, a lad who looked to have played high
school football, countered.

It sent the antiwar protestors into a frenzy. "Bloody
hands! Bloody hands!" they shrieked. "Motherfuckers! Rap-
ists! Baby killers! Enemies of freedom! Bastards!" The dark
epithets flew at them, mingled with the Communist rhetoric.

Slowly the bus inched its way between the nearly hysterical protestors and the confused, uncomfortable recruits while
Marino and Waters did a slow burn that they could not break
their cover and intervene. At the appearence of the bus, the
antiwar agitators went absolutely ballistic. They howled and
capered on the wide grass burm that separated Pacific Coast
Highway (US 101) from the three-lane loading lanes at the
Lindberg terminal. Several began to hurl rocks. In the distance, several sirens howled as the SDPD responded. Two
uniformed security guards came out through a pair of double
doors, hands nervously on the grips of their .38 Specials.

Abruptly, after the bus pulled away and a suitable amount

of film had been exposed, "Without equal time being given to the Navy," as Tonto Waters observed, the cameras were shut off and the media mavens departed to get their footage developed and printed in time for the noon news. Like a switch being thrown, the "demonstration" broke up and the young antiwar enthusiasts began to wander off without a backward glance.

"You gonna cut Soch this morning?" one dewy eyed blonde asked a scrawny kid of 19 or so.

"Sure, we just had our Sociology experiment for today, didn't we?" he responded. "Besides, Robbie has some boss pot. We're gonna go over to Bippy's and toke a coupla joints. Wanna come?"

"Cool. You bet I do," the blonde replied.

"Jimmy," called out another boy who had likewise miraculously clicked off his rabid outrage at the Navy recruits the instant the TV lights had gone off. "I ain't got a class until one. Let's go shoot some pool, huh? Somewhere we can get some beer?"

"Real cool. We can go to Butch's an' do some pitchers, he won't card us."

A sort of numb astonishment descended on Marino and Waters. Disgruntled by the hypocrisy and stage-managed nature of the calculated demonstration, Waters looked after the departing punks. "Just give me one night with those assholes in Tre Noc," he growled to his commanding officer.

BM/1C Charles Sturgis became a very busy boy during the day that followed the latest NVA attack. He spent most of the morning laying and burying long lines of coaxial cable. Then he settled in at the sandbag revetment that held one of two selected LMGs. The M60, mounted on an M122 tripod, covered the next most likely approach route.

"As you know, sir, there are only three accessible approaches to this place," he had explained to Captain Morgan. "The NVA used one of those this morning. Have you ever seen them use the same one twice before?"

"Only the first day. After we called in arty and air, they started alternating their attacks."

Anchor Head nodded thoughtfully. "So then, what I'm going to do is rig up coaxial machine guns on the two they did not use. They'll fire remotely, in five-round bursts."

"Why five rounds?" the Special Forces officer asked.

Sturgis grinned slyly. "Because I brought along an interrupter that will allow five-round bursts."

Considering what he knew would be happening in the compound when the machine guns opened up, Morgan asked seriously, "But won't they know there's no one behind those weapons when they continue to fire without traversing?"

"Well now, Captain, you've got a point there. What we need is a means for makin' them track across their fields of fire."

"Such as what?"

"A motor that will run until the last generator is blown up. Something that will make them move from side to side. Like an oscillating fan."

The two troop leaders fell silent a moment. At last Kevin Morgan brightened, his face beaming. "I think I've got something. We have an old-fashioned washing machine. Think you could do something with that?"

Surprised at finding such a convenience in a remote firebase, Anchor Head at last consoled himself with the thought that these blanketheads were known to be incredibly vain. Freshly laundered and starched uniforms were probably as important to them as hot chow. Sturgis dismissed his moment of frivolity and frowned, trying to visualize whatever the captain was getting at. "You mean an automatic washer, sir?"

"Nooo. This is an old ringer job. It has a dasher—or whatever you call it—that turns nearly three hundred sixty degrees, then swings back."

The light dawned. "*Yess!*" Sturgis enthused. "Perfect. We can rig the co-ax cables to the agitator—it's called an agitator—and then have our traverse. The interrupter will be cross-connected to the other lead, and that'll let us bust off caps like there really was a guy behind the gun."

Captain Morgan looked absolutely gleeful. "You can really do that?"

"Turn me loose, an' watch me go, sir."

Three hours after that conversation, Anchor Head tightened the last screw in a cable clamp that he had fitted to an extension on the trigger of the second M60. "There, that does it," he declared triumphantly. "Now we give it a try."

"You're gonna fire it?" asked the mystified gunner, a Special Forces corporal. "Won't that tip off what we're up to?"

"No. Just fire up the wash machine an' kick in the interrupter. Take the belt out of the loading tray an' leave the gun charged, okay? We'll hear the bolt fall forward and know we've got a winner."

To the immense pleasure of Captain Kevin Morgan, BM/1C Charles Sturgis, MSGT Hank Carter, and the corporal gunner, it worked fantastically. At least, after a little fine tuning and fidgeting. Now all they need do was wait for a night attack.

"I am sorry, Miss Song, but there is nothing more I can tell you. After all, the SEALs are an independent command." The duty yeoman for the 534th turned away from the counter dissuasively.

It had been like that throughout the past two days. No matter to whom Francie Song spoke or how she asked her questions, she could get nothing more. She had no more idea where Lieutenant Marino and Chief Waters had gone than when she'd begun her quest. So far she had hesitated at asking in her own department at the Riverine Force office. Now she felt that her lack of results compelled her to. Sighing in resignation, she crossed the hallway to the Operations Section and approached the walled-off cubicle that housed the CPOs desk.

The chief petty officer for Operations was in for once and he looked up, his youthful, freckled face reminding her of the friend of her Kentwelby, Archie Golden. "Yes, Miss Song?"

"Chief, I was wondering—that is, I do not recall processing any orders for Lieutenant Marino and Chief Waters of the SEALs. Do you know what their current disposition is?"

Chief Dawson—that was the name on his dungaree shirt—frowned. "I shouldn't be telling you this, but I know you have a close friend in the SEALs. Lieutenant Marino and Chief Waters are on administrative leave."

"Where?" Francie pressed.

"Lieutenant Marino has gone to Japan. Something to do with martial arts instruction, according to the request form. The chief is in Australia."

"Is Mr. Ott in charge now?"

"Yes, but he's not present at the compound."

"Where is he?"

"Ah—in Saigon," the CPO lied artlessly.

Francie's scornful glower would have curled the hairs of a lesser man. "No doubt on leave?" she snapped before making a hasty departure for her noontime meeting with Elmore Yates.

The sinister Marine sergeant waited impatiently for her when she approached the pagoda beside the carp pond in the small formal garden. Her eyes widened when she saw him and realized that his promptness indicated how badly he wanted the information.

"They are on leave," she told him bitingly.

Suddenly his hands shot out from his sides and gripped her by the shoulders. He shook her violently for several seconds, eliciting a gasp from the slightly built and very pregnant young woman. "I could have learned that myself. Where are they *really?*"

Fighting back tears, Francie tried what Kentwelby had instructed her to do. Quickly raising her knee, she slammed Yates in the crotch, then stomped down hard on his instep. Yates uttered a low groan and bent over, clutched his aching genitals.

"They are on leave. One in Japan, the other in Australia. And do not ever touch me again," Francie hissed in fury, before she spun around and stalked off past a trio of saffron-robed Buddhist monks.

General Trang Van Key stared with ill-concealed anger at yet another of the parade of politicians who had assailed his office in Hanoi over the past several days. This one in particular. Did the idiot not know that the primary purpose of this high-level meeting was to augment the military capability?

"Your plans are totally unacceptable, Comrade General. I must insist that you curtail much of your ambitious program to make the military the center piece of the meeting. The military simply must play a lesser role."

You pompous bastard, Key thought furiously. "Perhaps you fail, Comrade Minister, to realize that it is the military that is at the center of the topics to be discussed?"

"Not likely. However, protocol demands that not only at the banquets will the political leaders of our three nations be seated on an elevated dais, but also at all plenary sessions."

"That is entirely unacceptable," General Key growled in a low, menacing tone. "We are every bit an equal with the political arm of the Party."

"I suggest you learn to live with it," the Minister snapped, dismissing Key's argument. "After all," he went on with a disdainful sniff, "by nature, those of the political *apparat* are truly superior in every aspect to the coarse, unfeeling military. This is to be represented by their raised position over you martial types."

"Damned striped-pants cretins," Key snarled at his adjutant, as the minister exited the general's office.

A trail of orange sparks arched into the black night sky at the outer perimeter of Firebase Loadstone. Seconds later a soft pop sounded and a blaze of harsh white light erupted as the trip wired flare ignited. It was the first warning of the NVA assault. A Green Beret on duty began to crank the handle of a siren mounted beside the command bunker. Moments later, claymore mines began to detonate. Screaming as much to build their courage as to intimidate the enemy, the North Vietnamese soldiers charged the reestablished concertina wires.

That set off another series of land mines. Gouts of dirt erupted into the night air and the heavy machine guns of the artillery unit opened up. A Special Forces sergeant with an M128 flame generator hosed down the first NVA troops to throw themselves on the wire to provide a human bridge for their comrades. To a man, they died screaming, their bodies engulfed in fire.

More died as two M60 machine guns began to fire in five-round bursts, traversing the killing field with mechanical precision. They worked precisely as Anchor Head had intended. While they did their job, the plan of Anchor Head Sturgis, as refined by Captain Kevin Morgan, went into operation. Their exit covered by the guns of the Special Forces troops and the Hre CIDG strikers, the artillerymen left the compound on a marginally watched side.

Screened by the CIDG troops, the soldiers quickly crossed the open ground to the inner wire, there to wait for the Special Forces troopers and the SEALs. Behind them, preset demolition charges blasted with painful volume. They destroyed the heavier equipment that could not be taken out. Captain Morgan insisted that a part of his force be the last to leave. "A matter of honor," was how he'd put it.

"I can live with that," Anchor Head had responded without hesitation. Hell, this was Morgan's base the captain was abandoning to the enemy.

Now, Anchor Head and three of his squad slithered past the wire and the bare no man's land between it and the outer concertina. There they oriented themselves and set off for predetermined locations in the nearer screen of jungle. Dallas Goracke was first to reach his target.

Moving slowly so as not to draw attention from the NVA sentry posted like two others to keep watch on this side of the base while the attack was carried out, Tex Goracke raised the suppressed M22 Smith and Wesson and shot the Vietnamese soldier in his left ear. A sizable chunk of the right side of the dead man's head blew outward when the slow-moving bullet exploded shortly after impact and tore through bone and tissue. Goracke and Welby had each been given a box of "special" ammunition for this mission by Jason Slater. The CIA man had neglected to inform them that the slugs were a type of explosive hollow points, their cavities filled with fulminate of mercury and sealed with wax. Dallas Goracke grimaced slightly and then signaled that he had eliminated his target.

Each of the SEALs wore infrared night vision goggles and so Tex had no doubt that Anchor Head saw his thumbs-up gesture. Without waiting for an acknowledgment, Goracke moved off toward the trail that would be used to clear the area.

Off to the right of Tex Goracke, Little Pete Peterson crouched low as he moved in on a bored watcher. With all of the action going on elsewhere, the North Vietnamese had quickly become bored when darkness arrived and he could no longer see movement in the firebase. In scant seconds, he would pay the price for his inattention.

Little Pete struck with the swiftness of a cobra. One muscular arm whipped forward and encircled the NVA soldier's neck. The other pumped furiously, first into one kidney, then the other. Quivering in Pete's grasp, the stabbed man could only suck in a great gush of air as the intense pain washed through his body. His shuddering ended at the count of forty seconds. The inhalation burst outward as though expelling his very soul and he went rigid for a moment before collapsing like a wet blanket. Little Pete gave a thumbs up in the direction of Anchor Head and he too moved out for the designated trail.

Anchor Head Sturgis nodded his satisfaction. Two down and only his to deal with. *Whoever commanded the NVA troops must have a genuine hard-on for that firebase*, he mused, as he listened to the fury of enemy fire above and behind him. No matter. He'd win this time, only it would prove a hollow victory. *God, he must be high on something,* Sturgis thought. *He never talked fancy like that. Hollow victory, my ass.*

A moment later, the sound of 40mm grenades from Special Forces M79s rang clearly across the bare mountain top, the signal that the withdrawal had been completed. Anchor Head rose up out of the underbrush and shot his target in the chest, tearing a jagged hole in the aorta before it splashed the right ventricle of the heart.

CHAPTER 17 ─────────────────

JET LAG had caught up to Marino and Waters with a vengeance as they waited at an otherwise empty loading gate at Stapleton International in Denver for yet another change of aircraft. Lieutenant Marino glanced balefully at the ticket in his left hand.

"Next stop, Chicago," he announced glumly, with no effort to stifle the prodigious yawn that erupted immediately after.

"Yeah," the chief agreed. "Only to change again and fly to New York."

Marino covered the last of his yawn with a hand. "At least we go by land from there."

"You'd think they'd have scheduled in a stopover somewhere, right, Pope? We're gonna look like hell when we get to the White House."

"Yeah," Pope Marino quipped, "what's the President going to think of us? We're sure going to make lousy examples of sailors, let alone SEALs."

Other passengers began to wander in and their talk shifted from the reality of their situation to inconsequentials, such as team rankings. From New Jersey, Tonto Waters was naturally a Yankees fan. Pope Marino from Pennsylvania, favored the Pirates.

"Yer both fulla hot air," a gregarious fellow traveler interrupted to observe. "The Dodgers have it all wrapped up

178

this year. Wait an' see. They'll win the Pennant and the Series.''

"Says you," Waters retorted.

"Yeah, says I. I oughtta know. I'm their defensive coach.''

That settled the matter so far as the two SEALs were concerned. So far removed from the World for so long, they would soon be out of their depth in any discussion of current sports data. "You ever take in a hockey game?" Marino asked his companion.

"Naw. Just a bunch of guys on ice skates and a crowd so noisy in a confined building you couldn't hear anything that's going on. Give me football anytime," responded Waters. He rose abruptly. "I think we've got time for another cup of coffee."

"Make mine a double Scotch, rocks," Marino offered.

"If you're buyin', I'll take one, too," Watson said through a laugh.

At that hour they found the bar empty. When the bartender served them and withdrew a discreet distance, talk went back to their itinerary. "The Company will have a field officer meet us in New York," Marino repeated to Waters for the fifth time since their initial briefing by Jason Slater.

Fighting droopy eyes and a yawn of his own, Waters asked, "Why the involved run around?"

"Someone," opined Marino, "either among the President's men or in Christians in Action is exceedingly paranoid. They see an enemy everywhere."

Recalling what they had witnessed in San Diego, Waters remarked, "Considering the close collaboration between the TV people and the pcacc pukes, that doesn't sound very paranoid to me."

"American Airlines Flight number two-three-zero for Chicago is now boarding passengers at Gate nineteen," came an announcement that precluded a reply by Marino. The two SEALs downed their drinks and headed back to the loading gate.

*   *   *

In the heavy drape-shrouded study of the small villa he rented, Pyotr Rudinov entertained his superior in the KGB. It was not a welcome visit, Colonel Rudinov admitted to himself, yet the vodka brought by General Ludvinov was appreciated. Ludvinov spoke again, which drew Rudinov's attention away from the liquor.

"The primary responsibility for security at the meeting will be yours, naturally, Pyotr Maximovich."

"*Pozhalyista, tovarish!*" implored Colonel Rudinov, then repeated. "Please, Comrade, I would appreciate being spared the honor. I am concerned about the lack of professionalism on the part of the North Vietnamese government and the Army of the People's Republic. They are a little too enraptured with ideology. They seem to lack that policeman's instinct and craftiness that so often points to any possible threat."

Ludvinov sighed his agreement. "You will have to make the most of it."

"Ya gotta admit, these blanketheads are good at noise discipline. An' they don't smoke in the field," Anchor Head Sturgis whispered grudgingly to Long Tom Killian during a brief rest break.

They had made three klicks away from the firebase before pausing here in the jungle. By Anchor Head's figuring, they had to do at least ten more before holing up for three hours' rest. So far, he had no complaints from either the Special Forces men or their CIDG strikers. It was those dog-faces in the artillery outfit that gave him the ass.

Buncha crybabies and whiners is how Anchor Head saw them. Not that any of them were blubbering, or anything like that. But they complained mightily about blisters on their feet, the lack of cold water, and the pace set by Anchor Head's point man.

On the move again, Captain Morgan marched at Sturgis' side. More a brisk walk than a march step, their gait covered ground at a satisfactory rate. Anchor Head had no doubt that when the NVA found the firebase deserted, they would waste little time in putting out patrols to locate which direction had been taken by the Americans. They were headed southeast on a bearing of 130 degrees, which would carry them sometime the next day into friendly territory. Even so, they would have the VC to contend with. Which reminded Sturgis of something.

"Captain, have your troops secured everything that can make noise with black tape?"

"Oh, yes, Quartermaster. I even had them go among the artillery people and get them secured."

"That's good thinkin', sir. 'Cause the fuckin' VC can be all around us. Those little brown men in black pajamas usually don't come out during the day, so we can make better time after sunrise and noise discipline won't be so critical. Until then, we gotta keep it quiet . . . *real* quiet."

Morgan immediately got the drift of Sturgis' comment. "I'll take it up with Colonel Dotson right away. He's behind us a ways."

"Limpin' along with the rest of his doggies. No disrespect for the Army, sir, they *are* our brother service, but . . ." Anchor Head added with transparent insincerity.

"If we didn't have to keep it quiet, I'd laugh, Sturgis. There's some among us—blanketheads, do you call us? who don't think Sneaky Pete is a part of the Army. Or rather, that *we are* the Army. Us and the Rangers, that is."

"I understand, sir. Elite troops tend to see themselves as somethin' apart. Like the rest of the Navy is only there to move *us* from Point A to Point B."

"You got that right, sailor." Then, as though echoing Anchor Head's thoughts, he asked, "Do you think those NVA are on our trail by now?"

"I would imagine so," Anchor Head responded without hesitation. "If not, they'll come on at first light."

The colonel was furious. Unlike him, Lieutenant Gao Hip was not angry. He was deeply disappointed that they had failed to capture even a single American soldier. Worse, all of the valuable artillery pieces were destroyed, along with the radios and generators, the meteorological equipment, and the water refinement plant. *Scorched earth*.

Lieutenant Hip had heard the term before. He had never experienced it until now. Where were the Americans? He badly wanted to confront them, come into contact in an environment in which they did not have the advantage in equipment, technology, and weapons. In other words, face-to-face in the jungle. Through his company commander, Hip had made a request to speak with the battalion commander. He stood now before the furious major, who reflected the attitude of the regimental commander.

"Do I understand this correctly, Comrade Lieutenant? You are volunteering your platoon for the task of locating the route of retreat taken by the cowardly Americans and pursuing them as the spearhead of our entire force?"

"Yes, Comrade Major. I shall do so most assiduously. We have lost enough face for the rest of our lives. I would be honored to have the privilege of regaining some of that face for the People's Socialist Republic."

"An admirable outlook, Comrade Lieutenant. Ummm, yes, I see no impediment to your pursuit of the Americans. You will be provided with three types of radio. Each has a separate frequency and different range. Use them as needed. The moment you discover what trail they took out of here, contact my headquarters. Use the call sign 'Sunrise Valor' for yourself, and 'Seeking Dragon' for this command."

"As you order, Comrade Major. I am overwhelmed with gratitude for this chance to do my share in redeeming our honor."

Twenty minutes after sunrise, Lieutenant Gao Hip received the call he had been expecting from one of his squads. "Sunrise Valor, this is Valor Three. We have found what you seek."

"Excellent," responded Hip. "How do we find you?"

"There is a trail from where you are at the base along a compass reading of a hundred thirty degrees. We are a kilometer along that trail. Many people have been over this trail recently."

"You are to be commended, Comrade Sergeant."

"But sir, I am only a corporal."

"Not anymore. I will see that the commander of our Joyful Strength Company affirms your promotion. We will join you in minutes."

After their rest period, the SEALs led the troops southeast again. They made better time in daylight, albeit the column tended to spread out more than during the night. Anchor Head noted that and summoned Mickey Mouse Norton and Tex Goracke.

"We've gotta keep these people closed up. Mouse, you an' Tex here drop back and move the rear of the column along a little faster."

Twenty minutes later, the soldiers and their SEAL escort were no longer strung out along the trail and moved more as a unit. Captain Morgan caught up with Sturgis. "When do you figure we will link up with your people?"

Anchor Head paused only a moment before answering. "I reckon we'll join them around midnight, Captain. From here on it'll be a cakewalk."

A moment later, as though to mock him, a silent signal flashed down the line from the point man: *Enemy in sight!*

"What the hell?" Sturgis muttered under his breath. Stealthily he worked his way forward to where Long Tom Killian crouched in the bush. The squad leader put his lips up close to Killian's ear. "What we got here?"

Long Tom turned and addressed Sturgis in the same manner. "Damn near stepped right on top of 'em. There's about fifteen Cong out there in an open box ambush. If I hadn't spotted their flankers, I'd have walked right into it."

"Hold what you've got, we'll take care of it," Anchor Head promised, as he made ready to slide back along the route of march.

He went directly to Captain Kevin Morgan and explained the situation. "Are we going to have to go around it?" asked the Special Forces officer.

"Naw, we've got enough bodies to handle fifteen VC,

Cap'n. What we need to do is turn the ambush back on them.
It'd be nice to get some people behind them.''

"Yeah, but how?" asked Morgan, then an idea bloomed
in his quick mind. Quietly he went among his CIDG Hre
tribesmen and selected four whom he knew to be adept at
subterfuge. "Now, here's what I want you to do. Uh—Sturgis." He turned to Anchor Head. "Do you think you can
lend a couple of these men a pair of suppressed weapons?"

From his position at the center of the ambush, the Viet Cong
known as Xi Bao watched as four Montagnards approached
along the trail. They wore the traditional loincloth of their
people and chattered noisily as they gathered windfall
branches for either sale or a future cook fire. They appeared
to be alone and Bao waited to verify that. He knew it would
be disastrous to make their presence known to these mountain folk. They were somewhat far from their usual territory,
Bao thought, as the Montagnards drew closer. But then the
fighting had dislocated a lot of people.

Better to let them pass unaware and unmolested, Bao decided. He signaled his comrades and the ambushers went to
ground. With the M22s concealed in their diaper-like loincloths, the young Hre men looked harmless enough as they
gathered more deadfall and walked through the hidden line
of VC.

Unseen by Bao and his fellow Cong, the SEALs and Special Forces troopers, interspersed with the artillery unit,
spread out ready to assault the unsuspecting ambushers. Acting oblivious to the danger around them, the Hre cleared the
immediate area, their voices fading as they progressed down
the trail.

Silence returned to the clearing that fronted on the ambush
site. Bao fingered the handset of the radio which had brought
them word of the Americans. Should he report the presence
of the Montagnards? The distant sounds of machete blows
and breaking vegetation took his mind from that problem and
set his adrenaline flowing.

Gradually, individual voices could be distinguished, although Bao and the others could not understand the words spoken. They grew louder. Bao tensed; he would be the first to fire and trigger the ambush. He saw a blur of motion at the edge of the jungle across from him. Xi Bao tightened his grip on his Type 56 carbine and eased the safety off onto single fire.

A fraction of a second before his finger tightened on the trigger, a soft chuffing sound came from behind him. The crack of his Chinese-made weapon sounded cataclysmic in contrast. He lurched forward, eyes bulging as a 9mm slug exited through his left cheekbone. Three more swift coughs announced the return of the Montagnards.

At once, the Hre tribesmen dropped to the ground as a hailstorm of full metal jackets cracked overhead. Confused and off balance, the VC found themselves leaderless and the target rather than the shooters. Two Cong screamed as hot copper-clad rounds ripped through their bellies. One of the flankers turned outward to find himself facing a hideous apparition, a man with a green and black face. A snarl cut an ugly red gash where the mouth should be and not a sound came as the SEAL who wore the fierce expression struck with a powerful buttstroke that broke the jaw of the VC and slammed him to the ground unconscious and bleeding.

Not all of the Cong in the ambush lost their heads. Two of them shifted their fire selectors to full-auto and cut off short, disciplined bursts. One of the Green Berets went down with a bullet through the meaty part of his shoulder, another spun sideways as a round popped him in the belly, fortunately missing anything vital before it exited through his back. A gunner in the artillery outfit let go a piercing scream that cut short when his brain got the message that his heart had been blown apart.

For all of their controlled action under fire, the two VC paid dearly for their hits. One took four rounds from as many M16s and went down bleeding from two chest wounds, the back of his head blown off. The other took a 40mm projectile from an M79 grenade launcher in the gut and it literally shattered him. Viet Cong began to die rapidly in the brief, violent onslaught. As firing dwindled, Captain Morgan saw Anchor Head Sturgis standing over the final VC. A muffled burp came from the Swedish Carl Gustav in the SEAL's hands and the Cong jolted with the impact of the 9mm slugs.

"Not bad," Sturgis observed as he surveyed the killing field. VC three, us seventeen."

"Yeah," Morgan replied softly, suddenly very tired indeed. "Only one KIA on our side. Sergeant Gray. I knew him. He was a good kid."

"Shit happens, Captain."

"Right, Sturgis, only too right."

"We better get to humpin', sir. That firefight is gonna draw more of the Cong. We'll do five klicks an' then stop for chow. Can your wounded make it okay?"

"One's going to need to be carried. The other one is more pissed off than hurting. We bring out Gray, too."

"Damn right, sir. SEALs never leave anyone behind."

Morgan gave him a rigid thumb. "Boo-rah, Sturgis. And by God, I am going to go through channels and put you in for promotion to Chief."

For all his rough edges and unrefined language, Charlie Sturgis blushed. "Awh, hell, sir, don't do that. It'd take me away from my squad. Maybe even out of the platoon."

"It was your man who detected the ambush. I'll put you both in for a Bronze Star, at least."

"I ain't all that big on medals, sir, if it's all the same with you."

"No. It is a done deal as far as I'm concerned."

"Then we'd better put some distance between us an' these VC."

Captain Morgan readily agreed with that. He was aware of how intense the pain would be for the gut-shot man and the sergeant from one of his A Teams. He had refused treatment until his own medic had tended the newly wounded.

"Gotta change that field dressing, sir." He did it quickly and competently, then extended a hand to Kevin Morgan.

"Here, sir, take these."

"If I have to. But what is it?"

"Penicillin, sir."

"Damn, that makes me think I've flunked a short arms inspection and have to treat a dose of clap."

"You'd best do what he says, sir," Anchor Head made bold enough to say. "It's too easy to get an infection out here."

"Yeah, I know that. What do you give as odds that Charlie will catch up to us again?"

"Maybe three to five. No more than even odds, at best.

"Then lead on, McDuff."

" 'Into the valley of death,' sir?"

"No, that's Shakespeare."

CHAPTER 18 _____

A DIM yellow rectangle defined a window in the thatched palm wall of the small farmhouse. Raised on stilts, it had a roofed-over porch on three sides. Inside, Francie's Uncle Phan lowered the wick of the kerosene lamp and sighed softly. The boy, Thran, lay curled up asleep on a mat beside the table. Phan worried about him. He worried also about his niece.

Francie was involved in something dangerous. He knew that as surely as he knew the ways of the hogs he raised. It troubled him that she worked for the Americans. He did not believe for a moment Francie's story that she had to go to Saigon for a training course. There had been fear in her eyes. In her posture and gestures, too. He saw the foreigners as allies, but did not trust their different ways. They did not seem to respect their elders. Nor did they give proper thought to what words they spoke. Often, what they said was hurtful or insulting. Which brought him back to his concerns over Francie. Suddenly he stiffened. Had he heard someone under the house?

Perhaps one of his pigs had gotten out of the fenced-in hooch where he kept them. The first place they usually went was under the floorboards. He would have to go out and see in a minute. He hacked to clear his throat and spat into a chamberpot in one corner of the larger room attached to the central kitchen and living area.

Unseen by Phan, three short, dark figures ran away from under his house and the two outbuildings. Moments later flames erupted in the pigpen and the storage shed, followed by a *whoosh* and flare-up beneath the house. Phan smelled smoke immediately, and as the fire ate into the dry thatch walls, felt the heat. Swiftly he ran to his sleeping wife.

"Nimh! Nimh! Wake up. There is fire. Hurry."

Next he went to the boy. "Thran! There is a fire. Get up."

Thran woke with a start and heard the frantic squealing of the doomed pigs. With a sob he threw his arms around his uncle. Together they ran from the blazing building, Nimh ahead of them. Their shouts of alarm brought satisfied smiles to the faces of the three men in the darkness along the narrow trail that connected the farm to the nearby village.

The darkly tinted windows of a big, sturdy Chrysler station wagon prevented anyone from seeing details of those inside. It swung to a gate that gave access to the West Portico of the White House. There it halted, although the driver did not get out. One of the rear passenger side doors swung wide and three men climbed from the seat. The one in a neatly tailored suit led the way to an open gate in a low wrought-iron picket fence.

In stark contrast, the two men he ushered through the opening looked rumpled and half-awake, like a pair of panhandlers outside a liquor store. The fashion plate gestured downward and followed them down a short, steep set of steps that led to a door at the base of the big building.

"The War Room?" Lieutenant Marino asked.

Their escort said nothing. He used a key card to open the door and gestured for them to enter. Inside two capable agents gave the SEALs a thorough search.

"If you're lookin' for weapons, we didn't bring any," complained Chief Tom Waters, resentful of the over-zealous security procedures.

"What about a bomb?" asked one of the Secret Service types going over their persons, which was more than had been said by the CIA field officer who had met them in New York, and the nearest to any attempt at humor on anyone's part.

"Yeah, it's right up my rear."

CIA gave him a scowl. "Don't make jokes. These guys will take you seriously and you'll end up with a strip search."

"He does talk, after all," Marino quipped, his personal dislike of most of the spook clan rising to the surface.

"Over there to the elevator. The President is awaiting you in the Oval Office," directed one of the Secret Service agents.

"You're not coming along?" asked Marino.

"No. You will be met by another agent." He paused, then made a face. "The President has demanded that he see you alone with the deputy director for Operations."

Marino raised a hand in a deprecating gesture. "The Super Spook, eh?"

"We—ah—tend to avoid such terms of reference, Mr. Green."

They had been given false names when they arrived in New York, different ones than those used on their variety of airline tickets. Marino had become "Mr. Green," and Waters was "Mr. White." They forbore any conversation while the aged elevator groaned them upward to the second floor. There another agent escorted them down a hallway and stopped to open a door.

An attractive middle-aged woman sat at a desk in a small anteroom. She looked up as the door opened. "Mr. Green? Mr. White? The President will see you now."

The Secret Service looked uncomfortable as the President's secretary conducted the visitors to another, larger door. Beyond it, Marino and Waters found themselves in the most famous and familiar room in the world. Past the curved windows a screen of trees was clearly visible, as were clusters of manicured shrubs. The view was slightly distorted by the thickness of the bulletproof glass.

Brightness distorted the large figure seated at the huge

desk. When the President rose and walked toward them, his hand extended, his features became recognizable.

"Welcome, gentlemen. Have you met Preston Adams? He's deputy director for Operations at the CIA."

"Mr. Green. Mr. White. Nice to meet you."

"Sir, if it's all the same with you," Carl Marino addressed the President, "do we have to keep up this phony name thing? I have no doubt that this is a secure office."

"It is for a lot of things, Mr. Green. But Preston has assured me that the KGB has parabolic mikes that can pick up conversation right through a closed window."

"Even armor glass, sir?"

"We think so," Adams interjected. "At least it is not wise to assume the contrary."

"Very well. Is it possible to close the drapes, Mr. President?"

The President nodded and Adams let go a short bark of laughter. "And they call people in *my* business paranoid."

Without waiting for a White House staffer to enter and accomplish the task, Tom Waters stepped to the nearly floor-to-ceiling windows and pulled aside a panel of the gathered drapes. A puzzled frown bloomed on his face when he found no pull cord. Quick as ever, the President correctly identified his difficulty.

"They are motorized, Mr. White. The switch is right there."

A low hum filled the Oval Office as Waters activated the switch. Slowly the long, thick blue drapes glided across the expanse of armor glass, darkening the room. When they ceased their traverse, the presidential seal was picked out in the proper colors in the exact center. Preston Adams stepped to one of the paneled walls next to the door and touched a pressure plate.

Soft, indirect lighting illuminated the Oval Office from recessed sconces midway up the walls. The President returned to his desk. "Now then, gentlemen, let's get down to it. How many men are we talking about committing to this operation?"

"On the ground, one SEAL platoon, Mr. President," Pope answered.

"Twelve men and two officers, right?"

"Yes, sir."

"You said on the ground. What else is involved in this?"

"We need a distraction to cover our infiltration. We will be inserted by air, and an air raid would be nice."

"You mean bomb Hanoi?"

"Yes, sir, that is exactly what I mean."

"Well, hell, that's exactly what I've been pushing for the past week, isn't it, Preston?"

Adams chuckled softly. "Yes, it is, Mr. President."

The long, narrow face and lengthy nose turned on Marino. "You really think we should do it that way?"

"Navy pilots?"

"No, sir," Marino did not even hesitate to respond. "My scenario calls for a HAELO insertion. We'll use the new Paracommander 'chutes and jump from a B-52."

"Can you do that?"

"Yes, sir, I believe we can. Just has to be worked out."

"How many do you expect to lose?"

"None, sir," Marino answered soberly.

"Is that possible? I mean, considering where you'll be and the immediate tactical, not to mention strategic, advantage of the enemy?"

"Yes, sir, it is."

The President hadn't finished as yet. "Normal attrition rates would dictate a loss of at least ten percent."

Marino looked him in the eye. "Mr. President, a ten percent rate of attrition is considered an unmitigated defeat to a SEAL, sir."

Chief Tom Waters listened to this exchange with a growing appreciation. The president's questions indicated his knowledge of the situation and his grasp of military realities. Tonto mused that he would hate to be the bureaucrat who tried to bullshit this president.

"Perhaps Chief Waters could explain it better. After all," Marino admitted freely, "it's the chiefs who run the Navy."

"I know what you mean, Lieutenant. Please, go on and lay it out for us, Chief."

"Like Po—er—like the lieutenant said, sir, we would insert by HAELO during a bombing raid by B-52s."

"The Air Force will cooperate in this?" the President asked, intrigued.

"Oh, yes, sir. We have already liaised with them on it. And they want to bomb Hanoi again so bad they can taste it. They're eager for it."

"Go on, please."

"Once on the ground four of our people, our snipers and demolition specialists, will break off and set up for further diversions. The remaining ten will set off for the travel routes for the prisoners being moved from the Hilton."

"How will you know where these prisoners are, if there are indeed any?"

Waters glanced to Adams. "Blackbird and U-2 overflights, right?"

The CIA deputy director of Operations nodded. "If they are moving those people there will have to be communication between point and point and the vehicles. We can have ELINT tags on them almost the first time one of them opens up."

"And we would be provided with these routes and the volume of traffic in advance?"

"Right, through your station chief where you are located. Radio contact can be used once the operation is in motion."

"Okay, so it is our thinking that we make the bigwigs at this three-nation meeting think that they are the main target of our attack."

"By what means, Chief? I understand the air raid. But we can't do it around the clock until you make contact with the prisoners, free them, and get them out."

"The snipers will remove several select targets among the delegates, explosive packages will be distributed around the building where the meetings are held. Trip-wire mines and shaped charges will also be employed. That part takes some refining, but we can be sure of the general shape of how we keep the Vietnamese off balance.''

The president nodded thoughtfully as Waters outlined their plans. ''Is that all? How do we get out anyone you rescue?''

''Now's the time for the Navy. Or at least the Marine Corps. We'll chopper them out from inside North Vietnam.''

''I see. Well then, there appears to be only one factor still a problem with me. Which is, is there enough time to train for the operation?''

''Oh, yes, sir,'' Tonto Waters assured him. ''It's actually nothing we haven't done before. There's even a training scenario we have all been through for termination operations within the city of Hanoi.''

The president shot a nervous glance to Adams. ''Does he mean what I think he does?''

Preston Adams hid a grin behind one hand as he replied, ''Oh, yes, I think he does. But I didn't hear anything, did you?''

''No, you're right about that. We heard nothing.'' Although shaken by this discovery, the president made up his mind. ''I am going to give my approval to the mission. I think that because of the inter-service shifting of phase responsibility and the use of sleight of hand to confuse the enemy it is entirely appropriate to name the operation ''Shell Game.'' Thank you gentlemen for coming. You have certainly eased my mind.'' *And shaken it up some*, he added in his thoughts. ''Your transportation will be waiting at the east portico. Good luck.''

Marino and Waters came smartly to their feet. Dressed in civilian clothing they did not render a salute to their commander in chief, but their posture implied one. They left the room briskly, elated over what the future promised.

Once again on point, Long Tom Killian signaled to Anchor Head Sturgis shortly before sunset. A village in sight, his hand signs relayed. Sturgis came forward to study the situation. Bad time to stumble onto a village, he reflected: Charlie is about to come out to play. What were the odds that there were no Cong in this village? Anchor Head made a quick decision.

He returned to where Captain Morgan and Lieutenant Colonel Dotson waited. Quickly he explained the situation and gave his evaluation of what they might face. Immediately Lieutenant Colonel Dotson expressed his opinion.

"We can't be sure of the loyalties of the villagers. I say we had better find out if they are Cong sympathizers before entering the village, if at all. I think our only choice is to skirt the village, bypass it through the jungle."

"If your people . . ." Captain Morgan began, then cut off his intended criticism, although QM/1C Sturgis knew well what he intended to say about noise discipline.

"If my people what, Captain?"

Kevin Morgan smoothly changed gears. "If your people feel up to it, we have the firepower and the numbers. A show of force might cow them especially if they are VC."

"D'you think we could get your Hres to go in and sound out the locals?" Anchor Head asked.

Morgan shook his head. "Wouldn't work. These lowland people distrust and fear the mountain warriors."

Sturgis thought a moment again. "Screw it. You're right, Cap'n, we got the fire superiority, and the numbers. If everyone looks as bad-ass as they can, we can pull this off. I say we go right through the village."

"I'm with you. Colonel?" Morgan inquired of the artillery commander.

Dotson sighed. "I'll withhold open objection to the plan. And I'll tell my men to try to look as hard and mean as you SEALs and the Green Beanies here."

"You might," suggested Sturgis, on the verge of laughing in the face of the timid officer, "recommend they smear some cammo stick on their faces. It'll help."

Ten minutes later, Tom Killian, at point, entered the village. Silent throngs of residents streamed into the open space created by the juncture of the trail and the only cross street in the vil. Suspicious glances, looks of fear, and confusion

met the Americans as more and more of them cautiously
entered the village. Weapons at the ready, constantly alert,
they progressed to a point where the trail widened into a sort
of central square. There an elderly man, dressed in a
Western-style suit, with a fedora on his head, stepped forward.

"*Amérique?*" he asked hesitantly.

To the surprise of Anchor Head, Captain Morgan stepped
forward. "*Oui. Nous son soldats d'Americains,*" he declared
in flawless French, declaring them to be American soldiers.

Surprised pleasure, and a hint of relief flooded the old
man's face. He raised his arms and turned a full circle, declaring to all of the villagers, "They are American soldiers.
They are Americans!"

In brief seconds the tension abandoned the scene. The
people applauded the visitors, some rushed to bring refresh-
ment and offer stools and rickety chairs for them to sit and
rest. They chattered among themselves cheerfully and rapidly
in their own tongue, while some exercised old French grown
rusty from lack of recent use to address the welcome Americans.

"Do you play soccer?" some small boys asked Dallas
Goracke.

"Do you know baseball?" others inquired of Archie
Golden.

Archie, who also spoke French replied to their queries.
"No. I'm too short. But I am a Knicks fan."

A festive mood broke out in moments as the soldiers were
made welcome. Food and drink were pressed on the visitors,
including the ubiquitous Bahmibah beer. The entire popula-
tion of the village appeared to be genuinely happy to see
these allies—everyone except for two, that is, who slipped
silently into the bush and headed away from the village.

CHAPTER 19 _____

MARINO AND Watson, riding in a different car, passed a movie house in Virginia. They were on their way to National Airport, to take a flight to Atlanta, and from thence to Dallas, Phoenix, Los Angeles *ad nauseam* like their inbound journey. Tonto looked up and gestured to the marquee.

JOHN WAYNE
Starring in *The Green Berets*

"Look at that, will you? They get all the good press," Tonto complained.

Pope Marino looked at him with raised eyebrow. "You'd rather *we* got the spotlight?"

Tonto Waters considered that. "No, not really."

Marino checked the diver's watch strapped to his wrist. "The way I make it, we'll be back home in time for noon chow."

"Yeah," Waters observed, "tomorrow."

Elsewhere in Virginia, not 40 miles from where Pope and Tonto rode to their homeward flight, Betty Welby drove her convertible somewhat erratically along State 17 on the edge of Norfolk, headed toward the Causeway. Sudden confusion washed over her as a glitter of red and blue lights reflected into her eyes from the rearview mirror.

Automatically, Betty pulled into the right lane and continued on her way. It took a short growl of siren to make her realize that the police wanted her to stop. *Whatever for?* she wondered.

"Good morning, ma'am," the tall, lean, clean-shaven traffic officer addressed her as he stepped to the driver's side. He wore a light blue uniform with dark blue pocket flaps and epaulettes. His chrome-plated nametag read: "Sanford."

"W-what's the matter, Officer? Was I speeding?"

Virginia State Patrolman Larry Sanford ran fingers through the curly blond hair over one ear. "No, ma'am. May I see your licence and registration, please?"

"Certainly, but what for? If I wasn't speeding, why did you stop me?"

Patrolman Sanford remained silent while Betty dug into her purse to retrieve her driver's license. From the holder on the sun visor she produced the registration. The officer studied them both, made notations on his clipboard, and stepped back to his car. After transmitting the details on the documents to the dispatcher, he returned.

"Please," Betty began, even before he reached her. "I would like to know why you stopped me."

In his youthful good looks, Sanford actually seemed embarrassed by his answer. "You seemed to be having difficulty keeping in one lane, Mrs. Welby." He had noticed her rings and also the musty odor of alcohol on her breath.

"Why—I—I don't understand. Perhaps it is because I was up rather late last night. I'm still drowsy."

Radio static crackled from the patrol car and the officer excused himself. He returned with the information that there were no wants nor warrants for Elizabeth Welby. Still certain that she was intoxicated at only 9 o'clock in the morning, he asked her to step from the car.

"But, why? I don't understand."

"Ma'am, I think you might be otherwise impaired, rather than simply sleepy."

"Are you sha—saying I'm drunk?"

"Not at this point, ma'am. I just want you to take a simple

field test to verify or disprove that you are under the influence. Step back here behind your car, please.''

In a quick minute and a half, Sanford took her through the standard field sobriety test. Betty passed the alphabet routine easily enough, and with eyes closed, touched her nose with alternating forefinger tips. She utterly failed the heel-to-toe walk and the head-back-and-stand-on-one-foot.

''I've always had a balance problem,'' she attempted to explain away her deficiency. ''Really, I have. I could never play tennis well because of it.''

Patiently Officer Sanford explained what was in store. ''Mrs. Welby, you have scored only fifty percent on a standard field sobriety test. Our procedures are clear on this. I'm going to ask you to submit to a Breathalyzer test.''

Betty paled, her eyes suddenly wild and evasive. ''No, I cannot. Don't you understand?'' She peered at his name tag. ''Officer Sandborn, I am subject to dizziness, loss of balance.''

''It's Sanford, ma'am. Virginia law requires that if you refuse to submit to a Breathalyzer test, you can be detained for up to twelve hours and your driver's license suspended for up to a year. Do you have anyone who can come to the station to pick you up and to claim your car from the impound lot?''

''I can't take that test. You have to look at it from my point of view. I'm the wife of a naval . . .'' she started to lie and say ''officer,'' but refrained at the last moment. ''Of a SEAL,'' Betty concluded.

At first Larry Sanford thought she had lapsed into an alcoholic delusion, then he recalled the hush-hush Navy special warfare outfit stationed at Little Creek, near the Norfolk Naval Station. It figured, the conduct of the family members would reflect on such guys. They had to have security clearances up the wazoo. For a moment he debated writing her a warning and seeing her safely off the highway to a parking lot and calling a cab. It was a common practice. Then Betty's anxiety, fear, and early too-heavy consumption of vodka caught up to her and she bent over to heave wretchedly, spewing the contents of her stomach, mostly bile and liquor, onto the macadam surface of Highway 17 and the spit-shined black shoes of Patrolman Sanford.

When she had subsided, Sanford stepped forward and touched her lightly on one shoulder. "I'm sorry, ma'am, but I would like you to step over here, to the front of my cruiser. That's right. Now, put out your hands and lean forward and rest them against the hood. Good." He performed a quick search, certain he would find nothing incriminating or dangerous to himself, while regretting the necessity of this move. It was for her own safety and that of others, he told himself.

His search completed, Sanford produced a pair of cuffs and, relenting to her obvious humiliation, and somewhat to her good looks, violated regulations and cuffed her hands in front so she could sit comfortably. Then he helped her into the rear of his patrol car. Only after he pulled away did Betty begin to sob piteously.

Tired from a long working day, Francie left the base at Tre Noc with thoughts of a long, hot soak. The stair treads creaked as always as she climbed wearily toward her apartment. Inside she sighed, looked around in a forlorn way, missing Thran terribly. She walked slowly into the bedroom and bent to grasp the hem of her dress.

The garment had only ridden over the pert swell of her finely molded breasts when a soft knock sounded at the door. She drew off the dress and shrugged into a robe. Barefoot now, in anticipation of the communal bath on the shaded roof of her building, she crossed the woven matting to respond. When she opened the door it revealed her uncle and son.

"Thran! Oh, my darling, I so missed you." She could not restrain that, but gathered herself to look up at Thran and ask, "What?"

"There was a fire," the older man said. "It was not an accident. Someone set it. It is not safe for Thran at the farm."

Francie could not accept that. "It is not safe for him here, I told you that."

"It is safer than out in the country. Here are many friendly eyes to see that no harm comes to the boy."

"What 'harm,' *Maman*," asked Thran, using the French word for momma.

She drew the eight-year-old to her and held him close, stroking his hair. "Something . . . unpleasant could happen. But I want to spare you the details. I was just getting ready for a long, hot bath. Do you wish to join me?"

Thran looked eager. "Oh, yes, *Maman*. It has been so long and we are hot and dusty."

"Of course, Phan, you are welcome to stay. You can spend the night on the chaise."

"It is a pleasant thought, the family together. But I cannot. Nimh has secured a room at the hotel. She is downstairs waiting for me."

That surprised Francie on two counts. There were only ten rooms in the hotel and they were usually full. Also, although Nimh had never been overtly approving of Francie and her determination to become Westernized and raise Thran accordingly, she had never been so openly hostile as to refuse hospitality. She pushed back her concerns and thanked Phan. After her uncle had departed, her brave front dissolved enough to allow doubts to rush in.

What could she do? Where could she turn? Kentwelby was gone off somewhere, no way to reach him. Was Yates really trying to kill Thran? Or was he only threatening her? Tomorrow she would have to find out what she could do to protect Thran in any condition. Desperately she clutched Thran to her until she recovered her composure. Then she gave him a huge smile.

"Go along, get out of your clothes and we'll spend a long time in the bath."

Lieutenant Junior Grade Wally Ott sweated his way through the jungle. Still two hours to sundown, and the heat had only intensified. Inevitably, so had the humidity. He had been in contact with QM/1C Sturgis by radio earlier in the day. The range had been at the maximum. Anchor Head had given him bad news.

"Say again your coordinates?" Sturgis had asked. Ott gave them and silence followed. Then Sturgis came back. "Not so good. Based on where we are, we won't likely link up until early morning. You can forget a midnight waltz."

"Is everyone all right out there?"

"Yeah. One walking wounded and one in a stretcher, but everything's boiling along. Only thing, we got more people with us than anticipated."

"Why's that? Over."

"Never could get choppers in to evacuate the doggies. We got a couple of companies of them along, with the Blanketheads and their CIDG strikers."

"Wonderful."

"Yeah. I'm underwhelmed. We better get off the horn before Charlie or the NVA get a fix. Bravo-one out."

Which left Wally Ott with a quandary. He could not move Alpha along any faster due to possible exposure to an unseen enemy. Quiet and darkness were their allies. Nothing for it but to keep trying.

Much larger in size, and far cruder in manufacture and technology, the radios provided by the Soviet Union to the North Vietnamese, and disseminated downward to the Viet Cong, worked properly only part of the time. Static usually obliterated part of every message. Lack of solid state technology in abundance to share with their lesser client states meant the Soviet radios supplied used vacuum tubes—delicate under the best of conditions, absolutely fragile in the mountain jungles and swamplands of Vietnam. Failures to transmit or receive were daily occurrences. As a result, alternative means of communication had to be devised and relied upon.

While radios tried vainly to reach Colonel Voy at his headquarters, moped mounted couriers sped outward from the local VC command post where the two deep-cover Viet Cong agents reported on the presence of the Americans in the village of Dong Da. Telephones played a part as well.

From the remote area around the village, these were Russian made, leather-cased field telephones, which also functioned spottily. Closer to the largest city overwhelmed by the two regiments with Colonel Voy's spearhead, commercial instruments jangled stridently, their old-fashioned French design an anachronism amid all the implements of war. Within the invading units of the NVA, radio functioned normally. Especially those within the tanks and armored personnel carriers. The result was that the message received did not present a true picture of the American force.

Colonel Voy looked up furiously at his intelligence officer who had handed him the first contact report. "They have made that much progress?"

"Yes, that is what the courier informed us. Dong Da is over twenty-eight kilometers from the captured firebase. It is only a few short kilometers from a tributary of the Mekong that is navigable by the enemy's river patrol craft. Their—ah—PBRs."

"Which puts them that close to escaping us entirely. What is the composition and strength of this enemy force?"

"I believe, sir, that information is coming in as we speak. I shall return to my reconnaissance vehicle and learn the latest."

"Bring it to me at once."

Ten minutes later, Major Lao Nang returned. His face registered his concern. "The reports we have just' obtained indicate that the Americans are a hundred fifty to a hundred eighty strong, all Special Forces personnel. All heavily armed."

"Impossible!" snarled Voy, as he slammed a fist on the surface of a metal foldout table.

"Perhaps it is not those who fled the firebase. It could be a rescue force sent out to meet them. We need more information."

"Then get it. Facts, Comrade Nang, I need facts."

Voy drank lukewarm tea and stewed in his own frustration for half an hour. Maj. Lao Nang returned at that time, his face brightened by his encouraging news. "We have better contact and more reliable sources now, Comrade Colonel. For example, we know for a fact that the Americans came from the direction of the firebase. We also know that they are not more than eighty-five in number, most of them do not look like hardened combat infantry or elite Special Forces troops. Only one report makes this good news somewhat doubtful of its accuracy.

"This comes from a man who should know if any of the Viet Cong in the area would. He claims that there are Navy personnel with the Army troops. He says it is the Men with Green Faces, the Navy SEALs." Nung paused, frowned.

"They do not even share a common command structure."

"Never mind. I tend to believe the figure of the total number of enemy present. We can catch them and put an end to this insult to our superiority. Get my operations officer in here."

When the staff assembled, Voy announced his intentions. "We have water access to Dong Da. I want to dispatch three large sampans loaded with troops. At least a company to each. A fourth will provide mortar and machine gun support. They are to utterly crush these irritating insects."

The discussion lasted only a short while and the embarkation took less than an hour, much to the pleasure of Colonel Voy.

An hour and a half later, the sampans arrived at the indicated debarkation area. They offloaded their passengers and the troops quickly deployed. Two hours and ten minutes after leaving Colonel Voy's headquarters, his designated troops launched a surprise attack on the village.

Lieutenant (j.g.) Wally Ott turned to MA/1C Archie Golden. "I have a gut feeling that we should be on the move. There's something wrong out there, and the closer we get to Bravo Squad, the better off we will all be."

"No argument here, sir. We can cut down the time to link up by as many hours as we put on the trail starting now."

Ott nodded decisively. "Saddle 'em up, then, Archie."

"Aye, sir."

In an hour Alpha Squad had covered three klicks, despite the dense, clinging undergrowth. Zorro Agilar, at point, signaled a halt. Through his night vision goggles, Wally Ott watched Zorro raise his M16 above his head to signal "Enemy in Sight." Then he raised two fingers. Slowly Zorro swung one arm, first right, then left. *Two of them, one on each side of the trail*, Ott interpreted. He sent Archie forward to confer with Zorro.

"This is gonna be a cakewalk, *'mano*," Zorro advised. "They're in ambush position all right, but they're lookin' the wrong way."

"How's that?" Golden asked.

"They're watchin' the trail in the same direction we're goin'."

"We can just slip up there and waste 'em?" suggested Archie.

"Yeah, sure. Why not?"

"Positive there's only two?"

"Ummm, no, *'mano*, I'm not."

"What say you slide around one way and I'll go the other? See what we can find out first. Then, if they really are alone, we can take 'em out. Otherwise I'll bring up the squad."

In ten minutes they had returned to the trail near where Zorro had first sighted the Viet Cong. "I make it an El-shaped ambush," Archie declared.

"Yeah, that's the way I see it. Nine dinks out there. We gotta use the whole squad."

"Okay, but we gotta make it quiet." Archie returned to the rest of the squad and explained the situation.

Stealthily, Alpha Squad spread out to encircle the ambush. Kent Welby reasoned that the VC had been advised of Bravo Squad and the Special Forces people coming down the trail and were in place to ambush them. Too bad they didn't have all the intel they needed. Yeah . . . right.

Kent took the suppressed Browning HiPower from its over-large holster and eased a 9mm round into the chamber, careful to engage the slide lock. This would be easy. So long as no one made a noise before everybody was in position. He took a deep breath and edged forward. On his right, Wise Guy Santoro ghosted up behind his target, a large K-Bar knife at the ready in his hand.

Welby raised the Browning and sighted along the elevated sights that compensated for the bulk of the hushpuppy. The broad black-clad back of a Viet Cong filled the rear notch and Kent raised the point of aim until the dark blob of head under a rice straw conical hat brim came into focus, bisected by the front post. His finger tightened on the trigger.

Three other suppressed weapons fired a fraction of an instant apart as Welby discharged his own. In a flicker, Santoro circled one arm around the neck of his target and the other descended to plunge the knife into the Cong's chest. The tip slid off a rib and sank deeply through the intercostal muscle and into a heart suddenly accelerated by a jolt of alarm. In less than a full minute the ambush became a charnel house.

Only one Cong got off a shot, and that was fortunately from a suppressed Czech vz 61 Scorpion. Among the SEALs, only Bobby Santoro received an injury. He cut his thumb while pulling his K-Bar knife free of the body of the VC he killed.

"Put a dressing on that, Fil," Wally Ott told the platoon medic, HC/1C Filmore Nicholson. "Let's keep moving, guys. We've got a date with the Bravos."

CHAPTER 20 _____

WHEN THE first mortar round struck in the village, Anchor Head Sturgis rolled up onto his boots and stared into the darkness. "What the hell?" he wondered aloud.

"I'd say we were under attack," Captain Kevin Morgan answered in a droll tone.

"If you please, sir, I don't propose we stick around long enough to make a battle of it. Sounds like the regulars have caught up to us."

Morgan nodded approvingly. "Good. I'll get my people to form a rear guard and start Dotson's men on down the trail."

"Fine with me, sir. We'll be at point. I'd like to take all the Claymores your people have. We'll place them and your demo man can hook up those that cover the trail."

With quick, practiced efficiency, the 2 Special Forces teams engaged the two attacking NVA companies. Anchor Head sent Long Tom on point down the trail. After gathering the available antipersonnel mines, Brandon Mitchell, the squad demo man, went into the jungle on a line parallel to the trail, while Tex Goracke took the opposite side. Like the Special Forces troopers, SEALs are cross-trained in the skills of other team members, so Anchor Head had no doubts that their sniper would plant his Claymores in an effective manner.

YO/2C Dallas Goracke did not disappoint him. Backing

up the slightly curved Claymores with stout tree trunks, Goracke aimed them to cover the most logical routes of travel through the jungle that might be taken by NVA troops. He winced at the sounds emanating from the artillery outfit as the soldiers rushed by on the trail. There was little need for noise discipline when the enemy already engaged the rear guard, he rationalized. Within a minute and a half of stopping again, he was on the move once more, another mine in place. He noticed that he had caught up with the dogfaces.

Their initial pace, driven by a communal adrenaline rush, was beginning to burn out, Goracke observed. Well and good. It wasn't that he lacked the guts for the work, rather that it made better sense to be at the front rather than the rear under these conditions—hell, under any conditions. And SEALs always took the lead. He wondered if everyone had gotten out all right.

Captain Kevin Morgan was in a foul mood. He let his bad attitude spill out on Sergeant Carter. "Damnit, there's no reason for us to lose two men. They're better trained than that." Inside, his heart ached for the lives of the young men who had died in the effort to get their charges safely out of the village.

To Morgan's surprise the villagers had not betrayed them to the enemy; rather, when the NVA troops had been identified, the people of Dong Da had rallied behind the Americans. "Expel the foreigners!" the headman had yelled and his young men had joined in the rear guard with weapons provided by the Civilian Defense Assistance Command (CDAC), a project Morgan knew in which the CIA was heavily involved. Here, apparently, it had worked.

When the last of Dotson's artillerymen had time to make it at least half a klick down the trail, the Special Forces troopers broke contact with the enemy in pairs and disappeared down the trail. At Carter's insistence, Morgan did not remain to be the last to pull out. Now they trudged along the trail, conscious that the entire American force had barely managed to escape. A rustle from behind and to the left of them put them into a crouch, concealed by the underbrush.

Ba-wham! A claymore detonated off the trail by thirty meters. Screams followed, and the sound of retreating footfalls. Morgan grinned. *Those SEALs know their business*, he thought with respect. With a little luck, they might make it out of there after all.

Returned to Tre Noc at precisely 1145 hours, Pope Marino and Tonto Waters were immediately summoned to a meeting with an Air Force liaison team.

"We have problems," an Air Force Lieutenant Colonel informed the SEALs. "To deliver your people from B-52s is beginning to look impossible."

"Why is that, sir?" Marino asked.

"The only safe way to exit the aircraft is through a bomb bay. So far, our people working on the problem have tried several designs and types of material and all have been failures."

"Why is that?"

"In part because of the very nature of a bomb bay. It can't be pressurized. So when the doors open, the elements stream in. More accurately, slam in. The slide models we tried were torn to bits."

"What materials have been involved?" inquired Waters.

"We tried aluminum first. At our operating altitude of thirty-five thousand feet, at cruise speed, it curled up like a gum wrapper. Then we used steel. In the extreme cold it turned brittle and when we put a load on it, it shattered like glass. Plastic was worthless. It vibrated violently enough to damage the test weights we put on the chute. So far every form of fiberglass we've tried has whipped itself into shreds."

"Do you have written reports on this, sir?" Tonto asked.

"Yes, we do, Chief. Better than that, we have film of the tests."

Marino and Waters exchanged glances and Pope spoke up. "We'd like to study those test results and the film. Do you have it with you?"

"As a matter of fact, yes." The lieutenant colonel delved into a large old fashioned top-opening leather briefcase and extracted a loosely bound sheaf of papers. Next came three small metal cans containing 16mm movie film. "I'll have to remain, this is all classified Top Secret."

"You should be aware that we are all cleared for Top Secret," Marino complained.

"Yes, or I would not be discussing this with you. But these are Air Force documents, and regulations require I be present while you examine them."

Rarely the diplomat, Tom Waters soothed the rising tension. "Might be a good idea, Pope. We will no doubt have questions. If the Air Force people are on hand we can get an answer right away."

An hour and a quarter of careful study and questioning developed the germ of an idea in the head of Chief Waters. He began to lay out his concept by stating the obvious. "There has to be a lip protruding below the belly of the bomber in order to let us drop free of the tail. There's no alternative to that, as I see it. But it don't say that it has to be hanging out there all the way to the target. How about having it fitted with some kind of pistons to shove it into place at the last minute? Say hydraulic pistons?"

"Might work," allowed the colonel.

"Now, take the composition of the slide. What about fiberglass-coated aluminum? Maybe add some external ribs on the underside?"

A light of promise glowed in the eyes of the Air Force lieutenant colonel. His subordinates nodded and discussed the prospect enthusiastically. "You might be on to something, Chief. I'd like you to come up to Tan Son Nhut and show us exactly what it is you've described."

"Administrative liaison, Chief," Marino offered. "I'll have the orders cut ASAP."

Tonto shrugged. "Then I guess I'm on my way to Saigon."

*   *   *

"Comrade Captain, we have not far to go," a young NVA lieutenant sent forward to confer with the point element declared. "The enemy is actually within firing range."

Captain Xinh raised a hand in a restraining gesture. "Wait until we bring up more troops. And now that it is daylight, make certain that your advance element and the scouts locate all of the land mines and deactivate them. We have lost far too many to them during the night."

Twenty minutes later, Captain Xinh and his company experienced an unpleasant surprise when they charged through a screen of jungle growth into a clearing where their three-man point indicated a large number of Americans were resting and eating a meal. What they found was an empty clearing, covered by the guns of two SEAL squads and two A Teams of Special Forces.

Projectiles from M79 grenade launchers and XM-148 tubes whistled into the air to descend on the advancing NVA soldiers. The crackle of small-arms fire followed directly upon their detonations. Fifteen men fell as though cut down by a scythe. Whistles shrilled commands and the Vietnamese troops hit the ground. The only effect Xinh observed that it had on the Americans was a change in tactics.

A shower of M26 fragmentation grenades rained down into the grass to detonate with ear-shattering force. Here and there fires began. When the flames licked close, the NVA troops began to crawl frantically away from painful contact with the conflagrations. Individual shots cracked from the American positions, aimed toward the ripples this exodus had created.

Groans and screams rose up. From point to point, several NVA soldiers returned fire. The volume of American fire increased. The grenade launchers blooped again. Captain Xinh stared in consternation. He was certain he outnumbered the enemy, yet they had reduced his assault to a rout. How could that be?

Captain Kevin Morgan spoke softly to Quartermaster's Mate Sturgis. "I think it's time, don't you?"

"Right on, sir." Anchor Head turned to face the rear and raised an arm to signal Lieutenant Colonel Dotson.

At once the straight-leg artillery, small arms at high port, started forward. By the time the first rank reached where Sturgis and Morgan stood, they were at a fast trot. When they cleared the covered positions of the SEALs and Special Forces troopers, they were running.

"Yiiiiiiiaaaaah! Fieeeeeld Ar—tilllll'ry!"

They hurled grenades and fired their M16s as they slammed into the huddled, confused ranks of Captain Xinh's company. Captain Morgan wore a broad grin. The caisson crushers had upheld the honor of the Army, after all. Anchor Head summed up Morgan's feelings.

"They may be noisy in the bush, but they've got balls, sir."

"You got that right, sailor. Damn, we'd better call them back, or they'll kick ass and take names all the way back to Loadstone."

Captain Xinh and twenty-seven bedraggled survivors glumly contemplated their fate when they returned to regimental headquarters. He had lost three quarters of his command. They had been ill informed as to enemy strength, knew nothing of their tactical dispositions, and had been outsmarted by someone with a cold, murderous will. Colonel Voy would be certain to see that his failure was conveyed to Hanoi. His career would be terminated. Personal inadequacy of this magnitude could even result in termination.

That his own life might be at risk gave Xinh a moment of consideration of desertion. Throw off his uniform and become just another citizen of South Vietnam. It seemed so tempting.

Then visions of his childhood rose up, choking him with a weird mix of emotions. The cruel French nuns slashing his knuckles when he failed to write his lessons neatly enough. The bewhiskered old man who worked for his family as a gardener taking him aside and doing unspeakable things with him. When his father complained to the French authorities,

they had only laughed and made obscene gestures describing
the acts which had so humiliated him. Fury exploded within
him. Damn the French and damn the Americans, who must
be just like them. He would go back to Colonel Voy and
accept whatever punishment was decreed. That he had lost
all face went without saying.

All he would ask, all he would beg for, would be the
opportunity to avenge his dead soldiers on the Americans.
They still had a long way to go to escape a concerted effort
to destroy them. If only their army had air support, Xinh
lamented for the hundredth time in the past two and a half
hours.

The half-hour battle had been over for two hours. Surprisingly, only eleven casualties—two of Dotson's men KIA and
the rest wounded—had been sustained. For the NVA enemy
it was another story. Eighty dead, with half a dozen severely
wounded. After treating their own wounded, Hospital Corpsman Nicholson and the Special Forces medic worked on
them, left them with field dressings and penicillin tablets.
They could do no more. While they worked, the three unit
commanders held a meeting. Although arguably the most
subordinate, Anchor Head Sturgis was deferred to by the two
commissioned officers.

"That was a little costly, I'd say," Lieutenant Colonel
Dotson remarked, seeking agreement.

"That was less than one percent, Colonel," Anchor Head
answered him lightly. "I'd say it was a hell of a victory.
Now all we've got to do is make a short jaunt across country
to the Kaman River. From there a flotilla of our PBRs will
take us to Da Nang and we'll airlift out of there."

"All of us?" asked Captain Morgan.

"Just your people and ours. The doggies—er—Colonel
Dotson's men will be reassigned from Da Nang, or so we
were told when the plan was to airlift them out."

Lieutenant Colonel Dotson had another worry. "Do you
expect the North Vietnamese to attack us again, Petty Officer
Sturgis?"

Anchor Head considered that for a while. "I've been thinkin' about that for the past two hours. I doubt it. Bein' they were regulars, not VC, they had to be brought this far from their point of origin by boat. That limits the number that could have come along. It's a matter of logistics. Only so many men per boat. D'you follow me, sir?"

"Yes, I do. So what do we do now?"

"Take a comfortable little stroll to the Kaman, sir. And I suggest we get started right away. If the NVA has lost its stomach for a fight, it don't mean Charlie won't want to take a crack at us."

A bedraggled Betty Welby left the central jail building in Norfolk, Virginia. *My God, those people in there. Such filthy language*, she thought, as she dug in her purse for enough money to pay a taxi to the impound yard. *And what those two with the short-cut hair wanted to do with me. Ugh! Who does those horrid things?* She felt she would have to stay in the tub for hours to soak out the dirt. And it wasn't really her fault.

She hadn't really had that much to drink yesterday morning. Only a little bracer to make her ready to go shopping. Also, she'd needed something to dissolve the humiliation and guilt she'd experienced once more when *he* had called back yet again.

He had spoken so softly, a cooing whisper, really, reciting the wildly exciting things he had done to her and she to him. His words had aroused her as they had that awful afternoon when she had weakened. Images of his hard brow, naked body, and large, wondrous member made her quake. She had weakened, her heart had pounded, and at last she had breathlessly agreed to meet him. When? Where? The vodka had been to drive that assignation from her mind.

This afternoon! My God, she was to meet him at the Holiday Inn at three this afternoon. But she would not. She dared not. Never again.

*   *   *

Chief Tom Watson put aside the tray containing his empty soiled plate and crumpled paper napkin with its logo for the NCO mess. A real burger and fries. Not bad, almost as good as in the World, he mused, as he headed for a bank of telephones. His call from Ton Son Nhut would be by private company, not military lines. He found an empty stall and inserted a piastre coin.

Background scratches and clicks reminded him that telephone service was not the same the world around. The call was answered on the third ring. "Hotel Montleon."

"Room three-forty, please."

"Yes, sir."

Four rings and still no answer from Eloise Deladier's room. Tonto wondered if she had gone out for lunch. In the middle of the sixth, her voice came to him, somewhat distant and hollow. *"Bon."*

"Eloise, it's Tom." A long pause. "Hello? Can you hear me, Elie?"

After yet another pause, her voice returned, cool now and distant, though not from electronic inferiority. "Yes, I can hear you, Thomas. What for are you calling?"

"I'm in Saigon temporarily and I wanted to call you to say how sorry I am we missed our weekend together."

"I . . . see. And why is it, I wonder, that we did miss our rendezvous?"

"I was—well, there was this *thing* going on." He could tell her nothing about the visit to the President. Nor indeed anything about what had brought him to Saigon. He had carefully avoided mentioning where he was, saying only that he was in Saigon. Not that she constituted a security risk. The French were allies, somewhat lukewarm ones at present, but on the same side. That did not give them access to military secrets, Tonto satisfied his own mind.

"An operation?" Eloise queried with a chill.

"Yes, you could say that," Waters lied, his mind fixed on the rescue operation laid on for the Blanketheads.

Frost rimed her words. "I was told you were on leave, in Australia."

"Ah—well, that was the cover story. We were all off somewhere other than where we really went. You understand those things, so why the third degree?"

"Do you still care about me?"

"Of course I do, or I wouldn't be calling you now."

"Thomas—Thomas, I was most unhappy that we did not spend the weekend together. I am leaving in a few days— Friday, to be exact."

"Back to Afghanistan?"

"No, my editor is sending me to the Philippines. To follow up on a story of mysterious submarine sightings two months ago."

Bingo! French intelligence had caught on to Artful Dodger. "War jitters," Tonto evaded. "Even in a little one like this, all sorts of people, even in places far removed from the fighting, tend to see things that don't exist. Can we get together before you leave?"

"Perhaps. I will have to consult my schedule."

"C'mon, dinner and a night out? Is that too much to ask? I have to get back to what I'm doing, but I'll call later about plans for dinner."

Eloise sank her claws. "Provided you are not involved in some important operation?"

"That's not fair. I could get jammed up with the work I'm doing now, but I don't think so. I'll call you."

Eloise hung up without comment. *Damn.*

"I'm glad you came," he said, as he pulled her into his arms once the door to the room closed.

"I—I had to," Betty gasped. His mouth covered hers and his tongue slid inside to explore. Betty groaned as she felt the pressure of his erection through his Hang Ten shorts and her thin dress. Her knees went limp and she knew only breathless expectation of a wonderful afternoon. *Three times again?* she wondered, hopeful of the outcome. The farthest things from her mind were her drunk driving arrest and Kent Welby, her husband.

CHAPTER 21 _____

TONTO WATERS looked admiringly at the prototype of the exit chute that had been fabricated in the Air Force machine shop during the afternoon. Its lower lip hung two feet below the open bomb bay of a B-52 which had been brought over from the American base at Udorn Royal Thai Air Base in Thailand.

"Now, that's what I call fast work," he complimented the men who had worked on the aluminum and fiberglass contraption.

"We had to do it fast," growled one corporal. "Someone high up, they say a super spook, is gigging our ass to turn this out yesterday. Besides, we used one of the already formed frameworks, only delay until we could try mounting it was to let the fiberglass coating cure. We should have it tested and be outta here by twenty-three hundred hours."

"Okay. Then it's my treat. Burgers and brews on me at your Noncom club."

"Good idea, but they stop serving at twenty-one hundred hours. We'd have to go off base."

"Any problem with that?"

A tech sergeant looked at him glumly. "Midnight curfew without leave papers."

Tonto shrugged. "No liberty card, no go, huh? Well, an hour's better than nothing. What you say?"

The corporal grinned. "You're on, Chief."

"Oh, and I want to come along on this test flight," Tonto said, revealing the motive behind his generosity.

A Captain Wheeler came over to where Tonto jawed with the USAF mechanics. "Afraid not on this first one, Chief. Crew only. We don't want to take the risk of losing you in an accident. You can listen to it in air traffic control."

Waters frowned. "How do I know if what I came up with is right if I don't see it up close?"

"Next time, you can go, determine its suitability for deploying parachutists. I understand you've got a Master Parachutist badge."

"Yes, sir, I do."

Wheeler nodded his approval. "Good, then. Once we work out the bugs, you go."

Chief Waters joined an anxious group on the apron outside the B-52 hangar as full darkness descended with its usual swiftness in jungle country. Because of the lack of large quantities of dust particles in the atmosphere, there was no lingering glow of pinks, oranges, and magentas. One minute the sun was up, next came a protracted pearly opalescence on the western horizon, then bang-black night. Before the goat had pulled the bomber out of its hangar, the hydraulic pistons had retracted the slide chute into the bomb bay and the doors closed.

Now, with the engines spooled up, the bird turned onto the taxi strip and headed for the active runway. Tonto found himself snapping his fingers in anticipation, a childhood nervous habit he had abandoned with the onset of puberty. *Awh, shit, would it work?* The question haunted him. The navigation lights on the wingtips of the B-52 glowed steadily and the tail and belly mounted rotating strobes blinked rhythmically, lulling Tonto into a near-stuporous condition. Suddenly they all went out and the SEAL snapped back to the present, knowing that the bomber had turned onto the apron of the runway, ready for takeoff.

With a mighty roar, the B-52 sped down the wide concrete strip and lifted sharply into the night sky. The bellow of the powerful Pratt-Whitney engines quickly faded along with the orange glow of the exhausts. At once the assembly of Air Force types headed for the nearby radio shack that contained the air traffic control. Tonto joined in the rush.

Coffee mugs in hand, they waited a tense twenty minutes before static crackled briefly and cleared into the voice of the flight engineer. "This is Rincon One. We have reached assigned altitude."

"Roger, Rincon One. Squawk one-four-zero-niner and proceed with assignment." It had been agreed upon that no mention of a test or experimental equipment would be made. Enemy ELINT might not be all so good, but they could receive aircraft radio transmissions and they weren't dummies. In moments, the transporter had been adjusted to the new frequency and a blip appeared on the radar repeater scope, tagged as Rincon 1.

A strident mechanical whine backed up the words of the Master Sergeant flight engineer, who peered into the bomb bay through a reinforced Plexiglas window. He fixed a pair of wide-angle binoculars on what went on beyond the pressurized door.

"Opening doors. So far all is smooth. Standard buffeting in the bay. Hydraulics activated . . . so far, so good. Everything is holding."

Three minutes went by. "Chute deployed now."

Five minutes further into the test and he spoke again. "Weather is perfect. Low humidity, there is no mist over the sea, CAVU conditions all the way. We're ready to drop the load."

"Proceed, Rincon One," the air traffic controller responded after a nod from the lieutenant colonel in charge of the experimental project.

"Dropping . . . first one is down and away. Falling free. Second . . . third . . . smooth as silk. Fourth out. This is looking good." One by one the weighted sacks that simulated paratroopers slid down the chute and broke free of the aircraft. "Fifth and sixth away. No interference from the empennage. Seventh off. Eighth. Wait! From where I'm standing there appears to be a crack in the . . ." Quickly he censored his transmission. "There's something wrong."

While the flight engineer watched in stunned silence, a crack that had formed as the eighth dummy had slid free of the chute widened and the entire trailing edge of the slide began to vibrate violently. It swiftly tore free and whirled off into space. "Sorry, guys. Something broke."

"Back to the drawing board," the USAF lieutenant colonel informed the gathered watchers sadly.

Yuan Café was a favorite gathering place for late night supper dates. The noodle shop, one of several that had opened with the coming of the American Navy, prospered because of the quality of the food they dispensed. Kent Welby and Francie Song approached the softly glowing lights of the interior hand in hand. Not until they had been seated and a pot of tea brought did Francie speak of what troubled her. She had been obviously disturbed, Kent had noted when he picked her up at her apartment.

"Kentwelby, please put the menu aside. You can't read it anyway. I will order what you like most; the pork noodles with lemon grass, bok choy, scallions, and fresh coriander." She paused, then plunged on. "I am worried terribly about Thran."

"What's the matter with him?" asked Doc Welby, relieved that her obvious trepidation did not pertain to their relationship.

"He is not sick. I am afraid Thran is in great danger."

"Danger from what?"

"Not what . . . it's from who—er, whom."

"Well, go on. You've said this much. Tell me the rest."

"I am afraid for myself, too. I am afraid that if you know all the truth, you will hate me and I will never see you again."

"That's ridiculous. You should know better than that."

"But I have not been entirely truthful with you. When I talked about Sergeant Yates before, I did not tell you everything. I suspect that he does not want to know the things he asks for himself. I believe he works for the Viet Cong, or much worse, North Vietnam. I have . . ." Francie cast her gaze down to the snowy tablecloth. "I told him things I learned about you and the SEALs from the office. Secret things. He—he demanded it of me."

"Which is why I got so damned mad when you first brought him up. You can't blame me if I'm even more pissed off now."

"But you don't understand. I mixed up the things I told him, gave him only false information on those things that really mattered. I think he has found this out. He is demanding details of what is going on right now, and has threatened Thran. He says Thran will be hurt badly, maybe killed, if I do not cooperate. I was afraid to do it. I was afraid I would be caught and executed as a spy. Then I was afraid not to do it. Yates threatened Thran. I sent Thran to my uncle's farm. Yates had men set fire to the house and buildings at the farm. Thran is back home now and I am so afraid."

Aware of the entire situation, Kent's anger shifted to Yates. "I promise you this: you will have no more trouble with Yates. And neither you nor Thran will be endangered in any way. Don't worry. All we need to do is turn in Yates for espionage and likely a charge of treason. You'll have seen the last of him then."

Stunned by this revelation, Francie absently waved away the waiter and asked in a tight voice, "How can this be? How can we prove he is the spy?"

Welby carefully laid out a plan in his mind, then confided his idea to Francie. "All you have to do is wear a wire and get Yates to incriminate himself. Then we take it to Mr. Ott. He's not only the executive officer for the platoon, he's the team S-2 as well. He'll turn it over to the G-2 at Binh Thuy. When he does, he will explain that you have been working undercover for him and that will be that."

Tears filled the eyes of Francie Song, but she bravely blinked them back. "Will it work? Will anyone believe us and not him?"

"Oh, with a little help from Tonto Waters and a few other

SEALs, I think we can guarantee it. Now, let's eat, I'm starved."

Disappointment rode the shoulders of Chief Tom Waters over the failure of his chute. He stayed up until 0430 hours with pencil and paper, scribbling notes, drawing designs with ruler, triangle, and protractor. At last he looked at what he had accomplished and judged it to be little.

"Hell, I'm not an engineer, or a machinist's mate," he declared aloud. "What do I know about this stuff?"

The breakup of the first prototype mocked him. At least until he compared his most recent efforts with the drawings of the failed test chute. There it was, right in front of his face. Figuring the average weight of a man and his equipment, they had weighted the test drop subjects at 180 pounds. Reasonable enough. Yet it had to be the weight that cracked the trailing edge. They could do two things.

First, they could lighten the loads. Perhaps even do an equipment drop along with the personnel? And second, they could thicken the aluminum slide itself. And maybe another layer of fiberglass? Sure, it could work out.

By 0730 he had made his proposal to the Air Force team and they had set about producing a thicker slide frame. It would take the rest of the day and part of the next, so Tonto had time to burn. He called the Montleon.

"Eloise," he spoke in his most sincere manner. "I was going to call you and beg off dinner because something went wrong with what I'm doing here. But everything has changed. I've time to burn right now. What about a late breakfast? Then . . . well then we can probably think of something to do until dinnertime."

"You are a typical American male, Thomas. Gloom one second, glory the next. I will never understand you."

Encouraged by this, Tonto riposted, "I thought it was us men who could never understand women. Then I take it that is a definite yes?"

"Oh, yes. Brunch at the International?"

"At eleven hundred, my sweet."

All of a sudden the day was brighter, the air sweeter to breathe, and the world a better place to live. Tonto hung up the civilian phone receiver and listened to the piastre coin fall into the hopper.

Lyman Clark heard the President's remark with rising hope. He bounded to his feet, energy coursing through him. "Did I hear you right, Mr. President?"

"Yes, I'm afraid so. I'm seriously having second thoughts about this upcoming raid into North Vietnam. It would sure be egg on our faces if some of those troops on the ground got killed and their bodies were recovered by the enemy, or some of them were captured alive."

"I told you it was a mad scheme from the beginning, Mr. President." Clark came close to rhapsodizing in his response. "Shall I issue an order to terminate the operation?"

"You are entirely too premature," growled Preston Adams from CIA. "In fact, you are bordering on being far too negative. What the hell does it matter if we bomb Hanoi again? We did it before."

"Goddamn right, Preston. I like your outlook. I've wanted to bomb Hanoi since long before the election, let alone the inauguration. But there are some problems, and Lyman has brought up two of them. Are there assurances that any of our people killed in the north will be retrieved by our own forces? And what about captures?"

Adams glanced at the ornate carpet on the floor of the Oval Office. Then he glanced up. "Sir, the SEALs have a reputation, call it a tradition. They never leave any of their own behind. Only one time did that happen, and that was a long time ago. As to captives, they are trained to fight to the death. 'Death before dishonor,' that sort of thing, only they believe in it religiously. No, I see no danger in that. As far as the Air Force and Marine Air personnel laid on for the mission, they're over the north all the time and none will have advance knowledge of the purpose of the operation."

The President cut a questioning look at Clark. "Did you hear that, Lyman?"

So determined was Clark to keep the hands of his friend, the Chief Executive, clean that he dismissed a diplomatic response. "Yes, sir. But can we believe it?"

Adams picked up on it instantly. His tone of voice hovered on the edge of naked hostility. "Are you calling the SEALs liars, or are you calling me a liar?"

Swiftly Clark appraised his adversary. Here was a man who had been trained to kill quickly and quietly with a gun or knife, poison, a lead pencil, a rolled newspaper, or his bare hands. Word among the denizens of the Beltway had it that he had not just once or twice, but many times. But Adams was civilized now, a member of the team, an advisor to the President. Yet what would the price be for pissing him off? Clark swallowed hard before he made an answer.

"N-no—no. Not at all. Least of all you, Preston. I only maintain that we examine every angle."

"Only a waffle has holes on both sides."

Taken aback, Lyman Clark blinked. "What's that supposed to mean?"

Preston Adams gave him a look of condescension. "Inscrutible Oriental saying, Lyman, old man. Now, do you have any truly concrete objections to this operation going forward as the President has ordered? If not, trust me. Everything is okay." He turned his appeal on the President. "Trust me, Mr. President. If you have doubts about the efficiency of the SEALs, perhaps a trip to Little Creek, Virginia, to see firsthand how expert they are would prove efficacious."

"What's at Little Creek?" asked the President. "Enlighten me."

"First off, a Naval amphibious base, a Naval ordnance station, and the East Coast training base for the SEALs. The SEALs are in the James River estuary, which at that point is a quiet backwater where no one much knows they're there or what goes on."

"All right, only tell me how I can pull it off without all of those television vultures gnawing on my ass."

CHAPTER 22

LIEUTENANT (J.G.) Wally Ott peered across the small field desk at Kent Welby and the petite Vietnamese woman. "You are sure of this?"

"As sure as I am of anything, sir. Francie is not a spy. She is not a traitor to her country or to ours. Whatever she has done she has been forced into. And she swears she falsified every classified item she has been made to convey to this Sergeant Yates. Lastly, it is she who came to us, not the other way around."

"Might I add that had her performance as a spy been proper and effective, we would have known about it only by our losses," Mr. Ott added, already convinced. Silence followed while the young officer considered all that YO/1C Kent Welby had told him. At last he spoke his mind in an effort to reach the proper conclusion.

"If we do this, it will have to be the most squared-away operation in the history of the Navy."

"Touch every base, sir, square in the middle," Welby responded soberly, his expectations rising.

"No one will know the facts outside of you and me."

"What about the NIS?"

"The Naval Investigative Service won't know a thing until we have enough to make an arrest."

Kent Welby persisted. "Not even Pope?"

Ott nodded toward the closed door to Marino's office.

"You know how he feels about spooks and spook activities. The only one he's even cordial to is Jason Slater. He never asks me for my opinion as an S-2, although I give him an intelligence assessment along with my XO's report."

"I thought part of that was copping an attitude."

"Not with him it isn't. Not with any SEAL. You should know better. SEALs don't cop attitudes or strike poses. What you see is mostly what you get. Like Chief Murchison said when he ran us through BUDS, 'If they ain't genuine, they ain't in the teams for long.' Now, to get on with it. Will she wear a wire?"

Welby shrugged. "I don't see she has any choice. If she wants us to nail this son of a bitch, she has to set him up for us." Kent Welby snorted in disgust and spoke his mind. "A traitor right here at Tre Noc. Damn that redheaded bastard. How could a *Marine* be a fucking turncoat?"

Ott sought to calm the youthful SEAL. "Easy. None of us are more than human. And," he paused for effect, "Yates isn't a SEAL."

"Okay, Mr. Ott. Show me how to put this wire on a person."

"It's easy, Doc. Fact is it is not a wire as such. There's a small box, the transmitter, that fits a woman best just under her breasts. The 'wire' part comes from the antenna, which is a strip of copper encased in plastic and run down the body." Lieutenant (j.g.) Ott opened a drawer of his desk and removed a cloth bag. From it he took the concealable microphone and transmitter unit.

"Take your shirt off and I'll put this on you so you can see how it's done."

Kent Welby complied with only a slight twitch when the cool metal of the transmitter box touched his chest. "Don't look too hard," he observed.

"A couple of practice runs and you'll be doing it like an expert."

His mind on the trim, lovely body of Francie Song, Kent grinned. "I think I'll enjoy the practice sessions."

*   *   *

Thran Song ambled along the street on his way home from school. He was in a good mood; his teacher had praised his work and the neatness of his written assignment, which had been rewarded with a 4.0 grade. Thran hummed a snatch of a song popular among the sailors at the Tre Noc base. He glanced up suddenly from an absorbed study of how his bare toes wriggled in his sandals as he walked. A huge figure loomed over him and Thran skidded to a stop.

"Hello, Thran. You know me, my name is Elmore. I'm a friend of your mother."

Thran mustered his less-than-perfect English. "I do not know you, mister."

"Well, maybe not," the broad-shouldered redhead allowed, as he leaned down to put himself nearer on a level with the boy. "But I know you. And I know your mother real well. She sent me to get you from school, but I was a little late. You're to come with me."

Thran's lower lip curled outward in a disbelieving pout. "No, I am not. My mother said nothing about you or anyone coming for me."

"Listen to me, boy. You're coming with me, hear?"

"No!" shouted Thran, as he turned and bolted down the street.

Three fast, long strides caught Yates up to the youngster. His hand shot out and he straight-armed the boy between the shoulder blades. The slender child lurched forward and went down, skinned bare knees, the palms of his hands and the tip of his nose on the hard surface of the dirt street. Yates was on him in a flash. He balled his fist in the back of Thran's T-shirt and yanked him upright.

"You'll do as I say, you fucking little brat," he snarled.

Thran recovered himself quickly. Thrashing in the big Marine's grasp, he tore free. Swiftly he pivoted and delivered a side kick to the vulnerable floating rib portion of one side of the chest of Yates. The corrupt Marine grunted and tried to yank the boy back to him. Cloth tore and Thran fled between two persons in the small crowd that had begun to gather and disappeared into a tea shop. He left half of his shirt behind in the hand of Elmore Yates.

Suddenly aware of his situation and what might be reported back to the base, Yates turned on one heel and set off at a rapid pace for the base. Behind him a gossipy older woman made a caustic remark to one of her neighbors.

"Since they came here, I have learned many things about these Americans that I do not like, but this is the first time I have seen that they have a preference for little boys."

They clinked glasses in a rather dubious toast. For his part, Tom Waters was willing enough to make amends and take up their relationship where it had been interrupted by Eloise Deladier's reassignment to Afghanistan.

Eloise saw it differently. Perhaps in her absence Thomas had found someone else. His evasiveness on the telephone reinforced this entirely feminine, albeit entirely erroneous, intuition. She put a brave face on it, however.

"Ah, Thomas, to what are we drinking?"

"To us, of course," Tonto Waters replied. "For whatever time we have together."

Her eyes narrowed. "There is something that will interfere?"

"There is always something. Duty, your schedule; eventually we will be rotated back to Little Creek. Any number of things can happen."

She lowered long lashes over her pale amber eyes. "You could get killed, for instance."

"There is that, but let's don't go there, okay? Tell me about your new assignment."

"I will be chief of three agent—" She broke off as an obsequious waiter approached to take their order. "I will be in an office with three other reporters. Actually, it's a promotion, darling. I will be an assistant editor."

Tonto translated that as meaning she was being elevated to Case Officer in the Deuxième Bureau. He smiled—it was a bit brittle, but not remarkable to the bored young man in the white jacket and black tuxedo trousers.

"May I take your order, *Monsieur, Madame?*"

Eloise ordered for them both. After the waiter had departed, Tonto poured more wine and spoke in a low rumble. "You'd think they would hate the frogs so much they'd drop the French."

Eloise twisted her lips into a moue that turned to a pout. "*I* am French, remember?"

"You are beautiful, bright, and in love with me. That makes a difference," riposted Tonto Waters.

"And you? Are you in love with me?"

"Oh, yes, lady. Very much in love."

A sigh escaped Eloise. "I was beginning to wonder. After you threw over our weekend and then would not tell me the real reason."

"Eloise, honey, listen to me. You are ... what you are. And our operations are all Top Secret. I simply can't give you chapter and verse. If you're not involved on behalf of your government, you have no need to know."

She made a face. "I have a need to know where we stand, how you feel about me."

"Is this a quarrel? If it is, it would only be our second. I'd rather we enjoyed our dinner, took in the lounge show, and then ..."

"Thomas you are a naughty boy. I think you have in mind to make wild, ravishing love to me."

"I have *exactly* that in mind."

"Oooh, that tickles," Francie Song cooed, as Kent Welby inexpertly fitted the "wire" to her body. Through the backs of his hands he was intensely aware of the firm youthfulness of her breasts.

Warm and silken, they slid against his knuckles and instantly aroused him. His member swelled and arched upward as he tightened one of the straps that ran around her chest. The second band of cloth, which ran over her shoulder, went into place. Fully tumescent now, Kent bent to tape the antenna in place on her naked belly and left thigh. He winced as he did.

"Woman, do you have any idea how hard you're making things for me?" he teased.

"I think I do," Francie replied, as she reached out and squeezed the bulge in his trousers.

Urgently he clamped large, spatulate fingers around her upper arms and drew her tightly against his body. "You are all set. All we have to do is turn it on."

Francie wagged her head from side to side. "I don't think we want to do that right now." Her fingers fumbled at his belt buckle.

"No, I don't think so either. But maybe we'd better get you out of that before this goes any farther." He paused and gasped as Francie lowered his trousers and delved behind his Navy-issue boxer shorts. "Is Thran sound asleep?"

"Oh, yes, for hours now." She pushed away from him, her ardor cooled by the memory of what her son had told her when he came home from school, his shirt hanging down the front of his body, the back torn out. "I am still mad about what Yates did to him. I'm ready to wear this wire every day until we can get him to say something that will put him away for good. He tried to kidnap my son," he hissed, furious at the recollection. "Thran came home half-naked, his shirt torn off his back. What will the neighborhood say?"

"Frankly it is none of their damned business," Kent growled. "And as far as Yates goes, the only reason I'm not staking out the Golden Tiger to kick the crap out of him when he leaves is that I don't want to make him suspect anything is wrong. He must have scared the daylights out of Thran."

Francie smiled, more her usual self. "Actually he was—how you say, spitting?—mad. He said an ugly American tried to take him away. Next time, he told me, he would kick the redhead in the . . . in where I'm holding you."

"That should do it, all right. Thran has been learning his karate well." Kent chuckled. "Slightly built as Thran is, he has good muscles in his legs. Hell, he could have Yates singing soprano the rest of his life." He drew her close again.

''Here, let me get you out of that thing so we can do something else.''

Early the next morning something new came along to bother the men of First Platoon, SEAL Team 2. Pope Marino delivered the news with a straight face.

''The legend for our operation up north has been decided upon. The story will go out and paperwork will support it that we, First Platoon that is, are on a special R and R to Okinawa as a reward for our rescue of the Special Forces troops, and the artillery outfit.''

Tonto Waters raised a hand. ''Pardon me, sir, but we used that same cover story during Artful Dodger, right?''

''Yeah,'' Archie Golden added. ''That's right, sir.''

Marino arched an eyebrow. ''You have a problem with that, Archie?''

''Yes, I do, Pope. I got the feeling that this time it won't wash.''

''So what if someone tumbles to the fact we are on an operation? The key word is *where*. Where is this operation? Is it in our normal AO? Up in the mountains, like with the Blanketheads? Near the DMZ? On the east coast, say around Da Nang? Who would jump to a conclusion that it was in North Vietnam until it was too damned late to do anything about it?''

Tonto threw up his hands. ''All right, you've convinced me. We'll live with it. When do we begin rehearsals?''

''Right now. Sand table exercises first, then simulation runs until we get it right.''

Colonel Pyotr Rudinov paced back and forth in front of the floor-to-ceiling windows that comprised most of the narrow end of the Grand Ballroom of the former Metropole Hotel. Standing close by as though in a football huddle, three North Vietnamese colonels looked on with worried frowns.

Rudinov gestured impatiently. ''These are an invitation to disaster. Is there any way of closing them off?''

One colonel, a member of the Party Intelligence Committee, wrung his hands. "There are, there used to be, long, red velvet draperies. The policy committee of the Party declared them ostentatious and had them removed."

"Where are they?" Rudinov demanded.

"I do not know. Perhaps Colonel Thre could answer."

A pained look of extreme discomfort settled on the face of Colonel Thre. "They were cut up and made into curtains, then issued to peasants who had none."

"*Borgemoi*! My God," Rudinov repeated. "At least we in the Soviet Union had brains enough to know and appreciate quality workmanship. Even the Fabergé eggs of the Czars were preserved. We did not strip the gold leaf from the columns in the Kremlin. We did not crush the gold chalices of the Orthodox Church under our tank treads, we simply took them and used them to drink our wine."

All three North Vietnamese adopted blank masks of incomprehension. What was this Russian colonel ranting about? Even though he spoke their language with far better than average clarity, he made no sense. Loot the wealth of the capitalists? Preserve gaudy, wasteful trinkets? Beauty and gracefulness were the trappings of hateful capitalist opulence. Obedience, plainness, uniformity, these formed the mantle of true Communists. Was he perhaps a madman? Unfortunately they were unaware that Rudinov was KGB. He had been introduced to them simply as a Soviet security expert.

"Cover these windows," Rudinov demanded. "If you have no drapes or can not prepare them in time, use plywood, boards, anything that denies a view into this room. After that is done, we can address other security lapses that seem a plague around here."

Francie hummed to herself as she walked to work the next morning. Her Kentwelby had a liberty card that let him stay off base until daylight this morning. She and Kentwelby had enjoyed a long, sweet, tingling night of love. Her pregnancy was beginning to show, and again he had suggested that they forgo their energetic coupling for the safety of the baby. She had insisted once more that it was not necessary, then convinced him with her lips and tongue that even if they did abstain, there were other ways to share pleasure. Kentwelby had proved an apt pupil and serious devotee of the new-to-him exotic Asian practices. Her pleasure in recalling halted abruptly when she saw the signal that a message waited her in the dead drop established by Yates.

Although she had expressed fear of discovery by Yates and severe injury if she wore the wire, she had left it open that she would consider it and let Kentwelby know, and through him Mr. Ott, if she would. This morning, Thran had asked in a solemn vein if he really had to go to school. It chilled her and set her mind in favor of the trap her SEAL friends wanted to lay for Yates. Now, seeing the signal, she made up her mind. She turned abruptly and went back to her apartment.

In a matter of minutes she had placed the listening device on her chest and tightened it snugly. She quickly dressed and went to the dead drop as directed. She felt a little foolish when she read the brief note printed in block letters.

TUESDAY, NOON, THE PAGODA

She read it a second time. Now she would have to be uncomfortable all day in the harness of the wire.

CHAPTER 23 _____

TONTO WATERS met with Mouth in a small fishing village five kilometers south of Tre Noc early the next morning. Ranks of grooved wooden boards lined the riverbank, each with its spiked, deeply scored large herring draining liquids into catch pots. Behind the display was a small factory for the processing of *n°oúc móm nhí* fish sauce. Needless to say, the place smelled to high heaven. Tonto wrinkled his nose as he lifted a cup of coffee to his lips.

"I appreciate the danger this meeting puts both of us in, *dawi*," Vinh Nhon urged Chief Waters.

"You can say that again. Hell, half the guys in this ville are Charlie by night."

"True, but they do not know me, are not in my old cadre, nor the one I have joined now. I have most disturbing news."

"Which is?" Tonto Waters probed, eager to get away from the odor of herring cooking out in the sun. *Jesus!* he thought, *how could anyone eat that crap?*

Vinh drank of his thick, sweet coffee. "The Viet Cong militia battalion that I am a part of has orders to move northward to support the invading NVA force. We are to depart within three days, giving time to notify all tactical units and their members."

"Then they have changed their minds about the seriousness of this invasion?" Tonto asked.

"No. It is still a diversion. Many will die in an effort to

distract your people from the meeting in Hanoi. My only wish is that you can convince your superiors to do something about it."

Sincerity throbbed in the words of Nhon. Tonto Waters took note of it and reached out, uncharacteristically, to pat the hand of his operative. "You have done very well, Vinh. I appreciate the risk you have taken to travel this far south. Radio is out?"

"Yes. Every American frequency is monitored now, day and night."

"That radio I gave you is a very secure frequency," Tonto tried to impress on the Kit Carson Scout. He wanted to say it belonged to the CIA and was not in any available range for the unsophisticated scanners in the hands of the Viet Cong, or even the NVA. He refrained from doing so. "You have done far more than expected and provided excellent product—" *God, there he was, speaking like a spook!* "The time has come to get out, come in from the cold, while you still can. Come with me now. We can be in Tre Noc in an hour's time and you can rejoin your Kit Carson unit."

"You are most kind, *dawi*. But I must refuse. I still have valuable work I can do."

"What? Get your head shot off? I have to insist, Vinh. It is time to give up this assignment. There can be others. I know a man who would like very much to meet you and give you a very thorough debriefing."

"What is 'debriefing'?"

"Sort of what I'm doing, have done over our time together, only more intense. Will you come in?"

Vinh drank more coffee, though clouding his brow. At last he sighed, nodded curtly. "Yes. I will. A good soldier follows orders."

"Right two, up one," Dallas Goracke muttered to himself, after studying his latest bullet strike in the human-sized silhouette target positioned at 1,000 meters.

"You mean you're actually honing in on head shots?" asked Kent Welby, Alpha Squad's sniper.

Dallas wrinkled his freckled nose. "Yep, it's a no-fail technique. I remember one time a friend of my dad's took me rabbit hunting after the first big snow of the year. I had a four-ten shotgun and he had only a handgun. After a while we jumped up a rabbit and it took off running." The young SEAL looked embarrassed. "I fired way behind it. Before I'd got my shotgun to my shoulder for a second shot, he had that pistol out and fired one round. The cottontail leaped into the air and fell in the snow, with only a slight twitching.

"We headed for it, and I expected to see blood everywhere, the rabbit's guts blown out. Not so. There wasn't a mark on the rabbit, but he was deader than hell."

"What happened? Did it die of a heart attack?" Kent asked, somewhat sarcastically.

"No. Later, when we cleaned our bag for the day, that rabbit had a dark blood streak across its belly but no bullet hole. He had shot low and the high-speed bullet had done the rest. Hydrostatic shock, he explained to me, had broken the rabbit's spine. Instant death."

"No shit?"

"That's what he said, and I believed it. He said bullet placement was the most important part of shooting, whether at paper targets, or food animals, or men."

"How old were you, Tex?"

"Ten. The next year, following his advice, I won my first junior rifle competition."

"That's right, you've got all kinds of medals for shooting."

"And trophies and eventually prize money. The coolest thing I ever won was a Wichita Rifle Company stainless steel .375 magnum rifle. Custom made and worth over a thousand. It's a beauty and I would have liked to bring it along. It shoots a hell of a lot more accurately than these things."

Goracke looked down at his 700 Remington. Kent unconsciously did the same with his weapon. Truth was, the highly classified automatic ranging telescopes (ARTs) made by Bushnell were hard to zero and keep on zero. The slightest jar set them off perfect sight setting, which was 1 inch of

angle at 100 yards. Once set at that range, the sights were
intended to be adaptable to any range up to 1,000 yards without manual adjustment. Welby felt compelled to defend their
issue weapon.

"Hell, Tex, they're just fine if you remember to tighten
the adjustment lock screws. At a thousand yards," he began
one of his favorite sayings, "I can split a whisker on a coon's
nose."

Although at 20 the youngest SEAL in Team 2, the freckle-
faced auburn-haired Dallas Goracke grinned like a kid when
he replied, "I've got a year's pay to bet I can whip your ass
with my Wichita rifle."

Kent Welby opened both hands palms out in a gesture of
surrender. "Hey, man, no bet. You're the better long-range
rifleman."

Dallas grinned wider. "No sweat, man. We're both qualified Expert Rifleman an' SEALs and that makes us the best
dudes in this man's Navy or any other service. Now, I'll lay
you twenty dollars I can write my initials in the head of that
thousand-meter target."

While the two snipers practiced their skills, the remainder of
the platoon worked with representatives from the Joint Personnel Recovery Center. One of them, a Captain Ferrel,
seemed convinced of his infallibility.

"No, Chief, that is entirely the wrong way to go about
it," he brayed at Tonto Waters, after soliciting a rescue scenario from the platoon chief.

Tonto reminded himself of the difference in their rank.
"What would you suggest, sir?"

"You people are entirely too few in number to carry off
this sort of operation. When we go in, we must do it in force.
I would recommend at least a company of Special Forces
troops."

That did it for Tonto, although it was Pope Marino who
stepped in to make a point of the obvious. "With all due
respect Captain, we are only one platoon of SEALs, two
squads; twelve men and two officers. Yet we recently went

in and saved the asses of a company of Special Forces troops, and neither Chief Waters nor I were present for the operation.''

Ferrel's eyes narrowed. ''Why was that, Lieutenant Marino?''

''I'm sorry, sir, you have no need to know. Suffice that my XO, Mr. Ott, along with the squad leaders, went against two reinforced companies of NVA soldiers and kicked ass and took names for two days. They brought out an artillery company and the Blanketheads, also a bunch of Montagnards in the CIDG. I think we are capable of doing a rescue mission.''

Ferrel's jaw dropped. ''I—find that hard to believe.''

''I do not lie,'' Marino growled icily. ''I believe you are acquainted with a Blankethead captain name of Kevin Morgan? Ask him what Anchor Head Sturgis taught him on the way out of Firebase Loadstone.''

Ferrel's jaw sagged. ''Jesus, that was your people?''

Tonto wanted to laugh out loud but refrained from doing so. Instead, he asked a pointed question. ''Exactly how many prisoners have you extracted so far? Your unit, that is.''

''We—ah—that's also classified Top Secret. The enemy doesn't know we exist and we'd like to keep it that way.''

''By going in with a company of Blanketheads?'' Tonto challenged. ''With choppers, no doubt. This is North Vietnam we're talking here, not Pla Cu. A stealth approach is the only way to insert a rescue team and using as near a stealthy extraction as possible.''

''Stand easy, Chief,'' Marino cautioned. He turned to a master sergeant wearing the shoulder patch and flash of the Rangers on his right shoulder. ''Sergeant, have any of your people been inside North Vietnam?''

''Yes, sir, several times we have gone in and extracted downed pilots.''

''Have you ever been in Hanoi?''

''Uh—no, sir.''

''Well, we have. At least four of us were. I won't say it was a piece of cake, but we came out with whole skins. My point, Sergeant, is that we have been there, done that, lived to talk about it, although the latter is something we're not supposed to do.''

"All right," interrupted Ferrel. "So you can handle the diversionary aspect of the mission. I still say it will take a company of Special Forces or Rangers to pull our people out of there. They will be mobile. We can scoop them up easily. Look, we're not busting a prison, although there's talk of that on the table for the near future.''

Lieutenant Marino knew he had Captain Ferrel the moment the man began to appeal to reason rather than direct the course of their discussion. Although of equal rank, Marino was willing to bet his date of rank made him the superior. He acted accordingly.

"I'm sure Sergeant . . ." Marino looked at the dull black on green name tag on the sergeant's cammo jacket. ". . . Douglas here will agree that when it comes to moving quietly and quickly at night in the bush, there's no one does it better than us SEALs." MSGT Douglas flushed but nodded assent. "The fewer who go in, the less chance of detection. We can't get 'em all, as I'm sure you know, Ferrel. So we go for what we can get and extract them from one designated LZ at the same time. One close to the coast, so we are sure of air cover and naval bombardment, if necessary.''

Ferrel's mood altered noticeably. "You're sure of that cover? Well then, I think we can work something out. For instance, we can equip you with RF jamming equipment that will royally fuck up North Vietnamese communications. We probably have more, and definitely better, night vision equipment than yours. We can make it available also.''

Marino and Waters exchanged a glance. "Surprise, surprise,'' Tonto mouthed silently.

Ferrel continued revealing their space-age goodies. "We have some windup toys that will make noise in the bush in a wrong direction and when caught up with will explode. We can also provide you with flash-bang grenades that will stun but not kill, so they can be used right in with our people.

Also sleepy gas grenades to put prison guards and NVA troops out of action.''

From there on the atmosphere in the room intensified in a spirit of cooperation while both outfits laid out their best ideas for the operation. Marino and Waters left the meeting impressed with the rescue techniques that the gimmicks of JPRC opened for them. They admitted to one another that on their own they would never have come up with some of the methods used by JPRC. The session ended with a fully open discussion of how the operation would be put together. Only one condition was not shared by the SEALs: the very close personal interest of the President.

Despite her ongoing anger at Elmore Yates for his menacing of Thran, Francie Song wore the wire, which made her visibly nervous when Yates showed up at the pagoda. He studied her from his concealment behind a screen of tailored bamboo.

He noted her repeated fussing with the buttons of her light sweater, her licking of lips and short, jerky pacing. *Got to her,* he gloated. *She is still worked up over that little set-to with the brat. Probably imagining more of the same or worse. Time to go twist the screw a little more,* he decided.

"You are on time, for once," Yates snapped, when he walked up to Francie.

"What is it you want?"

"Now—now, take it easy. Nothing to worry about."

"Nothing? What about your attack on my son? Some of the neighbors say you tried to do—to do . . . impure things with him."

" 'Impure,' " he repeated in a mocking tone. "My—my what a cute turn of phrase. The answer to that is no. I do not prefer little boys. What I would have done, had I gotten the chance, is cut off his nuts as a warning to you. Now, listen close. The word is out that something big is brewing for the SEALs. I want to know what it is. You are to find any recent operations orders and anything pertaining to some hush-hush doings the SEALs are preparing for. I want dates, times, places. You have one day to get it all. Don't fail me, or Thran will be made into a capon. We will meet here again at noon tomorrow."

Abruptly he turned on his heel and stalked off, leaving Francie's acquiescence on the wind. "Yes, I will do as you ask," she said meekly, playing her part. Inwardly she rejoiced. *Now they will have what is needed. Tomorrow this terrible thing will be ended.*

Late that afternoon Jason Slater arrived in Tre Noc. He went directly into the tiny cubicle that served as an office for Pope Marino. There he perched his rear on the edge of the battleship gray steel desk.

"Got the latest from our friends up north. They report that there is increased activity around the Hanoi Hilton. Lots of coming and going. Also, there is a steady arrival of a large number of covered trucks. Zil-one-thirty-five-eight-bys that'll hold twenty men in back comfortably, up to forty if they rip out the benches."

"They won't jump the gun, will they?" Marino asked.

"I doubt it. There's also increased radio traffic between the Hilton, NVA headquarters, and several camps in the highlands. We've located them and know the destination for each group of prisoners to be transported. But time is growing short and you are to accelerate your training and make ready to move out at a moment's notice."

"In case they do move them early," Marino concluded the thought ruefully.

"Precisely." Slater rose, then reached into his bush jacket inside pocket. "I brought you some cigars. *Jolla de Monterey*, real Cuban stuff. Enjoy."

"Where did you get those?"

"You don't want to know. Actually, a couple of my field officers had a brief, violent, and successful encounter with some boys from *Spetznaz*. The Russians must be takin' eighty percent of Castro's tobacco crop."

"No doubt as collateral for all the money the Soviets are pumping into Cuba to keep Castro afloat," opined Marino.

Slater laughed. "You got that right. My bet is Castro would go tits up in a counterrevolution if the Soviets didn't keep the wheels of commerce well greased with the gold of the czars."

"Could be," Marino allowed, as he clipped the end from a cigar and wet it prior to lighting up. "All right, we'll double up on site rehearsals. I'd suggest you give this little pep talk to the Air Force types working on our deployment chute."

"Already have. They promise reliable results within twenty-four hours."

CHAPTER 24 _____

STATIC CRACKLED from the small speaker as Mr. Ott listened to the recording made the previous day at the pagoda. When Francie had contacted him to inform him of the meeting and to say that she would wear the wire, he had less than two hours to put a man in position with the receiver. To avoid discovery, he had utilized one of the Kit Carson Scouts assigned to the PBR River Section 534.

Dressed in civilian clothing, the middle-aged Vietnamese tended a wheeled cart at the edge of the park that surrounded the pagoda. From it he dispensed a variety of sweetened beverages to passersby. He also tended the concealed receiver. Now, early the next morning, Wally Ott tried to make perfect sense out of the imperfect recording.

"You're on time, for once," came the voice of Yates, growing stronger as he came nearer to the hidden mike.

Crackle, scratch, fizz. "—You want?"

More static. "—Easy. Nothing to—" A loud squeal.

"—Attack on my son? Some of the neighbors—" *loud buzzing, a scratching sound.* "—Impure things with him."

A long burst of static. "I do not—" *squeak-howl* "—little boys."

Wally Ott's frown deepened as he listened to the rest. He could contain himself no longer when Yates came in clear and sharp with these damning words: ". . . the SEALS are preparing for. I want dates, times, places. You have one day

243

to get it all. Don't fail me, or Thran will be made into a capon.''

During the burst of noise that followed, Ott exploded. "That son of a bitch! He's the one needs to be made into a capon.''

" 'Capon'? I do not understand,'' Francie responded.

Wally explained, blushing furiously as he did. "A capon is a neutered male chicken.''

Far from turning red, Francie blanched. "He would do *that* to my Thran? Oh, Mr. Ott, please, if you catch him,'' she rushed on, her fury near to choking her, "kill him. Such a monster does not deserve to live.''

"I think a noose will do just as well. We'll hang the bastard for treason. Actually,'' he went on, "this is pretty much sketchy, a bad transmission. It's too indistinct in places. Certainly not the sort of thing to take into a court of law. But it will serve our purpose. I am going to make arrangements for someone else to meet him at the pagoda this noon. I want you to go through the motions of keeping the meet, but stay clear of the pagoda itself, okay?''

"Yes, of course. But who . . . ?''

Mr. Ott raised a hand to restrain her rush of words. He lifted the handset of a telephone. "Give me the office of the Chief Master at Arms in Binh Thuy, please.''

When the CMA came on the line, Ott went on briskly, "Chief, Lieutenant Ott at Tre Noc. I have an arrest for you people to make down here. Yes, today, at noon.''

From an obscure point, Elmore Yates watched Francie Song walk along the smooth pebble path toward the pagoda in the center of the garden. When she passed the carp pond, he stepped out into the open and started for the doorway to the small shrine. He saw her walk inside without looking behind her to disappear into shadow.

Unbeknownst to Yates, Francie had overcome her unease and outright fear enough to press for the obvious. Yates always spied on her arrival at the pagoda. He would not show up unless she was actually there. Wally Ott tried to talk her out of it, but she remained stubborn. At last he agreed, especially after the CMA's shore patrolmen arrived and agreed with Francie that it was likely the suspect would bolt. Accordingly, they had her covered from several angles as she walked through the shrine and out the rear entrance. Still ignorant of all this, Yates followed her inside.

He stopped abruptly when he realized that it was not her shapely figure that blocked the light that streamed around the seated Buddha. Rather it was the broad-shouldered frame of a burly shore patrolman. A second SP stepped into his vision at his extreme right. *What's this shit?* The thought had time only to form before one SP spoke directly to him.

"Staff Sergeant Elmore Yates?"

"Yes I am, what is it you want?"

"You are under arrest on a charge of espionage against the United States of America."

Yates had several options open to him. He chose to react stupidly. "Bullshit I am!" he bellowed, as he launched himself at the shore patrolman blocking his access to an escape. Well schooled in hand-to-hand combat, Yates batted aside the black-painted hickory baton in the hand of the SP. He pivoted and lanced out with a side kick that doubled over the Navy policeman.

With a grunt, the sailor went slack in the knees and began to fall. His companion reached for Yates. He got a side hammer fist in the face for his efforts. Blood gushed from a broken nose. Yates delivered a set of one-two single knuckle punches to the SP's sternum and spun to make a high front kick at the head of the other policeman while he reached for a .45 pistol concealed under his civilian shirt.

In spite of his bloody nose, the other SP saw Yates' move and drew his weapon. He jacked the slide on the way up and the .45 Colt roared loudly in the confines of the pagoda. His bullet ripped into the chest cavity of Elmore Yates, deflated one lung, cut the aorta, and pulped his heart. Yates fell dead before he knew anything about it.

*   *   *

"That's it, sir," Wally Ott concluded, as he stood in front of the desk of Lieutenant Commander Barry Lailey in Binh Thuy. "He resisted arrest, went for a gun, and the shore patrol had to shoot him."

"Did they have to shoot so accurately?" asked Lieutenant Commander Lailey nastily. "Or should I say, so inaccurately as to kill Yates instead of wound him?"

"Yates is—was a Marine, sir. He was a traitor, but he was well trained, deadly with any weapon, dangerous with merely his hands. He broke several ribs for both SPs and broke one's nose."

"The one who killed him, if I'm not mistaken."

"Yes, sir. But I can assure you that it was not a revenge killing."

"Maybe not. But if Carl Marino had anything to do with setting this up, it might be another story." Which was in fact Barry Lailey's secret suspicion—that Marino had arranged for Yates to be killed to protect one of his own men who was actually the traitor. "NIS says your account of the incident stands, so we'll accept it for now. I believe you have a plane to catch?"

"Yes, sir."

"Well, then?"

"Permission to leave, sir?"

"Granted." As Ott passed through the doorway, Lieutenant Commander Lailey muttered a soundless curse aimed at Lieutenant Carl Marino.

With a ringing hiss the engines of the Gulfstream spooled up and the aircraft began its take off roll on the airstrip at Binh Thuy. Inside sat the entire First Platoon. Once the plane rotated and lifted free of the runway, the roar diminished with increasing altitude. Tonto Waters leaned close to speak to Pope Marino.

"I've never been to Con Son Island."

"There's not a hell of a lot there. That's why we have the target mockups set up there."

"That works for me, Skipper," Archie Golden injected, joining the conversation.

"Everything you'll need will be in place when we land. Remember, the plan calls for you to set demo charges to make it look like the only target is the meeting site. Don't blow the damn thing apart."

"Spoilsport," Archie faked a pout. "That goes for you, too," Archie reminded his counterpart in Bravo Squad, Brandon Mitchell. They hunkered together in side-facing seats and began to discuss their favorite subject, their destructive trade.

The Gulfstream banked steeply to starboard and lined up on the course to its destination. Off the south coast of South Vietnam, the island of Con Son waited for them in thick, verdant jungle and spectacular bare sand beaches. Two villages existed there, but both would be far from the training area. Lieutenant Carl Marino reviewed these facts in his mind while the converted biz jet whispered its way over its brief 175-mile journey. It would be after nightfall when they arrived. The SEALs would jump in, and after the joint training session with JPRC, they would be retrieved by boat from a remote portion of the island. The idea was that no one, neither friend nor foe, knew that they had been there.

It might work, in theory at least, concluded Pope Marino. He had seen too many clever plans turn to dog doo in the cold light of application. What was that famous saying by the Duke of Wellington? "The most brilliant tactical plan will not survive first contact with the enemy." Or was that Sun Tzu?

That might be, Marino allowed. But then, the duke had not yet seen Bobby Lee perform at Fredricksburg, Spotsylvania and twice at Manassas. And the Chinese philosopher had not been a SEAL. Yet, enough truth shined in the old saw that he was not willing to disallow it entirely. He had seen nearly six months of combat in the Mekong Delta and knew better. Before Marino expected it, the flight engineer came aft and swung open the over-large side door. It stowed inboard against the curved outer bulkhead.

Immediately, Chief Tom Waters assumed his position as jump master. With calm precision, he went through the jump commands and sent the platoon off into the night with only their Paracommanders for support and the pale glow of a one-cell penlight on the top of the parachute worn by Zorro Agilar to guide them. This would be a dry run for their insertion over Hanoi.

To everyone's satisfaction the jump went flawlessly. Assembled on the ground, their parachutes rolled and stashed in bags, the SEALs set off cross country for their AO. This particular area of operation had a mockup of the Hotel Metropole in Hanoi, constructed from U-2 spy plane photos and satellite views. Low level—flights by photo recon planes operating at under 50,000 feet altitude—added detail. A simulated road had been cut in the jungle to serve as a practice area for a rescue operation. First they would see a demonstration by the JPRC operatives.

What they saw was awesome, albeit awfully noisy and busy with surplus bodies bustling around on the ground. The "rescue" worked. A slick operation in which knockout gas was fired from 60mm mortars and M79 grenade launchers, followed by gas-masked troops who swarmed over the unconscious "enemy" soldiers and freed "prisoners." What impressed the SEALs most was when they learned after the exercise that the gas was real and the people had been out like a light. Had the gas not worked on everyone, the "rescuers" would have been "wasted" with blanks. Then it was their turn to go to work.

Arriving "diplomats" and "military leaders" were shot at but missed at the phony Metropole, escape routes and avenues of attack were mined with claymores and special satchel charges under manhole covers. Live ammunition added to the verisimilitude of the training. When the first live round cracked past the ear of a JPRC operative acting as an NVA general, he nearly panicked.

"My God, that's real."

"Sure," Lieutenant Marino told him. "We always load live for training exercises." It wasn't strictly the truth and definitely not so for training in the States, but it increased the respect for, and for some the fear of, the SEALs. A small armored scout car rushed toward the scene of the sniping incidents. One forty-pound satchel charge went off behind the vehicle, launching the manhole cover like a flying saucer. Had it been for real, the BRDM-2 would have been the object seeking higher altitude. A second later, pellets from a claymore slashed into a squad of cloth dummies in the rear of a truck. Then it came time to free some prisoners.

"Here is where we are definitely going to defer to your talents," Marino informed the major who commanded the JPRC unit.

"How is that?" Humor rather than rancor colored the major's voice. "I thought you SEALs had it all scoped out."

"We generally do, but when we learned what goodies you people had access to, we decided to incorporate as many as possible. We're never so good that we can't get better."

With speed and efficiency, the SEALs used gas and diverters to set up the rescue operation. When it was over, with only one SEAL declared wounded in action, the JPRC personnel, to a man, came over and expressed how impressed they were with the professionalism of the SEALs. One Special Forces sergeant summed up their attitude.

"Man, I didn't think anyone could move that quietly through the bush. And your kills were spectacular. On our best day, you're an arm and a leg ahead of us."

"Yeah," agreed another. "I wish I was going with you up north. This is makin' to be quite a party."

"Now hear this! Lieutenant Marino lay forward to the Captain's ready room."

Lieutenant Marino made it in record time, the CO noted, as the knock sounded at the side of the hatch. "Come."

Marino entered and halted in front of the desk aboard the *Horton*, DD-143. Light boats had picked them up from the beach and taken them to the destroyer where they were able to shower and get clean uniforms, and down enough solid Navy chow to feed the entire roster of the Pittsburgh Steelers.

"Aye, sir?"

The captain handed Marino a single sheet of paper. "I think this is what you have been waiting for?"

Marino glanced down and read the crisply printed words.

```
To: CO, 1st Platoon, SEAL Team 2
From: USAF Maintenance Depot
       Ton Son Nhut AB
       Saigon, RVN
Subject: Exit Chute

       1. The problem has been solved.
       2. Departure can be scheduled at
          your readiness.


                    (Signature)

                    Lt. Col. Norman Toller,
                    Commanding
```

Lieutenant Carl Marino looked up with a broad smile on his face. "Yes, sir. This is exactly what I was waiting for."

CHAPTER 25 ─────────────────

A HEADLINE in bold print on the front page of *Stars and Stripes* trumpeted part of the disinformation scheme devised by Jason Slater.

FIREBASE RESCUE REWARDED

The story, written by a well-known reporter, went on to reveal that due to the rescue by Navy SEALs of the besieged occupants of Firebase Loadstone, including Special Forces troops, CIDG strikers, and a reinforced battery of artillery and mortarmen, the leaders of the operation, Lieutenant (j.g.) Wallace Ott and QM/1C Charles Sturgis were to go to Saigon to receive a high decoration each, then on to a well-deserved R and R in Japan. The rumor mill at Tre Noc and Binh Thuy were rife with stories also.

Lieutenant Marino and Chief Waters were about to depart for Little Creek to pick up some new, super-secret equipment for use in the Delta. They would also take a short leave at home. The rest of the platoon was to be given a week's R and R on Okinawa as reward for assistance well rendered in interservice cooperation. There were other scenarios as well.

The entire platoon was to be rotated back to Little Creek early. Another had it that the platoon would be divided, with half remaining in the Delta, the other half going to the East Coast of South Vietnam. Yet a third had them transferred to a base near the DMZ to act as a counter-infiltration force. North Vietnamese frogmen, the story had it, were penetrating deep into the south by water and endangering the system of hydroelectric plants and flood control dams.

Slater explained it to the SEALs. "If a single legend won't fly, especially one that has been used before, drown the buggers in them."

"With Yates out of the picture, there's little chance of Charlie finding out what's really going on," Tonto Waters commented.

"Who knows what that fucking mole turned over in the past?" Slater complained rhetorically.

Wally Ott contributed his bit. "According to our under-cover op, he was fed a careful diet of disinformation. All the real stuff was outdated, old operations, rejected plans, that sort of thing."

Always the consummate spook, Slater mentally worried the revelation. "You'd think they would have figured it out."

"Who's to say an operation that hasn't yet happened had been previously rejected? What the enemy had to worry about, and prepare for, was if it would go off the next day," Ott defended Francie's efforts to confound Yates.

Slater considered that. "This was your doing? You directed the operative in what to say and to show to Yates? D'you ever consider a career with the Company?"

Wally shook his head energetically. "No way. That cloak-and-dagger shit scares me witless."

They shared a laugh, then Slater got to the important part of the meeting. "I hear you're going to make a trial run with this chute of yours."

"Right," Tonto Waters offered. "That happens later to-day. Tonight, actually."

"Good luck," the CIA man offered.

"Thanks, we'll need it. There's not that much time before that meeting in Hanoi," replied Tonto.

Bundled up in quilted coveralls, parachute backpacks, and oxygen masks, the SEALs of First Platoon resembled olive green snowmen as they shuffled up to the boarding ramp to the B-52 parked at a remote part of Ton Son Nuht airbase. The flight engineer spoke valuable, if not cheerful, words of advice.

"At seven miles up it's gonna be colder than a bitch. There's no way we can put you in the pressurized, heated part of the aircraft and get you out to the bomb bay when the time comes. You'll be in the bay all the way to the drop zone. You will have house air until time for the jump, then you're on your own oxygen mix. If anything goes wrong mechanically, there's a big wrench in a clip holder beside the access hatch. Just rap on the hatch and we'll abort."

"About how long will we have to signal trouble?" asked Wally Ott.

"Around thirty seconds," the flight engineer replied.

"That's comforting," Ott said glumly.

Ignoring Ott's mood, the Air Force sergeant spoke crisply. "Okay, gentlemen, that's everything. You can go ahead and board."

Ten minutes later, the B-52 rolled along the taxi strip toward the active runway. It pivoted on one set of wheels and paused briefly. Inside the bomb bay the racket made by the engines spooling up to full power punished the ears of the SEALs and brought water to the eyes of three of them. Then acceleration shoved them backward as the brakes were released and the bomber leaped forward.

Kent Welby, who was never fond of flying, watched the runway streak past under them, lighted by the actinic glare of the belly strobe light. He gripped his XM148 so tightly that his knuckles turned white. Would it be worse, he wondered, if that light was out? At the moment of rotation, all the navigational lights went out. *It is worse!* Doc Welby's mind screamed at him. It was going to be a long, long flight.

Tension mounted as the minutes ground past. With only a quarter waning moon, it was pitch black below the open belly of the B-52. It was small comfort that the flight engineer was with them to secure the chute after the jump. He studied the SEALs like specimens from another planet. Why would anyone deliberately jump out of a perfectly normal undamaged aircraft? If there was a fire, or half a wing shot off, it made sense, he pondered. But to do it from such a high altitude and in such a cockamamie way. To him, bombers were made for dropping bombs, not lunatic sailors. A soft red glow suffused the bomb bay and he gathered in his thoughts.

Jury-rigged jump lights blinked to life, the red one, at least. The burly SEAL chief stood up on the narrow catwalk and gave hand signals for jump commands. Each man followed his lead like a monk in a religious ritual. When they switched over from the bomber's air supply to their oxygen masks and adjusted the face plates that would protect them from cold, the Air Force sergeant shuddered involuntarily. Suddenly the red jump light blinked out. Then flickered back on. Went out once more, then came on green. The flight engineer pointed at the slide. The first SEAL lay down on the chute and pushed off. Immediately the green light went off.

Driven by palpable urgency, the flight engineer pounded on the tricked-up light system. It came on red, then turned to the green lens. Another SEAL lowered himself onto the slide. He sped away into darkness. Quickly the next eleven SEALs followed, one at a time.

It looked to the flight engineer as if it might work perfectly. Then the last crazy guy got into position on the slide and made ready to shove off. The loud crack of metal could be heard over the rush of air and the howl of engines. Partway down the chute the SEAL hung up. Suddenly it became necessary for him to do something, the flight engineer thought in a flash.

He freed himself from the harness that had held him secure and bent forward over the gaping maw of the bomb bay doors. Stretching to the maximum, he gave the pale-faced SEAL a hard shove. The Air Force sergeant felt rather than heard something tear and the SEAL dropped away out of sight. At once the flight engineer regained his seat and signaled the pilot to bank onto their return course.

*   *   *

Early the next morning, in the low cinderblock barracks at Tre Noc, Tonto Waters stuffed a black hooded sweater into his ditty bag and made a face. "It's gonna be hotter than hell in this stuff."

"It will also make us nearly invisible, as you well know," countered Archie Golden.

Along with the other SEALs of First Platoon, the two friends packed the clothing they would need for the operation in and around Hanoi. In order to perpetuate the myth of going on a prolonged liberty, the SEALs would be packing their suitcase-sized liberty kits and the smaller ditty bags used for temporary absences from one's duty station. It consisted of little more than their "ninja suits," black and green face paint, and personal sidearms. The snipers would take their rifles, disassembled and wrapped in cloth. They were very personal weapons, far more so than those taken off a company arms rack.

Everything else they needed would be packed and ready at their end destination. Although it took only twenty minutes for them to prepare for departure, the SEALs took the next five hours to leave Tre Noc. First to leave were Lieutenant (j.g.) Ott and Anchor Head Sturgis, who choppered out to Binh Thuy and from there to Saigon. Pope Marino and Tonto Waters hopped a ride in the back seat of an L-19 direct to Saigon and from there by commercial airline to Singapore. The remainder of Alpha Squad choppered to Ton Son Nhut. There they took an Air America flight to their staging area. The rest of the platoon, including Hospital Corpsman Nicholson, came last, stopping briefly in Saigon before grabbing a Thai Airlines puddle jumper to Bangkok. There they took a variety of transport to their destination.

Seven hours after the initial phase of Operation Shell Game began, First Platoon was reunited in a blacked-out hangar in the middle of a cluster of identical buildings at Udorn Royal Thai Air Force base outside Bangkok. Dim, night-vision red lights provided the only illumination.

"You look a little travel worn," quipped Zorro Agilar to Tex Goracke.

Although the tropical sun had given Dallas an extraordinary dark tan, his experience in the air had brought on a whiteness to his skin that rivaled the most extreme condition in his native Kansas. "You would, too, Zorro, if you'd been through twenty-five downdrafts in an hour and a half in a damned twin-engine turboprop."

"That many?" Zorro riposted. "We only went through eleven. But what's a few bumps among buddies?"

"A couple of full airsickness bags," grumbled a white-faced Kent Welby.

Chief Watson brought an end to the byplay. "All right, let's form up, guys. When we fall out, form a line over at that counter and draw our equipment." He sucked in a deep breath. "Platoon . . . at'n—hut!"

Lieutenant Marino rounded the corner of the formation and stopped in front of his men. "You know I think inspirational pep talks are a lot of crap. Where we're going it'll be dangerous as hell. Some of us might not make it, but we'll all be coming out. And we hope to bring out some of our captured people with us: Navy, Marine, and Air Force pilots and weapons officers, flight crew personnel also, unlucky Blanketheads who got caught where they shouldn't have been. The poor bastards have been sweatin' it out in the Hanoi Hilton, and now we've got a chance to free 'em. Doc, Tex," he singled out Welby and Goracke, "if you snipers happen to waste a few NVA generals none of us will shed a tear. If you blow away a few Russkies, I'll put you in for the Big Gong."

That drew laughter from the entire platoon. They well knew that a super-secret covert operation like this would never be written up in a nomination for the Medal of Honor. When the amusement subsided, Marino ended abruptly. "All right. Good luck, and do your best. I know you will. Chief, fall 'em out and draw equipment. Then we get on our magic carpet and haul out of here."

                    *   *   *

Tonto Waters stopped at the rigger table that Zorro Agilar bent over. He watched in silence a moment while Agilar lifted suspension lines and folded the skirt of the Paracommander in the proper manner. Next he handed the young Mexican-American a single-cell flashlight.

"Here, Zorro, attach this at the apex of your 'chute. Don't forget to turn it on before you put it in the deployment bag."

Porfirio Agilar swallowed-as though he had a sore throat. "I'm gonna be first out?"

"Yep. For the rescue team stick, anyway. Archie Golden's riding first slot for the demo and sniper team."

"Why not Doc Welby for that team?" Zorro asked. "He's a sniper and can cover the landing."

"Yeah, but he's honcho on that team. He goes last." Tonto moved on and repeated his instructions to an outwardly calm, though inwardly crawly critter nervous, Dallas Goracke.

Tex Goracke put on a clownish, big-eyed kid look. "Gee, y'mean I'm gonna be on the ground, all alone, in the middle of Hanoi?"

"Sure, for about forty seconds, Tex. Try not to attract too much attention."

"I'll be good, Chief, promise."

"You'd better be. I won't be close enough to twist your ear."

"Banner two-niner, you are cleared for flight level three-five. Squawk two-five-two-niner until you make rendezvous. Good hunting. Udorn departure control out."

"That's it, ladies," Pope Marino declared on the intercom over the noise inside the bomb bay fifteen minutes into the flight. Not that anyone could have heard him except for their connection to the intercom. "Tonto, break out the green goo."

Chief Waters nodded and produced a plastic tube of bioluminescent gel. It would provide further command control and indicate the location of each jumper, once outside the aircraft. He applied an "X" mark to the top of the cover of each SEAL's Paracommander main 'chute and the backs of their gloves. Once exposed to air, the soft green glow could be seen for 200 meters and would last forty minutes. At an air speed slightly over 600 knots, that would allow ample time for the tiny living organisms to serve their purpose.

His task completed, Tonto made his precarious way back to his jury-rigged seat and strapped in. The narrow benches that had replaced the bomb pickling mechanism and carry racks were far from substantially attached to the curved bulkhead of the plane. The hydraulic rams that would shove the drop 'chute into place and hold it there were mounted under the legs of the two sticks. Tonto checked his diver's watch, as did Marino. The lieutenant spoke over the intercom.

"In about ten minutes we will begin a large orbit in order to join up with the rest of the bombers. Ten of them took off with us, the rest will come up from Ton Son Nhut. We are due over the target, and our DZ, at nineteen forty-five hours. The North Vietnamese radars will not be able to tell that there is anything different about this bombing run."

"What about triple-A?" asked Archie Golden.

Marino looked sobered behind his oxygen mask. "Expect plenty of it. Most of what'll be fired at us can't reach seven miles in the air, so it'll just be for show, calm the local folks, you know? They have a few missiles that can reach this altitude, but the ECM equipment on these babies is up to it, and there will be a low-level attack on their radar sites by Tomcats off the *Coral Sea*."

"That'll be cool," Zorro Agilar observed. "Does that mean we won't have any missiles scootin' up the rear of an engine?"

"If one gets through, you'll never know it, Zorro," Archie suggested with gallows humor.

"Yeah, it'll be wham-bam, thank you, ma'am," Tex Goracke quipped.

"Thanks, awfully," Zorro glumly replied.

Archie Golden looked forward to Operation Shell Game. The chance to set off a few big bangs right in the middle of

Hanoi, sort of thumb his nose at Poppa Ho Chi Minh, was irresistible. HAELO jumps were a piece of cake. The trick was to breathe slowly and rhythmically, and keep an eye on team members and on your altimeter—too bad there wasn't a barometric automatic release for the 'chutes, he thought wistfully—and at the last moment, orient their surroundings before hitting the ground. Yeah, and be lucky enough not to land on a gook in a conehead helmet with a rifle and a big-ass bayonet.

Archie's thoughts shifted to the Claymores and satchel charges stowed in his GP bag. There were also trip flares and nut-cutter mines to spread confusion and terror among the NVA troops and the State Security force of that guy General Tri. How long could they survive on the ground in the middle of Hanoi?

Pope thought they needed only half an hour. Archie considered fifteen minutes a better idea. Then steal a truck and haul out of there. The mission briefing had included where the rest of the platoon would be landing, and the location of the LZ from which they would be extracted. All they had to do was get there.

What was he doing here? The question mocked Hospital Corpsman 1C Filmore Nicholson. Not that he hadn't jumped before, not that it wasn't absolutely necessary to have a corpsman along to tend any prisoners that were freed or any of the platoon who took a hit. But he was not a trained SEAL, not even a combat element of the platoon; he was a medic. It did not strike him as contradictory that he had a Browning 9mm HiPower strapped to his waist and a Carl Gustav SMG slung in a Griswold bag at his right leg. The Communists, both the North Vietnamese and the Viet Cong, had not the least respect for corpsmen, supposedly protected by the Geneva Convention. So he was prepared to shoot back, if necessary. Yet how had he come to be here?

It was sure a hell of a long way from the sunny beaches of Southern California. Fil had grown up there, become a blond-haired golden boy from the age of 10; surfing, diving for abalone, doing scuba, and growing brown, hard-muscled, and handsome. All his life he had had a soft spot for injured critters or hurt humans. After high school, he sought to attend pre-med at UCLA, only to not make the grade in his junior year. He joined the Navy then and after boot camp and basic seamanship training, put in for medical corpsman school. He was accepted and graduated at the top of his class. To his surprise, his qualification in scuba and his civilian license as a diver brought him an unusual assignment. He was shipped to Coronado, on the long neck of an island outside San Diego, California, and assigned to the SEAL base there. He received additional training at Fort Sam Houston, along with a class of Army Special Forces medics. After two years with the SEALs, he had felt the urge to see more of the world than the West Coast and put in for a transfer. He was granted a change of station and attached to Seal Team 2 at Little Creek NS, Virginia. Which, of course, was why he was where he was now. But jumping out of a B-52 at 35,000 feet? Somebody was friggin' nuts.

Dallas Goracke had sweaty palms inside the thick gloves he wore. It had been like that at every rifle match he had attended as a boy. This was different, though. He was about to jump into an enemy country, exactly the kind of thing he had been trained to do. He had done this sort of thing in Puerto Rico, and in the mountains of Colorado. God, the time they had spent with the Rangers.

Even if they were Army, those guys were damned good. They had kept the SEALs humping to keep out of sight during the escape and evasion phase of the course. High-altitude survival had been tied into it also. They had been issued two canteens of water, water purification tablets, and their weapons, and that was it. No food. Everything they ate came from nature. That, or go hungry for six days. Shit! If he lived another hundred years he'd never forget the taste of armadillo, or rattlesnake, or ground squirrel, for that matter. Nor would the bitter flavor of chewed pine needles and weird roots and berries leave him. Which still made him wonder how a good little Kansas Catholic and altar boy could wind up sitting in the belly of the most deadly bomber in the world, armed to the teeth and ready to kill or maim any number of people when he got on the ground. *If* he got on the ground in one piece.

His faith in Chief Tom Waters was absolute. Although he had to wonder how competent an engineer Tonto was. The SEALs, save for Tonto Waters, had remained blissfully ignorant of the damage done on the test jump. All the same, the drop slide resting below their heels looked mighty flimsy to Dallas. He devoutly wished he could rub his palms against the legs of his jumpsuit. They were still sweating like Niagara Falls.

Chief Tom Waters heard the scratchy voice in his intercom and snapped back to his surroundings. He had been thinking about the last letter from his father. Although the old man had not said so directly, Tonto could sense his declining health from his choice of words and the topics of the missive.

''Five minutes to target and your DZ,'' came the voice of the flight engineer again.

Tonto sprang up and signaled the rest of the platoon to disconnect from the intercom and the ''house'' air. After the test drop, it had been decided that jump command lights were unnecessary due to their previous failure and the compromising of the structure of the bomb bay bulkhead to mount them. Only he, as jump master, would remain connected with the flight engineer to receive the commands. Zorro Agilar and Dallas Goracke were last to fasten their oxygen masks and face protectors in place. A moment later the bomb bay doors rumbled open. More hydraulic motor whining put the slide 'chute in motion.

It immediately became incredibly noisy inside the bay. A rumble came from the forward bomb bay as the bombardier pickled the load. All around them the other B-52s unloaded their first salvos of bombs. Tonto signaled the first stick to stand up and check equipment.

Quickly Doc Welby checked out Wally Ott, who did the

same for Brandon Mitchell, who checked Tex Goracke, who saw to Archie Golden's gear and tapped him clear. Pope Marino checked Doc Welby. When the signal for all okay went forward, Tonto signaled for Archie to take his place at the chute. Archie shuffled into position and lowered himself. A moment before he pushed off, he raised the corner of his face mask and shouted to the others at the top of his voice. "Don't none of you guys beat the bombs to the ground."

Then he was gone. Swiftly he was followed by Wally Ott, Brandon Mitchell, Tex Goracke, and Doc Welby. The roar of the B-52s slackened, then faded to absolute quiet, save for the rush of air past their ears. All around was total blackness. Three minutes after the first stick had gone, Tonto Waters directed the remainder of the platoon out. Theirs would be the more difficult task: to find and free as many prisoners as they could securely transport out of the country. Last to leave, Tonto watched the horizontal stabilizers of the B-52 flash past the upturned toes of his boots. Dark smudge against dark smudge in the absolute blackness. Tonto recalled that at an altitude of 26,000 feet it had taken him 112 seconds to descend to an opening altitude of 800 feet, so this would be an even longer free fall. According to the book, 122 seconds in which something could fuck up. Hell, he chided himself, he had done this a number of times before, but he still could not keep his gut from wrenching as the B-52 squadron made a sharp turn and headed back for the second bomb load to be dumped on Hanoi.

CHAPTER 26 ———————————————

THERE IT was! Diffuse and fuzzy through a thin screen of high altitude cirrus clouds, Kent Welby spotted the faint green glow of the Xs of bioluminescence on Archie's 'chute cover and gloves. He quickly reoriented his flying position and tightened up on the demo man. The insubstantial gossamer of vapor whisked past and Doc Welby saw the dark form of Archie, spread-eagled and rapidly accelerating toward terminal velocity. He knew the others were doing the same.

They had 117 seconds more before opening. *Breathe deep, slow*, Doc reminded himself. *Keep your count.* The last of the bombs burst below him. That brought a wash of relief to Kent Welby. Dropping from an aircraft along with a stick of bombs had not sat comfortably in his mind. The green luminous hands of the altimeter strapped to his chest pack unwound as he fell toward his moment of truth with physics: each action has an equal and opposite reaction.

When the Paracommander opened at last, with his acceleration at 120 feet per second per second, it would hurt like hell. But it was survivable. He'd done it twenty-five times before.

Archie Golden rigger-rolled his 'chute and squatted on it, to free his XM148 from its position around his neck. His head swiveled as he took careful note of the first 90 degrees of the perimeter of the DZ. He turned and did it again. Archie heard Brandon Mitchell come in to a slightly rough standing landing. Nimble on tiptoe, Brandon ran around his 'chute and contained it, then activated the quick-release box to free himself from harness and parachute. Archie shook his head and swiveled farther to scope out the whole perimeter.

"Cover my six," he whispered, when Brandon completed rigger-rolling and stowing his Paracommander.

"Gotcha."

"Ain't supposed to come in standin'."

"So see the chaplain, will ya?"

"Screw you."

A moment later, Kent Welby hit the DZ in the same manner. Quickly the black silhouette of the booted feet of Dallas Goracke came into view and he spilled air, chin tucked tight in the approved manner as he completed a perfect PLF.

"At least one of you can get it right," growled Archie in a good-natured tone.

Chad Ditto watched the sudden disappearance of the green X on the back of Zorro Agilar and the rapid appearance of the tiny pilot light at the apex of the Mexican-American's Paracommander. My God, they'd fallen fast! Not really, he reviewed through the turmoil of his mind. After a quick check around him, Chad closed his hand around the D-ring and pulled. A moment later he heard the familiar ripple and tear sound that came from a deploying canopy. A soft pop and a hard tug at his crotch told him his 'chute had opened. He counted four seconds and undid the straps holding his Griswold bag and lowered it on its nylon cord.

Around him the darker forms of trees loomed over the small clearing toward which they steered. Chad pulled on the right control knob and steered the Paracommander to more closely follow Zorro's onto the ground. Now, legs together, knees slightly bent . . . toes pointed. Reach up and spill the air from the trailing edge of his 'chute as he heard the thud of Zorro's landing. Suddenly the ground lightly smacked his feet as Chad made a perfect, albeit unauthorized, standing landing.

They had chosen their DZ well, a wide field across the Hung (Red) River from the walls of Hanoi and the Hilton. It was the same field they had been required to cross to reach their CIA contact, Johnny Yu, during Artful Dodger. The Texas-raised Chinese had come in from the cold, and his bakery now belonged to the state. Too bad, Lieutenant Carl Marino thought, as he watched the SEALs police up the drop zone in preparation to burying their parachutes and getting quickly off the DZ. Like Jason Slater, Johnny Yu had been one of the few spooks who got things right. Which was high praise from Pope Marino. The last of the bombs had fallen, the B52s departed and only the fires remained.

In the flickering red-orange of one of the nearer blazes, Pope Marino checked his compass while Zorro and Chad shoveled dirt into the hole that contained their Paracommanders. "Close it up, cover it good and move out. We're headed this way, on a bearing of two-seven-four. We'll come to the road in half a klick. Next thing is to grab a truck and close the gap between us and the prisoner convoy."

Polkovnik Rudinov and the NVA General Staff huddled with Soviet diplomats, one general colonel of the Red Army, several PRC diplomats, and two generals of the People's Liberation Army in a shelter deep under the Central Defense Ministry in Hanoi. General Colonel Deguriev was furious at the audacity of the Americans.

"How dare they bomb Hanoi?" he asked rhetorically for the twentieth time since the sirens had wailed over the city and the B-52s had begun to drop their deadly cargo. "Our friends in their State Department, in the Senate and Congress assured us that this would never happen again. They are aware of what the media would do to them," he went on quietly to Rudinov. "Our agents from *Otdil Dezinformat-sayia* (Department of Disinformation) would flood the newspapers and their television news programs with condemnations of the president and the military. What is that phrase the OD people created to discredit their military and filthy capitalist barons of industry? Oh, yes, the Military-Industrial Complex.'' His mood abruptly changed. ''We could all be killed.''

''Take it easy, Comrade General,'' Rudinov urged.

Across the room from them, calmly sipping tea from gayly decorated handleless cups, the two generals of the PRC Liberation Army inwardly sneered at what they saw as cowardice on the part of the *qui fan loh* (white barbarian) Russians. ''If another bomb falls, I fear our brave General Colonel will dampen his uniform trousers,'' one suggested to the other in their singsong Mandarin.

His companion snickered. ''Perhaps he has already filled his drawers from the backside. Or is it that all *qui fan loh* smell so badly?''

Nodding his agreement with that, General Trang Van Key added his observation. ''It is most surely the latter, I assure you. They all eat too much meat. Their bodies stink of it.''

''You are most astute, Comrade Key. I must congratulate you.''

''Thank you, Comrade General Xiang. I do not deserve such praise. Perhaps I can put their worries to rest. My apologies and those of my country, Comrades. This is an unfortunate occurrence,'' Key advanced to the diplomats and military men in the shelter. ''Most unusual. And the bombing is going on a lot longer than ever before,'' he added as more bombs exploded above ground at some distance, accompanied by the frenetic, terrier-like *thud-thud-thud* of antiaircraft.

''Why is that?'' General Colonel Deguriev asked, somewhat rhetorically.

One of the striped pants set from the PRC broke the mythical pretext of Oriental inscrutability with a nervous, stammered question, thus revealing his nervousness to be under a bombing. ''Do you think they know we are meeting here?''

''Of course they do,'' snapped General Key. ''There has

no doubt been a leak. Someone too weak to keep his mouth shut.''

''But—'' the Minister of the Interior for the People's Republic of China blurted, then winced when a bomb fell much closer. ''But we made every effort, in all three nations, to make sure the meeting remained a secret. They cannot be so clever as to discover its existence.''

''Their intelligence services are not fools, even if our allies among their media do all they can do to make them appear so.'' Key turned to Rudinov for confirmation.

''It is indeed the operations that the world never hears about that are a measure of the success of the CIA, not the occasional failure or blunder. But it is a blessing indeed that *Dezinformatsayia* has so deeply infiltrated their media.''

While the nervous Chinese minister digested this, uncertain as to what the Russian word meant, the bombing dwindled. After two minutes the all-clear sounded.

Doc Welby put Brandon Mitchell on point as the small group of SEALs set off for their designated positions around the old Hotel Metropole. The bombing had ended only a few seconds ago and the streets remained blacked out and clear of anyone other than antiaircraft crews. Their night vision destroyed by the muzzle flash of their guns or exhaust flame from their missiles, General Vu's men would effectively be blind to their surroundings for several minutes more. That worked well for the SEALs. Archie Golden and Brandon Mitchell placed explosive packages and Claymore mines in concealed positions along the route they traveled. When the four SEALs reached the park opposite the Ministry of Defense, Doc Welby pointed out a suitable tree and Tex Goracke trotted over and began to climb.

Doc situated himself near the top of a public monument which gave him a clear view of the old hotel beyond. Archie and Brandon fanned out and began to place more of their nasty surprises. Some went into the park, while others they distributed down the street that would be their escape route.

By the time they returned to the park, Hanoi was coming back to life as the all-clear sounded.

With the streetlights on they could see that several of the spokelike streets that radiated out from the park had been blocked by rubble. Archie picked himself a spot from which he could cover one of those that remained open. Brandon chose another to cover. The four SEALs had every approach within their fields of fire. Tiny earpieces scratched and vibrated as Kent Welby spoke into a small handheld transmitter.

"Everyone, stand fast. Remember, Tex, you are to shoot and move, don't even wait for confirmation of a hit."

"Roger that, Doc. We're vulnerable as all hell in this park," Dallas responded.

"Archie, you have all of your goodies out?"

"Negative, Doc. Saved some for our extraction."

"Same here," Brandon acknowledged.

"Good. This'll be the last transmission until we're on our way out, unless there's danger. Doc out."

Twenty minutes into the mission, the snipers had their first targets. Activity started up around the portico entrance to the Metropole. Automobile engines started up and the cool night air revealed plumes of exhaust gas. Dallas Goracke eased his Remington 700 into position and peered through the light-gathering ART telescope. The crosshairs flicked past a uniformed enlisted man and centered on the tall double doors of the main entrance. Suddenly the high portals swung wide and a chest emblazoned with ribbons filled the scope reticle.

"A word with you, General Dao," Colonel Rudinov requested as he caught up to the departing head of the People's Militia in the opening of the main entrance.

"Yes, Colonel. What is it?" came a cool reply from the short, stocky Vietnamese.

"Sir, I am not entirely satisfied with the security arrangements made by your government. Would it be possible, in light of this bombing attack, for example, to enlist the use

of some of your militia units to serve as an adjunct to the
forces of General Tri?''

Dao frowned slightly. Such an undertaking would cause
an enormous loss of face for Nguyen Tri—something over
which he would not shed a tear. Dao privately harbored a
deep dread of the faceless, nameless agents of State Security.
To bring Tri down a notch would be a good idea. Dao erased
the furrows on his brow and smiled.

''Why, certainly, Colonel, I'm sure that we can arrange . . .'' He said nothing more as his head exploded into
a shattered mass of bone, brain, and flesh, a distinct rosy
halo surrounding the exit wound.

Bits of General Quon Dao smacked into the face of Colonel Rudinov, who dived for the paving stones. Foolish, he
recognized an instant later. He had succeeded only in making
himself a stationary target. Who the hell could be shooting
at them, and from where? Dimly he perceived shouts of
alarm and the big doors slammed closed.

One down, Tex Goracke thought, as he lowered himself from
the tree. Bent double, he sprinted to his next position. From
his right he heard the soft sound of the Sionics suppressor
on the rifle fired by Doc Welby. Almost immediately a terrible prolonged scream came from the direction of the Ministry of Defense. *Doc shot low*, Dallas thought fleetingly.

Doc Welby lowered his night-vision goggles into place as
he slid off the bronze rump of a cast metal horse. Through
them he could see one man in a medal-bedecked uniform
lying still under the canopy of the front entrance. Another
man lay on the flagstones under the portico writhing on the
ground. In the green glow of the goggles the profusion of
blood looked black. Doc's bullet had ripped across the target's belly and spilled his guts onto the stone-paved drive.
He had meant it to be a head shot.

The damned sight must have vibrated out of adjustment
during the jump, he thought angrily. Low and left, he reckoned the bullet strike. He'd have to compensate or he was
out of action. His next stop put him in line with a set of

windows on the second floor of the Metropole. Lacking curtains, drapes, or shutters, the windows gave a clear view of any lighted room. In one, Kent Welby saw the profile of a man from the shoulders up. The thick-necked Chinese was in the uniform of an officer of the People's Liberation Army. He had a blank look of concentration on his face. It must be a bathroom, Doc decided, as he watched the man through the scope. He remembered to aim high and slightly right.

Stout recoil drove the butt plate of the Remington into the shoulder of Kent Welby. A split second before the rise of the barrel took the scope off target, he saw the Chinese officer fly sideways out of the window frame. No doubt he finished his business all over the room, Doc speculated, as he rappelled down out of the tree.

General Chang Yee Gee lay on the floor of the tiled men's room of the Metropole. Shot through one shoulder, he had the bullet lodged in his spine, paralyzing him. Although he could breathe, he could not draw enough air into his lungs to shout for help. Numbness crept over him and his mind raced in a treadmill panic at the realization that he could no longer feel his fingers or toes. Better the bullet had hit him in the head, he thought. He heard the door open and rolled his eyes upward.

He saw the poor-quality boots of a Vietnamese Army enlisted man. How demeaning, he thought, to be lying here totally helpless in the presence of this common soldier. The loss of face brought tears to his eyes.

"General!" the NVA soldier exclaimed in his own language.

To the horror of General Chang, the private rushed to his side and knelt. Before the Chinese general could gasp a warning or protest, the dolt grabbed him by the good shoulder and lifted his body clear of the floor. Intense pain speared through Chang's body; his heart raced a moment, then faltered. Blackness swept over him as his autonomic nervous system shut down.

*   *   *

Polkovnik Rudinov sprang to his feet and rushed for the double doors. He struck them with both palms on opposite sides of the dividing line. Rudinov nearly lost his balance as they sprang open with little resistance. At once he began shouting orders in Vietnamese.

"Get troops into that park. That's the only place a sniper could be situated. I want armored cars on all open streets. Security Service agents are to be trucked in here now. I want them here yesterday!"

Faintly from the second floor he heard the tinkle of glass. Had the idiots not listened to him at all? Or was the sniper firing blind into drape-covered windows? No time for that. Then he heard a voice shouting in panic from the direction of the broken glass.

"General Chang is shot! General Chang is dead!"

"*Borgemoi*! One of the dignitaries." Ludvinov would have his ass for this.

Brandon Mitchell eyed the letter bin outside the Defense Ministry. He had placed his final charge in it shortly before the all-clear had sounded. It was a special job, with a tripwire, plunger-type detonating device, which he had fastened to the lid of the bin before closing it. Then he took up the slack, snugging the wire so that any pull on the lid would set off the twenty-pound satchel charge inside. People had been slow coming back onto the streets after the siren had blown, the first being military and police types. One of those, an NVA lieutenant, approached the letter bin with a package wrapped in brown paper and tied with string. Without a thought or hesitation, the young officer yanked the lid open.

Instantly he was blown to bits. Fragments of the bin hurtled through the air with thin whistles and sliced into vulnerable flesh as it cut down drivers standing by their recently abandoned vehicles. The shockwave sped across the wide green grass that fronted the former hotel and blew out the windows of the facing wall.

*   *   *

With a huge bone in her teeth, the USS *Coral Sea*, CVA-43, plowed through the waters of the Gulf of Tonkin off the coast opposite Haiphong, People's Republic of Vietnam. Although in international waters, and despite the pitiful inadequacies of the North Vietnamese Navy, all countermeasures were operating. Helicopters circled like fat locusts, the umbilicals of their sonobuoys trailing from their bellies to the surface of the sea. Hunter-killer aircraft orbited beyond them, ECM and radars tuned to pick up the slightest indication of missile activity on the part of the NVA. On board, Naval and Marine pilots waited in their ready rooms, tensed to man their planes for the second phase of Operation Shell Game. The briefing was strained.

"These are the three roads along which extended traffic has been spotted. I refer you to the enlarged photos taken by Blackbird overflights only last night," the briefing officer said briskly. "See here, here, here, and here, these are trucks. Now look at the faces in the back of the uncovered truck. They're either gooks who have been scared shitless or they're white men."

"What about that one there in the middle?" one large, very black pilot asked as he pointed to a black face.

The navy lieutenant commander chuckled. "There's no doubt he's an American. Right, then. We go in and fly low cover while the Jarheads take in their Hueys to extract any prisoners that are rescued."

"Who's doin' the rescue?" asked an eager red-haired lieutenant (j.g.).

"Nobody's said, but I'll lay money that it's a SEAL outfit."

"Go Navy!" an enlisted flight crewman cheered.

Indulgent laughter answered him, then the briefing continued. Shortly after the last run-through of their approach, overflight, and return, the gray squawk box on the wall crackled with static and a voice, low and steady came across the airwaves.

"Bailbond check," it said.

The squadron's XO, a young lieutenant seated in his F-

4J Phantom, clicked his mike switch twice, which sent out a carrier wave but no sound on which a fix could be made. In the ready room, the lieutenant commander squadron leader huddled with his pilots. "I say we give 'em an hour, and then the brown smelly stuff will hit the fan."

CHAPTER 27

AT HIS usual position on point, Tonto Waters was first to see the object of their search. A high-sided 8-by-8 Zil truck had been parked under a castanopsis, nut-bearing tree, apparently for the night. He signaled the platoon to halt and snaked his way forward to get a look at the vehicle. To his relief he found that the ignition did not require a key. He returned to the waiting SEALs.

"We've got a truck. It's big enough for everyone."

"Good," Pope Marino declared. "Any sign of the driver or any troops?"

"Nope. None that I saw."

Tonto's assurance proved inaccurate they discovered when they neared the Zil. The driver had returned and along with him seven uniformed soldiers. Pope Marino quickly organized an attack pattern. He pointed to each individual in the platoon and indicated where he was to go. They did so in such a silent manner that the enemy remained totally unaware of their presence. In effect then their assault formation became an ambush. When everyone reached their positions, Zorro Agilar popped the driver with a Mark 22.

He went down at once, only seconds before four other suppressed weapons took out the seven NVA soldiers. At once the SEALs came into the clear. Wise Guy Santoro discovered one had taken a poor hit and still lived. He writhed on the ground and made small mewing sounds. Bobby Santoro stepped up to him and put the end wipe of the suppressor an inch from his forehead.

"No—no," the wounded man pleaded. Santoro shot him between the eyes.

"Our chariot awaits; mount up, troops," Tonto Waters invited.

Tonto took the wheel and studied the map with its overlay from a spy plane photo, then he fired up the 8-by-8. The Zil truck rumbled off down the narrow roadway toward the north. "Th'way I figure it, we should cut Highway Four in about three klicks. Then we turn left and head for Viet Tri."

Highway 4 figured prominently in the most recent photos from U-2s and Blackbirds. Also Viet Tri, which the infrared photos marked out as the last place that the masses of men moving into the mountains from the direction of Hanoi remained in a single large body. From there they divided into three columns that took separate roads to the prison camps where the Hanoi Hilton's prisoners were to be housed.

It was beyond that point that the SEALs would make their attempts to rescue as many as possible. The smaller columns would mean fewer guards. First they had to get past Viet Tri. The distance to the provincial town proved to be a bit over three and a half klicks. Tonto saw the lights glowing on a slight overcast and killed the headlights of the truck. Twenty minutes later, the Zil ground up a steep grade to the top of a high hill and the SEALs saw the village of Viet Tri in the valley below.

"There it is," Tonto announced unnecessarily. "I'd sure like to pull a detailed reccee before we blunder in there."

"That works for me, Tonto," Pope offered. "When we get in closer, take Zorro and go for a look-see."

Halfway down the hill, Tonto took the truck out of gear and cut the engine. The Zil coasted to within 300 meters of Viet Tri, then braked to a stop. The SEALs waited in silence for any evidence of discovery. When no outcry came, Tonto dismounted and called Zorro to him.

"We're gonna go do some sneakin' and peekin' over in

that village. That's Viet Tri where the prisoner columns are split up.''

"Okay, Chief. We just walk in there an' say, 'Hi, guys, seen any American POWs lately?' ''

"Don't be a wise-ass, Zorro. Just like always. A wide loop first, closer in, and then even closer. If we find what we're lookin' for we hotfoot it back here.''

"Gotcha.''

This couldn't be any more dangerous than standing on the sand, in the middle of the arena, while a 360-kilo *novillo* thundered toward you. In his life before becoming a SEAL, Zorro had been an *afficionado practico*—an amateur matador. For as far back as he could remember he had been fascinated by the panoply and ritual of the art of bullfighting. The music stirred his blood, especially such classics as *La Vergin de la Macarena* and *Cielo Andaluz*. The bold bray of the trumpets, the vibrant thud of the bass drum made him feel truly alive. He still followed the *Fiesta Brava* in such magazine publications as *Torro* and *El Rey Dondel*. Rightfully, then, no one could call Porfirio Agilar a coward. He grinned at Tonto.

"Let's go, then.''

They moved off through the thicker undergrowth of the foothills, where ferns and palms gave way to thorn bushes and prickly berry vines. Sawgrass had adapted instead of dying out and become even more treacherous in this cooler climate. It made the going more difficult for Tonto and Zorro, but provided excellent concealment. On their second pass around Viet Tri, Tonto spotted something that centered his attention.

"Over there,'' he mouthed to Zorro. He pointed to where several pinpricks of light seemed to waver in and out of visibility.

"Let's get in closer.''

Tonto nodded and led the way.

More little yellow spots of light appeared the nearer they came to the dead black bulk of a low mound. Tonto suddenly realized that what they were seeing was a cave. It had to be.

No doubt vines and tall grasses had grown over the entrance and the slight breeze blew them to and fro, obscuring then revealing the kerosene lanterns lighting the interior of the cavern. At a distance of thirty meters they could distinguish voices.

Tonto cut his gaze to Zorro, who nodded. The young Mexican-American cupped one hand and put it on his opposite forearm to signify a cave. Tonto nodded. They started forward again and the voices grew louder, more distinct. Some of them, Tonto realized with a start, were speaking English, colloquial American English.

"We found them," Tonto reported to Pope, back at the truck. He related the details of their search, the discovery of the cave and the voices from inside. "I estimate there's some twenty to fifty inside. Maybe fifty to sixty guards."

Pope Marino looked unhappy. "We can't take them there, too close to town and the army garrison. Besides, we could never get them all out in the safety window the whiz kids in Ops aboard the *Coral Sea* say we have."

"So what do we do?"

Marino seemed not the least deterred. "I have an idea. What we do is skirt the town and advance along the two nearest roadways. When the time is right, we hit the convoy on that route, free all we can, and head for the LZ."

"Suits," Tonto agreed.

"Wally, you'll take the nearer column, using half the men."

"What about we all hit them one column at a time?" suggested the executive officer. "The stronger the force, the quicker it's over, right?"

Marino thought it over a second. "All right, Wally, you're right. Even Jeb Stuart got his tit in a wringer when he split his command at Gettysburg. We'll do it that way. Mount up, ladies, we've got a ways to go."

Police type sirens wailed in the streets of Hanoi. Civilian and military vehicles dashed from place to place in an effort to locate the unseen gunman who had shot at the distinguished visitors at the Ministry of Defense. One BTR-60 Soviet-made armored personnel carrier pulled to a stop directly over one of the mined manhole covers rigged by Archie Golden.

Golden grinned wickedly as he fingered the small transmitter of a radio detonator. ''Well, Comrades, kiss your asses goodbye.'' He raised the arming cover and pressed the fire button with his thumb.

Forty pounds of C-4 went off in a cataclysmic roar. The shaped charge sent most of its force upward, lifted the manhole cover, and continued its powerful thrust. Engulfed in flame from the explosion, the eight-wheeled BTR-60 raised off the ground and hurtled precariously to the height of a second story window. It seemed to hover there a fraction of a second, then its 9.82-ton weight obeyed the law of gravity.

It struck the cratered pavement with tremendous force: enough to break legs, spines, necks, and skulls among the fourteen soldiers and the three-man crew. Fuel spilled from the ruptured tank, quickly ignited by the flickering flames of the burning tar that had formerly sealed the outer ring of the manhole. Within two minutes the screams of the trapped occupants reached the ears of the SEAL diversionary unit. Archie hardened his heart to it, as did Doc Welby.

A rush of pity and a queasy feeling in his stomach troubled Brandon Mitchell, but he fought down the rebellious empathy. Dallas Goracke could not contain the fiery emotions that roiled his stomach and tore at his sense of fairness. It took all of his conscious mind to fight back a spew of bile. *Don't be a pussy*, his mind growled at him. *They are the enemy, let them fucking die.* Time to get back to business.

From his vantage point, Dallas scoped out an NVA general who reached for his sidearm. A quick adjustment in his breathing and Tex Goracke's trigger finger twitched. Immediately he lowered himself to the ground and coiled the ropes he used. A quick glance showed the general on his knees as though in prayer, his huge, Soviet-style flying saucer hat blown off along with the back of his head. They had to pull out, Dallas silently urged his teammates.

*   *   *

Special Security Police swarmed through the streets of Hanoi, among them Cam Liang, a young man proud of his recent promotion to lieutenant. Excitement coursed through his veins at the prospect of actually finding some enemy right within the capital city. *How had the sniper gotten to Hanoi?* Liang puzzled over that. *Could it be an airman?* One of the pilots of the bombers that had returned without warning to drop their deadly cargo on his beloved hometown.

Liang sat not in the back, as was his privilege as an officer, but beside the driver of the GAZ-58 half ton utility truck as the jeeplike vehicle approached one corner of the square outside the People's Liberation Park. Liang let his chest swell with pride as he envisioned the capture of the international bandit. Liang would parade the American pig directly in front of General Tri and receive the accolades of his grateful people.

Unseen by the daydreaming, inexperienced officer, the front bumper engaged a trip-wire. As the GAZ-58 continued forward it caused the firing pin to be drawn from a claymore mine. Cam Liang saw only a momentary flash of bright yellow before the thousand metal pellets flew out from the shaped charge and shredded the occupants of the vehicle. Driverless, the GAZ-58 careened across the square and crashed into the base of a statue of Ho Chi Minh.

Under direction of Lieutenant Marino, the rest of the platoon used the captured truck to block the road, some five klicks northwest of Viet Tri. At the suggestion of Tonto Waters, the SEALs had brought along one of the corpses of the NVA troops who had been killed when the truck had been liberated. They draped him over the steering wheel. Tonto Waters considered that they'd cut it mighty close when the sound of grinding gears and laboring engines came to their ears not five minutes after maneuvering the stolen vehicle into place.

"Heads up, they're comin'," went the warning along the quickly established ambush.

Another minute went by and dim yellow light washed over the bush. It failed to pick out a single SEAL. A Zil hove into view and groaned its way up close to the obstruction. Cursing in agitation, a burly NVA sergeant climbed from the passenger side of the cab and advanced on the apparently abandoned vehicle. At sight of the figure who might be asleep at the wheel, the sergeant bellowed an imprecation.

"Wake up, you diseased son of a scabrous Haiphong whore!"

Of course, the dead man did not awaken. The sergeant stepped closer and banged on the metal door. "I said, wake up and drag your sorry ass out of there!"

Following typical Soviet military convoy doctrine, the first element was a truck, or APC, filled with troops, second in line came the real purpose of the train, followed by the command unit, and the remainder of the vehicles. This NVA column did not deviate from that practice. Thus it took them several minutes while the sergeant argued with a corpse for the major commanding this shipment of prisoners and their escort to reach the noncom's side.

"What is it, Comrade Sergeant?"

Stiffened to attention, the sergeant made an effort to answer, only to have his features go slack and a halo of scarlet form around his head. Stitched up his spine with a three-round burst from a suppressed Carl Gustav Model 45, he was dead before the first splash of his blood ruined the major's uniform tunic.

Small *clinks* sounded in the bush to one side of the roadway, followed by thuds as sleep gas grenades flew through the open tailgates and landed on the floorboards. Contained by the canvas covers, the colorless, odorless gas concentrated enough to halve the allotted time it took to render all occupants unconscious.

More silent weapons went off to deal with the drivers and assistant drivers and armed guards outside the enclosed trucks. In two minutes it was over.

"You did a four-oh job, guys," Pope Marino praised his men. "Good work. Now, get that truck clear of the road, finish off the gooks, and let's get on the way. Tonto, I want a count of how many prisoners we have."

"Aye, sir."

"Anchor Head, pick three men. When these people come around, you'll set off with them to the LZ. Keep them together and use a truck as long as you can. The rest of us are headed for what is called Road 47 on this map the spooks fixed up for us."

Within five minutes only the dead NVA troops were left behind. Eighteen Americans had been recovered. Three suffered from old wounds and one man was so maltreated by his captors he was a basket case. Nine of the former prisoners were in good enough condition that Lieutenant Marino relented and allowed them to come along on the attempt to recover even more POWs. They armed themselves from the weapons of their former captors. After their departure, silence fell over the road to Phon Phon Containment Camp 31. Their new guests would not be arriving, although they did not know it yet.

CHAPTER 28 _____

CONFUSION CONTINUED in Hanoi, had in fact intensified with the unforeseen disasters enchanted by the Security Service. Colonel Pyotr Rudinov paced in the small communications office at the Ministry of Defense. In this crisis situation the North Vietnamese deferred to him as the most experienced in security matters, unaware that he was in fact KGB. The reports that crackled in rankled him to the point of cursing silently in Russian.

"Company Three of the Security Service is proud to announce that we have located the enemy force and are engaging them."

"No—no, stop, you idiots," came on the same frequency, accompanied by the crackle of 7.63mm fire. "We are not the enemy. We are Company Seven."

Rudinov slammed a fist into one palm. The Americans had a phrase for this sort of incompetency. What was it? Oh, yes, "Fucked up like a Chinese fire drill."

"We are under fire," came another bleating report. "Company Five reporting. The enemy has landed in force. This is an invasion."

"Nonsense," Rudinov snapped to the radio operator, who looked anxiously at him for instructions. "Tell them that. Tell them they are shooting at one another."

Quickly the RTO relayed that information. "That cannot

be so, they have armored vehi—'' The message ended in a burst of white noise.

An NVA signals officer approached Rudinov's temporary desk with a report form in his hand. ''We have an intercept of a scrambled radio transmission, Comrade Colonel.''

''Let me see that,'' Rudinov snatched at the yellow sheet of paper.

''But, Comrade, if it is scrambled, what good is it?''

Colonel Rudinov spoke patronizingly, as though to a small but stupid child. ''It means there is someone inside the country who should not be here, and if he transmits again we can pinpoint him to within a hundred meters. Deploy listening equipment at once.''

A major contribution to the confusion came from the release of the first of the windup toys provided by JPRC. They sent several units of the security force and army to the wrong side of the park, where the noisemakers went off with loud bangs and a lot of smoke. The result was that the North Vietnamese troops opened up on one another. Under cover of this bedlam, Kent Welby led the way out of the park, taking the point.

None too soon, he and the others found out two minutes later, when they had disappeared into the darkness of a narrow alley across from the park. Claymores and boobytraps left behind went off with staggered roars. The outcome of that was more pandemonium. For all these pleasant distractions, Archie Golden felt as though eyes had fixed on his back as they moved soundlessly through the litter of the alley, their feet clad in professional basketball shoes. The rubber soles reduced noise to their labored breathing alone.

''Tex has the back door. Keep alert for anyone on either side of us,'' Archie cautioned Mitchell over their private radio net.

Responsibility for that fell to him and Brandon Mitchell. All Archie knew was that they had a hell of a long way to go to get to the designated LZ in time to be extracted with the rest. With all these gooks running around, they might not make it.

Earmuffs protected the hearing of the flight deck crew as the engines of a squadron of F-4J Phantoms spooled up onboard the *Coral Sea*. Powerful lights that illuminated the launch catapults glinted off the light gray paint on four sleek AIM-7 Sparrow missiles fixed to the outboard hardpoint under the right wings of the Phantoms. Each was also armed with four AIM-9 Sidewinder infrared missiles on a hardpoint pylon under the left wing, and a rack of three one-thousand-pound bombs under the belly. Lieutenant Commander John Piper, squadron commander of the F-4s, recalled the closing words of his briefing.

"We will be the second strike on Hanoi tonight. We will go in low, under the radar horizon, then pop up and unload our ordnance and scoot the hell out. We are not there to hotdog. We are not the Blue Angels. We want to have everyone come back in one piece. Good luck and good flying."

Anchor Head Sturgis put Long Tom Killian at point, and chose Randy Andy Holt from First Squad, along with Zorro Agilar. They had the three walking wounded with them and one former prisoner so badly treated by his captors that he had to be carried in a litter. Some of the prisoners had armed themselves from extra weapons brought in by First Platoon and some from the arms of the NVA troops who had guarded them. All of them expressed the wish that they had been allowed to go along on the second phase of the rescue mission.

Anchor Head treated their low-key grumbling lightly. "Look at it this way, you're gonna get outta here faster, and if you went along, you might not get out at all. Besides," he told a slightly irate USAF captain, "we ain't all that sure there won't be some NVA shooters around where we're goin'."

Captain Frank Howell nodded agreement. "You've got a

point. You guys are good, but four men aren't a match for, say, a company."

An inordinately modest man, or so he claimed, Anchor Head refrained from recounting their recent set-to with a regiment of NVA. He put a good face on it. "You got that right, Captain. And we're glad to have you along with us."

"How far do we have to go?"

"About ten klicks. This truck isn't going to last us much longer. We'll have to hoof it from wherever we run out of road or get too close to a settlement."

With Tonto Waters on point in a GAZ-58, the remainder of the platoon, enlarged now by the volunteers, set off by truck for the two lane highway noted as Road 47. Guided by the photo overlays for the basic map, provided by overflights of OH-10 Blackbird spy planes, Pope could clearly make out that the narrow trail they followed would join Road 47 at a point that should let them once more outdistance the enemy and set up an ambush.

"I should be ashamed to admit this, sir," a young Marine lieutenant in remarkably good shape confided to Marino, "since I've only been in the Hilton for a week, but I can't wait to get my hands on some of those slope bastards who had me locked up."

Marino gave him a mild smile. "Understandable under the circumstances, Lieutenant."

"No, sir. You don't understand how truly awful conditions are in there. The cramped, filthy quarters, no sanitation, the brutality of the guards, the humiliation, and especially the torture. Those fuckers are nothing but animals, sir."

Pope Marino longed to be able to tell this soul-damaged young officer that he had indeed been there, seen that, and it was why he had insisted on being the one to lead the effort to rescue as many as possible. Screw it. He made a snap decision. "Lieutenant, would it surprise you if I told you that three of my men and myself were inside the Hilton not long ago?"

"Yes, sir. To be completely frank, sir, I think it would be impossible for you to have been there."

Marino avoided the confrontational tone. "We were after something, about which you have no need to know. We could not do a damned thing to help any of you locked inside. Not even leave a message. It so demoralized all of us that to be honest, we've been brooding about it until this operation came up."

The Marine flyer's eyes widened. "Jeez, sir, you really mean it?"

"Yep." Then Marino went on to describe the interior of the infamous Hanoi Hilton. When he concluded, silence held for a while.

"I'm sorry I doubted you, sir. You've really been in that hellhole. And . . . I'm damned glad you wanted to come back. Freedom never felt so good as it does now."

Lieutenant Commander John Piper tilted the starboard wing of his F-4J Phantom and caught a vista of black water, the crests of lazy waves foamed with whitecaps. They screamed along at 640 knots toward the coast of North Vietnam, at a dangerously low altitude of ninety feet. The shockwave of their passage generated a simulacrum of a rainstorm in reverse as the deadly birds roared across the distance that separated them from the mainland and Hanoi. Ahead and to starboard he could see the glow of the lights of Haiphong, and beyond it by eighty kilometers north and east, Hanoi. Which put the capital city right off his port wing. He keyed his intercom mike and spoke to his weapons officer seated behind him.

"What do you read?"

Lieutenant Travis spoke tersely. "No air traffic. We're all alone up here."

Piper noted that their target lay only six minutes away. He pressed the button on his stick that activated the transmitter tuned to the squadron frequency.

"Up."

A firm, smooth pull on the stick sent the F-14s screaming

up to attack altitude and Hanoi bloomed on their immediate horizon. So swiftly and stealthily had they approached that the AAA crews did not have time to react. The only response came from the far side of the city. A tweedling note came from the weapons officer's warning monitor. Piper checked it out in his HUD (head-up display) and identified the location of the acquisition radar that had painted them.

"Break right and left," he commanded his squadron. "You are free to engage ground targets. I'll get the SAM site."

In going for his setup, Lieutenant Commander Piper flashed directly over the Ministry of Defense. Travis triangulated his target, locked on, and toggled out a single AIM-7 Sparrow missile. The cautionary warble ended as the control truck for the radar ceased to exist. Piper banked to starboard and did a tight turn around a point.

There! A hundred meters from the targeting radar he saw the SAM emplacement. Time for a pair of Sidewinders. The large, deadly missiles came to vibrant life and a hum told the Navy pilot and his weapons officer that its guidance package had locked on to the infrared signature of the target. Release.

Eleven seconds later the explosion lighted the entire northeastern edge of Hanoi. Following the mental image of the photos they had studied in both the mission and attack plan briefing, Piper screamed his F-4J up into a loop, leveled out, and pointed the nose toward a tall building in midtown Hanoi.

The rooftop sported a forest of antennas. It was the communications center of Central Command and Control for the People's Revolutionary Army of North Vietnam. Piper keyed his mike. "Red Rover One, form on me, line of ducks, echelon left."

In a startlingly short time, half of the F-4s formed up to make a run on the targeted building. Piper's Sidewinder, and those of the three aircraft immediately following, would wreak havoc on the brick structure because of delay detonation fuses. They were designed to penetrate deeply into the

structure and cause the maximum destruction of enemy communications equipment. For all its power, the Phantom rose
slightly at release, Piper noted.

A hard, sharp turn to the right put more distance between
him and the racing missile. Piper spoke again. "Red Rover
Two, take out that clothesline array," he advised the other
element of his squadron, indicating the antennas as their target. Another radar painted the squadron and the first element
sent two Phantoms to dispose of it.

"Red Rover Two, take out your primary target."

After a shower of bombs that eliminated the antennas, the
F-4s of Red Rover Two turned to deliver their remaining
AIM-9 Sidewinders on the former Metropole.

"Okay, guys, TO time," Piper advised, after the run on
the Ministry of Defense, indicating they should expend their
remaining stores on targets of opportunity. It would never do
to return to the deck of the *Coral Sea* with leftovers.

Phantoms darted like fireflies in the sky over Hanoi, rain-
ing hell down on tanks and APCs and a large power substa-
tion, which plunged half of the city into darkness. Then it
was time to go home to the *Coral Sea*.

Archie Golden and the other three SEALs crouched in a
steel-lined concrete culvert on the edge of town while the
Phantoms visited Hanoi. When the explosions ceased and the
sound of jet engines faded, Archie spoke for all of them.

"Who the hell forgot to tell us about that?"

"Look at the bright side," suggested Tex Goracke. "With
this blackout, it's gonna be a lot easier for us to steal some
wheels."

Archie gave him grudging agreement. "You've got a
point, kid. Let's move out and find some."

Within five minutes they had located a whole lot of transportation, most of it blasted to ruin by the Phantom raid. One
light truck had rammed into a concrete power pole, its driver
unconscious and bleeding behind the wheel. Archie dragged
the Vietnamese free of the seat, and together with the others,
assessed the damage. Their decision was unanimous.

It would not take them far, not with the radiator caved in. But all agreed that it might take them far enough from town to find a functional vehicle. They piled themselves and their gear into the truck and set off across the grid of streets to where they would take Highway 4 to the north.

AH-1M Bell SeaCobra gunships lifted off from the fantail helipads on the USS *Justin Foster*. After forming into line-ahead formation, they slid along at fifty feet off the waters of the Gulf of Tonkin, their wasp tails turned back toward the ship which immediately cut the landing lights.

"Good hunting, Green Giant, this is Homeplate clearing you from our control." Now came the tricky part, thought Major Garth Holden, USMC, the flight leader, as he extinguished his navigational lights.

Everything had better work letter perfect, his musing continued. They had a 180km flight to the area where they were to fly cover, and even with maximum fuel aboard, that did not allow for much orbiting time. As it was, he considered that they were cutting it a hair too fine. But it was not his call. Theirs was not to reason why, eh? Who in hell, he wondered, had the clout to put together such a hairy big operation? If someone had told him the Commander in Chief, Major Holden would have laughed in his face.

Lieutenant Vinh Huang chewed nervously on his lower lip. At 21, he was one of the youngest commissioned officers in the NVA. The inherent responsibility weighed heavily upon his shoulders. Something inside him, some gut feeling, told him that the brief, interrupted message relating to an incursion by the American enemy and the escape of prisoners was correct. And also that the hated Americans were close at hand. Huang could sense them. Better than that, he could hear them.

He and his platoon, Third of the Sixth (Red Moon Rising) Company, continued to close in on them as he considered this stupendous turn of fortune. He knew that two kilometers ahead, sealing the fate of the cursed foreign mercenaries, was the platoon of Lieutenant Nguyen Cau. Huang could almost taste the sweet fruit of victory. Yet anxiety clawed at him as he considered the hard reality of the cold, unrelenting numbers in the brief message his company commander had received before all communication with and through Hanoi ceased abruptly. Eighteen prisoners escaped, freed from captivity, according to the officer from the general staff, by a force estimated to be no larger than seven or eight men, who left behind twenty-eight soldiers of the People's Army of North Vietnam; all were dead.

"Who could these enemy soldiers be?" Huang asked rhetorically, unaware he spoke aloud.

"Sir?" asked Sergeant Ming.

"Uh—nothing, Sergeant." But the question remained. What sort of fighters could they be, to exact such a bloody toll? A moment later he abandoned his worry as the whispered word came down the line to him from his point man, Cpl. Binh. They were within seconds of contact with the enemy! To his misfortune, Huang was totally unaware that there were actually three independent units of the enemy operating within his country, and that this one was unemcumbered by debilitated prisoners and decidedly the strongest.

Zorro Agilar served as Tailgate Tommy for the SEALs' route of march. In country as hostile as this, watching the backdoor was as important as being point man. Zorro frequently paused to do a 360-degree turn, eyes darting side to side, up and down in the darkness, in an effort to see what, if anything, lay out there in the bush or on their trail. He had lost count of the number of times he had done this when he stiffened and sharpened his focus.

A sudden, unguarded movement had attracted his eye. Zorro continued to hold his freeze until the movement repeated itself. He then sank into the deciduous undergrowth of this mountainous region. His thumb found the Send button on the walkie-talkie he carried and clicked it three times. A single soft burst of carrier wave static acknowledged. *Good,* he thought, *Marino knows*. Now for the tricky part, Zorro considered, bugging out without being spotted.

A broad smile spread on the flat face of Lieutenant Huang as he deployed his platoon across the trail and into the brush to either side. Then, giving a silent arm signal, Vinh Huang led the advance in a staggered line abreast. His plan was to engage the rear of the enemy column, then swing in from the flanks and crush them. It was, he had learned in his officers' school, the favorite tactic of the almost godlike Ho Chi Minh.

Houng could almost hear the cries for mercy of the Americans as his men heroically slaughtered them without quarter. There would be glory to share from their victory. A sudden chatter of an AK-47 carbine shattered his reverie.

"What idiot did that?" he demanded.

Immediately following upon it came a sharp crack and shortly after the pop and hollow boom of a 40mm grenade.

Huang had no choice. At once he shouted, "Attack! Attack! Press in on them!" he yelled, certain with a sinking sensation that the element of surprise had been lost. A most costly mistake. When he learned who was responsible he would flay him alive.

Zorro Agilar felt the tug of a bullet in the webbing of his A-frame backpack. Instantly he heard the crack of more slugs flying in the night around him before the sound of the weapon that fired them reached him. Conditioned to such situations, he dropped to the ground, did a roll, and came up facing back down the trail. He ticked off a 5.56mm round on single fire, then grounded the butt of his CAR-15 and triggered the XM148 grenade launcher mounted under the barrel.

The 40mm tube uttered its familiar *pop! . . . bloop!* and the small though deadly projectile arched into the air. At the last second he remembered to close his eyes and turn away slightly. A lot of good that would do, he reflected the next instant, his night vision had already been screwed up by the muzzle flash of his CAR-15.

The blast of the grenade brought satisfying screams of agony, which grew in volume and changed to rage as yelling and screaming the NVA soldiers charged in a line of skirmishers formation.

At once Zorro Agilar dropped to his belly and crawled rapidly backward as the other SEALs opened up from their hastily occupied ambush positions, which they had taken at the sound of the first shot from the nervous NVA soldier.

"Bailbond, this is Green Giant. We see some flashes down there. Is that you, Bailbond? Over."

Relief filled Carl Marino and turned the sweat he had been pouring out cold. "Roger that, Green Giant. Excuse my brevity, but it's a little hot right now."

" 'Gators are gnawing yer behind, right?"

"You got it."

"Can you light up the bad guys and we'll lend a hand?"

"Sure can, Green Giant. What you guys packin'?"

"We came in three flavors," Major Holden replied with a chuckle. "One is with a seven-point-six-five Minigun and a Honeywell remote fire forty mike-mike launcher, number two packs, a thirty mike-mike auto-cannon, and seventy-six Duce-seventy-five rockets, third is eight TOW missiles and a twenty mike-mike Gatling. Do you have a use for any of that?"

"Does a bear shit in the woods? We'll illuminate, you bring it on. Won't need the TOWs."

Seconds later, bright flashes from white phosphorus grenades lit up the stalled line of attacking NVA soldiers. Flare rounds from an M-79 tube and the two XM148s added overhead illumination as they floated serenely under their parachutes. Quickly the SEALs stuffed plugs in their ears and covered them as the Sea Cobras bore in, their 2,050-shaft horsepower T400 WV jet engines screaming.

Sunrise seemed to come from the middle of the sky as yellow-orange shafts of light flickered as the six-barrel 20mm

Gatling guns aboard the AH-1Ks unleashed their fury and a short salvo of fifteen 2.75-inch rockets ripple-fired from the outboard stores pylons under the belly of each of the nine Sea Cobras. Hell had come to settle in the Black Da Valley.

CHAPTER 29 _____

SUDDENLY THE sweet taste of victory had turned to the bitter gall of annihilation for Lieutenant Huang. Rocket rounds burst on all sides, and shrapnel shredded his soldiers, turned them into rag dolls. A deadly wasp burned his cheek, ripped it open, and exposed shattered teeth and his tongue. Only belatedly did he realize that it had been a very close encounter with a 20mm round. With eyes that dazzled and teared from a sudden wash of pain, he staggered unsteadily into the concealing bush.

Actinic shafts lanced from the halogen lights in the bellies of the gunships, adding to the glare that revealed every crouching, thoroughly cowed NVA soldier. Huang's small radio howled with static, as it had since the sudden cessation of broadcasting from Hanoi. His eyes were blinded from the light above. The roar of the T400 WV engines combined with the dragon roar of multi-barrel cannons to deafen him. With shaking fingers he changed frequencies and found enough silence to communicate.

"Break off, take to the bush," he shouted in garbled alarm to his comrade, Lieutenant Cau, whose platoon had rushed forward in the moment of imagined victory over the Americans.

Instead of running, Cau opened up in defense of his brother officer, directed his men's fire toward the angry dragonflies that harassed them from above. It only served to cause half of the Sea Cobras to turn in his direction and lash his platoon with a deadly rain of metal.

On the ground, Carl Marino and Tom Waters watched as the enemy fire dwindled to a dozen or so pinpoints, then blanked out entirely.

"Cease fire," Lieutenant Marino commanded their unexpected but thoroughly welcome air support. "And thanks, Green Giant."

"Always glad to oblige, Bailbond. We've lots of stores left—you have anyplace else you want busted up?"

"Not at the present."

"Then we'll orbit until we have to hotfoot it back and refuel. Good luck, Bailbond. Green Giant out."

In the silence that followed their departure, more of the former prisoners waded in and armed themselves from the corpses of the enemy. "If we're goin' after those other guys, we'd best have all the ammo we can carry," observed one grinning ex-POW. "Me, I figger on usin' a whole hell of a lot of it."

Marino addressed his reinforced unit. "All right, it's time to tell you exactly where we're going. About five klicks from here is another road, no connecting link, that's why we're on foot. It's our suspicion that at least a dozen more of your fellow prisoners are there in the custody of some twenty NVA soldiers. Now we could handle this easily enough ourselves, but why spoil your fun?"

A ragged cheer broke out as Tonto Waters set off at point.

Reports began to filter in to Hanoi, delayed by the destruction of the central communications complex. Many were relayed by the short-range radios of small units in the field. Among them were more details regarding the ambush of the prisoner transport column. As it became clear to those in the third sub-basement situations room that all eighteen prisoners had been released, General Nguyen Tri engaged Colonel Fong Xguyen in a contest of shouted imprecations that bordered on a full-blown temper tantrum.

"You are a pitiful incompetent," Tri shrieked at Xguyen for the tenth time. "Your men are an undisciplined, untrained rabble. If you had let me provide the security force for escort duty, none of this would have happened."

" '*Let* you,' " Xguyen sneered. "May I remind you, Comrade General, most of the prisoner escort was comprised of regular army units and that you refused to allow Security Service troops to be provided. They were needed here to protect the conference." Xguyen, who saw his career going the way of his predecessor's, waved around the war room deep underground. "What a marvelous success you have made of that."

"I do not control the United States Air Force!" Tri screamed.

General Bac, G-2 of the People's Revolutionary Army, took up a spirited defense of Xguyen. In a voice heavy with scorn he enumerated Tri's failures. "Two of our generals shot by a sniper, a Russian diplomat similarly slain, a general of the PRC dead, two drivers killed. An APC blown to bits. A GAZ half-ton truck ripped apart by those infernal claymore mines of theirs. These were not the doing of the American air arm. Where, Comrade General, are the ones responsible for this massacre? Has your vaunted Security Service made any arrests, captured any military personnel? Perhaps there are traitors within our own ranks? If so, why have you failed to find them before this—this disaster?"

Stunned by the vehement fury of the regular army officer, Tri swallowed his own rancor and faced the fact that so far he had no answer for any of these questions. He produced a weak smile and dissembled. "I am confident we will be acquiring answers to your inquiries in short order, Comrade General."

"Comrades . . ." the voice of Pyotr Rudinov inserted a note of calm and reason into the hot exchange. "Let us examine the alternatives that are open to us. I suggest, General Tri, that you designate a young Revolutionary Guard officer to make a personal evaluation of the ambush. He should have sufficient rank to compel immediate and truthful responses from all he questions. Another, similar man should be assigned to determine the cause, number, and whereabouts of those attacking this facility. I would assume it to be a simple matter to apprehend them. Failure to do so should be rigorously punished." This last Rudinov leveled directly at General Tri, his face a stony facade.

The KGB officer started to say more, only to be interrupted by the sound of powerful explosions and the vibration of the ground that not even this deep bunker could escape. Far above the situations room, Lieutenant Piper's squadron had returned for a second pass. The intensity and volume of explosions increased.

Panic erupted among those above ground in the Ministry of Defense as windows blew inward, admitting the nose cones of missiles that exploded with devastating results. Underground, Rudinov and General Major Ludvinov heard the blasts, and the floor shook beneath them. Concrete dust filtered through the light from shielded bulbs, which then blinked and went out. Moments later, an auxiliary generator kicked in and feeble illumination filled the room again.

Colonel Rudinov seized upon it at once, his fury rising with each detonation. "Where is your early warning radar? Where is your antiaircraft? Where is your air force?" he demanded. Then, for a moment he lost it and railed at his Vietnamese comrades in provincial Russian, thick with a peasant accent. "You disgust me, you stupid, incompetent, slant-eyed barbarians."

Astonished at this display of a loss of control—it was the first time he or anyone had witnessed Rudinov come so close to losing control completely—General Major Ludvinov could only gape for a moment, then moved to take his subordinate and old friend by one elbow.

"Pyotr Maxim'ich, old friend. Take it easy. Get a swallow of vodka, eh? It is all inevitable, is it not? After all, have we not devised scenarios in which the Americans resumed bombing Hanoi?"

"Yes, but in those, these cretins provided at least minimal resistance from their Strategic Rocket Service. And their

AAA has been effective in the past." Rudinov was not to be easily mollified.

"Come," Ludvinov urged, leading the way to a side table. There he swept away a white tablecloth and waved a hand over a bowl of caviar, with its attendant condiment dishes of chopped hard-boiled egg yolk, onion, and toast points. Beside it rested a platter of Imperial rolls, and another of spiced prawns. Flanking these delicacies was a rank of bottles. Ludvinov reached for one containing vodka, then winced as another bomb went off above and the bottles collided and rang musically.

It seemed as if they had been in North Vietnam forever. Actually, they had been on the ground less than one hour. So much had happened in so many places in such a short bit of time. Even madcap Archie Golden had a creepy-crawly feeling. The maps and overlays had proved excellent and far more accurate than anything available to the locals. They had made good time along Highway 4 in the stolen truck. Right where it was supposed to be, the narrow, rutted auxiliary road branched to the east, toward the coast.

Dallas Goracke, at the wheel, cranked it and nosed the vehicle onto the irregular trace and gingerly fed it throttle. At an indicated 27 kph the steering wheel began to vibrate violently in his hands. The front wheels fought the hard ruts of earlier monsoon seasons and acted as though they possessed a mind of their own.

"Can't you control this thing, kid?" Archie groused.

"Want to give it a try?"

"Naw. How about you, Doc?" Archie Golden asked Kent Welby.

Welby shook his head. "He's doin' okay, for a boy."

"Where d'you get this *boy* shit? I don't see you havin' to shave more than every other day."

"Yeah, but that's because I have such fair hair," Doc Welby defended himself.

"Watch it," Archie warned. "There's a water buffalo over there. Spook him and he could turn us over."

"Stow it, all of youse guys," Brandon Mitchell grumbled. "How far is it to that LZ?"

Kent Welby consulted the map. "Best guess is ten klicks. The rest of the guys went farther north and west. We're comin' at it from below. Which means we should get there first and secure the landing zone."

"Think we'll run into any resistance?" asked Goracke.

Archie nodded energetically. "Count on it."

Pope Marino and Tonto Waters benefited from the excellent maps provided by the CIA. They now waited along the right drainage ditch and across Road 47 some three kilometers northwest of the advancing column of closely guarded prisoners. Made much stronger by the freed prisoners who had armed themselves, they felt quite confident of the outcome.

Grinding gears and engine whines gave them ample advance warning when the prison detachment grew near. Safeties came off weapons, in the case of the non-SEAL element, and every man drew a breath, eager to finish this and get safely out of this hostile country. Slowly the trucks of the column rolled into the ambush. To those with nerves already drawn to extreme tightness, it seemed to take forever. Then came the sharp crack of the first round that triggered the ambush.

Darkness washed away in a torrent of muzzle blast. The two lead vehicles became enveloped in balls of flame. Carefully aimed shots took out the drivers of all the other vehicles. Zorro Agilar's eyes widened when a squad of NVA soldiers stood upright in one truck and aimed their weapons not at the ambushers but at the helpless prisoners.

He wasn't all that hot on shooting a man in the back, but this was another matter. His finger ticked off precise three-round bursts. The slugs bit into flesh and cut down the would-be executioners mercilessly. More soldiers disgorged from the Zil 8-by-8s, this time to engage the ambushers.

A grenade erupted along their line, one armed by an NVA soldier and dropped when he was shot through the head. Chad Ditto recognized that there was a lot of stored-up hunger for revenge among the former prisoners when they broke from concealment on the ambush line and charged directly into the NVA soldiers. Many turned their attention on those who had been their guards, others simply slaughtered North Vietnamese indiscriminately. The fighting was as vicious as it was brief.

Less than ninety seconds elapsed from the first shot to Lieutenant Carl Marino bellowing, "Cease fire! Back off, guys. It's all over."

A quick count disclosed two dead ex-POWs among those previously liberated. Two others had wounds that Fil Nicholson diagnosed as from mild to moderately severe. They would survive and could move under their own power. The best news came from one of the trucks, out of which emerged another eleven liberated POWs. One of them, in the tattered remains of an Air Force major's uniform, did not hesitate to push forward to where Pope Marino rested against a tree.

"I don't know where you guys came from, or who you are, but you're damned welcome. There's another column, on Highway 17, I think—we've got to go after them."

Quick agreement came from the jubilant freed men. Bitter regret filled Pope Marino as he studied the eager faces. Slowly he held up a hand. "I hate to have to say this, but we can't do that. We have to leave at once. We've already overstayed our welcome."

CHAPTER 30

LIEUTENANT COLONEL Minh Sahtay, the Security Service officer selected to inspect the scene of the ambush and liberation of the prisoners, did not know what to expect. What he saw stunned him. What he heard from a dying soldier angered and confused him. At first he dismissed the account as the phantasm of a dying man. Then he debated with himself and decided to include it in his initial report at least. Accordingly he relayed the now dead NVA soldier's description, albeit prefaced by his opinion that it was a hallucination.

"What is it?" Rudinov demanded. "What is this hallucination?"

Hesitantly, Minh stuttered out a reply. "G-green skin. He said the men who attacked them had green skin, green . . . faces, is how he said it."

A rage of fire exploded in the head of Rudinov while a spike of ice rammed down his spine. SEALs? "Those *blyo-odetvii* (fornicating) SEALs!" he bellowed into the handset of the radio. "Wait where you are," the KGB colonel demanded. "I will come at once."

After abandoning the truck, Kent Welby and the SEALs with him took off on foot, Archie Golden at point. They moved in a northeasterly direction. It was with considerable relief when Archie checked three landmarks that could be recognized even at night, triangulated them on the map he carried, and informed the others that they had indeed arrived.

"Yep, this is it, all right," he declared with justifiable pride. "I suggest we take five, pig out on some C-rats, and then we can fix the locator beacon for the Hueys." He turned and looked around. "Anybody want to volunteer to climb a tree?"

"What's wrong with putting it on the ground?" asked Dallas Goracke.

"Range. The higher up it is, the farther the signal will travel. The way I understand it," Archie explained, "it's a line of sight, FM, transmitter. So we want to make real sure those chopper jockeys find us soon."

Doc Welby shrugged out of his backpack harness and set it down. He delved into the interior and came out with four olive green boxes. "Okay, so who wants Vienna sausages? How about sausage patties and scrambled?"

"Got any ham and limas?" Dallas Goracke asked hopefully.

"Jeez, you mean you can eat that stuff?" Archie asked the young SEAL. At a nod from Dallas, he went on, "That's disgusting. I'd sure go for some anchovies, though."

Even Brandon Mitchell joined in making gagging motions and sounds.

Colonel Rudinov headed for the site of the ambush by helicopter, the same as Lieutenant Colonel Minh Sahtay. The straight line journey took only eleven and a half minutes. On the way he received a tap on one shoulder from the copilot and followed directions to tune his radio to a different frequency.

"Rudinov," he identified himself brusquely.

Over the headphones he received a grim-voiced report on the ambush and massacre of the search patrols looking for the intruders and their liberated prisoners. "Two platoons. Wiped out with only eleven survivors," General Bac informed Rudinov in his stilted Russian. "It is obvious there are entirely many more enemy in our country than we first suspected." Bac remained silent a while, then spoke crisply. "It is our belief now that the true objective of this incursion is to rescue those prisoners. Any attack on the Ministry of Defense is only a diversion."

"How astute," Rudinov answered acidly. "I had come to that conclusion the moment we received the first reports of prisoners escaping." Positive now that it was indeed the SEALs, he spoke tightly. "I am convinced that this is an American Navy operation, led on the ground by their elite SEALs. I had an encounter with them not long ago. I am afraid I completely underrated their abilities. That mistake will not be repeated."

Two minutes later, the Mil Mi-1 helicopter began to descend. Rudinov exited the aircraft before the wheels touched the ground. He ran out from under the whirling rotor blades and was greeted by the Vietnamese lieutenant colonel, Sahtay. His face reflecting his misery, the NVA officer waved an arm around to encompass the carnage.

Rudinov's normally thin lips drew to nearly invisible as he took in the sprawl of bodies. He blamed himself in part for this slaughter. When he had experienced his meeting with the SEALs, it had been over the matter of the bomb. They had the upper hand and had let him go. He had not made any effort to obstruct their withdrawal, taking the bomb with them. This time, as he had promised General Bac, it would be different. This time he would crush them.

Lieutenant Carl Marino led the armed former POWs away to the southeast in one of the recovered trucks from their last ambush. The rutted side road made movement so slow that his SEALs could provide a screen to the flanks as well as a point element—one SEAL, three very revenge-hungry ex-POWS—in a GAZ-58. The map was clear, the LZ marked. All they needed do was keep on the present road. Many among the American force actually began to relax slightly.

In the lead truck, Marino's radio crackled. "Boss man, I think we've got company," came the voice from Zorro Agilar in the last vehicle.

"What do you have?"

"I caught a flash of headlights behind us. Weren't too clear. This mountain undergrowth is even more dense than the bush in the Delta. Over."

"Zorro, get ready to hide and watch. Then close the back door."

"Roger that." Zorro, also in a GAZ-58, directed his vehicle off the road and into the thick brush. Darkness would hide the broken limbs and raw stubs of damaged branches. Two minutes later, the first vehicle of the pursuing column came into view.

"I got a GAZ with four occupants. There's three trucks, all with soldiers in back, no canvas covers. Looks like a platoon." Zorro continued a whispered count of the enemy force as it lumbered past his hiding place.

Pope Marino listened with growing concern. He quickly decided that he could ill afford to allow that large a force to get between his small band and their LZ. Quickly he formulated his plan. He used hand-and-arm signals to give hasty instructions to the SEALs and the occupants of the trucks. Then he whispered to Zorro.

"Hey, Fox, when the last one goes by, get back on the trail, rig a couple of claymores to cover your six and move into position to support us. We're takin' them out."

"Hot damn."

Long minutes passed. Then, in flashes of brightness, claymores detonated. They slashed waves of steel balls into both sides of the enemy trucks. Immediately the newly free Americans and their SEAL rescuers opened fire. Witheringly accurate, they cut down all of the enemy before the lieutenant in command could get off a word on the radio in the GAZ.

His straw hat clutched in sweaty hands, the frightened peasant farmer stood before the sleepy-eyed figure of the local commissar. He stammered his news under a cloud of fear for his own safety.

"It is true, Comrade Commissar," he concluded. "There

has been some fighting, a lot of gunfire, and loud explosions three *lan* from my rice paddies. Many soldiers have been killed. I have seen them myself.''

''I am sure your information is correct,'' he said placatingly. ''We will contact the authorities in the morning. They will perhaps send someone to investigate.''

Confused and hurt by such obvious indifference, the peasant asked plaintively, ''What is happening to our homeland? Who are these enemy soldiers who have attacked us far from the fighting in the south?''

Containing his impatience, and his insistent, strong urge to return to the warmth of the silken legs of the preteen girl waiting in his bed, the bureaucrat dismissed the peasant and stifled a yawn. A growing awareness of some of the details given awakened a gnawing sense of caution. Better that he make a report now than to be found wanting later on. If the peasant really saw dead soldiers it could be a problem. He padded barefoot across to his office and lifted the handset of his telephone.

''Radio room?'' he asked when the other end answered.

Who else? thought the bored signals NCO on duty. ''Yes, Comrade Commissar.''

''I have a message for you to transmit to Hanoi.'' Quickly he gave the gist of what the old farmer had told him. The response he got surprised and worried him.

''I am sorry, sir, but we cannot transmit to Hanoi. They have been off the air for thirty minutes now. But from what you want sent, sir, there is someone closer who will want to hear of this. It is one of our Soviet comrades, sir, a Colonel Rudinov.''

Their C-rations a fading memory, the SEALs of the diversionary team set about deploying the antenna for the marker beacon. Tex Goracke volunteered to climb the designated tree, rigged a pulley device from a rappelling D-ring, and guided the beacon into place as those below pulled it up. He lashed it to the trunk and then spread out the two long panels that formed the arms of the antenna. Satisfied with that, he turned on the transmitter. When the transmit light glowed green, he lowered himself in three swift drops.

"Somebody comin'," were the first words to greet him on his return to ground.

He looked startled at Doc Welby. "Any idea . . . ?" He let the question hang.

"We don't want to be standin' out here in the open when we find out," Doc suggested.

They faded into the bush, no sign of their presence left in the clearing. Tensely they waited, weapons at the ready. A rustling at the far edge of the clearing alerted them to the approach. A crouched form, bent low, weapon leading the way, appeared through a screen of ferns. Fingers tightened on triggers. Sweat popped on four foreheads. Then a harsh whisper reached the ears of Archie Golden.

"This is it, Pope. No sign of the guys."

"Jesus! Don't move, repeat. There's a claymore rigged to do you if you hit the wire."

"Archie? Are you fuckin' nuts?"

"No," Archie replied through a chuckle. "Just cautious. There's only four of us, remember?"

Chad Ditto bent low and lightly fanned his fingers over the ground at ankle height. He located the wire and released it from its triggering position. He sidestepped until there was a lot of slack in the wire, then followed it to the shaped charge mine. After he had inserted the safety pin, his hands began to shake. God, how he wished he was a kid again and could bite his nails.

No sooner did the long file of freed prisoners pass on through the opening in the defenses and the trip-wires reset than shots blasted through the jungle growth around them. Although some distance away, the nearly spent bullets clipped leaves and smacked into tree trunks. Instantly everyone went to ground.

It took all the efforts of the SEALs to get the rescued men to get out of the open and into the brush on the far side of the clearing. Marino knelt beside his RTO and took the handset from Chad Ditto. "Taxi, this is Bailbond, over."

Out on the *Coral Sea*, the message was relayed to the cockpit of the lead Huey in the extraction flight. "Roger, Bailbond," he replied over the secure scrambled radio circuit. "What do you need?"

"Taxi, we're ready for a pick-up." He continued by giving the coordinates for another clearing some half a klick away, but in direct line with the locator beacon. "That is half a klick southwest of LZ Hotshoe."

"Roger, Bailbond. Taxi is on the way. ETA is fifteen, I say again, one-five minutes."

"Better make it quicker than that. We're up to our ass in alligators."

"Bailbond, we have some friends still in the area who can fly over. Cobras, do you dig?"

Marino grinned. He had momentarily forgotten the Green Giants orbiting out there. "Send those sea snakes, brother."

"You got 'em. ETA for them, about 6."

Hands clasped behind his back, his body ramrod straight in a long black leather trenchcoat, Colonel Pyotr Rudinov struck an impressive figure as he listened to the peasant recount his version of what had happened. He turned his sharp gaze to the left and spoke crisply.

"You did right in contacting me, Commissar. I believe this man. Now, I want maps of the area."

For ten minutes, Rudinov pored over the map of the region. He was able to see and interpret what was there as easily as it had been for Marino. What he quickly discerned was a suitable clearing, near the coast of the South China Sea, but inland enough not to be covered by the coastal defenses.

"There is where they will be going," he declared. "There is where we will destroy them." He turned to the radio operator of the helicopter that had brought him. "Contact the nearest army unit. Find out from them where the nearest helicopter assault unit is located. I want them moving within the next ten minutes."

*   *   *

With Tonto Waters and all but two of the SEALs acting as rear guard, Pope Marino moved with all the speed he could muster from the weakened former POWs to the edge of the secondary LZ. Chad Ditto hunched down beside the platoon leader and held the radio handset ready. Marino reached for it.

"Taxi, this is Bailbond. Better speed it up, buddy, we don't have much time left. We are in place and waiting."

"Be there in ten. Have my friends arrived?"

"Not yet," Marino replied, then blinked as bright flares exploded over the distant primary LZ. The volume of fire increased dramatically and he could hear the howl of the Sea Cobra engines. "They are now."

"Hang in there. We'll be with you soon."

While Marino talked with the flight leader designated Taxi, ten Mil Mi-8 twenty-eight passenger helicopters settled in the rice paddies outside the large village from where the commissar had contacted Rudinov. The KGB colonel strode briskly to one and boarded. The side door slid closed and the twin Isotov TV-2-117A engines spooled up. Rudinov was not in his seat when the troop transport lifted off. After he fitted the headset and boom mike, Rudinov contacted the pilot.

"We will reach the clearing you indicated in nine minutes, Comrade," he was told in response.

"Make it faster."

"Bailbond, this is Taxi. ETA is three minutes."

"None too soon, Taxi. The Cobras have gone back home."

"They do enough for you?"

Marino chuckled. "They didn't leave much behind. The rest of my people are coming in now. It's odd, but if you're still three minutes out, why can I hear your rotors now?"

"Weather conditions, Bailbond?" suggested the Navy pilot.

"Could be. Open those throttles, Taxi. Bailbond, out."

Marino called over Tonto Waters, who had only then arrived from the inoperative LZ. "Hear those choppers? Our transportation says it isn't them."

Tonto listened a moment. "He's right, those aren't our choppers. They're Soviet made."

A roar of gunfire ended their speculation as the Mi-8 "Hip" helicopters swung into line and opened up with their 12.7mm heavy machine guns.

"Hang on," the Huey flight leader of Taxi informed his pilots. "We're going into a hot LZ."

When he got a look at the situation, he realized exactly how bad it would be for the guys on the ground. A third of the Hips had grounded and discharged their troops. They met a scathing counterfire from the American forces. *Who are they, anyway?* wondered the flight leader. At their briefing they had been told that they were to go in and extract some escaped POWs. Well, what was going on was sure not a JPRC operation. Time to get some help.

"Green Giant, this is Taxi. We've got a hot situation, over."

"Where, Taxi?"

"Half a klick southeast of where you went last time. Are you able to help? Over."

"Roger. But not much. We have only a quarter of our stores left and we're about to start running on fumes."

"Then get over here ASAP. There's gonna be two companies of NVA soldiers crawlin' all over our folks if you don't."

"On our way."

"Bailbond, this is Taxi. Help is on the way."

More of the Mil Mi-8s had grounded and disgorged their complement of troops by the time the Sea Cobras returned. From that point on it became a turkey shoot. Blazing exhaust from their missile pods, the attack helicopters fired salvos of 2.75-inch rockets into the thin-skinned Soviet helicopters on the ground. Thirty millimeter autocannons slashed the lightly armed choppers, blasting them to bits, some with the passengers still aboard.

"Taxi, Bailbond, the cavalry has arrived. This is Green Giant. We've got it in hand. Taxi, you can move in at will."

One Mi-8 burst into a black-tinged ball of red-orange flame, the nose broke free and cartwheeled across the ground. Swiftly the Sea Cobras swept over the enemy craft, unloading a cargo of destruction. They swung into position to bring death down on the Vietnamese troops. With the excellent cover of the Sea Cobras, the Huey slicks darted in and flared out, hovering some five feet above the ground.

"Go! Go! Go!" shouted the SEALs. For once unmindful of the former prisoners' less than robust condition, the SEALs forcefully urged them forward to board the waiting helicopters.

Polkovnik Pyotr Rudinov seethed with fury. The superior firepower of the Americans threatened to undo his plan. He shouted into the boom mike, choking in his outrage.

"Down. Get this craft on the ground before it is blown out of the air."

When the Mi-8 reached a point some three feet above ground, the KGB colonel bounded out of the open door, expecting the Vietnamese troops to follow; he did not look back. He made it only a dozen yards before the Soviet helicopter was struck by multiple rockets. It blew in a tumult with a rain of sharp-edged chunks of skin and frame that whirred through the air with a banshee scream.

Without orders or prior agreement, the SEALs remained behind to fight with the aid of the Cobras until the last of the freed men boarded a Huey. Then they scrambled into open doorways and the birds lifted off.

Behind them they left a smoking ruin that comprised a full third of the helicopters in the NVA and the bodies of two hundred soldiers.

*   *   *

Of necessity, security was extremely tight at Ton Son Nuht three days later, when the helicopters from the *Coral Sea* brought in the rescued ex-POWs. There was restrained jubilation and a brief address by General Westmoreland. When it was all over, Pope Marino and Tonto Waters repeatedly asked everyone in authority the same question.

"Where are Wally Ott and the rest of the platoon?"

No one seemed to know. Bobby Santoro shrugged when they pressed their query. "Did they get off the ground at all?"

"I don't know, Chief. I was too busy dodging slugs from those Russian machine guns," Santoro answered.

It began to appear that there was only half a squad that had survived. At last one of the surface fleet types from the *Coral Sea* offered what he could. "They had to divert, they were unable to return to the frigate designated as their landing target."

"Were they shot down?" Marino demanded.

Again, no one knew the answer.

Agitated, and in a glum mood, Pope Marino and Chief Waters returned to Tre Noc along with Bobby Santoro and Chad Ditto. With seeming reluctance, they climbed from the interior of a Huey.

There on the edge of the helipad to greet them were Doc Welby, Archie Golden, Zorro Agilar, and Lieutenant (j.g.) Ott. Shouts of surprise and relief filled the air. The SEALs rushed to clap big hands on broad backs and express their joy. When the reunion wound down a bit, Marino asked the important question again.

"Where are the rest?"

"Tough break, Pope," Wally Ott told his superior. "Little Pete bought it. Second squad's sniper, Tex Goracke, and their demo man are in the hospital at Binh Tuhy with minor wounds. The others are over there visiting."

Colonel Pyotr Maximovich Rudinov found himself on the carpet with his superiors. With an embarrassed and decidedly

uncomfortable General Major Vladislav Ludvinov standing
by, General Colonel Deguriev delivered a world class dressing down.

"I hold you personally responsible for the destruction of
much expensive equipment which we had loaned to our client state of North Vietnam. More so the loss of the lives of
many of our allied comrades.

"You acted precipitously, Comrade Colonel. By proceed-
ing on your own initiative you have seriously compromised
the regulation governing the conduct of Soviet officers. You
are, after all, KGB, not a commander of tanks on the Eastern
Front in the Great Patriotic War. Perhaps your superiors in
the *Komitet* have erred in promoting you? Perhaps you need
a time for reflection, a period of self-examination and re-
education? Perhaps you are in need of a period of self-
criticism, like in the old days of Beria? You are relieved of
your duties here in North Vietnam. We shall take all these
questions under advisement, and in due time, convey to you
our decision."

It was a word for which Lieutenant Commander Barry Lailey
had no clear mental image. Yet to himself he literally
faunched in silence as he reviewed the after action reports
of Operation Shell Game and noted its astonishing success.

More than a hundred million dollars' damage done to the
Strategic Rocket Force missile sites, the antiaircraft batteries
around Hanoi, and the Ministry of Defense in North Vietnam. Millions more in destroyed helicopters. And best of all,
twenty-seven prisoners freed and delivered in more or less
satisfactory condition. Quite a slap in the face of the NVA.

"Quite a slap in my own face," Lailey softly grumbled
aloud. Not even with the loss of one man in his command,
and with two wounded, and two of the freed prisoners KIA
could he paint a sufficiently dark picture of Lieutenant Carl
Marino. So much for his plans of making a blistering negative endorsement on Marino's next fitness report. Who would
believe him now?

SEALS
THE
WARRIOR BREED

by **H. Jay Riker**

The face of war is rapidly changing, calling
America's soldiers into hellish regions where
conventional warriors dare not go.
This is the world of the SEALs.

SILVER STAR
76967-0/$5.99 US/$7.99 Can

PURPLE HEART
76969-7/$6.50 US/$8.99 Can

BRONZE STAR
76970-0/$5.99 US/$6.99 Can

NAVY CROSS
78555-2/$5.99 US/$7.99 Can

MEDAL OF HONOR
78556-0/$5.99 US/$7.99 Can

MARKS OF VALOR
78557-9/$5.99 US/$7.99 Can

Edgar Award Winner
STUART WOODS

New York Times Bestselling Author of
Dead in the Water

GRASS ROOTS   71169-/ $6.99 US/ $8.99 Can

WHITE CARGO   70783-7/ $6.99 US/ $8.99 Can

UNDER THE LAKE
70519-2/ $6.50 US/ $8.50 Can

CHIEFS   70347-5/ $6.99 US/ $8.99 Can

RUN BEFORE THE WIND
70507-9/ $6.99 US/ $8.99 Can